OUT O

ROBERT F BARKER

Paperback Version first published in 2018

Copyright@Robert F Barker 2018

All Rights Reserved. No part of this book may be reproduced in any form other than that in which it was purchased, and without the written permission of the author.
Your support of authors' rights is appreciated.

All characters in this book are fictitious.
Any resemblance to actual persons,
living or dead is purely coincidental.

By Robert F Barker

The DCI JAMIE CARVER SERIES

LAST GASP (The Worshipper Trilogy Book #1)
The last time Jamie Carver let a would-be victim as bait for a serial killer, it ended badly. Now they want him to do it again, only this time the 'victim' is a dominatrix.

FINAL BREATH (The Worshipper Trilogy Book #2)
A monstrous killer, safe behind bars, but just how safe is 'safe'? An archive of debauchery and murder, poised to ruin reputations, carers, lives. A detective, running out of time to find what he seeks

OUT OF AIR (The Worshipper Trilogy Book #3)
One City; Paris. Two killers, one in hiding, the other stalking the streets. An innocent young couple, bewitched into the deadliest danger. The detective who must find them before the worst happens.

FAMILY REUNION
How do you save a family from slaughter when you don't know who they are, and you're not allowed to find out?
A killer is coming, and Jamie Carver has to to stop him. But how?

DEATH IN MIND
"Five minutes before she killed herself, Sarah Brooke had never had a suicidal thought in her life."
A mind-bending psychological thriller with a terrific twist. 'A treat for all Derren Brown fans.'

OTHER TITLES

MIDNIGHT'S DOOR

A novel of nightclub bouncers, Russian mobsters, and serial killing. Introducing Danny Norton, the man who runs the door at Midnight's, the hottest nightspot around. When it all kicks off, you'll want him by your side.

A KILLING PLACE IN THE SUN

His 'Place In The Sun' is simply a house. But to this Englishman, it's his castle, and he wants it back. "An action-packed international thriller that grips from the start, and ends with a gut-punch that pulls at the heart."

FREE DOWNLOAD

Get the inside story on what started it all...

Get a free copy of *THE CARVER PAPERS* - The inside story of the hunt for a Serial Killer - as they feature in LAST GASP, Book #1 of The Worshipper Trilogy. Visit **www.robertfbarker.co.uk** to find out more and get started.

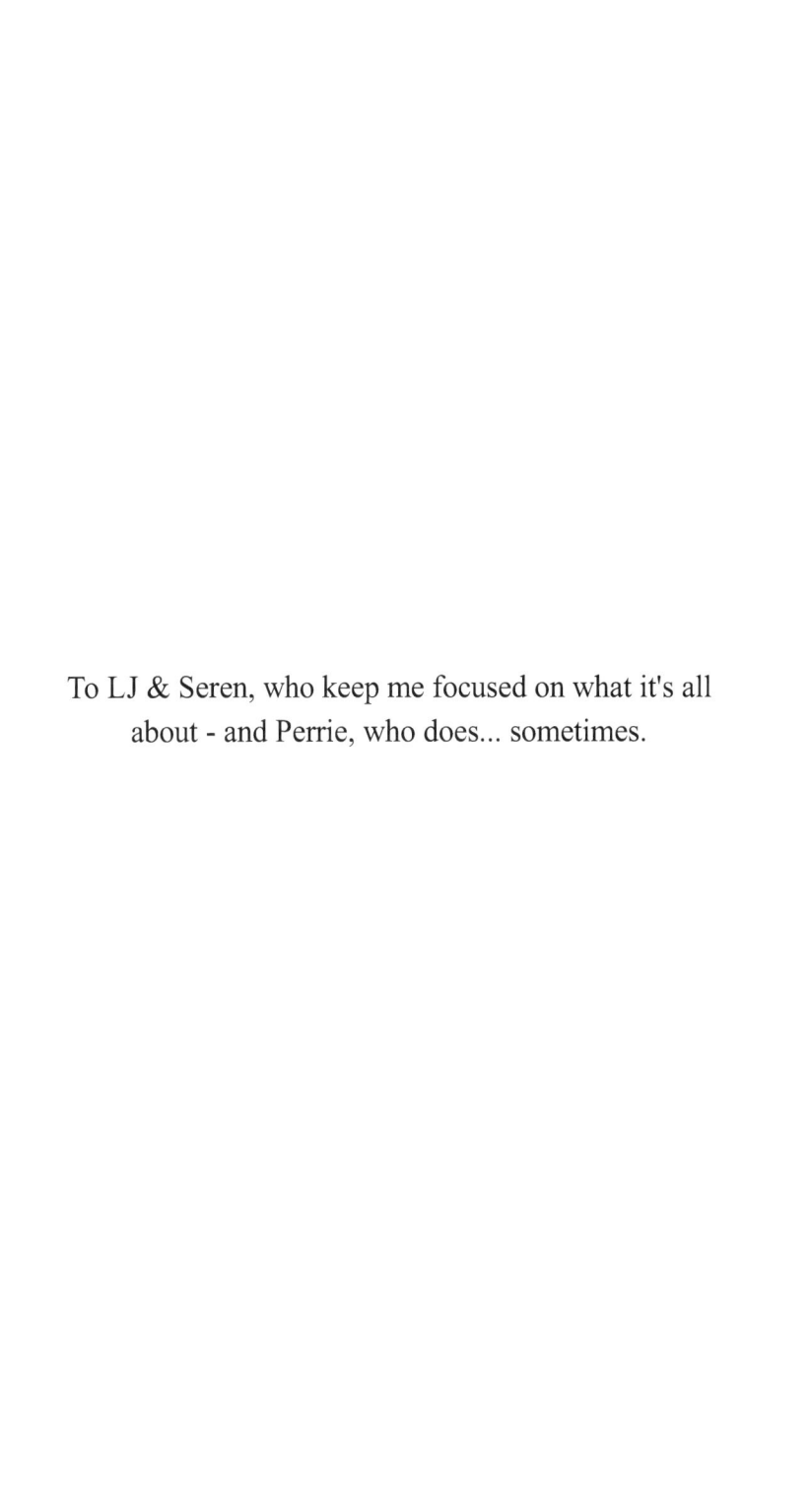

To LJ & Seren, who keep me focused on what it's all about - and Perrie, who does... sometimes.

Prologue

The room is pitch black. The boy sits on the middle of the bed, hugging his knees to his chest and rocking, back and forth. He is crying, though silently in case he misses the sounds he is straining to hear. They are those that tell him that tonight, like other such nights, there will be no respite from the evil.

It is later coming than usual. From his bedroom at the back of the house, he can just hear the church clock in the town. It chimed the half-hour some time ago. And while he knows he cannot escape the evil that is a part of his life, nor can he ignore the flicker of hope that sparks every once in a while. The hope that tonight, it will not come. That something has happened to stop it. An accident of some kind. Perhaps the unexpected arrival of an unlikely saviour who even now is making ready to bear him away somewhere safe where the evil cannot reach.

But the boy's eleventh birthday draws near. By now the experiences of birthdays past lie on his bony shoulders like a weighty shroud, restricting expectation, suffocating hope. In any case, hope has blossomed before, probably every time truth be told, only to be dashed on the rocks of reality that seem to rise like devil's teeth as the inevitable storm hits.

A bright boy, he knows what date it is, its significance. Over the past weeks his thoughts have turned more and more to what this day will bring. Or rather, what the night will bring. During those times he has thought often of running. Of spiriting from his plate such scraps as might not be missed until he has sufficient to sustain him long enough to reach the city, many days travel hence. Perhaps there, he imagines, he will find refuge from his pursuer.

For there lies the problem.

If he runs, the evil will follow after. And when it catches him, as it surely will, he will suffer even more. By not running, he knows that at least by tomorrow the evil will have passed. Until the days run their course and the time comes round for it to show itself once more.

So instead he rocks, back and forth. And cries.

Eventually there is a sound. A metallic scrape. A click, then another click, followed by a rattle. A key in the lock. It is here.

He stops rocking.

He tries to stifle the sobs. His breathing slows to a sort of panting-gasp. 'Huhh... Huhh.... Huhh....' He keeps listening.

The creak of a hinge in need of oil. The scrape of boots on tile. The first heavy planting of foot on stair, followed by others, slow and steady.

He counts the thuds. One, two, three... In his mind's eye he observes the evil's ascent as clearly as if he were outside on the landing, witnessing its approach. The count stops at thirteen. For several moments there is only silence. But not entirely. As he strains to hear, the sound of laboured breathing comes to him. It is mixed with the low, throaty rattle that in those not used to physical exertion speaks of too much drink.

The pause lasts almost a minute. During it, the heavy breathing subsides while the boy stares, wide-eyed towards where he knows the door is. The sound of shuffling steps is followed by the squeak of a handle, turning. A crack of dim light appears. For a moment it remains just a crack, as if tempting him to hope the door will shut again. But he is not fooled. He knows it will not. This is the way it happens. Every time. The crack widens.

A whimper escapes the boy's throat and he scuttles back on the bed until he reaches the wall and can go no further. A man's head and shoulders, huge it seems in the now semi-dark, appear round the door. Guttural breathing and the odorous smell of stale beer fill the room. The figure is framed against the light so the face is in shadow. Even so, the boy imagines the flabby lips and drooling mouth twisted into the black-toothed snarl that passes for a smile as he hears the greeting that marks the evil is upon him once more.

'Hello boy. Happy Birthday.'

CHAPTER 1

The man the *flics* who make up the Paris CID had taken to calling The English Detective stared, hard, at the screen. The past hour, his gaze had barely shifted from it. At its centre, still pondering his response to all he had heard, Henri Durcell, the self-styled Comte de Vergennes sat, upright, correct and composed. Dressed in a shiny petrol-blue suit, white silk handkerchief peeping above the breast pocket, he looked every inch the aristocrat he purported to be. The silver-topped cane and carefully-trimmed goatee, complemented the look. Had DCI Jamie Carver not read his intelligence file, he may even have taken him for a real count.

But while Durcell was the operation's designated target, the greater part of Carver's attention was on not him but the woman half-sitting, half-reclining on the chaise, just out of shot at the top of the screen. Rather, it was on her legs, which were all he could see of her and which explained the frustration gnawing at him. It had been that way since she had settled there, shortly after arriving in the fourth-floor bedroom of the Grand Hotel Edouard VII in the heart of Paris's fashionable Opera District.

They had been expecting that Durcell would be

alone. That was what he had intimated when he rang, three days before, to confirm his interest and his attendance at the time and place stipulated. When he first stepped out of the taxi that bought him and Carver heard the transmission confirming there was a woman with him, his heart had skipped a beat. When someone described her as having dark hair and being, 'Très, va-va-voom,' it skipped several more. If it was *Her*, his mission to Paris could end right here, provided no one cocked up and let her slip through their fingers when he called a strike.

Earlier, as the hidden mics relayed the knock on the door of the room directly below theirs, Carver had hovered in front of the screen like an expectant father. All he needed was a glimpse. Seventeen months isn't that long, and unless she'd resorted to cosmetic surgery - highly unlikely - he would have no difficulty identifying her. The camera concealed in the ceiling rose didn't cover the door, but it did the chairs set up in the middle of the room. During each of the five meetings previous to this, the subject's faces were clear. On those occasions it hadn't mattered that whoever provided the Paris CID with their Tech Support had chosen to use a fixed camera without tilt-pan-zoom capability, God alone knew why. *Well it bloody mattered now.*

The moment he saw her legs enter the shot at the top of the screen and realised what she was about to do, he let out a strangled groan. 'Don't. PLEASE don't.' But she did.

Carver had no way of knowing whether her decision to choose the chaise over the chairs resulted from a desire for comfort, or some animal instinct that made her suspicious of situations that smacked of contrivance.

It didn't matter. She had settled there, and had not moved since. Apart from a muted 'Bonjour' when she arrived, she had said barely a word since. And though he had seen Durcell turn towards her several times - s*eeking approval, guidance maybe?* - she had played no significant part in the proceedings. It made him wonder if someone had somehow seen through their deception and had arranged things just to thwart him. *Is it possible they know*?

But then reason kicked in. If, by some strange twist, it *was* Her, and she *did* suspect it was some sort of set-up - police or otherwise - she would hardly risk showing herself. She would know that they would have everything well-covered. Officers would be everywhere. Then he remembered. She had done exactly that three years before, *and* got away with it.

There was only one way to be certain. He needed to see her face.

Which was why the hour that had passed following their arrival, had been one of the most exasperating Carver had ever experienced. He'd sat through many a frustrating stakeout in his time. None held a candle to this. Most of the hour he spent mentally willing her to move, as if through some telepathic means he might influence her to change her position, leave her seat, get up, walk around, do something, *anything* that might bring her face within range of the camera.

She did none of those things. All she did was sit, and observe. Now and again she crossed or uncrossed her legs. Each time she moved, Carver sat forward, fists clenched, hoping this was it. Each time, he made ready to give out the triple 'strike' command that would send Remy and his team in. Each time, he had to ease back as she stayed put, face tantalisingly, out of view. It got to the point where he didn't dare shift his gaze in case she moved and he missed his chance. Which was how he'd ended up rooted to the chair, head in hands, staring wide eyed at the screen, hardly daring to blink. As a result, he'd barely given Durcell anything more than fleeting attention.

At one point, the door behind Carver opened then closed again, quietly. He didn't shift his gaze. The whiff of Gitanes Brunes wafted over his shoulder.

'Well?' Remy had said. 'Is it her?'

'Can't tell,' Carver said, not turning. 'I still haven't seen her face.' He waited a moment before issuing the rebuke he'd been rehearsing through his vigil. 'If we have to do this again, make sure whichever tosser you use for tech support uses TPZ.' Then, realising it may be lost in translation, he added, 'That's Tilt-Pan-Zoom to you.' For once he didn't bother to tone down the Northern twang that in the early days had confused those among the Paris CID who thought they had a good grasp of English. The response that came, was typical Remy.

'Mais, Oui.'

In his mind's eye, Carver saw the thin smile he knew would be there if he had been bothered to look.

Despite his frustrations, Carver was still reading the encounter taking place beneath them. 'I think they're close to finishing,' he said. 'You better get down the lobby. I'll let you know when they're on their way.' Behind, he heard the door open. 'And Remy?'

'Oui?'

'It would also help if we could hear something apart from the bloody pigeons shagging on the window ledge, and frigging traffic.'

There was a pause, then, 'Très bien.' The door closed. Carver refocused.

In the foreground, the two women comprising the other party to the proceedings sat with their backs to camera. On the left, Carissa Lavergne, the older of the pair, had done most of the talking, as usual. Today she was wearing her thick, auburn hair up, secured at the back by a wooden peg. Her sultry looks spoke of her Mediterranean origins. And though her younger companion, Ingrid, was darker-skinned, she was possessed of a fresh-faced prettiness that contrasted with Carissa's exotic beauty. Carver thought that considering what they were selling, the combination was about right. By now, both were sufficiently practised at their pitch he no longer felt the need to follow it in detail. They were convincing, which was what mattered.

Nevertheless, Durcell had now spent something close to two minutes in silent contemplation, a good deal longer than any of his predecessors. Carver was not surprised. If 'Monsieur Le Comte' *was* representing The Woman's interests, as intelligence suggested could be the case, he would want to be certain before committing himself. Certainly, he had grilled Ingrid on her story in more detail than any of those before him. Seeing the way Durcell's gaze stayed on her as he weighed her answers, Carver was thankful for the hours the women had put in making sure Ingrid could play her part convincingly. Carissa, of course, needed no rehearsing.

Eventually, Durcell rose from his chair to come forward, proffering a hand to Carissa as she rose with him. After an appropriate pause, Ingrid also got to her feet.

Pressing the rocker-switch on the console, Carver spoke into the mic. 'They're getting ready to move. Remy, are you there yet?'

The voice in his ear said, 'I am here. Tell me when they leave.'

For the next few minutes, Durcell nursed Carissa's hand in both of his as if she were an old friend, huddling into her as they spoke together, though too softly for the mics to pick up. Several times, a nod in Ingrid's direction indicated they were talking about her. For her part, Ingrid stayed in role, waiting in silence while doing her best to look suitably flattered by his attentions. Carver was impressed. For a detective, she wasn't a bad actor. All the more so considering how she hated the part she was playing, the sorts of people it demanded she meet. She had told him so, many times.

Eventually Durcell let go Carissa's hand and turned towards the door. At the top of the screen, his female companion finally stirred, rising to her feet, making ready to depart. Carver held his breath and waited, just in case. His disappointment stayed as she slid to her right and out of the camera's view.

'Bollocks.'

Then they were gone.

'Remy,' he radioed again. 'They're leaving.'

'Oui.'

Carver headed for the door. He was on the fifth floor. The door through to the back stairs was twenty yards down the corridor. It wasn't a problem. When they first set the operation up to run from the hotel's fourth and fifth floors he'd rehearsed the descent, timing it to the second. He hadn't yet had to make it in earnest, but he knew that the Comte and his lady would take the lift, which was old and slow. It was easily do-able, provided none of the hotel staff had chosen that particular moment to start shifting beds between floors or anything.

CHAPTER 2

Marianne Desmarais stood at the kerbside, arms rigid at her side, eyes closed, mouth set in a thin line. She was fighting against the temptation to give in to the voice telling her she should abandon her mission, *right now,* and return to her hotel. All she had to do was cross Plâce Madelaine then walk the two hundred metres that would take her to the St Augustin Metro. From there she could head straight back to Montmartre. She could be checked out and on her way to Gare St. Lazare within the hour. By late evening she could be home, safe in the arms of her husband, Guy, her children, Marie-Rose and Thierry, at her side. But warming though the images were, Marianne knew she dare not follow the voice's directions. To do so would mean abandoning them all to the ruination she had brought upon them. How could she carry on, knowing she had come all this way, only to give up with her goal in sight? No, she had planned too long, travelled too far, to even think such a thing. Steeling herself, she turned to face her enemy.

The stretch of grey cobble stared back at her, waiting. Though the warming sun had now broken through, damp patches from the morning's showers still showed between the brickwork. On the other side of the railings to her left, the broad flight of steps led up to the church's great bronze doors. In her conflicted state, Marianne imagined the cobbles themselves daring her to make another pass, to attempt once more what she had failed to do three times already. On each of her previous tries, the cobbles had defied her intentions, carrying her past the gate through which she meant to turn. The thought came that perhaps the stones themselves were imbued with some divine power by which they could see into people's minds and deny access to those deemed unworthy. But even as it formed, Marianne recognised it for what it was, a faint-hearted attempt to cast blame from where it truly lay. She knew full well that the enemy was not the ground beneath her feet, but her own fear. But by transposing her guilt in such a way, she hoped she might strengthen her resolve.

She clenched her fists at her side. 'This time,' she said. 'This time, I *will* succeed.'

A particular cobble, opposite the opening and slightly raised above the others, marked the point at which she should turn. Fixing her gaze on it, she set off once more.

As she bore down on her target, Marianne felt the familiar wave of panic starting to rise. Her heart pounded. Her breathing quickened. *Please God, give me the strength to do what I must.* She did not dwell on what would happen if her prayer went unanswered. She would not find the resolve for another attempt. *It has to be this time... It must be.. Now.*

Suddenly she was mounting the steps, one foot in front of the other, advancing towards her goal. Finally she had succeeded in getting her legs to respond to her brain's commands. As the realisation came, a joyous feeling came over her, banishing the doubts of a few short seconds ago. She *was* going to succeed. As she neared the top of the steps, exhilaration almost drove her to run, but she controlled it. For all that she was young at heart, her fortieth birthday had come and gone. In France, Paris especially, women of such years do not run. Certainly not into church.

Gaining the plateau at the top, Marianne joined with the tourists and worshippers filing through the high portal. As she crossed the threshold, a shudder of anticipation rippled through her. Once inside, she stopped to let her eyes adjust to the sudden gloom. Before her, the wondrous interior that many around had travelled far to see, seemed to stretch in every direction. In that moment, the fears and doubts she had carried with her so long melted away. And for the first time since she'd arrived in Paris, Marianne Desmarais relaxed, confident in the knowledge that she had, for once, made the right decision.

She had no way of knowing how wrong she was.

CHAPTER 3

Out in the corridor, Carver jogged down to the door at the end bearing the sign, "Sortie De Secours." Pushing it open, he took the stairs down two at a time. On the ground floor, the door to the left was marked, "Reception". Pushing through, he found himself in the lobby. Remy was over at the desk, going through the motions of registering. As Carver passed behind, the Frenchman muttered, 'If it is her, remember. We must take her.'

Carver didn't respond. He needed no reminder that on French soil he had no jurisdiction. But he didn't resent his friend's prompt. Remy had gone out on a limb just running the Op. In the event it *was* her, common sense demanded that they avoid any legal complications.

Grabbing the day's edition of 'Le Monde' off a table, Carver headed for the three leather sofas arrayed around the huge stone mantelpiece. Settling himself in the one facing the reception desk, he opened the paper at eye-level and waited. Half-a-minute later, the 'ping' from around the corner to his left announced the lift's arrival. Seconds later the couple came into view, making straight for the hotel's main entrance.

'Fuck.'

Almost inevitably, the woman was on the Count's other side, his gangly frame blocking her from Carver's view. Not daring to strain for a better look, Carver could only hunker behind his paper as they passed. Nevertheless, the half-glimpse he managed to grab set his heart pounding. The woman was tall, even allowing for her heels. And her hair was certainly very dark. Not quite as black as he remembered, but close enough he couldn't rule her out. The way she carried herself, poised and confident, was also in keeping. But he was still missing the clear view he needed. Their backs to him now, Carver dropped the paper and sat up, craning in case she turned his way. *Just a glimpse...* But even as he thought he might catch her in profile, she turned away to peruse the contents of one of the several jewellery displays littering the lobby. He stood up. The pair were almost at the revolving door. Once outside, he would have to go some to get to a position where he could see her without being spotted. If the operation ever came to run its course, it was important that he remain unrecognised. He took a few steps forward, peering after the couple. Beyond them, over by reception, he saw Remy, still waiting on his signal. *Yes or no?*

Carver shook his head. *Not yet.*

The couple slowed to negotiate the door capsule. As a gentleman should, Durcell stepped aside to let her go first. Carver held his breath. The upper halves of the doors were glass. The doors revolved anti-clockwise. So long as she kept looking ahead, he should get a decent view of her before she passed out of sight. To his left, he was conscious of Remy, gesturing, wildly. *Yes or no?*

Carver ignored him. Two more seconds and...

He froze.

Expecting to catch her right profile, he got more than he'd bargained for. As she negotiated the door, she turned towards him. Their eyes met. For a split-second, their gazes locked and held. The sort of contact people remember. Then she was gone, through the door and out onto the Avenue De L'Opera, the Count following right after. Carver turned to Remy. The Frenchman's stare was wide, expectant. *Well?*

Carver let out a long breath, before shaking his head. *No.*

Deflated, yet also relieved in a way he couldn't even begin to explain, Carver watched as the couple came together on the pavement. Pausing only to link arms, they turned left towards the Opera Garnier, before passing out of sight. In his ear, he heard Remy relaying his instructions to the rest of the team, this time in rapid French. 'Ne les arrêtes pas. Je repete. Ne les arrêtes pas.' *Do not stop them. Repeat. Do not stop them.*

A couple of hundred metres away as the crow flies, Marianne Desmarais blinked and squinted as she stepped out into the bright sunlight. The morning clouds had cleared and as she looked up into the cobalt sky, she experienced a lightness of spirit she had not felt in a long time.

Since arriving in Paris two days before, she had spent much of her time casting furtive glances at people on the bus, the metro, in the hotel. The past few days her guilt had built to the point where she had convinced herself that despite the city's vastness, she was bound to bump into someone from her home town. They would, she was certain, have heard about her grandmother's 'sudden illness.' They would want to know why she was here, instead of tending to the old lady's needs in Provence.

Now, buoyed by her new-found feeling of freedom, Marianne had no time for such fears. She was even thinking of catching the train home that evening, rather than staying over another night. She was surprised to realise that she was actually excited by the thought of seeing Guy again, something she had not experienced in months.

Such was her good-heart, Marianne had no thought for others as she almost skipped down the steps that earlier had proved so troublesome. Even if she had, she would not have given the figure in the dark coat, halfway down on her right, a second glance. Holding a mobile out at arm's length, the figure's only interest seemed to be in capturing the perfect symmetry of the view down the Avenue De Medici, and across the river to the imposing, Assemblie Nationale. But once Marianne was past, the arm lowered. A second later the device disappeared into the coat's side pocket. At the bottom of the steps, Marianne turned left in the direction that would take her back to her hotel. The figure waited until she rounded the corner into the Plâce and out of sight, before descending, rapidly, and following in her footsteps.

CHAPTER 4

Jess Greylake returned to her new apartment's first-floor living area to find her three visitors admiring the view from the picture window. She couldn't blame them. It was the view of the stream at the bottom of the garden and the surrounding woodland that had swung her decision to rent in the first place. That and the 'special deal' she had managed to work out with the property's well-off insurance broker owner.

When her visitors first arrived, she had been in the middle of one of the difficult telephone conversations with her mother that had become more regular since the chemo began. Leaving them to see to themselves - 'You know where the kettle is,' - she excused herself and retreated into the main bedroom. There, she spent several minutes reassuring her mother on the matters about which she needed reassuring. Yes, she would pick her up early enough the next morning that they would get to the hospital in good time for her ten o'clock appointment. And yes, she would stay over as long as necessary if the much-feared-but-so-far-absent worst effects of the poisons being administered kicked in the way Mrs Kathily, the oncologist, had warned could happen any time. Jess didn't even try pointing out that the treatments so far had gone well and that there was no reason to believe that tomorrow would be any different. They both knew that could change. And Jess had learned the hard way that when it comes to cancer, especially when the patient is your mother, the path between remaining optimistic about the future, and appearing dismissive of the risks and/or patient's fears, is a narrow one. In the early days, she had slipped off that path a couple of times. She had no intention of doing so again.

As she came back in and saw the three men stood in line, she ignored the two on the end and made straight for the one in the middle. Wrapping him in her arms, she hung onto him, tightly. And when she realised she was struggling for words, she settled for tightening the hug further. It must have gone on longer than she realised, because when she did eventually open her eyes, it was to find Alec Duncan staring at her with one of his cock-eyed smiles on his face. Finally letting go, she stepped back to look at the man who, the last time she saw him, was still bed-bound and only just beginning to speak again. The scar running down the left side of his face pulled his eye down a little, same with the corner of his mouth, and she could see a lot of his previous vitality was yet to return. But apart from that, he looked *so* much better than last time. She patted his stomach.

'You've lost weight. You either need fattening up, or to get back in training.'

Detective Sergeant Gavin Baggus made a point of looking offended. And when he spoke it was all Jess could do to keep from smiling at the slight lisp that crept in every now and then and which she knew the doctors had said would pass in time.

'Well that's nithe,' he said. Turning, he addressed the older man who still towered over them all. 'You were right, thir. She's not bloody changed at all.'

As Jess turned a pointed look on him, Detective Chief Superintendent John 'The Duke' Morrison rushed to defend himself. 'I didn't actually say that. What I said was, he'd probably find you more like your old self.' Seeing her eyebrows starting to rise, he tried again. 'What I meant was he'd- Ah, fuck it, why should I worry? You two work it out.'

As Jess brewed them all coffee - mint tea for Baggus - Alec and The Duke brought up the boxes of documents that were the main reason for their visit. When Baggus made to help, Jess ordered him to stay where he was. 'You're on light duties, remember?' About to argue, he must have seen the look in her face and didn't. They stacked the boxes next to the others in the corner of the room. Jess could see they carried the by-now familiar customs and transit stamps, some in French, some English. When they were finished, The Duke nodded across at the dining table the other side of the room. It was completely hidden under bundles of papers and photographs.

'How's the analysis going?'

She put on a pained look. 'Making progress, but there's a lot of ground to catch up. It's a pity we weren't in at the start.'

'Have you spoken to Jamie lately?'

'Not since last week. I'm due a call soon, I think.'

The Duke harrumphed. 'You and me both. Talk about out of sight out of mind. If you hear from him before I do, tell him I'd appreciate an update.'

'Will do.'

Their first visit to the place, Jess gave them all the tour before Alec and The Duke had to head back to Warrington, leaving Jess to put Baggus on the train back to Gloucester when he/they were ready. As Jess anticipated they were impressed, and suspicious.

'It's a hell of place, lassie,' Alec said. 'Yer very lucky'

The Duke was more direct.

'I never realised a DS's wages can stretch so far. Or must I hope that Professional Standards don't get wind of it?'

She gave him a straight look. 'With all respect, sir, if anyone else had said that, I'd tell them to fuck off and mind their own business.'

Alec and Baggus shied at her boldness, but The Duke just nodded. 'Fair enough.'

Later, as they were leaving, The Duke noticed the room downstairs, next to the garage. Jess hadn't included it in their tour. Boxes of flat-pack furniture were stacked outside the door. When The Duke asked about it, Jess was non-committal.

'I've not decided what to do with it yet. It's either going to be a work-out room or an office.'

'Got the furniture already though, I see.' Jess could see him scrutinising the boxes. 'Not going for Ikea then?'

She gave a half smile. 'It wouldn't fit with the surroundings.'

The Duke nodded. 'Hmm. Probably not.'

After waving them off, Jess turned to the young detective whom she once thought she would never speak to again. For several seconds they both just stared at each other, as if neither were sure where to start.

Jess's head was a jumble of thoughts and feelings. She had no idea what was in his. The last meaningful conversation they had had, the day he was attacked, they had talked about relationships, their feelings for certain people. She wondered how much of it, if any, he remembered. But then she reminded herself. This was his first proper venture out since leaving hospital. She ought to treat him gently... for now at least.

Slipping an arm through his, she turned him back towards the house. 'I think me and you have got some catching up to do.'

And as Gavin Baggus let himself be guided by her, he felt the stir of something he thought he remembered, but could not be sure if it was a false memory.

In the heart of Montmartre, on the fifth floor of the Pension Turec on Rue De Grave, Marianne Desmarais paused in her packing to stare across at the door. The double knock had been gentle, inquisitive almost. Arriving back at the hotel, she'd asked the young man at the desk to wait an hour then send up a porter for her bags. He was early.

'Moment,' she said.

Taking the blouse off the hanger, she folded it neatly into the case before turning to the door. As she rounded the bed, force of habit made her check herself in the dresser-mirror. As her mother had always cautioned her, lone women in hotels must always guard against giving out signals that could be misinterpreted. Imagining she was showing too much of herself, she adjusted her top, before opening the door.

It wasn't the porter.

CHAPTER 5

As in a great many Paris restaurants, a trip to the washrooms of the Café Rive Gauche in the heart of the Eiffel Tower district involves negotiating winding walks, twisting stairs and dimly-lit corridors. Inside the restaurant, the flowery wallpaper is barely visible under the blanket of photographs, posters and movie memorabilia that reflect the owner's long fascination with Hollywood's 'Golden Age' and the stars he claims have visited the place. The two features combine to confuse and distract, which is why it took Tory Martinez so long to find her way back to the outside table where Scott, her fiancé, waited. They had chosen that particular table especially for its evocative view of the City's most famous landmark, poking above the grey-slate rooftops opposite.

As she emerged back into the sunlight, Tory knew at once that Scott had not been bored during her absence. The state-of-the-art Nikon he'd bought especially for their European back-packing trip was up and trained. Only it wasn't aimed at the structure towering over them. Instead, it was pointing across at another table. The one, *She* was sitting at.

Earlier, after they had arrived, settled, and ordered

drinks, it had taken Tory a while before she became aware of the woman's presence. To begin with, as they spoke of their plans for the next few days, she assumed Scott was admiring the views as his gaze kept slipping away over her left shoulder. Which of course he was, of a sort. But as the discussion headed towards the argument it was destined to become, Tory realised his attention wasn't on her as much as it ought to be. She turned to check the source of his distraction, which was when she saw her for the first time.

The woman was sitting at a front corner table, shielded from the afternoon sun by one of the large, burgundy shades. Angled, so she was facing away from them, she was nevertheless in Scott's direct line of sight. Tory noted at once how the plain, black dress complemented her tanned complexion and coal-black hair. Her legs were crossed at the knee, a glimpse of toned thigh showing through the slit in the side. Although the fashionable, wrap-around sunglasses hid much of her face, Tory put her at around forty, albeit a well-preserved one. She understood the reasons for Scott's distraction at once. Before coming away, Tory had heard much about Paris's beautiful women. And this particular example of the genre, posed with a glass of rosé in her left hand, a bottle of Perrier water on the table next to her as she flicked, idly, through some glossy magazine, was as eye-catching as any Tory had seen so far.

But though her fiancé's Pavlovian response to a woman old enough, probably, to be his mother irritated her, Tory stayed focused on their discussion. It involved an important point of principle, and she wasn't going to let herself be distracted by her fiance's wandering eye.

Turning back to him, she pinned him with the look she used those times she wanted to register her displeasure. For several seconds, Scott's expression was that of a little boy caught with his hand in the cookie jar. Then it morphed into the cheeky grin that, even after so long, she still found hard to resist.

Another time, Tory may have caved into giggles, an exasperated smile at the very least. But on this occasion, she managed to hold it together, just. Since becoming officially engaged, she had grown more and more aware of just how often she allowed him to charm her into giving way to his view - though he was yet to succeed with regard to, *all the way.* Well not this time. Ignoring the cause of the distraction, she dug in.

'Nice try Babe, but it isn't going to work. I'm not giving on this one.'

Scott Weston must have realised that for once, his Ivy-League looks and boyish charms were set to fail. Crossing his arms, he leaned back in his chair. His face set in a scowl.

'Well I'm sorry, but I'd like to stay and see more of Paris.'

Tory stared at the young man who had loved her as long as she could remember. At the same time she tried to gauge if his uncharacteristic insistence on, 'having his own way for once,' marked a fair preference, or was just the latest of the worrying signs she'd seen of late. They had agreed long ago that the by-word for their relationship would always be, Equality. Nevertheless, she was beginning to wonder if there weren't times when he expected that she should defer to him for no reason other than he needed reassuring that he hadn't yet been emasculated. For Tory's part, his balls on a plate were not, and never would be, on her agenda. She had known Scott and loved him back ever since she was six, when she and her family moved in next door to his in the affluent Boston suburb of Newton. But if Scott had any thoughts that their long familiarity meant she would let him push her around, simply to assuage some latent male insecurity, she needed to rid him of the idea, and quickly. Certainly before the wedding. Twelve months sounded a long time, but she knew from her sister's experience it would flash by. Before they knew it, it would all be upon them. Too late then to start laying down ground rules. Still, for the time being she was happy to rely on the, 'Training In Making An Argument,' that had been part of both their lives these past three years.

'Okay. So we stay over in Paris a few days. What do you think that'll do to our budget? You've seen how expensive everything is here.'

He shrugged. 'We re-jig it. It's no big deal.'

She repeated his last words, calmly, 'No big deal,' at the same time, giving him a long, even look. Reaching down to her backpack, she plucked out the plastic wallet containing the itinerary they'd worked so hard on together. She ran her eyes over it.

'Let's see. Monaco... Rome... Madrid... Barcelona.... Hmm... No. I guess you're right. It *is* no big deal.' She slid it across the table. 'You decide.'

'Decide what?'

'Which of those places we agreed were, 'musts' we're going to cut out.'

Scott rolled his blue eyes. 'Aw, c'mon Tory, don't be melodramatic. We don't need to cut anything.'

'No? So what do we use for money when we get to

all these wonderful places we want to see and find we spent it all in Paris and can't afford to stop? You've seen how much just a coffee costs here. How much do you think we'll spend in a week? Or are you thinking we'll just dangle our feet in the Seine, gaze up at the Eiffel Tower, and be so taken in by the romance of it all, we won't need food, drink or a bed to sleep in?'

He began to bristle. For a lawyer-to-be, he was yet to master how to deal with a direct challenge.

'There's no need for sarcasm. All I'm saying is, we both agree there's something magical about Paris. We've been here a day and a half and we've barely scratched the surface. There's still so much we both would like to see. And we can if we knock a few half-days off some of these other places. I know they're all wonderful, but let's face it, there's nowhere like Paris. And who knows when we might be here again?'

About to come straight back at him, Tory hesitated. For all her opposition to the idea, Scott was right about one thing. Once married and settled in the legal careers that awaited them it would, in all likelihood, be a long time before they saw Europe again - unless one of them did so spectacularly well as to land a job in one of the firm's three European offices, London, Paris or Milan. It was why they had planned the trip so carefully, agreeing exactly what they wanted to see, where they would stay, how they would travel. The attention to detail was essential they'd agreed, if they were to keep to the budget that would leave them enough for the down-payment on the Greenwich Village apartment they'd set their sights on. Thanks to Scott's real estate buddy, Greg, they already knew it would be coming on the market the month after their return. Over the past few weeks, thoughts of clinching the property had dominated almost as much as scheduling the trip they had long dreamed of. Using the architect's blueprints that cost them a bottle of Greg's favourite Jim Beam, Tory had even worked out the colour scheme for the nursery, though they'd both agreed they should wait a few years before even thinking about kids.

Apart from breaking the budget, the thought of not seeing some of the places they had planned to, worried Tory more than she expected. Her Norwegian-born grandmother had travelled throughout Europe before heading to the USA and marrying an enterprising Mexican. Thanks to the old woman's tales, Tory had grown up yearning to one day see the places her grandmother used to describe so graphically.

But Scott was also right about Paris. It *was* magical. She *would* love to see more of it. But if they broke their budget now, what would it mean later? Okay, she only had to pick up the phone and speak with her father and the money thing would stop being an issue. But she wouldn't do it. Nor would Scott. It was something they both felt strongly about. *Emergency only.*

She glanced across the table. One look was enough to see that, in the face of her silence, he was already softening. He wasn't the only one who knew which buttons to press, though she did so less often than he. She knew that if she really stuck it out, chances were, she would prevail. But she could also see that he really, *really* wanted to see more of Paris.

It was at that point she decided a toilet break might give her the time needed so she could consider the conundrum.

By the time she found her way back, through the

maze of staircases and corridors, her thoughts were already turning to a compromise. The last thing she wanted was to remember Paris as the place they fell out. If they cut out Monaco altogether, they might manage at least a couple more days in Paris. Truth be told, it wasn't so much her grandmother, as her fondness for Grace Kelly in the old Hitchcock classic, To Catch a Thief, that she'd included the tiny Principality at all. But as she arrived back at the table and saw where his camera was focused – on the woman in the black dress - she wondered if her consideration for his wishes wasn't premature.

As she took her seat – Scott was still peering into the viewfinder – she made a point of clearing her throat, loudly.

'Ahem.'

Scott turned towards her, though the camera stayed up. The cheeky grin again.

'What, may I ask, do you think you're doing?'

Taking a last look at the screen, he lowered the instrument.

'I'm shooting the sights and sounds of Paris, what do you think?'

She pointed up, and across the street. 'It's over there. Or hadn't you noticed?'

'I shot that yesterday. And I took a few more from here while you've been gone.' He threw a glance across the tables before leaning into her, conspiratorially. 'It's just-'

'Just what?'

His tongue made a strange clicking noise. 'That woman-'

'What about her?'

'Well, looking at her, sitting there. Don't you think she's so... typically *French*?'

'Er... Hello? Aren't we like, in *Paris*?'

'I know *that*. What I mean is, isn't she just how you imagine a sophisticated Frenchwoman should look? Like, maybe she's a countess or something? She reminds me of one of those women in that Italian guy's paintings. What's his name, Vetrano?'

'If you mean Jack Vettriano, he's Scottish.'

'Really? Jeez, I'd never have thought. Anyway, it makes no matter. You know what I'm saying. She's one for the scrap book.'

'Nice,' Tory said. 'In years to come, we'll be showing our friends the snaps of our European trip and I'll be saying, "It was all soooo romantic and, oh yes, this is the woman my husband got the hots for outside a Paris street café." Great.'

'Aww-' He turned to her and suddenly his arms were round her, pulling her into him, burying his stubble into her neck the way she both hated and loved. 'You're the only gal I'll *ever* get the hots for Tory. You know that.'

She tried pushing him away, feigning hurt. 'I know no such thing.' But he was too strong. 'And if I ever did, I'm definitely having serious doubts now.'

They were still wrestling when a soft voice said, 'Excuse me?'

Tory stopped struggling to turn and look up.

Scott did the same. His jaw fell open.

CHAPTER 6

As the two women exited onto the Avenue de L'Opera, they cast teasing smiles at the concierge who responded, swiftly, to help them negotiate the revolving door. Turning right, they headed south towards the river, heels clicking on the pavement. The concierge was not the only one whose head turned to follow their departure.

Across the road, in the recessed doorway of Foucher, the famous chocolatier, Carver carried on pretending to peruse the displays of succulent but ridiculously-expensive delights while following their reflection. The convenient curve in the glass and the Avenue's arrow-like precision meant he could track their progress all the way down to the Louvre if necessary. As it was, he judged a slow count of thirty enough. Turning from the window he crossed the road and headed south.

Fifty yards ahead, the women's sashaying progress was still turning heads. But Carver's interest lay not with the women themselves, but with those following behind, whether on foot or by vehicle. Half-an-hour had passed since Durcell and the woman he'd never seen before had left the hotel. On balance, Carver doubted that, having turned up for the meeting, Durcell would go to the trouble of arranging to have them followed. If he had doubts, all he needed to do was walk away, as a couple of the early marks had done. On the other hand, if his and his lady's interest was genuine, they had nothing to lose by waiting for word of when and where the event they were seeking to buy into would be staged.

Carver's initial sweep of what lay between him and the women in front raised no alarms. In the case of those on foot, they all fitted with the expected profiles - tourists, shoppers, business-folk. As they progressed he spotted none of the give-aways that most often expose surveillance - double-backs, sudden direction shifts, masking behaviours. It was the same with vehicle traffic, the only exception being a white van, which slowed as it drew level with the women. But even as Carver came on alert, the muscled forearm that appeared from the driver's window and the accompanying gesture, reassured him he was seeing nothing more than that worldwide phenomenon, White Van Man, in action. Carissa's immediate response, a raised middle finger, confirmed it.

Satisfied there was nothing that warranted further investigation, he slowed his pace to match that of the women, and settled down for what he anticipated would be an uneventful stroll across Paris.

Fifty yards behind Carver, the heavy-set man in the black leather jacket and jeans also slowed his pace to that of his subject's. He'd had no difficulty matching the English detective with the description he'd been given. He marked him the moment he saw him in Foucher's doorway. And it was hardly a chore having to loiter so long in the shop's back-room. The chocolatier's taste-before-buying policy saw to that. He had no idea where the trail he was now following may lead, or even what use that information would be to those paying for his services. But the way the Englishman appeared oblivious to the possibility he may be followed, it stood to be the easiest piece of work he'd undertaken in a long time.

CHAPTER 7

Standing over their table, and with the sun behind so that it framed her in a halo of light, Tory's first thought was she was seeing some saintly vision. Her second was, *She's beautiful.*

As she untangled herself from Scott's embrace and came around straight, Tory's angle changed enough so she could see the woman was wearing a half-smile that brought to mind the one in the disappointingly small portrait they'd perused in the Louvre, the day before.

'I am sorry. Please excuse me' the woman repeated. Tory tried to place her accent. Somewhere between French and English. 'I hate to interrupt at a private moment like this, but-'

Gathering herself, Tory tried to respond as she thought a polite American girl should, at the same time hoping she wasn't blushing too much. 'I'm sorry if we disturbed you. It's just, this is our first time in Paris and we-'

'No no,' the woman said quickly. 'Do not apologise. It is wonderful to see young people in love. It is exactly how it should be in Paris.' She turned her gaze on Scott. The smile grew.

Tory turned to her fiancé. His mouth was hanging

open as he looked up at the woman who had interrupted their tomfoolery. As if sensing his girlfriend's stare, he snapped it shut. For once, he seemed lost for words. Tory turned back.

'Can we help you?'

The woman put a hand to her face, bit her lip. Tory sensed embarrassment.

'Well it's just... I am sorry, this will sound so silly.'

'Please, go on.'

The woman looked around, as if she was torn, facing a difficult decision. One or two of the customers at other tables seemed to be taking a casual interest, in what or who exactly, Tory wasn't sure. As if aware of it, the woman said, 'May I sit for a moment?'

'Please.' Tory pulled out a chair. She sat down.

The woman hesitated, took a deep breath then turned her gaze full on Scott. 'You were pointing a camera at me. Were you by any chance... taking my picture?'

Scott rocked back, eyes wide. Tory's stomach lurched. *Uh-oh*.

Much of their final semester had been given over to considering the complexities surrounding privacy entitlements, harassment, and related subjects. Tory had celebrated when their finals were over and she had finally got to put her books away, for a little while at least. Now, in the space of a single second, it all came swooping back. Her head filled with thoughts of subpoenas and invasion-of-privacy suits.

'I'm sorry, my boyfriend was only-' She stopped. If she lied now and was found out, it would make matters a whole lot worse.

Scott looked wary, almost vulnerable. 'I was just-' He stopped as the woman's hand came up. An emerald the size of a quarter flashed in the sun's rays.

'Please, do not worry. I do not wish to complain... exactly.'

Wary, Tory waited. Silence was the least damaging course while they figured out what she wanted. Money? A quick pay-off? Between them they probably had a couple of hundred Euros, cash. She remembered passing an ATM down the street. She flashed a warning to Scott. It said, *Wait till I get you back to the hostel*.

The woman continued. 'But I saw you pointing a camera in my direction while you were taking pictures. I am just interested to know if by any chance I appear in any of them?'

Scott had been brought up to be as honest as the day is long. His tutor at Yale had noted it on his Graduate Portfolio, under "Areas of Potential Weakness." He barely hesitated before reaching for his camera.

'I'm sorry. I'll delete them at once. I meant no offence. I was just trying to capture the, uh... ambience of Paris.'

Tory thought, *Scott, shut the fuck up*.

At that moment and for the first time, the woman unleashed the full force of her smile. And as she did, the world changed. In that moment Tory knew she had everything wrong. This woman meant them no harm. Everything was going to be fine. The woman reached across Tory to place a soothing hand on Scott's arm. A fragrance, heavy and heady, wafted.

'It is alright. I did not mean to embarrass you.'

Scott stopped fiddling with his camera. His mouth gaped again. Tory thought that if she listened closely, she would hear his heart thumping. Then she realised. The way the woman was leaning across her, her face close to hers, her heart was racing as well. She had even paused in her breathing. However old she was, she had an amazing complexion.

The woman pulled her hand away, leaned back in her chair. Tory breathed again.

'And I am flattered that you seem to think me a worthy subject.' The smile was still there. Scott looked like he might melt through the chair's cane weave. 'But I am afraid I have this silly phobia about having my picture taken. I get anxious and have panic attacks if I think someone has taken my photograph without my permission.'

Scott seemed to sense he may be about to be let off the hook. He snapped out of whatever had him. 'No problem. Like I said, I'll delete them right now.'

The woman seemed to hesitate, then said, 'Would you mind letting me see them before you do?' She held out a hand. In some way Tory couldn't quite grasp, it seemed more like a command than a request. 'I am trying to treat myself to get over my affliction. Seeing them may actually help.'

Scott beamed. 'Of course. Here, let me show you.' For what seemed minutes but was probably only seconds Tory found herself trapped in the middle as Scott showed the woman the viewfinder, demonstrated how to scroll through the images. 'Like this, see? Here, take it. Have a look.' As he passed the camera across, Tory glared at him. Far from the 'couple of shots' he had spoken of, she had glimpsed several, and there were more he hadn't got to.

For the next couple of minutes, Tory and Scott waited and watched in silence as the woman examined the pictures, turning the camera as they changed aspect from portrait to landscape and back again. Tory counted well over a dozen presses of the 'back' button before the woman handed the camera back to Scott.

'They are very good. I do not mean me, of course. I am nothing. I mean the quality of the pictures. Are you a professional?'

Scott chuckled, falling for it. 'Nah, I've just graduated from law school.' He remembered Tory. 'We're *both* law graduates.'

Tory smiled. And thank *you* for remembering. She turned to study the woman who moments before had given her such a fright but now seemed so amiable. Which was when she realised. Their new found companion seemed to be scrutinising *them*, her gaze passing over them, up, down and back. Though she couldn't say why, Tory experienced the same sort of feeling she'd had that day when she'd sat before the firm's three senior partners, doing her best to give the answers they wanted to hear - the feeling of being *assessed*.

'Law graduates? You are American, yes?' They both nodded. 'Did you study here, or at home?'

Again, it was Scott who responded first. 'The US. We just graduated. From Yale. We're on holiday. You know, travelling around Europe?'

Tory could hardly believe it. Scott hadn't talked so much since they'd left from JFK.

'Really? How interesting. Listen, I am sorry for intruding on your privacy. And I apologise if I startled you with my questions. Please, may I buy you both a drink?'

Tory smiled at the woman's offer, relaxed now that she knew there was not going to be a problem. But their afternoon was already set aside for Sacre Coeur and the Montmartre district. From what she'd heard, the quarter's Bohemian ambiance sounded fascinating. She opened her mouth to speak. She wasn't quick enough.

'That's swell of you,' Scott said. 'Do you know if they sell Bud here?'

CHAPTER 8

When the door to the apartment opened, Carver could tell that for Carissa Lavergne at least, the morning's business was already history. Without the restraining peg, her hair was about her face and shoulders in a way that for her bordered on tousled. In place of the expensive Italian heels were a pair of gold mules, though he suspected they were probably no less expensive. On her face, the haughty-bored expression he knew so well. She made a point of hesitating before admitting him, as if he had called at an inconvenient time and she was considering telling him to come back later. Eventually, she stepped aside and opened the door, just wide enough he might slip through. As he brushed past her, the unmistakable fragrance of Shalimar acted like a trigger and he had to force the memories away. When he first realised the coincidence of her favouring that particular fragrance, he'd been more than a little unnerved.

Inside, the apartment was as elegant and plush as a residence on the fringe of the Jardin De Luxembourg ought to be. Stopping in the middle of the spacious living area, he turned to her, only to see her crossing to the drinks cabinet next to the full-length window that looked out over the park. Lifting a decanter containing something with deep, velvety undertones, she showed it to him. Much still to do before the day was done, he shook his head. 'But don't let me stop you.'

'Do not worry, Jamie. You won't.'

As she poured a second glass - for Ingrid, presumably - bathroom noises filtered through one of the doors. He nodded to it. 'How is she?'

Placing the decanter down with deliberate care, Carissa made a half-turn towards the bathroom, as if choosing her words. She rocked a hand, indicating uncertainty. As she did so, the several stones on her fingers glinted and flashed in the sunlight streaming through the windows. 'She is okay, I think. But it is hard for her. Each time she feels the need to cleanse herself after.'

He nodded. *Understandable*.

Standing there, he was conscious of the seconds stretching as he groped for something to say. His discomfort surprised him. Given the past, and especially the nature of their enterprise, there was much about which they could have spoken. At the very least he could ask after her family. Only that risked dredging up memories for which, he was sure, she would not thank him. They had only ever spoken once of the matter that had brought them together. The murder of her stepsister, Anna, the third victim of the so-called Worshipper Killer. That was on the day she agreed to help him draw her sister's killer from hiding. They had not spoken of it since, though there had been occasions when he'd thought about delving. Their joint mission meant that they met regularly to assess progress. Nevertheless he was yet to discover what she really thought about what they were doing. In the twelve months that had passed since he first sought her out - after coming across a reference to the the parallel nature of the sisters' interests whilst trawling through the remains of Megan Crane's burnt-out archive - he'd never heard her express hatred towards the woman who had taken her sister from her. Even so, he knew it was there.

An expensive-looking handbag, tan leather festooned with gold chains and straps, rested on the table. Reaching into it, Carissa drew out the now familiar gold cigarette case and lighter. Taking out one of her thin cheroots she lit up, drawing on it deeply while still keeping him in her gaze. She blew smoke away over her shoulder, then stood there, cradling her smoking arm in her hand while regarding him with the sort of expression that says, 'Well?'

Carver felt the need to break the silence. 'How do you think it went with Durcell? Did he buy it?'

She considered it. 'Who knows? He said the right things. But he will want to be careful. We will know better when we hear from him again.' She paused before adding, '*If* we hear from him again.'

He nodded. *What did he expect? A signed contract?*

'Besides,' she continued. 'You saw. What do *you* think?'

His turn to ponder. 'He *seemed* interested. The way he kept looking at Ingrid...' He caught Carissa's smirk. Her opinions of men were, he now knew, low. 'But whether it was enough to make him buy in...' He shrugged. 'As you say, we will see.'

For a moment longer they stood there, looking at each other. Carver sensed as much as saw the amusement in her eyes. Then, just as the silence was beginning to stretch too far, the bathroom door opened and Ingrid came out.

Paris CID Detective Sergeant Ingrid Prideux was wrapped up in a fluffy, white-cotton bathrobe. Her still-wet hair hung in clumps around her face and down her back. Seeing Carver she stopped. He wasn't sure if the flush in her face was the result of having just stepped from the shower, or finding him there. She looked first at Carissa, then back at him.

'I thought we were meeting later?'

Carver felt Carissa's amused expression as he replied. 'We are. I, er... just wanted to check you were... That you are both... Okay.'

Ingrid forced a smile. 'I am. We are.'

As he saw the glance that passed between them, Carver suddenly felt like an idiot. They were due to meet later anyway for a structured de-brief. Whatever excuse he gave, there was no good reason for his turning up now. None he cared to mention, at least. 'Good,' he said.

About to make his excuses and get the hell out, there was a knock on the door. He checked with both women. Ingrid looked blank. Carissa shrugged. *I have no idea.* He crossed to the door, opened it.

Remy didn't wait to be invited, but strode straight in. 'Where's Ingrid? I need Ingrid.'

Seeing the two women he stopped. When he turned to address Ingrid, Carver noticed how he seemed to make a point of ignoring Carissa.

'I've just had a call. There's been another one.'

Ingrid's face fell. 'Merde.'

To his shame, Carver felt the tingle of opportunity.

'Where?'

'Montmartre.'

Ingrid headed for one of the bedrooms. 'Give me two minutes.'

As the door closed, Carver turned to Carissa.

'Carissa, this is Remy Crozier. He is-'

'The Police Inspector who is helping us. Yes, I know. A pleasure to see you again, Remy. How are things?'

The look on the Frenchman's face as he met Carissa's gaze was unreadable. 'I am well, Madam. Merci.' He turned back to Carver.

'I have a car waiting. Now you will be able to see for yourself what this maniac does.' Carver nodded but made sure not to show enthusiasm for the task. Remy threw another glance at Carissa - it was as unreadable as the first - before leaving as suddenly as he'd arrived.

Carver turned to her. Traces of a smile lingered at the corners of her mouth. 'You didn't tell me you know him.'

She feigned a light-hearted air. 'There are still many things you do not know about me, or my sister, Jamie.'

A minute later the bedroom door opened and Ingrid stepped out. She had thrown on a black skirt, red top, short black leather jacket and black boots. No makeup. Her still-damp hair was pulled into a pony-tail, held by a black velvet scrunch. She looked terrific.

'Where's Remy?'

'Waiting downstairs.'

She headed for the door. 'I will call you later Carissa.'

As he made to follow, Carver threw a last glance back at the woman standing alone in the middle of the room. Mischief mingled with features that were designed to seduce. He gave her a scolding look, then closed the door, firmly, behind him.

As Carver followed Ingrid's determined strut towards the stairs, he hoped to God that Carissa Lavergne wasn't seeing it all as a game. Things were bad enough as they were.

CHAPTER 9

Carver stood in the corner furthest from the bed, his back to the wall. They had agreed at the outset that if he ever found himself at the scene of one of *Le Boucher's* atrocities, his part would only be to observe. He had been observing since they'd arrived an hour earlier, watching the detectives and forensics going about their grim business. In that time he had learned much. Unfortunately, none of it was of any immediate help towards finding whoever had butchered the woman still tied to the bed in the way he had seen thus far only in photographs. Marianne Desmarais's blood was everywhere.

One of the things he *had* learned, however, was that there was a side to Ingrid he had not seen before.

In the slightly more than four weeks they had known each other, most of their time together had been spent planning out and rehearsing the series of meetings of which the one that morning was the latest, usually with Carissa present. Most days, he also got to see her working with the rest of the investigation team, in the unique surroundings of the offices of the Paris Police's, 'Premier De CID' in the heart of the Ile de la Cité. But it was usually from a distance, and in circumstances that meant he had little chance to gauge how she operated in her more usual working environment. Her closeness to Remy and the obvious trust he placed in her, had to mean she was more than just competent, but beyond that, Carver had no real feel for her capabilities.

The opportunity that had been missing came as soon as they drew up outside the simply titled, 'Pension Turec' in the heart of the Montmartre District. The moment she stepped out of the car, Ingrid changed in a way that made Carver hope to God he hadn't been guilty of patronising her these past weeks. For though he could follow little of what she said, it was clear she knew all about managing crime scenes. A couple of glances up and down the cobbled street that sloped down and away from the glory that was the dome of Sacre Coeur, were all Ingrid needed to assess things. Police vehicles, parked at all angles and with their blue lights flashing, were still strung along the street, their occupants milling around, singly or in pairs, talking to each other or into their radios, all the while trying to look like they knew what they were supposed to be doing. Unlike them, Ingrid did. As they made their way towards the hotel's narrow entrance, she barked commands and pointed, first at the officers, then at both ends of the street, waving her arms and issuing directions in a way that left them all in no doubt she was not happy. No one argued. Carver was impressed. As they'd turned in, his first thought had been why the road hadn't yet been blocked off. It continued inside.

The hotel reception was little more than a walk-round counter built into the cramped hallway. Even as her eyes darted here and there, noting the layout, those present, she was throwing questions at the uniformed

Policier guarding the stairs. The way the young man coloured as he stammered his replies, Carver guessed she was pointing out what she considered to be failures in his attempts at scene control. Reaching into the breast pocket of his blouson, he took out pen and paper, and there and then began the log he should have started the moment it became clear it was a crime scene. Even as she was instructing him, she interrupted herself to hail two detectives, about to ascend the narrow, winding staircase. The rapid-fire exchange between them, accompanied by the hand waving and gestures that in France characterise even the most minor exchange of views, were enough for Carver to imagine an approximate translation.

'Where do you think you are going?'

'We're just going to take a look at-'

'No you are not. Get back down here.'

'But we need to-'

'No you don't. There are enough people trampling over this scene as it is without you adding to it.'

Or words to that effect.

Carver had had the same conversation many times. He also noted how Remy, the senior detective present and clearly the more experienced of the two, didn't interfere. He seemed happy to leave to her the job of making sure that the controls needed were in place and operating. It left him free to absorb the sights and sounds of their surroundings, which is just what Carver liked to do. As he watched her in action, Carver mused on how the way she was now, assured, confident and in complete control of things, contrasted with the role she had been playing earlier that day. It made him wonder which was closer to the true Ingrid.

The second thing that Carver's observations taught him, was that after years of being stuck in the dark ages, the French Police had finally woken up to the realities of managing crime scenes in the modern world. The last time he'd attended a French murder scene, during the month-long exchange that came at the end of the European Crime Investigation Course at the Dutch Police Academy where he and Remy first met, he had been shocked by the police's scant regard for even the most basic contamination-control procedures. But now, as he noted the care being taken by those present, pathologist, scene manager, Remy and the videographer, to work together and make sure nothing was overlooked or inadvertently contaminated, he was quietly impressed. As he stood there, alone, he paid mute respect to the French police's willingness to admit its former mistakes, and to bring their efforts at managing scenes up to standard.

Enough time spent re-ordering perceptions, Carver turned his attention to the matter in hand.

That Marianne Desmarais had suffered before she died, was obvious. The amount of blood testified to the fact that she was very much alive when her killer began to carve out the meticulous pattern of lacerations Carver recognised from the photographs and videos of the other scenes. Even from his place in the corner, he could make out the burns to her wrists and ankles where she had strained, ferociously but in vain, against the leather thongs securing her to the bed. But he avoided the trap of letting himself be drawn into dwelling on what she had gone through. To do so ran the risk of not focusing on the things that were important. Turning his gaze to the wall above the bed he re-read the message written in capitals in Marianne Desmarais's own blood. "PRIEZ POUR LES ENFANTS" *Pray for the children.* There had been much debate over its meaning. If Marianne Desmarais fitted the profile of the other victims, she would have young children. But whether the message related to them, or other children, no one could yet say.

Even as he pondered on it, the pathologist working next to Remy, squatting beside the bed, rose to get something from his box across the room. Looking over his shoulder, Remy beckoned Carver to join him. It was the first time he had sought to involve him since they'd arrived.

'You see?' Remy said, as Carver squatted beside him. 'The cuts? All between three and five centimetres. Not too deep. Made by something very sharp. A razor perhaps.'

'How about a craft knife?'

Remy thought about it. 'Perhaps. Razor or knife, his aim is to cause great pain. He likes his victims to suffer.'

Carver nodded. He'd once dealt with a gangland revenge-attack where the victim was cut all over his back with a Stanley Knife so badly he'd needed close to five hundred stitches. It wasn't an attempt to kill or even maim, but a warning. He switched his gaze back to the message above the bed.

'So what about this? Where does, "Pray for the children" fit in?'

Remy shook his head. 'We cannot be sure. Presumably it is something to do with why he kills. Have you had any thoughts on it?'

'I'd say it depends whether your killer simply enjoys inflicting pain, or has some other purpose.'

'Such as?'

Carver shrugged. 'Maybe he sees himself as inflicting a form of punishment. Like a religious zealot who murders a prostitute but claims it is simply God's retribution on 'fallen women'.'

Remy looked unconvinced. 'So far, none of our victims were prostitutes, and she doesn't have the look of one either. And one of the victims was a man, remember?'

'As I said, just a possibility.' Carver pointed to the wound in the victim's side. The only one visible that appeared to be a stab wound as opposed to a cut. 'Same position as the others?'

'I would say so.'

'Are you religious Remy?'

Remy shot him a glance. 'Not since I watched the cancer take my mother. Why?'

Carver stood up. Remy rose with him. 'Look at her. Arms stretched out. Ankles together. Like she's been crucified. Wasn't Christ finished off with a spear in the side?'

As Remy returned his gaze to Marianne Desmarais's torn and bloodied form, his eyes narrowed, as if seeing her for the first time.

At that moment the pathologist returned, prompting Carver to resume his position against the wall. After a few minutes, Remy joined him. He nodded towards the pathologist, now instructing one of the forensics over bagging the victim's hands before moving the body.

'He says the cause of death will most likely be the internal damage to the spleen and liver from the wound to the side, like the others. I mentioned your Christ theory. He thinks it is interesting.'

'We'll see.'

Remy turned to him. 'Is your analysis showing anything yet?'

Carver hesitated. He was yet to raise the matter Jess had spoken of during their last telephone conversation. 'I won't know until it's finished.' He turned to face his friend. 'With this one Remy, I'd like to speak to those who knew her myself. I need to see their faces when they answer the questions.'

Remy looked at him, long and hard. They had talked about it before. They both knew the examining magistrate would never authorise his becoming actively involved in the investigation. 'I understand,' he said before continuing. 'I must find Ingrid. Are you coming, or staying?'

'I'll stay and have a look around, if that's okay? Get a feel for the way he likes to work.'

Remy smiled his thin smile. 'Trying to get into his mind, eh, Jamie?'

'Something like that.'

In truth, Carver had little time for the so-called 'psychological approaches' to investigation beloved by writers of TV drama and crime fiction. In his experience, success most often came through plodding police work, assisted, now and then, by a little helping of luck. 'I'll head back when I've finished. See you back at the office.'

'As you wish. It may be late before we return.'

'I'll wait.'

CHAPTER 10

Later, slumped in the back of the car taking him back to the Prefecture, Carver's thoughts pulled in different directions. A new death was no cause to celebrate, God forbid. Assuming the victim's profile aligned with the others - he was certain it would - there was a loving family somewhere. Right now they would be wondering where their wife/mother/daughter/was, why she was not at home. He veered away from imagining their torment when they learned what had happened. But a new murder held out the promise of things that simply weren't possible working from statements and police reports, some of which were now eighteen months old. It was why his Pinnacle Analysis was progressing so slowly.

Carver had come up with the Pinnacle Inventory during his time at the National Crime Faculty. But he'd designed it to be used on live enquiries, not using historical data. To be effective, the questioner needed to be able to see and read the responder. Marianne Desmarais's death, tragic though it was, raised the prospect of using it the way it had been intended. And when Carver pleaded with Remy to be allowed to speak to the witnesses directly, his response had fallen short of a clear, 'No'.

Like Carver, Remy was not averse to a little rule-bending, when needed. On first meeting, it was their mutual distrust of 'tried and tested' procedure that drew them together. Still, Carver was aware that, under the French system of investigation, ignoring the Examining Magistrate's dictats counted as more than simply bending the rules. It was why he'd always been glad the British system of policing had developed independently of those of its continental neighbours. When it comes to investigating crime, the ability to operate without a representative of the judiciary breathing down your neck was a God-send. And while the relationship between the police and the Crown Prosecution Service in England may be heading that way, the CPS mandate was still only to advise and make charging decisions. It played no part in directing investigatory effort, unlike France's more active Examining Magistracy.

But Marianne Desmarais's bloody murder wasn't the only thing preying on Carver's mind as he passed by the sleazy sex-shops and gaudy light shows that, at night, are Montmartre's defining feature. Today was always going to be significant, however it played out.

Carissa and Ingrid's meeting with the Comte de Vergennes and his striking 'friend', whoever she was, was the most important step so far towards the goal that had brought him to Paris. The night before he had barely slept, excited, but also nervous over the 'what-ifs'. As he'd lain in the dark, staring up at the black void where the ceiling should be, his hyperactive mind had played out in advance how things might go. And he'd managed to conjure up any number of possible outcomes before dropping into the fitful sleep that was to be as good as it would get that night. For all that he told himself, over and over, it was never going to happen, he could not jettison the slim hope that The Woman herself might show. When he learned that the Comte had a woman with him, his excitement had bordered on the adolescent. Stupid, he knew, but given the circumstances and how much it meant, inevitable. A bit like a child the first Christmas after they begin to suspect the truth about Santa. It doesn't stop them going to bed on Christmas Eve, hoping.

As Carver's thoughts turned to the darkness that was his primary mission in the city, his mood turned sombre. And as the sights that tourists the world over come to marvel at merged into a montage of flashing images, faces loomed and faded, each one bringing with it its share of remorse and regret.

The Worshipper Killer's six victims.

Gary Shepherd.

The Hawthorns.

And so nearly, Rosanna.

Worst of all, there was Angie. The remorse that came with her memory was greater than the rest put together. As he felt the familiar void opening up once more, he realised he needed an escape. He chose Rosanna.

Right now Rosanna was back in Lisbon, secure in the bosom of her family. Her last words to him, three weeks before in a fraught telephone call that tore him apart and left him feeling wretched, confirmed what he had long sensed about their chances of a future together. 'Call me when you have found her Jamie. Not before.' And Rosanna wasn't the only casualty.

Part of a close family, the once regular phone calls home to see how his sisters were doing, particularly the wayward one, Sally, were now rare. They used to be lengthy. Now they lasted only as long as it took his father to drop some reference to the 'help' that is freely available to officers affected by their work. Which is when Carver usually found an excuse to end the conversation, or hung up. Still seeking a refuge, he turned his thoughts to Jason, now back with his grandmother, Sue, for whom Carver remembered most days to thank God.

Now seven, Jason was still ignorant of the events that had shaped his life more than any other. But Carver knew that the time would come when he would want to know more about the mother who had loved him, what happened to her. When that time arrived, he needed to be able to put his hand on his heart and know that, whatever responsibility he bore for Angie's death, he had done everything in his power to set things straight with her memory as was possible. Even as the thought came, he realised. He had gone full circle and now his thoughts were back with Angie again.

But then, out of the gaudy light show beyond the car, another face loomed. It was that of a woman with coal black hair. And by then the feeling of regret had turned to something else. Anger, and a grim determination.

'Monsieur?'

Carver jumped as someone shook his shoulder. He turned. The car door was open, the Police driver looking down at him, trying to hide the amused smile.

'Nous sommes arrivé, Monsieur.' *We are here.*

Inside, Carver found the CID office deserted save for Claude, the young office clerk, jabbering away on the telephone. The way he raised his eyes to the ceiling as

Carver passed, he guessed he was having difficulty getting the caller to understand why, at that moment, there were no detectives about. As he made his way to the stairs that would take him to the attic-storeroom he had been allocated as an office, he had to pass through the Murder Control Room, with all its trapping of a multiple murder investigation in full flow. It too was empty apart from one of the indexers, an ebony-skinned woman tapping away at her keyboard. Intent on her data-entry, she didn't pause to acknowledge Carver as he went by.

After negotiating the ancient, spiralling, stone stairs, he dropped into his chair, suddenly aware of the tiredness creeping into his body. A weary sigh escaped him. It was coming on eight o'clock. They'd begun the day with a six o'clock briefing over coffee and croissants to plan the forthcoming meeting with the 'Comte de Vergennes.' And it wasn't close to over yet.

At that moment, undecided about where to point his attention, his gaze drifted to the bottom drawer of the desk. It was locked, but he did not need to open it to visualise its contents - a thick manila folder, secured by a stout rubber band. About to reach for his keys, he stopped himself. He knew the folder's contents by heart already. The various documents, the information contained within them, the photographs. Especially *one* photograph. The past weeks he'd fallen into the habit of turning to it every once in a while, mainly those times he felt the need to refocus his attention on his principle reason for coming to Paris. But he also knew how easy it was to lose himself in it, the trains of thoughts it was capable of triggering. If he wasn't careful, the file would consume hours of his time before he even knew it. *Not tonight.* Turning to the tray marked, '*Entrant*' he picked up the topmost piece of paper, a translation of a statement from a supposed witness to the third murder, and began reading.

CHAPTER 11

Carver dropped the account he was reading so it floated down to join those scattered over the huge desk that Remy had got someone to dig out of the basement the day he arrived. Made of some fine, dark wood with decorative edging, it bore the marks of decades of use. It made him wonder about who may once have used it, the events it would have witnessed over its lifetime. He'd heard that during the war, the Gestapo had commandeered the rooms now being used by the CID.

Leaning back in the old office swivel chair that definitely didn't match the desk, he rubbed fists into his eyes before stretching his shoulders back, easing the stiffness of the past couple of hours. He checked his watch. Nearly ten thirty. He had no idea when Remy and Ingrid may return. If the pathologist had decided to start the PM that night, it could be a long time yet. In which case he needed a break.

He pondered about making his way down and grabbing a coffee. But he didn't relish the thought of negotiating the dimly-lit stone steps with a scalding-hot drink in his hand. The week before, he'd managed to purloin a water cooler. It would do.

Plastic beaker in hand, he crossed to the small leaded

window behind his desk. Far below, the lights of the city's famous *Bateaux Mouches* reflected off the Seine's glossy-black surface. If he leaned out and bent round to his left, he would see the Eiffel Tower with its hourly, flickering light show. All around was the spectacular sight of Paris at night, laid out for his inspection, should he be so inclined. He wasn't. When Remy first showed him the room and asked if it would suit his purpose, Carver was blown away by the views it offered of a city he and Gail, his ex-wife, had once regarded as their favourite. The novelty wore off quickly. The combination of the stairs and the amount of arriving paper – stacks of cardboard boxes, neatly labelled and all of which he was committed to reading - saw to that. Now, he barely gave it a thought. After a couple of minutes spent taking in the cooling night air, he returned to his desk.

Dropping back into the chair, he considered the time. It was an hour earlier in the UK. He reached for his mobile. She answered on the second ring.

'Hello you,' Jess said.

'Not disturbing you, am I?' he said.

'As it happens, I'm just starting on the batch that came today.'

'At this time? Shouldn't an unattached young woman like yourself be out having a good time, rather than sitting at home analysing Pinnacle data?' He imagined her in the new barn conversion she'd moved into just before he left for Paris, perched on the huge sofa she'd bought second hand from some warehouse, surrounded by statements, reports, graphic scene-photographs, a DVD playing on the TV, maybe.

'I've got a visitor,' she said.

'Who's that then?'

He expected her to say it was her mother, and was surprised when she said, 'Gavin.'

'Really? How's he doing?'

For the next few minutes he listened as she brought him up to date with the young detective's slow recovery. But when he asked to speak with him she told how he was already in bed. 'He still gets tired easily.'

'Well give him my best when he wakes up. But it sounds like he's coming along?'

'Seems that way.'

'I take it he knows about Rossi?'

'He does,' Jess said, sounding regretful.

Three months before, the body of Alessio Rossi, the second half of the professional hit team Anne Kenworthy had tasked with keeping her sordid past secret, had been dragged out of a canal in Amsterdam. No one knew who was responsible for his death, or the reasons behind it. It meant he would never now be charged with the series of murders that included Alistair Kenworthy MP, or the attempt on Baggus's life.

'And?'

'I think he's happy the bastard's paid his dues without him having to sit through a trial.'

'And what about you?' Carver said.

'What about me?'

'What do you think, now that you've had a chance to think about it?'

'My views haven't changed. Why do you ask?'

'I seem to remember you were disappointed that events that night at Kenworthy's would never be examined in open court.'

'I was. I still am. Why wouldn't I be?'

'No reason,' Carver said. 'Just wondering.' In that moment Carver decided he would never raise it again unless she did. It was only fair to her. Time to move on.

'Right,' he said, preparing her, 'I've got other news.'

'Go on.'

'There's been another killing.'

'*What*?' He imagined her coming bolt upright. 'When? Why didn't you tell me?'

'It only came in this afternoon. I'm telling you now.'

'Oh.' Then, 'I'm listening.'

He told her about Marianne Desmarais, what he'd seen, what they knew so far.

When he finished she asked, 'Did you mention to Remy about the crucifixion thing? Had they thought about-'

'I did, and no, they hadn't. They're doing so now.'

'Good. I still can't believe no one picked up on it. I thought France is big into Christianity?'

'Not so much in CID it seems. Besides, it's still only one theory.'

'Fair comment. How many others are there?'

'Other what?'

'Theories.'

'Er... none.'

She let the silence hang long enough to do its job. 'So who is this Marianne Des-whatever? Any indication why she was in Paris?'

He sensed her impatience. More like the old Jess. 'Not yet. I left them working the scene. I'm still waiting on an update.'

'You're not there?' She sounded incredulous. 'I thought you don't rate French crime scene management?'

'I didn't used too, but it's getting better. And I saw enough to know Remy and Ingrid will make a proper job of it.'

'Speaking of Inger, how's she shaping up?'

'*INGRID'*. Carver shook his head, though he was beginning to suspect she did it deliberately, just to wind him up. 'And she's doing fine. You'd like her. She's impressive.'

'Hmm. You said that about someone else once.'

It was his turn to let the silence speak. After a moment she realised.

'I'm sorry, Jamie. That was stupid. I'd never-'

'I know you wouldn't. Forget it.'

But he knew she would not. By now they were as much attuned to each others sensitivities as any married couple. They had both suffered loss since it all started. Both had seen their lives change, if in different ways. Some of those changes were obvious, others not. Some, he was sure, were yet to reveal themselves.

Now, hearing her breathing in his ear, Carver knew that like him, she would be remembering and reflecting. He let the few moments silence reinforce the things that lay between them, the knowns and the unknowns. Eventually, he said, 'How's the analysis going? Any more progress?'

'Some,' she said, as if waking up. 'I finished the Inventory for the fourth victim, Catherine Duchamp, this afternoon. I'll start running the correlations tomorrow. The problem is the gaps. If we could plug some of them it would help a lot.'

'Remy's doing his best. He's got a team revisiting the victims' families and friends and asking the questions that weren't asked first time. But it's a lot of work and three of them are way out in the provinces. This latest murder will slow things down even more, especially if Remy has to pull them in.'

'Which is exactly what shouldn't happen. From what I can see, completing the inventories ought to be the priority.'

'I'd agree, but that's where the politics comes in. If Remy's Examining Magistrate gets wind that he's got detectives running around on the say so of an English cop who, officially, isn't even supposed to be here, there'll be hell to pay. Remy's right behind it, but he can't say so openly.'

Jess's terse, 'Tch,' summed up both their feelings. 'God help us if we ever get in that state. The CPS are bad enough.'

'It's France Jess. Everything's different here. Not all of it's bad.'

'I'll take your word for it.' She moved on. 'The good news is, our victim's secret hypothesis looks like it's still holding up.'

'Does it now? Tell me more.'

It was while analysing the second murder, that Jess first reported signs of the pattern she'd since labelled, *The Victim's Secret Hypothesis*. When she went back, she found it was there with the first murder as well, just harder to spot. In each case there were significant and unexplained gaps in the victims' private lives. Some of the reasons that the victims had given for being away from home were hazy, to say the least. When Jess first mentioned it, Carver was excited. Apart from anything else, it showed that his inventory worked.

When, the week after he'd arrived, Remy met him to ask if he would be interested in assisting, unofficially, in the investigation into, 'Les Massacres de Pension', as the French media were dubbing the series, Carver had doubts. He had not designed his inventory to be applied retrospectively. But seeing as how Remy had already by then pledged his assistance to Carver's own mission, he could hardly refuse. When Jess first mentioned what she was beginning to see as she went about the painstaking task of combing the hundreds of statements from witnesses, family and friends to extract the answers to the Inventory's three-hundred-plus questions, he confessed to feeling the sort of tingle he realised he'd been missing for a long time. If it did turn up something here, in Paris, it would be a real plus. Not for any credit that may come his way, but if there was a chance of putting the Paris Judiciary in his debt, even to some small degree, it would put him in a stronger position when the time came to ask for the support he may need to pursue the matter that had brought him to Paris in the first place.

As Jess described her most recent findings, he listened closely..

'I was beginning to think it was just coincidence, or even that I was subconsciously skewing the process. But the last batch of statements you sent over, the ones that included Catherine's closest friend and her sister, showed the same as the others. None of them can say exactly what she was doing in Paris. They also show the same sort of gaps in her personal life we see in the others. Blank spaces no one ever seems to have noticed, let alone had a theory about.'

'And which points to some big secret?'

'It's a possibility, don't you think?'

Carver played with it. 'I'm not discounting it. I'll bear

it in mind as we get stuck into this latest one.'

'That sounds like you are expecting to be involved?'

'I've seeded it to Remy enough times that if there's another one and there's even half a chance of letting me run the Inventory myself, then he should. I mentioned it again this afternoon. He didn't say, "No."'

'It would make sense.'

'There's still the politics to get around.'

'I'll keep fingers crossed.' She switched track. 'How's the other thing going? Managed to arrange any more meetings yet?'

'We had one today. We were about to wash-up when this latest murder came in.'

'What's that now? Four, five meetings?

'Five.'

'Are they going for it?'

'The last two did. We'll wait and see about today.'

'Christ. What does that say about today's society?'

Carver hesitated. 'We already know the answer to that.'

There was a pause, then, 'I suppose we do...' After another moment's hesitation she went on, 'So how far will you go setting it all up?'

'As far as I need to. Carissa has a friend who owns a place, a chateau or something, on a lake out near Rennes. He's told her we can use it if we have to.'

'A chateau? That sounds a bit grand.'

'It fits with what we are offering.'

'I guess. But then a good convent girl like myself wouldn't know.'

'Hmphh.' But before he could continue, noises on the stairs drew his ear. Remy and Ingrid were back.

Before she rang off, Jess said she would ring him

when she'd run some more correlations. About to ring off he suddenly remembered. 'How's your-?' But it was too late. She'd gone. 'Bugger.'

As they reached the top of the stairs, Remy and Ingrid were chattering away. To Carver, it sounded as it often did like an argument, though he knew it wasn't. They finished their discussion before turning tired faces on him.

'How did it go?' he asked. 'Progress? Witnesses?'

Remy shook his head. 'Nothing so far. But it is early. We will see.'

For the next half hour they talked the international police language of murder investigation. Knocking on doors. Appealing for witnesses. Victim background. Forensic. Running the Murder Control. Continental Europe police procedures differ markedly from those of the UK. Nevertheless, Carver was pleased there were enough commonalities he didn't have to worry too much. Eventually, Remy made ready to leave. Carver knew what he would be thinking. *One last, good night's sleep*. If it came.

'The autopsy is set for seven in the morning. You would like to be there?'

Carver was eager. 'You bet.'

'Good. Now then -' He clapped his hands. 'I need a drink before home.' He headed for the door, started down the steps. 'Are you two coming?'

Not quite ready for sleep then.

As the echo of his descent dwindled, Ingrid stopped looking at the floor and lifted her head so her cool gaze was on Carver. She leaned back against a table, arms folded. He waited. Her face was unreadable as she said, 'Yes. It is time you bought me a drink, Jamie.' She didn't wait for his response but turned and headed after her boss.

Carver watched as she disappeared through the door. He waited a moment, then he grabbed his jacket off the chair and followed.

CHAPTER 12

The moment he entered Les Deux Chats Noirs, Carver knew why Ingrid and Remy had ignored the many bars they'd passed on the way there. The acknowledging nod from the stern-faced man behind the bar and the flashing smile from the pretty waitress holding aloft a tray of drinks spoke volumes. And as he followed Remy and Ingrid through to the tables at the back, the several faces he recognised from his travels around the Prefecture De Police confirmed it. *'Les Deux Chats'* was a police haunt.

The busy little bar lies across the Pont Au Change from the Ile de La Cité, on the Seine's right bank. Tucked away down an alleyway off the fashionable Marais district's Rue Des Rossiers, its carefully contrived look of dowdy neglect deters all but the most inquisitive tourists. Those strangers who do venture within - usually tourists in search of a more authentic experience than those mentioned in the guide books - tend not to linger. Non-smokers quickly discover that even today, there are pockets where the smoking ban is enforced only loosely. On the other hand, puffers who think they have dropped lucky soon realise that the level of service on offer is worse even than the infamous disdain some Paris waiting staff are reputed to show towards, 'Les Touristes.' For that reason, the place is well known to officials of The Paris Tourist Authority. During the summer season especially, they receive a steady stream of complaints. They are all acknowledged, either in writing or, in the case of those that come via telephone, with studied concern. Reassurance is given that notification will be passed to the, 'Appropriate Authority.' In the case of '*Les Deux Chats,*' the Appropriate Authority is the office of the *'Prefet de CID'* who dutifully reads every letter, notes every call, then stores the details in the buff folder he keeps in his bottom desk-drawer. Whenever it seems that the bar's Alsatian owner, Gustin's, antisocial ways are in danger of drawing too much 'official' attention, the Prefet instructs the duty CID Inspector to mention the fact on his next visit. That usually means the same evening, when the cohorts of off-duty police and detectives retire there for their cognacs and whiskeys before wending their way back to their partners and lovers. The feedback loop works well and ensures that those members of the CID who like a Gaulloise with their after-work drinks continue to enjoy the privilege. Unlike the rest of Paris.

As they settled at a table near the back, Carver took in his surroundings while Ingrid dug in her shoulder bag for her cigarettes.

'Seems a nice place,' he said.

Remy misread envy in Carver's casual observation. 'But you must have places like this in England, Jamie? Somewhere you can talk over the happenings of the day in private?'

Carver nodded, an image of The Bells forming. 'Of

course.' As Ingrid lit up he added. 'They're just not always so...'

'Friendly?' Remy offered.

'I was going to say, liberal.' Carver nodded at the fug surrounding the neighbouring table where two older *flics* were puffing away.

Remy smiled, raised his glass. 'Salut.' Carver returned it.

For the next few minutes they talked over the plan for the following day. Following the seven o'clock postmortem, the investigation into Marianne Desmarais's murder would commence in earnest with a full investigation team briefing at ten.

'An early postmortem will at least give me something I can tell my *Legionnaires*,' Remy explained. Carver nodded. By now he knew how Remy often referred to his team as *Legionnaires*, particularly when things were hotting up. Carver suspected it helped propagate the mystique that already surrounded Paris's 'Premiere de CID'.

Carver asked Remy about some points of procedure, interested in how their countries' differing judicial systems impacted on major crime investigation. The answer was, not much. The way he described it, Remy's approach would be little different to the one Carver would use. Much emphasis on the victim, her habits and movements before she died. And of course her family. As they would in the UK, teams of officers were even now combing the streets around Pension Turec, knocking on doors, seeking out witnesses. Forensic examination of the scene would continue for a couple more days yet. The main difference, as far as Carver could tell, was in how Remy planned to use – rather not use - the media. In Britain, one of the first calls an SIO makes is to the Force Press Officer. Remy barely mentioned the press at all. It made Carver think of the infamous Madeleine McCann case and the Portuguese Police's catastrophic failures to share the little information they had at the time with the public. It always amazed him that parts of Europe still haven't learned the lesson. Carver thought about mentioning it, but pulled back. He was enjoying local cooperation on the understanding that he did not involve himself directly in operational matters. More to the point, he could remember times he'd been gearing up for a major investigation when some outsider-SIO-type started trying to be 'helpful.' Invariably, they weren't.

After half an hour spent going over things, Remy recognised someone at the bar behind Carver. Carver turned in time to see a middle-aged man with a vaguely middle-eastern look about him return Remy's nod. Squarely-built and with close-cropped hair he was dressed all in black and wearing a leather jacket.

'Excuse me,' Remy said, rising. 'I need to speak with someone.'

Seconds later, Carver found himself alone with Ingrid for the first time outside of 'work.' Looking up, he saw she was regarding him through half closed eyes as she drew on her cigarette. As earlier that afternoon at Carissa's, he felt suddenly self-conscious. He reached for his glass.

'Have you and Remy worked together long?'

She managed to hide a smile before answering. 'A couple of years, but I met him before that, when I worked in Marseille.'

'You worked Marseille?'

She nodded. 'Vice. Drugs and Sex Trafficking.'

Carver was impressed. She had more history than he realised.

'Have you met Remy's wife, his family?'

'Yes, I know Sylvia. And their little Jasmine.' The smile broke and she giggled, almost girlishly.

'Have I said something funny?'

She drew on her cigarette again, gave him another look. 'You want to know if we are lovers.'

Carver spluttered into his beer. 'No I don't.' He felt himself starting to redden.

Ingrid shrugged. 'Yes you do. It is the first thing men think about. A man like Remy, with a younger partner like me. They like to think we are having, *'Une affaire.'*

'What you and Remy do or don't do away from the office is none of my business.' But even as he said the words he remembered when he first took on Jess as his partner. The whispers that started. They were probably still doing the rounds.

Ingrid shrugged. 'If you say so. But for what it is worth, we only slept together once. Now, it is just work.'

Caught off guard by her stark honesty, Carver opened his mouth to say something, but nothing came out so he shut it again. He'd heard how Ingrid was known for speaking her thoughts and wondered if there was a French equivalent of the English expression for someone who, 'wears their heart on their sleeve.' If there was, it applied to her. She read his thoughts.

'Do not worry, Jamie. I am not giving away secrets. Everyone knows, including Sylvia.'

'Oh,' Carver said. 'Right.'

Ingrid chuckled. It was throaty, sensuous. 'That is so English. "Oh. Right". I love it.'

About to say, 'Right' again, Carver realised she was making fun of him. He settled for a pointed, 'Hmm,' and drank his beer.

There followed a few minutes' quiet during which Ingrid smoked, Carver drank and Remy stayed talking to the man at the bar. Eventually Ingrid reached across to stub out her cigarette. She glanced over her shoulder towards where Remy was still engaged at the bar, before coming back to Carver. She leaned forward, elbows on the table, cupped hands supporting her face.

'I have told you about me, and Remy. Now it is your turn.'

'For what?'

'This woman we are trying to lure. This Megan Crane. There is a story there as well, I think.'

Carver kept his face neutral. 'Not really. She's a fugitive from British justice. I'm here to find her and return her to prison.'

She dismissed it with a flick of a hand. 'Not that story. The other story. You and her.'

Carver gave her a long look, saying nothing. Through everything that had happened, no one had ever asked the question the way she had just done, outright, *you and her?*

There'd been plenty of enquiries over that time of course. And inquests, formal and informal. By Carver's reckoning the accounts he'd provided to various parties - Chief Officers, CPS, Prison Service, Coroner, Parliamentary Sub-Committee on MP's Ethics – would fill a book. But the focus of those accounts was always on the facts. The history between Megan Crane and Edmund Hart. The 'Worshipper' series of killings that occurred after Hart hanged himself in prison. The investigation that led to her unmasking. The complex web of events and the conspiracy surrounding her escape from custody. None of them touched on what lay beneath the surface. The motivations of The Woman herself. The way she'd played with and manipulated those she met along the way. The mistakes and misjudgements by police and others that allowed her catalogue of depravity to go undetected so long. Such matters remained out of sight, known to and understood only by those closest to the story. Those such as himself, Jess, and their boss at the time, The Duke. And not forgetting Rosanna and, of course, poor Angie.

Now Ingrid had just asked the question everyone else avoided, either deliberately, out of sensitivity, or because they didn't realise its significance. *You and her?*

As if she had somehow read what was in his head, Ingrid backed off, suddenly 'I am sorry. There is still much pain there. I didn't mean to-'

'It's okay. It's just that... There's so much to tell. It's hard to know where to start.'

'Another time perhaps. When you are ready.'

He thought about it. Was her backtracking itself a ruse? Testing to see if he was vulnerable? It was only natural she would want to know more than what he had given them so far. In reality it was little more than what was in the official reports. Ingrid's part in what they were trying to do was key, and not without its dangers. He knew what could happen, had *seen* it, *experienced* it. And the way she had offered to help right off, 'I will do it,' without asking for more detail or guarantees for her safety, she was entitled to something for God's sake. How much?

He began to talk.

CHAPTER 13

As always to begin with, Carver stuck to what had been written about, either in the official accounts or the press. They were the easy bits. Less painful. It helped him get the other elements in the story lined up and exercised. Like a pianist stretching fingers before a concert. It isn't what the audience pays for, but it improves the flow. Logic demanded he begin with Edmund Hart.

Carver was pretty sure Ingrid would know of the infamous serial killer and the seven high-class escort girls he butchered in and around England's North West. Apart from the publicity at the time, Carver had been asked to provide the French Authorities with chapter and verse just to get the authority he needed to pursue his mission across the channel. And not just about Hart and Megan Crane. He'd also had to state his grounds for believing that she was being given sanctuary somewhere near Paris, as well as spelling out his argument as to why the Case Officer himself should oversee the search, rather than leaving it all to the local police. That was where he'd had to be his most imaginative. It wasn't easy couching it in a way that didn't read, 'They're not up to it,' or which explained in too much detail how a Case Officer had come to have such insight into how his quarry's mind worked.

Ingrid would have read most if not all of it by now, he was sure. She would be familiar with the background. But she hadn't asked about background. Still, she stayed quiet and attentive, sipping her cognac and smoking her way steadily through her Marlboros as he laid it all out, building on the facts, edging closer and closer to what she wanted to know, but which he wasn't at all certain he would be able to tell. From Edmund Hart, Carver moved on to the Worshipper Murders, and how they eventually led him to Megan Crane's doorstep. He described how, after enlisting her to aid in their hunt for the killer, she proceeded to insinuate herself into not just the investigation, but his and Jess's private lives. At this point he interrupted the story to take a drink. By now he too was on cognac. It wasn't his usual, but in the absence of a good Jameson, it would do.

Perhaps sensing hesitation, Ingrid tried easing it out. 'You and this Megan Crane. You became, involved?'

Carver glanced up from his glass, threw the rest down. 'Not in the sense you are thinking. We were never lovers, or anything.' Ingrid waited. 'But there was something... There must have been some sort of... connection.' He glanced up again. Ingrid was regarding him the way she might if he were a suspect about to confess. He felt the need to explain.

'You need to understand. Megan Crane is a woman of unique qualities. And I mean, *unique*. When you... If, you meet her. Then you will understand.'

'She is beautiful, yes?'

'Not so much that, it's more to do with... I mean, yes, she is beautiful, very beautiful, But many women are beautiful-' About to reference Ingrid's own qualities, he checked himself. 'There's something about Megan Crane that is...The only word I can think of is, captivating. Not in any romantic sense. But when she enters a room, heads turn. Men and women's. I've seen powerful men fall silent when she speaks. Even the judge at her trial allowed her the sort of leeway I've never seen him grant any defendant.'

'You sound a little in awe of her.'

He considered it. 'Maybe I was. I think we all were. None of us had ever met anyone like her. I don't think there *is* anyone like her. As I said, she's unique.'

'Which is how-'

'Which is how she managed to blind us to the truth. About what she really was. Is.' His face grew dark. 'And what she was up to.' As he paused again Ingrid stayed silent, giving him time. He shook his head. 'I still don't know how we didn't put it together. Over time we began to pick up that she'd been involved in some dark stuff in the past. We just had no idea how dark.'

'Stuff?'

'Things she was involved in. Her activities.'

Ingrid nodded, beginning to understand.

'Believe me Ingrid, I've met some twisted people in my time. You hear stories about serial killers and you wonder how anyone can get off on the sorts of things they do. But her and Edmund Hart... I've never heard of anyone who got their kicks the way they did.'

For several seconds neither spoke. The buzz of bar-room chatter and drinking noises swooped in to fill the silence that fell, suddenly, between them. The two men at the next table were discussing the previous night's Champions League game. Had they known what was being talked about a few feet away, they too, may have fallen silent.

Eventually Ingrid whispered across. 'You were her real target.'

He nodded. 'Me and Angie, the escort who helped us trap Hart. The whole thing was a set up from the start. The series of murders, the ritualistic way the victims were killed. She knew that because of my background I was bound to get sucked into the investigation. And because she made herself fit the victim profile, she also guessed that I would find her, look to involve her like I did with Angie. It gave her the opportunity to get close to me, and her other target.'

Ingrid leaned forward. Though her voice was barely a whisper, he had no problem hearing her. It was as if they were the bar's only customers. 'And she did. Get close I mean.'

Another nod. 'Yes. She got close.'

'She tried to kill you.'

Carver swallowed, his throat suddenly dry.

'Yes.'

'But she failed, Jamie.'

For a long time he stayed silent. When he looked up his eyes were dark.

'No, Ingrid. She succeeded. In part at least.' He fell silent. Ingrid waited. For Carver, this was always the hardest part. Facing up to it. 'She didn't kill me, but she did manage to-'

'What are you two talking about so close together?'

Carver turned just as Remy slid past to drop into the chair next to Ingrid. Ingrid tried to recapture Carver's gaze, but the moment was gone.

Remy read the sudden silence. 'Am I interrupting

something?'

After a moment Ingrid said, 'Jamie was just telling me about this Megan Crane creature.'

Remy showed surprise, turned to Carver. 'Is he now?'

Carver said nothing but sought distractions amongst the bar's sights and sounds. If Remy was conscious of Carver's discomfort, he masked it.

'Well I must go. We have an early start tomorrow. What are you two doing?'

Carver reached to empty his glass. 'I'm going to have another drink then call it a night.' His room was in the Bastille district. Walking distance.

Remy turned to Ingrid. 'If you want me to drop you at home, come now.' He didn't wait for an answer but headed for the door. 'Goodnight Jamie.'

For a moment Ingrid looked like she might linger, scrutinising Carver's chiselled features. But then she made her decision, and her face changed. Rising, she leaned over to stub out her cigarette in the ash tray. As she did so, she stared deep into Carver's upturned face.

'I look forward to hearing the rest of your story Jamie. How it ends.'

He nodded, smiled, weakly. *Ends? It never ends.*

'Have a good night's sleep, Ingrid.'

The smile she returned him was a little sad. 'You too.'

As he and others watched her follow after Remy, Carver's thought was, *She knows*.

He took another drink at the bar before heading out.

CHAPTER 14

The night was mild, the air still and calm. All around were the sights and sounds of Paris, closing down for the evening. Barmen stacking tables and chairs, bringing in the chalk menu boards with their tempting offers, job done for another day. Neighbouring proprietors bidding each other, 'Bonne Nuit.' The smell of garlic hung heavy in the air. Somewhere across the city the plaintive wail of police sirens gave rise to harsh images involving street violence, blood spilling into the gutter. Shouting young men being bundled into the back of police vans.

It had been a long day. But whereas an hour earlier he could have gone straight to bed and slept, his conversation with Ingrid had left his head full of thoughts he knew would not disappear easily.

Instead of heading back to the Police lodgings where he was billeted, he took a meandering route back towards the river, hoping the exercise may provide the diversion he sought. It didn't. As he sauntered through the streets and out onto the bridge across the Seine, his mind re-ran the day's events meandering over what they may bring in their wake.

To begin with, poor Marianne Desmarais was

dominant in his thoughts. Her brutal murder meant that the next few days would be hectic. But for all the opportunities her death may present in terms of gathering evidence, he didn't want to take his eyes off the main reason for his being in Paris. With all that had happened, there had been no time to consider the meeting that had taken place in the fourth floor suite of the Hotel Edouard VII that morning. He wondered what Carissa might say now that she'd had a chance to reflect on it. Each of the previous meetings had been followed by a de-brief during which they had pooled their thoughts and observations. Looking to see what they could learn from the encounter. Questioning if it had taken them any nearer to their goal. He'd used those occasions to challenge what they were doing. Not on moral or ethical grounds, but simply asking whether the bait was still the right one. How likely was it that what was on offer would reach their quarry's ears. And if it did, would it be enough to draw her out? Megan Crane was no fool. God knows, he had learned that lesson. She would know the police were hunting for her. She would be ultra-cautious about exposing herself. It was why their charade needed to stand up to rigorous scrutiny, why he'd kept himself out of things. She was too clever to be tempted to break surface herself to examine the hook that carried the bait. If she did so at all it would be through a third party. Someone like Henri Durcell. Which is where Carissa came in. Without her contacts, gathered over twenty or more years providing her particular brand of specialised services to those who could afford them, the operation stood little chance of success. Wherever Megan Crane was right now, she was buried deep. Calling on those who had once been part of her circle and asking them outright if they knew where she may be found would be like trying to catch fish by diving into a river. But dangle the right sort of bait. . . Which is where his own unique knowledge came to the fore. No one alive knew more about how Megan Crane's mind worked than him. They all knew that if anyone outside their immediate circle learned of the nature of the bait they were using, the issues raised could be enough to force them to drop it. But Carver also knew that what they were offering was about the only thing that stood a chance of prising Megan Crane from her bolt hole. It would, he hoped, be more than she could resist. She may even-

Carver stopped, suddenly aware of where his legs had taken him. As he'd mused and walked he'd assumed his wanderings were aimless. Wrong. His subconscious had returned him to the one spot where he might find solace, of a sort.

He looked about him. The street was lined with Cypress trees, tall and elegant. Just like the high townhouses and apartments of the Rue de Luxembourg itself. To his right, the grey stone steps he had mounted once already that day stood waiting.

For more than a minute he hesitated, debating within himself. It was such a cliché, turning up like this on the doorstep, late into the night, feeling sorry for himself. And not just sorry. Insecure, needful of reassurance from someone who would tell him that what they were doing was right, that the ends justified the means. Someone who understood what he went through night after night. Someone who had experienced similar loss, who could relate, at the personal level, to what they were doing - and why. Someone who may, for a while at least, give him the succour he needed to sustain himself through what he hoped but also feared would soon come.

Deep inside he knew that what he ought to do was to turn round, cross back over the river and head back to his lodgings. Okay he may not sleep well but at least it didn't run the risk of complicating further a situation that was already of Gordian Knot proportions. But Carver wasn't stupid. He hadn't arrived here by accident. He knew full well that tonight, especially after his conversation with Ingrid, he wasn't strong enough to do what was 'sensible'.

Mounting the steps, he pressed the button showing the number of her apartment. At the same time he turned his face to the CCTV camera above the door. Eventually there was a buzz and a click. Pushing the door open, he stepped inside and closed it, gently, after him. He mounted the stairs slowly, conscious that within him the debate still raged. Not for long. As he reached the third-floor landing he saw that the dark-green-painted door was already ajar. Crossing to it, he pushed against it, but did not move to step inside. The heady smell of Shalimar wafted from within.

As the door swung back against its brass hinges, he had a clear view through into the living area. In the middle of the room, almost in the exact spot where he had left her earlier that day, Carissa Lavergne looked radiant in a crimson satin robe that followed the contours of her body. If she had been asleep when he rang the bell, it wasn't apparent. For a moment they stood there, looking at each other. The expression on her face was neutral, neither inviting nor rejecting, simply waiting.

Carver hesitated one last time, then made his decision.

CHAPTER 15

The early-morning postmortem on Marianne Desmarais turned up nothing unexpected. In layman's language, cause of death was renal bleeding and liver failure, exacerbated by the multiple stab wounds to just about all areas of her body apart from her lower legs and arms. The pathologist counted thirty nine wounds in all, one more than the last three victims and two more than the first couple. There was no way of knowing if the extra wound was deliberate, or a slip of the knife.

Afterwards, Carver listened as Remy briefed the detectives, scene investigators and support staff who had gathered in the Prefecture's impressive 'Grande Halle.' Carver estimated some sixty plus heads. More than he expected. The briefing itself fitted the usual pattern for such things. A perfunctory and suitably grave welcome, followed by a run down of the salient facts - the wheres, whens, and hows. A summary of the PM findings. What they knew so far about the victim. Then Remy gave a broad outline of the approach they would be taking to the investigation. It was as they'd discussed the previous evening. He named the officers who'd been delegated specific responsibilities. Scene. House-to-house. Victim background. In the latter case he told the nominated Inspector he would need to brief him later about, 'other matters.' Though he didn't look at Carver, sat in the front row, when he said it, Carver nevertheless felt a tingle of anticipation. Remy then handed over to his immediate superior, the Prefect de CID, a lanky but immaculately dressed Superintendent of police who possessed a suave manner and what Remy had described as a 'deceptively-gentle' delivery. Carver had met him a couple of times, but each time came away unsure whether the man was a committed policeman, or a wily politician. Whichever, he captured the attention of his audience the moment he began speaking and held it as he spoke, gently but nonetheless persuasively, of the urgent need to catch the killer whose exploits were spreading fear through all of Paris. Though Carver understood few of his words, the way in which he addressed his audience, solemnly and with studied deliberation, Carver was in no doubt of the gist of it. He'd listened to many such speeches. He would be reminding everyone to be on their guard at all times so as not to miss the vital clue that may turn the case. That he expected their full commitment to what was rapidly becoming one of the most infamous investigations in the history of the Paris Police. Eventually, he passed the baton back to Remy to wind up and send everyone away to get on with whatever it was they were supposed to be doing. Despite his doubts, and all things considered, Carver was impressed. He'd seen none of the cynicism or muttered but misplaced jocularity he sometimes witnessed on such occasions. Then again they were talking about the sixth in a series of horrific murders. By now it had been confirmed that, like the others, Marianne was indeed a wife and mother.

Afterwards, Carver waited, patiently, as Remy huddled with his deputies and team leaders, giving them further direction where needed. When the last departed and they were alone in the Halle, Remy turned to him.

'Come, Jamie. I must introduce you to someone.'

Leaving the Prefecture, they crossed the square to the historic, Palais de Justice. After negotiating the several layers of security, they took the lift to the fourth floor. Remy was clearly known to some of the officers stationed at the various check-points along the way, but no concessions were made. Passes and Identifications were produced at each barrier. As they walked the corridors, Carver's gaze was everywhere. The building reeked of history and momentous events. Many of the paintings decorating the walls depicted scenes from France's several revolutions, though which particular ones, Carver had no idea. Eventually they arrived at an impressive double door. On it was a brass nameplate proclaiming in capitals, M. Marc Couthon. Beneath it, written in brush script, was the legend, *Juge D'Instruction*.

Remy turned to Carver. 'Be on your guard, Jamie. He is a smart one. And his English is better than he makes out.' He knocked once, and went straight in.

The office of Paris's Principal Examining Magistrate was pretty much as Carver had expected. Expansive, traditional, well appointed. The dark wood panelling, shelves of leather-bound books, paintings, antiques and other accoutrements reflected the room's historic setting. Beyond the leaded window and across the square, Notre Dame's twin towers stood, proud and magnificent. To the side of the huge desk, two leather Chesterfields faced each other across an elaborately-carved stone and wood coffee table. Carver was reminded of the time he'd visited the office of the British Parliament's Speaker in the Palace of Westminster. It also oozed status, privilege, and apparently bottomless government budgets.

As they came in, the man behind the desk rose and came round to greet them. His smile was welcoming, the eyes less so.

Marc Couthon was shorter than the two detectives by several inches. But his eyes were sharp and they honed in on Carver at once, taking him in with a sweeping down-up glance. He greeted Remy with a flurry of French that Carver had no chance of catching. He was younger than Carver had expected, early fifties maybe. Balding on top, the hair at the sides and back was dark, and suspiciously free of grey. The face was dominated by a hooked nose and dark, deep-set eyes, hence the nickname Remy had told him. '*L'Aigle,*' - The Eagle. Carver could well imagine that what he lacked in physical stature, he made up for in shrewd intelligence. Word was, *L'Aigle* never missed a trick.

Remy introduced Carver in English. Couthon switched language at once, though he made a show of hesitating through his sentences, as if it was a real effort. 'I am... pleased we meet at last Monsieur Carver. I have heard... much about you.'

'Not from Remy, I hope.'

Couthon took a moment to get the joke. 'Mais-non. He speaks... well of you.'

'I'll bet.'

Couthon flashed a polite smile. 'Forgive us,

Monsieur Carver, but I must... discuss with your colleague over this latest atrocity, and my English is not good.'

'Of course.' *Sounds good to me.*

For the next ten minutes Carver made himself comfortable on one of the Chesterfields while the two men spoke. A young woman, blond, pretty - Carver assumed she was the magistrate's PA – brought in coffee. Carver drank his while doing his best to follow as Remy briefed Couthon on the latest murder.

Remy had once tried to explain to Carver the role the Examining Magistrate plays in cases such as murder. He still wasn't sure he got it. In reality, it seemed that the magistrate played little part until a suspect came into the frame. Nevertheless, in the case of a notable crime or a series like this, the Officer leading the investigation is required to keep the magistrate updated on progress, presumably so he has a good grasp of the case if and when a suspect is identified. Carver also knew that the days of the *Juges d'Instruction* were numbered. Some weeks before he'd read an article describing how the French Government were planning changes that would see the Examining Magistrate role transferred to the Office of the State Prosecutor, the French equivalent of the CPS. It made him wonder what M. Couthon, comfortable in his elegant office, thought about it. Hearing mention of his name, Carver tuned back in to the conversation.

Couthon was regarding him with studied interest.

'Marc was just asking about the part you are playing in all this Jamie,' Remy said. 'I have explained that while you are simply observing, you have some experience in cases such as this which you are sharing with us.'

Carver took his cue, meeting the magistrate's enquiring gaze. 'That's about it. I happened to be over here on another matter and Remy asked if I would be interested in following the investigation. To compare notes as it were.'

Couthon gave a sly smile. 'I suspect, Monsieur Carver, that with your particular experiences it is a little more than, comparing notes, *n'est ce pas?*'

Carver came on guard. Either Couthon had taken the trouble to research his background, or Remy had briefed him on Carver's case history. 'Remy and I are aware of the protocols involved here, Monsieur Couthon. We are taking care to ensure I am not directly involved in the investigation.'

'Of course,' Couthon gushed. 'I did not mean to suggest otherwise.'

To this point formal and stiff, as befitted his position, Couthon suddenly signalled a change. Draping his arm across the back of the Chesterfield and adopting a more relaxed pose, he turned to Carver. 'I hear that your other assignment in Paris is an interesting one?'

Resisting the impulse to swap glances with Remy - *heard from whom?* - Carver played it straight. 'Not particularly. I am just following up information that a fugitive from British Justice may be in the Paris area.'

'But not just *any* fugitive, I believe?' Couthon's gaze locked on Carver. *Lie to me if you dare.*

'A woman,' Carver said. 'A convicted murderer who escaped from prison.'

'Come, come, Monsieur Carver,' Couthon, said, too smoothly. 'From what I hear, this woman you seek is hardly just another murderer.'

Carver clung on. 'Whoever they are, whatever they do, they are still criminals.' He gave what he hoped was a casual shrug. 'She is no different.'

For a moment, Carver thought Couthon might press him further, force him to name her – *he already knows* – but then he backed off, cloaking himself once more in formality.

'I am sure you are right. Anyway, I wish you good luck in your search.' He stood up, signalling the meeting was over. 'Keep me informed Remy.'

Ten minutes later, the two detectives emerged through the gates onto the bustling Boulevard de Palais.

Carver turned to Remy. 'He seems well informed.'

'I told you he is a smart one.' But if Remy felt the need to speculate on how and where Couthon came by his information, he resisted it. 'Come. We have work to do.'

As they headed back to the Préfecture, Carver reflected on his meeting with Paris's Principle Examining Magistrate. He could not escape the feeling that despite Couthon's attempt to get him to open up - half-hearted though it was - he already knew more than he had let on. But even had the magistrate pressed him further, he would have skirted round the steps he was taking to locate his, 'fugitive from British Justice'. Provided he stayed within the bounds of protocol, it was none of Couthon's business. Nevertheless, Carver wondered where he was getting his information. So far the operation had involved only Remy's small team, all of whom had Remy's complete trust. The only non-police officer who knew any of it was Carissa, and she was the most discreet person Carver had ever known. There were, of course, the several 'invitees', but none of them had met with, or even seen Carver, with the exception of the woman with Durcell, the previous day.

In the end, Carver didn't need to worry as to whether Remy would let him have early access to Marianne Desmarais' family. After their visit to Couthon, Carver left Remy to get on with the business of making sure the investigation was gearing up the way it should. To begin with he sought out Ingrid, who was patient enough to interrupt her phone calls to give him a rundown on how the Murder Control Room was being expanded to encompass the latest crime. Several weeks since the last murder, the past couple of weeks it had been ticking over rather than running flat out. But now Carver could sense the urgency was back again. Ingrid filled him in as to who had been designated to the various key positions in the Room. At first, Carver wondered if she might try to pick up their conversation from the night before. But if it was in her mind at all, she ignored it in favour of the more urgent business of the day. When Remy called Ingrid into a meeting, Carver mooched around, talking to those detectives who spoke reasonable English, watching as the various processes kicked in, observing but at the same time making sure he didn't get in the way to the point of being a nuisance.

By lunchtime Remy was free enough to beckon across for Carver to join him and Ingrid in his office. Closing the door, firmly, Remy came round his desk.

'I am putting Ingrid in charge of victim background. She and two of my team will be travelling to Marianne Desmarais' home town this afternoon. You may wish to go with them.'

What Carver had been hoping for, he remained cautious. 'Aren't you worried someone might see that as me becoming directly involved in the investigation? I wouldn't want to be cause of Monsieur Couthon climbing all over your back.'

'Do not worry about Couthon, Jamie. I am in charge of the investigation. I would like you to apply your Inventory yourself this time.'

Carver needed no further encouragement. 'Fair enough.'

Two hours later they were heading south west on the E9 towards the small provincial town of Souterraine where Marianne Desmarais had lived.

CHAPTER 16

It was nearing six o'clock when Carver, Ingrid and the two other detectives, one a trained Family Liaison Officer, arrived at the hotel where the local police had booked them rooms. Dumping bags, they made their way straight to the Desmarais family home, a modest dormer bungalow-type property on the outskirts of town. With a tended garden resplendent with blooms of many colours, its normality belied the fact that less than twenty-four hours before, its mistress had suffered a horrific death at the hands of a serial killer.

Inside, they found Marianne's husband, Guy, together with their two children, Thierry, twelve and Marie-Rose, fourteen. An older, married daughter was, they learned, about to board a plane at Athens airport that would bring her back from the holiday she had been enjoying with her husband of less than six months. *What a journey that will be*, Carver thought. The local priest was also present, as were an older couple whom M. Desmarais introduced as neighbours and family friends. Between them, they were doing their inadequate best to offer succour to the grieving family.

The first hour was every bit as heart-rending as Carver expected. Words such as 'distraught' and 'devastated' barely did justice to the state the family were in. News of their wife and mother's death had been brought to them the night before by the local police, but this was their first contact with officers involved in the actual investigation. Not surprisingly, between the tears, they had questions. Some of them, the detectives could not answer. One in particular escaped them.

'What was she doing in Paris? Guy Desmarais demanded to know. 'She was supposed to be visiting her mother in Provence?' Carver noted it for later. And it took all their combined skills of persuasion and sympathetic cajoling to convince the grieving husband that if he wanted to see his wife's killer brought to justice, he needed to find it in himself to grant the officers the time they needed.

For a murder victim's family, the first few hours are, inevitably, the worst of times. Along with the numbing shock and overwhelming grief, there is the awful task of having to inform others, be they relatives, friends, or work colleagues. Even experienced police officers find it difficult to ignore the natural instinct that makes them want to lighten the load by not intruding on their grief. But Carver knew the truth of it. Though understandable, such instincts are misplaced. In the long term, what haunts the family more than the loss itself, is the absence of closure that an arrest followed by conviction can bring. Contrary to what many imagine, knowing the details of the murder, even in circumstances as horrific as that of Marianne Desmarais, can be more settling than the years of uncertainty families face when the killer is never caught.

Carver also knew that for a variety of reasons the first few hours are critical to bringing about that outcome. Some are to do with the way the scene is managed, or not. Others concern the quality of early decision making, or whether key witnesses are spoken to and their stories captured before they drift away, not realising they hold vital information that could turn an investigation. As critical, particularly in cases where the victim is in some way identified and selected in advance as opposed to being randomly chosen, is getting to family and friends of the victim and tapping into their knowledge before the impact of the death sinks in. Sometimes knowingly, sometimes not, a relative or close friend is the only person able to point to why a victim may have been targeted. Often that knowledge relates to an aspect of the victim's life he or she chose to hide from the rest of the world. Detectives know that the likelihood of such information being discovered decreases with the passage of time. As those with the relevant knowledge come to terms with what has happened and begin to think rationally again, they sometimes choose, misguidedly, not to disclose what they know, preferring to think that is what the deceased would prefer. Unfortunately, such withholding substantially decreases the chances of identifying the killer. Which was why Carver had no qualms over pressing a grieving husband to let him run his Pinnacle Inventory so soon after learning of his wife's death.

But having acceded to the detectives' request – 'If it will help find who did this terrible thing, then let us do it,' – it was not long before Guy Desmarais began to show impatience, questioning the relevance of some of the questions.

'Why do you want to know what she likes to eat?'
'How will knowing her preference in films help?'

As always, Carver responded by describing the basic purpose of the Inventory as being to provide an in-depth profile of all aspects of the victim's life. But he resisted explaining more. The more the subject understood the process, the more they could be tempted to give what they imagine to be a 'right' answer. If it happens too often, the responses could skew the whole profile to the point where it becomes useless. It was another reason why Carver liked to get the process underway early. Heartless though it seemed, someone still reeling from shock – as opposed to being 'in shock' – is more likely to provide honest and open responses, if only to get the process out of the way so they can return to their grieving.

But while Guy Desmarais appeared to answer Carver's questions openly, there was nothing in his responses that pointed to why or how she had been targeted as a murder victim. He described his wife as a loving partner, mother and home maker. She had no vices apart from the cigarettes she had managed to cut down to five a day. She was well-liked and took part in a wide range of social activities with friends and family in and around where she lived. A devout Christian - as were some of the other victims Carver remembered - she was an active member of the local church, hence the priest. As far as Guy knew, there was nothing about his wife's life that would have made her a target for a killer, whether he was known to her or not. Yet still, there was the question neither he nor any member of his family could answer. What was she doing in Paris? Leaving home three days before, she had said she was visiting her ailing mother in Provence, a story that unravelled the moment they rang the old lady upon receiving the dreadful news. Far from being ill, Marianne's seventy-eight year old mother was in relative good health, though concern was now growing over how what had happened might change that. The last time she had spoken with her daughter – the previous week – Marianne had said nothing about a planned trip to the capital.

By the time they came away, leaving the Family Liaison officer and her colleague to start their work of building trust with the family, Carver and Ingrid were exhausted. They had both found the process of trying to stay focused through so much grief and sadness draining. But as they sat in the car, commiserating with what the family were going through, Carver's brain was working. At the forefront of it was Jess's analysis of the previous murders, and her remarks about each of the victims having a part of their lives that seemed, 'closed.' He mentioned it to Ingrid.

'Closed in what way?'

'We're not sure yet. But Jess thinks it may have been something they were keeping hidden from their families. A personal secret perhaps.'

'Like Marianne's reason for being in Paris?'

'Exactly.'

'But surely it cannot be the same thing? There is nothing we are aware of that connects the victims in any way. We looked for such a connection, but could not find one.'

Carver thought about it. 'Whether they knew each other or not, *something* connects them. All but one of the victims were visiting Paris. Maybe the fact they were visitors is something to do with why the killer chose them.

'So where do we go next?'

Carver thought on it. The last half-hour with Guy Desmarais, they had spent talking about his wife's close friends and acquaintances. She had many, though one stood out. Veronique Guillot had been Marianne's closest friend since their school days. They needed to speak with her next.

'Tonight?' Ingrid said, checking her watch. It was now past nine. They had barely eaten since a snatched lunch on the way down.

'Tomorrow,' Carver said.

As they headed back to their hotel, Carver's hope was that Veronique Guilot and Marianne had been close enough friends to share secrets.

CHAPTER 17

Rising from the kitchen table, Simone Bessette crossed the cottage's old stone floor to the door to the living room. Pushing it open a few inches, she peered out. Her family had not moved. Fabienne and Estelle were still snuggled up against their father, Oliver, on the old battered couch. He was reading to them from the latest 'Horrible Histories' book that had arrived in the post from Amazon that morning. Rapt, the girls were the picture of how eight and ten-year olds should look whose father finds time to read to them after a hard day at work. Letting go of the door so it swung shut again, Simone returned to her chair. She was safe, for a few minutes at least.

On the table was her handbag. Reaching into it she took out a folded envelope. It was crumpled and marked as if it had been much-handled. Yet it too had arrived in the post only that morning. Through the day she had taken it out, opened it and examined its contents, several times. She did so again now. It contained two slim pieces of card; train tickets, valid for a return journey to Gare St Lazare from her home village, one hundred and eighty kilometres outside Paris. The date showed the eighteenth of the month. Less than two weeks away.

She bit her lip, wondering if she would go through with it.

Rising from her chair, Simone crossed to the window to look out over the patch of garden that was her pride and joy. Colourful, ordered and with just the right mix of flowers and shrubs, it reflected all the love and attention she had poured into it these past seven years. At that moment a profound sense of guilt closed in on her. She shuddered. Would that she could say the same about other things.

The sky was darkening to night as she leaned on the worktop, staring out. She thought again about how stupid she had been. How close she had come to ruining the lives of so many. As happened easily now, her eyes started to moisten. Her breath caught in her throat. Realising the danger, she forced herself to turn away from the window, back to the room that all her friends and family spoke of, enviously, as being the 'beating heart of the perfect home.' She shook her head to rid herself of the melancholy. 'Stop it,' she hissed at herself. 'We have been over and over this. We made our decision. It is behind us. It is time to make things right again.' Remembering the envelope still in her hand she stared at it, the promise that lay within. Then she straightened, calling on her resolve. She *would* go through with her plan. She *had* to.

Returning to her handbag, she stuffed the envelope deep down within it. It would be safe there. Oliver would never dream of rifling through her bags. Raising her hands to her cheeks, she pinched and patted them to bring back some colour, then ran her hands down the front of her dress, gathering herself, making sure there was no visible trace of her momentary lapse.

Pinning on a smile, she pushed open the door and stepped through. Three pairs of happy eyes looked up to greet her.

'Now then, family, what would you all like for supper?'

CHAPTER 18

The woman who'd introduced herself as Madame Michelle Chartier shared the last of the bottle's contents between the couple's glasses before rising from the table.

'Now, if you will excuse me, I must leave you alone for a few minutes while I attend to a few things. Can I get you anything else before I go? More bread, or cheese perhaps?'

Tory cast her eyes over the kitchen table. Crumb-strewn plates and the remains of several different breads, cheeses and fresh fruit testified to one of the most pleasant suppers she'd had in a long time. She patted her stomach. 'Not for me thanks, Michelle. If I have any more I'll burst.'

Michelle turned her smile on Scott. 'And what about you Scott? I am a bit worried that a strong young man like you needs more than bread and cheese. I am sorry I had nothing more substantial. Tomorrow I will send to the *boucherie* in the village for some good, red meat.'

As he had done several times already that evening, Scott flushed at the older woman's attentions. 'Thanks but I'm fine, Michelle. Not all us Yanks live on burgers, you know.'

She threw her head back and laughed, throatily, as she seemed to do every time Scott attempted a funny. Tory didn't think they all merited it.

'Right then. I will be back soon.' With a girly wave of her fingers, she breezed out of the kitchen, shutting the door behind her.

Scott waited until he was sure she was out of ear-shot before turning to his fiancée. 'So what do you think?' he said, eyes bright with enthusiasm. 'Have we fallen on our feet or what?'

Tory blinked and shook her head, as if still struggling to come to terms with their stroke of good fortune. 'I don't know. Don't you think it seems a bit O.T.T.? Free bed and board as well as guided tours of Paris? And just for helping her plan a trip to Boston in the fall? I'd have thought that living in a house like this, she could afford to just pay an agent to tailor an itinerary? At the very least, all she has to do is go online and download one?'

But Scott wasn't for quibbling. 'You heard what she said. She wants to see Boston as the locals see it. And she likes the company of young people and loves to show off her home city. What's wrong with that?'

'Depends what she means by, 'company'.'

He picked up on her pointed look. 'What does that mean?'

'Now don't tell me that the famous Scud hasn't noticed the way she looks at you.' 'Scud' was the moniker Scott had acquired at College; an amalgam of Scott and Stud that also referenced, amongst other things, the missile of that name. 'They don't make beefcake like you in France, you know.' She smiled as she said it, though it wasn't entirely natural. But the smile he returned her was.

'You mean she only wants me for my body?' His eye twinkled. 'I can live with that.'

She slapped his arm. 'Don't be getting any ideas. You're taken, remember?'

'How could I forget?' He reached for her but she ducked away from his grasp.

'Not here,' she hissed. 'We're guests in someone's home.'

'And what a home.' He looked about him. The farmhouse-style kitchen and adjoining living area – the 'play room' Michelle had called it – could have graced any of the home interiors journals they'd poured over before coming away. 'If this was mine, I wouldn't want to move, would you?'

'Probably not, but then from what she said, she's only here temporarily while she finds somewhere more permanent. I wonder if it belongs to that Count guy she spoke to on the way here?'

Scott leaped on it. 'And what about that? A real French count.' Did you catch what they were talking about?'

'Only the odd word. I got the impression it was something to do with some show that's coming up in the next week or so. As far as I could make out, she was trying to work out if she should go.'

'What sort of show? Maybe she'll take us.'

'I think she's giving us enough, don't you? Besides, we'll be long gone by then.'

Scott pulled a non-committal face. 'Hm-hm.'

She read it. 'Three nights we agreed, remember? Then we're moving on.'

'Hm-hm.'

'And we're supposed to be calling on Jacques on the

way out of Paris. Have you spoken to him yet?'

'Mmm, not yet but I will.'

Tory eyed him, suspiciously. Jacques was a French-born fellow graduate. His parents still owned a property in a small town to the south and east of Paris. He and his family were summering there before he returned to the US to take up his place with one of the bigger Boston Law firms. Hearing of their trip, he'd insisted that Tory and Scott visit on their way through. After days of badgering, Scott had had to promise they would, and they had duly written it into their itinerary. Only now Scott didn't seem to be assigning it the same priority as before. Tory decided not to push it. Yet.

She changed the subject. 'So what do you think was going on with the house maid or whatever she is when we arrived? I had the feeling she wasn't too pleased to see us.'

'I had the same thought about her driver when he picked us up. Maybe they don't take kindly to unexpected guests.'

'But what sort of hired help argues back they way she did? Did you see Michelle's face? I thought she was going to hit the roof.'

'Yeah, but she certainly put her in her place. I guess they're right what they say about the French being a bit arrogant sometimes.'

'That's another thing.' Tory looked puzzled. 'When I asked whether she was French or English she was a bit vague, almost like she didn't want to say.'

'Maybe she likes to cultivate a mysterious side.'

'Well if so, it's working. I can't get a handle on her at all. I keep wondering if she's an actress and still performing.'

'I know what you mean. And what about her asking us not to connect or use our cells while we are here? Do you believe all that about having had trouble with a stalker and not wanting anything showing up on social media that may give her location away?'

'Well, it does sound a bit extreme, but if you've had that sort of trouble and are worried about some psycho finding you... maybe it makes sense.'

'So as well as being paranoid about having her picture taken, she's also paranoid about people posting on Facebook? She doesn't come across like that in person.'

'Hey, we both know people who are wary of social media. Michelle wouldn't be the first.'

'Moving off some social platform isn't the same as making your property a digital free zone. My cell doesn't even show a network, and I haven't seen anything that looks like a router.. Who doesn't use the internet *at all*, these days?'

'Well her, apparently. Maybe the French don't connect like we do. And don't forget, she's older than us.'

'Not *that* old. Hell, our parents are online more than we are.'

'That's true. So what are you saying we should do?'

'Do? Nothing. I think we should just accept her hospitality in the spirit it's offered and not worry. Not many back-packers get to stay for free in a house like this.'

'In that case, we'd better make sure we're spot on with whatever steers we give for her trip.'

'If there is a trip.'

'What do you mean?'

He mused a few seconds. 'Hmm, well, I dunno... It all sounds a bit pat, don't you think? She bumps into us just as she happens to be planning a trip to Boston? Then when she hears us talking about what to do, she offers to put us up in return for helping her plan her trip? Bit coincidental, don't you think?'

'And I thought I was the sceptical one. I never even-' She stopped as the door opened and Michelle Chartier returned to take the seat between them at the head of the table.

'There, that's your room sorted. Ursulla is just making up the bed then you can unpack. I'm sure you'd like to freshen up. There's a shower in the room, so you'll have plenty of privacy.'

Conscious of the doubts they'd discussed in her absence, Tory decided to check one last time. 'Before we do that, Michelle...' She glanced at Scott. 'We seem to be putting you to an awful lot of trouble for no great return. Are you sure you're happy to put up with us for a few days? We don't want to stop you doing... whatever it is you would be doing if we weren't here.'

The woman turned suddenly serious. Reaching out, she took a hand off each of them in hers.

'Believe me, it's no trouble at all. Right now I'm between projects and was planning a few days' relaxation before moving on. You being here will force me to not get involved in things that can wait. Besides I have another, selfish reason. As you can see, right now I'm on my own here. I have to confess I have been missing company. Having two such young and vibrant people as yourselves around will do me the world of good.'

Scott joined the conversation. 'We got the impression

your staff didn't seem to like the idea of others staying here. We wouldn't want to be the cause of any friction.'

She gave a dismissive wave. 'Pay no attention to Alain and Ursulla. I have already spoken to them about their attitude. They're both in training and I'm afraid they've a lot to learn. I shall be sending them back to the agency when I leave. And with suitable reports I may add.'

Tory and Scott exchanged worried glances. 'Oh dear,' Tory said. 'I hope-'

Michelle's hand came up. 'Enough. It is not your fault it is theirs. Let us not talk of it again. I just want that you both enjoy whatever time you spend here.'

Finally, Tory accepted it. 'Okay. If you're sure.'

'I am.'

'But just to be clear. We'll just stay the three days as we discussed, then we'll move on and leave you in peace.'

The attractive face took on a conspiratorial air. 'As you wish. But let me tell you now so that you know. I will be hosting a leaving party next week for some of my friends. Nothing grand, just a small gathering. I would love for you to stay until then and meet them. I am sure they would love to meet you. I will say no more about it for now but please, think about it.'

About to reply, Tory stopped herself. It had been a long day and they were both tired of debating what-ifs. She looked at Scott, could see he thought the same. 'Okay,' they said together.

'Now let me show you to your room. I'm sure you could both do with a good night's sleep. It will be a long day tomorrow. There is much to see in Paris and we must make the most of your time.'

Neither argued. Michelle Chartier smiled at them. Already, they were learning.

CHAPTER 19

Over a late dinner at the hotel, Carver made sure that conversation with Ingrid stayed focused on the business that had brought them to Souterraine - Marianne Desmarais' murder, her family, and what the next day might bring. Running the inventory with Marianne's best friend, Veronique, would call for clear thinking. He did not need other distractions. Nevertheless, one came. Halfway through the evening, Carver took a call from Carissa. He excused himself to take it just in case, and went back through to the lobby. He needn't have. It was business.

She told him that earlier that evening she had heard from Henri Durcell. He had confirmed his interest in what they were selling. He wished to take up six of the eight places still available. When Carissa enquired who they were for, 'Just a name, for admission purposes you understand?' Durcell gave himself, a 'Madmoiselle Jacqueline,' whom he identified as the woman who had accompanied him to their meeting, a Monsieur and Madame Gerrard, and two others whose names he said he would confirm within the next couple of days.

Carver asked her if any of the names rang a bell.

'No, but that doesn't mean anything. There are so

many, I could never have hoped to know them all.'

Carver responded with a vague, 'Hmm,' before voicing what was in his head. 'We've said all along that if she took the bait, it would likely be through a third party, and using an assumed name. Durcell is still the only contact we've had who we know for definite knows her. The two other places could be for her and a companion.'

'Maybe, maybe not. We also said we most likely won't know until on the night.'

For all that he craved certainty, Carver knew she was right. The game they were playing was bound to remain an uncertain one. By its nature, those showing interest would be wary about doing anything that may later link them to it. Nevertheless, Durcell's confirmation was the most promising development so far.

Carver breathed deep. 'We've got the twelve confirmed places we said we would aim for when we started all this. I think we should go with what we've got. Is your friend with the house still on board?'

'Of course.'

'Then let's fix a date and get on with it.'

'You are sure, Jamie? Once we set a date, we must be prepared to see it through?'

He didn't hesitate. 'If we don't, we could end up going round in circles waiting for the certainty that may never come.'

'Alright. I will let you know when I have spoken to him.'

After Carissa rang off, Carver breathed out, long and slow. At last, the plan that had formed during a long dark night of even darker discussion and deliberation, months before, was about to roll out. Three people had

had a hand in forming that plan. All had a personal interest in seeing Megan Crane brought to justice; himself, Carissa, and Jess. But while they were all party to it, the decision to execute it was for him, and him alone.

He had known from the beginning that the moment would come when he would have to grit his teeth and make a decision. That moment had just arrived. And having made it, he was acutely conscious that he was taking the biggest gamble of his life. It was why he hadn't hesitated when Carissa had asked if he was sure. If he thought about it too much, he may have wavered.

In truth, there was never any question that they would seek someone else's authority or approval for what they intended. No one in their right mind would give it. Even if they did, it would be subject to so many riders and caveats, it would make it impossible to execute. Besides, there was a better than even chance that come the time, they may need to go further than any official, police or otherwise, would be prepared to countenance. And for all that everyone agreed that Megan Crane needed to be recaptured, no one would risk their career or worse to make it happen. Not unless they had already lost something so precious as to make considerations such as career, reputation, maybe even personal freedom, irrelevant. Now, five in all knew of the plan's details. And while Carver knew he could count on the other four's support, he had decided long ago that responsibility for anything that might happen had to lie with him. It was why he had made Remy agree that, in the event something went horribly wrong, Remy would claim that Carver had deceived him into believing that the plan had been sanctioned by his superiors in the UK. And getting Remy's agreement, had taken some time.

When Carver returned to Ingrid, she seemed to sense the change in him. She asked what had happened. He told her, and what he'd told Carissa to do.

Ingrid put down her knife and fork, sat back in her chair. 'So we are going ahead with it.' A statement, not a question. The look on her face made Carver's stomach churn.

'It's not too late to back out. We can try something else.'

For all that he meant it, her simple reply didn't come as a surprise. 'No.'

There was a moment's silence, then her hand slid across the table, seeking his. She squeezed it. And though she said nothing, he read its meaning.

Look after me.

He returned the squeeze. *I will. I promise.*

CHAPTER 20

As it turned out, Veronique Guillot knew as much English, as Carver did French. For that reason Ingrid conducted the part of the Inventory headed, *'Victim's Close Friend - Non-Familial*. It meant she had to translate Veronique's responses word for word, in case Carver saw the need for a follow-up. Carver was finding the process as tortuous as it was frustrating. The disconnect meant he had virtually no chance of picking up on the subtle changes in language or inflection that might mark a change in Veronique's established pattern. Not for the first time, Carver wished he'd stuck with the Conversational French Course Rosanna had enrolled them on the time she thought she may be about to break through into France's burgeoning folk music market.

There was one compensation. Not having to ask questions and note answers meant he could concentrate on Veronique's body language. Which was why he noted at once the way she spread, then re-clasped her fingers when Ingrid posed the question, 'Did Marianne share any personal secrets with you over the past three months?'

'No,' Ingrid translated her reply, though Carver had no trouble reading Veronique's terse, 'Non.'

As the silence that followed lengthened, Carver knew that Ingrid was following the guidance attached to many of the questions. In this particular case it read, *"If the response is negative, remain silent, do not move on to the next question until satisfied no further response is forthcoming."*

The silence did its job. After long seconds, Veronique bit her lip. The detectives waited. Eventually she spoke. Ingrid translated. 'What sort of secrets?'

Carver was on it at once. 'The sort a woman only shares with her best friend.' Ingrid relayed it.

The next silence was as long as the first. Veronique's pale complexion began to take on a pinky hue. Carver's pulse quickened.

CHAPTER 21

It was something Carver had witnessed many times, a man doing his best to make it look like he has nothing to hide, whilst at the same time trying to mask growing anxiety.

Paul Dupont and his architect partners shared a suite of offices in a neighbouring town, not too far from the Desmarais family home in Souterraine. When Carver and Ingrid first arrived, Dupont made a show of being eager to help, '-Anyway I can.'

Earlier, when Ingrid phoned to let him know they were on their way and told him it was to do with the death of Mme. Marianne Desmarais, he apologised, saying he was unavailable and citing an 'urgent meeting with clients.' When Ingrid suggested it may be in his interests to cancel it, that they were coming anyway and she expected that he be there to greet them, he gave up trying to dissuade them. When he greeted them at reception, summoned by the receptionist's guarded call – '*Votre visiteurs sont arrivés*' - he was all smiles and handshakes. But his muttered aside to the girl as he showed them up the stairs to his office, - '*Pas d'interruptions, Elyse,*' contained an edge that made Carver wonder if the sharp-witted receptionist might already have some idea as to the reason for their visit.

Dupont's manner changed the moment he closed his office door and turned to face them. It was obvious he was nervous. And when Ingrid introduced Carver and asked if he minded if they spoke in English, he consented, readily.

'How may I help?'

Carver got straight to it. 'We understand you and Marianne Desmarais were having an affair?'

Dupont flushed a deep shade of red. 'Who told you that?'

'I'll take that as a "yes". How long were you seeing each other?'

For several seconds Dupont hesitated, eyeing first Carver then Ingrid in a way that suggested he was weighing his chances. It didn't take him long to work out what they were. Collapsing into his expensive looking leather chair, he told them everything.

Dupont and Marianne had become lovers ten years before, after meeting at an anniversary celebration of mutual friends. It was both passionate, and frequently stormy. Marianne made clear right at the start there was no question she would ever leave her husband. A staunch catholic, divorce was out of the question. Often ridden with guilt, Marianne tried several times over the years to end it. But whether driven by the thrill of illicit sex, or just bored with the secure but unexciting life she shared with her salesman husband, she always crept back to Dupont's bed. Six weeks earlier, Marianne had finally declared it over - 'For good this time.' According to Dupont she could no longer live with the guilt that comes with skulking around, lying to her husband about her movements in order to snatch the odd afternoon in some hotel room. He claimed that the last time he'd seen her was four weeks before, on a supermarket car park when Marianne returned to him the locket and chain he had given her years before to mark his 'commitment.' After pressing as to whether he had seen her since – he denied it – Carver believed him. It matched what Veronique Guillot had told them. She had heard it direct from Marianne during an emotional confession when she unburdened herself to her best friend. Dupont said he was wholly unaware of the anguish Veronique described Marianne suffering through the last few weeks.

By now Dupont's jaunty facade was in tatters, replaced by a quivering mess of remorse and self-recrimination. Ignorant as to why she was in Paris, the thought had clearly occurred that her death may, in some way, be connected with the end of their affair.

'Tell me, monsieur,' he asked Carver, anxiously, 'Do I bear some blame for her death?'

Carver thought on what to tell him. Through the interview, Carver had seen nothing in the Frenchman's responses that set any alarms ringing. He had given the detectives the names of the several clients he had said would confirm his whereabouts throughout the day Marianne died. Right now, Carver was as satisfied as he could be that Dupont was not a murder suspect. But, like Marianne, Dupont was married, with children. Listening to him, Carver had formed an impression he was one of those men who like to have their cake, and eat it. His guess was that Dupont had only ever wanted one thing from Marianne Desmarais. He let one word suffice as his answer.

'Probably.'

Back in the car, Ingrid turned to Carver. He was staring through the windscreen, focusing on nothing.

'Okay. We know that Marianne was having an affair, but not why she was in Paris. What now?'

He looked at her, thinking. 'Just a minute.' Pulling out his mobile, he rang Jess, putting her on speaker. It rang out several times before she answered.

'How's it going?'

'I need an intuitive guess.'

'Go on.'

'This hidden aspect of the victims' lives thing?'

'Yeees.' Wary, wondering what was coming.

'How about extramarital sex?'

'You mean an affair?'

'Isn't that the same thing?'

She snorted. 'Not necessarily. Which victim are we talking about?'

'All of them.'

'Bloody hell. Hmm. Let me think.' There was a short silence, then, 'Possibly. I can't think of anything that would rule it out. What have you got?'

He filled her in on what they'd learned. After another short silence she said, 'Sounds good to me. But if you want to confirm it, you're going to have to revisit the other victims' families and dig for it.'

'I know.'

For Carver's benefit, Remy confirmed his instructions over the phone to Detective Martin in English. Remy had assigned Martin and his partner, Brigitte, to revisit the previous victims for the purpose of re-running Carver's Inventory. 'That is right. Whether they were having an affair. . . Yes. . . I do not know. That is what you need to find out.' Shaking his head, he mimed exasperation to Carver and Ingrid. 'We cannot say. Some time before they were killed. . . It could be any time-'

Carver chimed in. 'Tell him, it probably ended within the six months before.'

Remy relayed his advice. 'Yes, not too long. Guilt festers quickly.' He listened a moment then repeated the thing about guilt, in French this time. 'Oui, Martin, Ça va.' He hung up.

'They will revisit the victims again as you ask. It will take a few days, but Martin and Brigitte are two of my best. If they know what to look for and it is there, they will find it.'

'Good.' Carver turned and headed for the door.

'Where are you going?' Ingrid said.

'Downstairs.'

'What for?'

'To find out what else the victims may have had in common.'

CHAPTER 22

The Paris Police Crime Laboratory is situated in the Préfecture's vast sub-basement. It comprises a series of interconnecting rooms, each separated by a graded system of anti-contaminant and isolation technologies that converge, through five tiers, to the centre where the 'one-hundred-percent sterile' area is located. The room they were standing in was one of the three that form the second tier. Spaced around the outer wall were rows of ceiling-high storage racks. They were full of plastic sacks and cardboard boxes, all neatly labelled and marked. Each set of racks corresponded with one of the 'Pension Murders.' Between the racks, white-topped examination tables were littered with plastic evidence bags, documents and index sheets. The last rack and table in the row lacked the studied order of the others. It contained the exhibits from Marianne Desmarais's murder, which were still being processed. Carver's gaze roamed over them. Every now and then he picked up a bag, perused its contents, put it down again. At the same time, Ingrid patrolled up and down the other tables, as if reminding herself of the previous murders. At the end of the room nearest the entrance, two scene analysts were updating the Exhibits Database. The first, whose name was Ali, was tall and angular. He had gelled, spiky hair that made Carver wonder about contamination. He was reading items off a clipboard. His shaven-headed partner, Firisat, was entering the data. Firisat was several inches shorter than his colleague, and barrel-shaped. They made a contrasting pair. After showing the detectives where to find what they'd asked for, they'd returned to their task.

After several minutes, Ingrid wandered back to Carver.

'What is there?'

He pulled a face. 'Not much I'm afraid.' He indicated several items he had pulled from the pile, each in a see-through plastic bag. 'There're some cash receipts from cafés and restaurants which our friends over there-' he nodded in the analysts' direction, 'tell me are in the vicinity of her hotel. A two-day métro pass, which the Transport Authority is checking to see which stops she used. A credit card receipt for some items she bought from the Samaritaine.' Ingrid nodded, but didn't register anything. Most provincial women who visit Paris find time to visit the equivalent of London's Harrods. 'And this.' Carver indicated a piece of A5 size paper. Bright pink, it was printed both sides.

'What is it?'

'It looks like it might be something to do with a church. An order of service maybe?'

He passed it to her. She read the closely-typed script.

'It's from La Madeleine. The Church of Saint Mary Magdelene.'

Carver nodded. He'd once visited the church that is also one of the city's most famous tourist spots. He recalled learning how it was a place of pilgrimage. And not just for Roman Catholics but many other faiths as well.

Ingrid continued. 'It is a guide to services. It shows the days on which services are held. Mass, Communion, Confession.' She became thoughtful. 'I wonder...'

She turned to the other tables, hesitated, then spun on her heel and approached the two analysts. She showed them the piece of paper. There followed a three-way conversation which Carver could only observe as the analysts looked from Ingrid, to the paper, and babbled at each other. Firasat became animated. It looked to Carver like he was chiding his colleague over something, indicating the paper with an open hand like he was making a point. Carver translated his body language as, '*You should have raised it.*' Eventually Firasat broke off and headed down the room, passed the racks containing the exhibits from the previous murders. Ingrid followed. So did Carver. They stopped at the middle table of the five. Firasat rooted amongst some plastic bags then pulled out one containing a yellow slip of paper.

'Voilà,' he said with a flourish.

Ingrid stepped forward and took it from him. Carver saw at once that it was similar to the pink one in Ingrid's hand.

'This is the same,' she said. 'Also from La Madeleine.' She smiled at the young man next to her and said something Carver assumed was complimentary. Firasat beamed and reddened the way some technicians who spend most of their day focused on processes do when certain types of women address them. As they were examining it, a call came from Ali down the other end of the room. 'Ay!' He was pointing to his screen.

Firasat retraced his steps to join him. There was another animated conversation, though shorter this time. He returned to the second table in the line, beckoning Carver and Ingrid to join him. Rooting again in the pile of plastic bags, he checked reference numbers, eventually pulling one out. It contained a small cardboard slip. He showed it to Ingrid.

'What is it?' Carver asked.

'A Métro ticket. To St Augustin.' Carver looked blank. 'The nearest stop to Madeleine.'

Carver's eyes narrowed as he remembered what Jess's analysis had revealed. All the victims were Christian church-goers, though she hadn't mentioned if she'd tied them down to a particular faith. In his mind's eye, he pictured the large scale map of Paris on the wall of the Murder Room upstairs. It showed the location of the hotels and guest houses in and around Paris where the murders had taken place. All but one were on the north side of the Seine. The same side as La Madeleine.

'What are you thinking?' Ingrid said.

'I'm thinking about how long it is since I last went to church.'

CHAPTER 23

Jess Greylake stared across at the man whose words were still bouncing around her head. She had wondered why Arthur Carrington had been so keen that they meet over lunch, rather than talk on the phone. Now she knew.

Jess had experience of being propositioned, by both sexes and in a variety of circumstances. In her early days, it most often took the form of a clumsy lunge or quick grope, usually involving alcohol. As she matured, the fumbles and lunges gave way to bare-faced, up-front 'offers', often from people already in a relationship. Apart from the embarrassment and disappointment such incidents invariably generated, Jess always took them as signalling a lack of respect, both for her and women in general. Where, as it sometimes did, it involved someone senior in age or position, she also regarded it as creepy and amoral.

She was surprised therefore when she realised that the proposition just made left her feeling neither disrespected, nor creeped-out. In fact, as she digested the words, she realised that the feelings it was triggering were more to do with amusement and flattery, than outrage or offence. She also knew that without her experiences of the past couple of years, her response would almost certainly have been the reverse. It had a lot to do with the man making it.

Looking at Arthur Carrington now, smartly dressed, at ease with himself, sampling the Rioja while awaiting her response, it was hard to imagine him as he was the first time they met. On that occasion he'd been wearing nothing more than a pair of shiny briefs, actually little more than a thong, covering the bare essentials, and a tight fitting hood with zippers over the eye and mouth holes. He was kneeling, chained to a wall, in Megan Crane's 'play room'. Next to him, also naked apart from a leather body-harness and similarly hooded and chained, was a younger, blond haired woman. Her name was Tracy Redmond, a 'switch' who was then even more under Megan's spell than Arthur was.

What none of them knew at the time, was that Megan was setting Tracy up to take the fall for the Worshipper Murders, including Angie and Jamie Carver. Thankfully for Tracy, Megan's plan failed, though her career as a barrister was ruined. After, her life fell apart. And it was what befell Tracy, that led, eventually, to Jess renewing her acquaintance with, 'the man in the shiny briefs.'

Arthur was also a barrister, attached to the same Manchester chambers as Tracy. Over the course of the five years they worked together, Arthur, a widower since his fifties, came to believe he loved her. Sadly that love was never to be requited, Tracy's being reserved, solely, for Megan Crane. It was Tracy who introduced Arthur to Megan, encouraging him to join them both in Megan's playroom whenever work allowed. There the two women, both experts in their craft, taught Arthur how to exorcise the desires that drove him. For Arthur, innocent and ignorant of the truth behind the woman he knew only as 'Mistress', it was a happy time. When, a year or so after Megan's escape from custody, rumours came to his ears from other 'acquaintances' about Megan possibly living somewhere just outside Paris, he saw the opportunity to help the woman he once loved gain at least some closure. He contacted Jamie Carver.

Since then, Jamie, Jess and Arthur had met several times, cross-checking the rumours Arthur was hearing, against other possible clues to Megan Crane's whereabouts. It was Arthur's sporadic confirmations that she was still in the Paris area, that led, eventually, to Jamie deciding that his best chance of hunting her down was to go to Paris armed with a plan to do so. In this regard, Arthur's knowledge of Megan's past interests and activities would prove useful. Unfortunately by then, Jess's mother's cancer treatment had begun, which was what kept her from accompanying Carver to Paris.

With hindsight, Jess should have seen Arthur's proposal coming. Following lunch - they both passed on dessert - Arthur fell to philosophising about the way both their lives had been changed by events of the past couple of years. After some reflection, he put down his glass, looked Jess square in the eye and in a matter-of-fact tone that contained not a hint of pleading, threat, or anything else that may cause a woman half his age to take offence, said, 'Talking about these matters, it has been in my mind to ask something of you, Jess.'

'And what would that be, Arthur?' she said, though the suspicion grew in an instant.

'I wonder if you might be interested in exploring what it means to be in a D/S relationship, by agreeing to partner me in an occasional scene?'

So casually did Arthur deliver the words, it took Jess a few moments to realise that what she thought she heard him say, was correct. It then took several more to get her head around the fact that a man old enough to be her father was actually proposing that they enter into a relationship in which they would act out the sort of activities with which she had become all too familiar these past years.

Reaching for her glass, Jess took a sip of her wine. At the same time, she returned Arthur's steady gaze, gave a wan smile and said, 'I will take what you have just proposed as the compliment I suspect you intend. And while it raises issues we could spend some time going over, I'll respond by pointing out that right now you are, effectively, acting as a police informant, albeit an unregistered one. For that reason if no other, I must pass on your proposal. But thank you for asking.'

Arthur Carrington waited another moment before returning the same wan smile she had sent him, nodding an acknowledgement to himself, then drained his glass, and placed it down in front of him.

'Thank you for letting me down gently, Jess. I'll not raise the matter again. Now, would you like a liqueur to see us on our way, or ought we to call it a night?'

As much to show she bore him no ill feeling, Jess opted for a Cointreau. It was clear to her now why Arthur had pressed for a meeting, and why he had spent so long skirting around the subject that was the only reason for them meeting in the first place - Megan's whereabouts - about which he had no new information, and could easily have confirmed in a telephone call.

But later, in the taxi home, Jess found herself pondering over the question that she already knew would return to her over the coming days.

What would her response have been had Arthur Carrington not been an intelligence source, and if he had been twenty years younger?

CHAPTER 24

Taking his coffee out on the terrace in the morning sun, Scott Weston stared out across the swimming pool at the Maison De Floret's well-stocked gardens. Several times over the past days, Scott had imagined what it would be like to vacation here during high summer, what it would cost. He had no idea of rental values in France, but the house was only a thirty minute drive from Paris' centre. It had to be worth quite a bit. He had thought about messaging Greg and getting him to check it out on Google Earth, but then remembered his host's concerns about going online and forgot about it. But right now Scott's thoughts weren't on property values, vacationing or anything else to do with the house. He was pondering on the position in which he found himself, and trying to work out how he felt.

By rights of course, he should be blessing the luck that had brought them here. Instead he was contemplating his dilemma, what he ought to do about it. He wasn't yet at the point of regretting their decision to break their trip, but his thoughts were beginning to turn that way.

To be fair, the last few days had been amazing. The big old house on the outskirts of the small village outside the capital evoked everything Scott imagined as 'French.' In particular, it reminded him of the old, French art-house movies he and Tory had latched onto during their first year at college. This was before they realised that watching a boy and girl angst over whether they were meant for each other before discovering they were actually siblings, wasn't that riveting. And they had certainly seen a side of Paris they would never have discovered on their own. Each day Michelle's driver-handyman, Alain, had dropped the three of them off outside the Opéra Garnier for a day's sightseeing. In that respect, their hostess's knowledge of the city's fascinating history as well its quirky, and darker, elements seemed boundless. She knew things about Paris the guide books never even touched on. But after four days, Scott was growing anxious.

By now he'd admitted to himself that it wasn't just the chance to see more of Paris while enjoying free bed and board that made him leap to accept Michelle's generous-sounding offer. There was another reason, though not one he could ever share with Tory. Not even after they were married and Paris was merely a fading memory.

The truth was Scott had found the woman instantly fascinating. And not just her exotic beauty, even if it was enough to set any red-blooded male's pulse racing. There was something about her that started to act on him the moment he looked up from embracing Tory and found her standing over them. There was an air of mystery about her that was almost palpable. He saw it in her eyes that first time he stared into them. The sure sense that there was something beyond her story about not liking having her photograph taken. At the same time, and more weirdly, she exuded an aura of vulnerability that was completely at odds with her appearance. She *seemed* the sort of woman who would be capable of taking charge in any situation. Her calm assurance and measured manner sometimes bordered, almost, on the severe. Nevertheless, whenever he caught her eye, he could swear the message read, 'I need someone to look after me.' It was like nothing he had encountered before. And it swung his decision, not that it needed much swinging. And for all that Tory later took him to task for not consulting her before deciding to change their plans – 'Is that all it takes? A pair of fluttering eyelashes, a French accent and our whole trip goes out the window?' – the moment she saw the house, its grounds, her attitude changed. And right now it was Tory's change of attitude that was playing on him.

As long as he had known her, Tory had always had an independent streak. 'Strong-willed,' her father called it. 'Stubborn,' was Scott's take. Either way, he had discovered long ago that for all that they were a couple in every sense of the word, Tory had a side that sometimes left him wondering how much she needed him. Not in the 'living together' sense, but *really* needed him, deep down, the way he knew he needed her. From an early age, Scott had always known that for him, Tory was his 'missing appendage.' The one that some search for all their lives and never find. It always reminded him of the line in Tory's favourite old film, Jerry Maguire, when Tom tells Renee, "You complete me". Tory knew it of course. And Scott liked that she knew it. They talked about it, joked about it. 'Hey, third leg,' he would call to her. 'What's up, second head?' she would respond, though he'd never been brave enough to challenge her as to whether she really meant it. Nevertheless, aware of his dependence on her, of the insecurity that was deep within him but which no one who knew him could ever imagine, Tory always behaved so that whatever the circumstances, whatever the choices they faced, independently or together - lives, careers, families - he would know that he was her number one priority. And it had worked. Ever since the time she found him upstairs in his room, alone in the dark, distraught because he'd imagined her New-Year's Eve party flirting with Brad Wilson hinted at something more serious, there had never been a moment when he'd had cause to believe Tory's focus was anywhere but on him.

Until now.

The irony of course, was that while *he* was the one who had jumped to accept Michelle's offer, and in so doing gave Tory probable cause to fear she may need a crowbar to prise him away, the reverse had happened.

To begin with, Tory had been cautious, even suspicious enough to question the woman's motives. 'What does a woman like her want with a couple of kids like us?' Thinking of other things, Scott did his best to play it down. 'It's a quid-pro-quo, Tory. Like she said, she needs our help, we need hers. Simple.' The way Tory looked at him, disbelievingly, he knew it was anything but simple. It hadn't escaped him, and nor would it have escaped Tory, that the woman in whose company they had now spent the best part of five days looked like she knew how to enjoy life, in every sense of the word. From what they could tell, she lived alone, though they'd seen and heard plenty pointing to a wide circle of friends. There were no rings on any fingers that might signify a work-away husband, or other claims on her affections. A woman like her had to have needs. And not just the, 'someone to mow the lawn', variety. While Scott knew that Tory often liked to make out she only put up with him grudgingly, 'until I find someone more deserving,' they both knew the truth of it. With his ice-blue eyes, quarter-back physique and blond locks, Scott's 'Scud' tag was apt, and in all sorts of ways. And while he and Tory knew almost nothing about Michelle Chartier, one thing was clear. There was nothing wrong with her eyesight.

Which made it all the more surprising when, on the third day of their stay, something strange happened.

Right from the start, Scott had been conscious of the spark he felt every time Michelle paid him attention. On the odd occasion they were alone together, whether for minutes or seconds, he experienced the sort of near-panic a burgeoning adolescent sometimes feels when he suddenly finds himself alone with a pretty girl. As some older women are with a younger man, Michelle was teasingly tactile. She was not averse to emphasising a point by laying a hand on his arm, playfully rubbing shoulders, nudging elbows. For Scott, each contact was like an electric shock. Immediately after, it was all he could do to talk without squeaking. He was grateful that during the day at least, it was warm enough that he could put his sweating brow down to the late summer heat. Michelle knew the effect she was having of course, of that he was sure. And she played on it to the point where, time and again, he felt the need to convince Tory there was absolutely nothing going on.

That the playful banter was nothing more than that. The looks and smiles simply diplomatic US-Franco relations. At every opportunity, he made sure to include Tory in their tomfoolery. Not to would have been dangerous. Besides, there was a spin-off benefit.

However it worked, and regardless of whether Tory would ever come to admit it, the sexual chemistry that existed between him and Michelle and which simmered through each of those first three days, seemed to act on Tory like an aphrodisiac. The bedroom Michelle had given them was the other side of the house to hers. It was as well. Tory had always been capable of letting go when the mood took her. But the transformation Scott witnessed that first night as they went at each other under the canopy of the slightly-musty but oh-so comfortable four-poster bed, cushioned, thank God, by the deep feather mattress that smelled of heather, was nothing short of startling. Later, as they lay together, spent, covered in sweat, looking out through the floor-to-ceiling windows at the clouds passing across the crescent moon, he turned to her. All he could manage to convey his awe at what had just occurred was a single word. 'Jesus.'

The next night was the same.

It changed on the third day. At breakfast, he sensed something was different, but could not work out what. Michelle seemed as attentive as before, seeing to their needs, asking what they'd like to do that day, talkative as ever. But Scott felt a change in the atmosphere that made him wonder if something was distracting her. The amount of eye contact between them wasn't as frequent as it had been, the smile not quite as quick. He noticed it more as the day went on. On the boat trip along the

Seine which Michelle insisted, embarrassingly, on paying for, rather than sitting between him and Tory so they could benefit equally from her commentary, as she had done on the open-top bus tour the day before, Tory ended up in the middle. As they took their seats, Scott sensed Michelle waiting to see where he was going to sit before parking herself on Tory's other side. He spent much of that day trying to work out if he had said or done something to offend her, gone too far perhaps in his jokey asides and sometimes-loaded responses. But he could think of nothing. He wondered if maybe she had realised she may be going too far, and had decided to rein herself in. But he had been scrupulous at making sure that his responses to her flirting - no other word for it – conveyed what he thought was the right message. *I'm happy to play, but that's all.* There was, therefore, no reason he could see why she might think a change was called for. By the time dinner rolled around – Michelle insisted on taking them to an atmospheric but slightly seedy backstreet bistro in Montparnasse - he was certain. It wasn't that she was ignoring him, far from it. But for some reason the spark was definitely gone, turned off like a lamp switch. It was almost as if she had taken a conscious decision on waking that morning to not play the game anymore.

The penny dropped at bedtime.

The previous night, as they'd swapped the continental, kiss-kiss he had quickly come to look forward to, the spark had still been there as she bade him, 'Have a good night.' To his shame, the image returned to him unbidden, halfway through his and Tory's romping. It was partly the reason he was so quick to note the change at breakfast. But as they made ready to wend their way to bed that third night, Michelle placed herself so that she would bid him, 'Goodnight,' before doing the same to Tory. Both the previous nights he remembered, it had been the other way round. And as she turned to Tory, taking her hands in hers and leaning in for the ritual exchange, Scott saw what he'd been missing. The spark *was* still there. Only now it was aimed at Tory. As he now suddenly realised, it had been all day.

Like a drowning man, the day's events replayed before his eyes. The flashing glances and smiles as, sailing past the amazing church of Notre Dame, she and Tory joked about the Hunchback's less well-known deformity. The touching and close body contact as she drew Tory's attention to some famous bridge or building. The girly banter as she pointed out Paris's most famous department store, La Samaritaine. Thinking back, he now realised that throughout the day, Michelle had been acting *exactly* as she had the previous two days. The difference was, it was all now directed at Tory rather than him.

The realisation hit him like a sledgehammer. So much so that later, in bed, he had to work hard to push it from his mind as he tried to remain focused on repeating his performance levels of the previous nights. He wasn't altogether successful.

'Not wearing you out am I?' Tory pouted when she realised he didn't seem to be recovering as quickly as he had the night before. 'Want me to-?' she said, reaching for him.

'No need,' he said quickly. Calling on all his resources, he managed, just, to not disappoint her.

It continued the following day. Michelle ministering

to both their needs as before, but definitely more towards Tory, Scott could see now. The same yesterday. The trouble was, Scott noted to his disappointment, whereas he'd gone out of his way during those first two days to make sure Tory had no reason to feel excluded, the same wasn't holding true for her. In fact the more Michelle turned it on for Tory, the more Scott felt Tory turning her attentions away from him, to the older woman. By the end of the fifth day, each time they leaned into each other, laughing and giggling, touching foreheads, Scott found himself wondering just what, or who, they were laughing at.

But what really got him thinking, and worrying about what was going on, was what had happened last night, after they got to bed. For the first time in days, Tory's new-found form seemed to desert her. As he tried, playfully, to reignite the spark of carefree abandonment that had marked their previous night's lovemaking, Scott sensed it wasn't there. Instead of launching herself at him the way she had been doing, the moment she emerged from the bathroom, she'd trooped, almost dismally, over to the bed. She'd even yawned, for God's sake.

'What's up?' he said, trying not to sound critical.

'Nothing. Just tired is all. We've had a heavy few days.' Kissing him quickly on the lips, hard but without passion it seemed, she turned on her side, away from him. He stared at her.

'What's going on?' he asked.

'What do you mean?'

Taking her arm gently, he pulled her round. 'You seem-' He stopped, unsure what it was he wanted to say. What he *could* say. He chose a different tack. 'Listen.'

'What?'

'We've been here five days. Maybe it's time to move on.'

The speed with which she sat up surprised him. A moment before, she'd been bushed.

'Why? Aren't you enjoying Paris?'

'Sure I am, but we can't stay here for ever. We've still got a lot to see, remember. And we've still got to fit in a visit to Jacques before we leave France.'

'Of course I remember, but there's still plenty of time. Like you said, all we need to do is re-jig the schedule. Right now we're having a great time here. Aren't we?'

He stared at her. 'Are we?'

Puzzlement showed in her face. 'I thought we were. I thought you were too.'

'I was until-'

'Until what? Has something happened?'

He hesitated again. What was he going to say? *Until Michelle started paying you more attention than she does me*? 'No nothing's happened.'

'So what then? What are you saying?'

He dropped to lie beside her. 'Nothing. I'm not saying anything.'

She leaned over him, her hair falling across his chest like a curtain. She looked into his eyes. 'Hey?'

'Hey what?'

'We're still good aren't we?'

'Of course we're still good. Why shouldn't we be?'

'Exactly. There is no reason.' She kissed him again. 'G'night.'

And that was it.

That morning, everything had seemed normal again.

Getting ready to go down for breakfast, Scott was careful not to bring it up again. So was Tory.

'It's a beautiful day,' she said, pointing out the window.

Scott turned. The sky was a clear blue. 'It certainly is.'

Downstairs, he found Michelle the same as the day before. The spark still there, but directed elsewhere. But she must have waited until she saw him tearing into the croissants she had delivered fresh from the village pâtisserie each morning, to make her announcement.

'Has Tory told you?'

He looked up. There was a twinkle, not just a spark, in her eye. He turned to Tory. She was smiling, but nervously he thought. 'Told me what?'

'Of our plans for this morning?'

He put down his croissant. 'What plans?'

Tory came in quickly. 'Michelle says she has something she wants to show me this morning.'

'What sort of something? You mean on your own?' Tory's gaze switched to Michelle. It was almost like she felt she needed the other woman's permission to speak. Scott was confused. 'And where is this, 'something'?' He turned to Michelle. For the first time, he sensed some sort of battle going on, but for what he was unsure. But it was enough to scare him into what, when he said it, sounded almost like a challenge. 'Are you planning on taking Tory somewhere without me, Michelle?'

The smile it produced was every bit as disarming as the first time he saw it. The effect however was much reduced. 'Do not worry yourself, Scott. I would not dream of taking your beautiful Tory away from you. I wish only to show her something here, in the house.'

He started. 'Here? And I'm not allowed to see?'

The smile again, but mysterious this time. 'Oh you will see, have no fear of that. But after. When we have finished.'

'Finished?' He turned back to Tory. 'What are you two up to?'

It was Tory's turn to beam at him. Whatever it was, she seemed excited. 'Be patient, baby. You'll see soon enough.'

And that was as much as he could get out of them. A few minutes later, Michelle rose from the table. Taking her cue, Tory did the same. Turning to him, Michelle said. 'Now, while I show Tory what she wants to see, you make the most of this beautiful morning.' Taking Tory by the hand, she led his fiancée towards the hallway.'

'See you la-ter,' Tory sung to him, over her shoulder. She was still smiling. The last he saw was of them ascending the wide staircase, Michelle in front, Tory following, like a puppy dog.

Now, as he finished his second coffee of the morning, reflecting on all that had happened these past days, Scott was aware of a growing sense of unease. Where it came from and what was driving it, he wasn't sure. He knew only that almost two hours had passed since he'd seen Michelle leading his Tory up the stairs to... he knew not where. In that time he had seen and heard nothing but had sat in the garden, enjoying the sun as best he could, dozing occasionally between musing. Lifting an arm he checked his watch. Where had they got to? What the Hell were they doing? A sudden thought came, adding to his fears. For all he knew, they may no longer even be in there. While he'd been dozing they could easily have-

At that moment a low murmur, followed by girlish giggles sounded from the direction of the house.

He sat up.

The sun was just a little higher than the house's roof, but to one side, shining directly at him, making it hard to see. After so long lying in its harsh glare without sunglasses, his vision needed to adjust. Lifting a hand to shield his eyes, he peered forward. Over by the French windows that led into the breakfast room, he could just make out two shapes drifting, first together then apart, now together again. Who the hell? He leaned further forward, seeking out a clearer view. As his eyes started to adjust, he could just make out the women's forms, making their way towards him. But something was different, though he couldn't quite put his finger on what it was. As they neared he became more certain the one to the left was Michelle. At least, it was her height and build. But the other... It couldn't be Tory. She was far too tall. For no reason he could explain, a panic started to rise in him. He jumped up, shouted across.

'Is that you Michelle? Where's Tory?'

Years before, Scott had read the Iliad. An image from the famous story had always stayed with him, materialising to infiltrate his dreams now and then. It came to him now. The Sirens. Deadly sisters drifting, ghostlike, towards their prey. Luring them in. The thought came that he had drifted off in the sun, that right now, he was dreaming.

'Tory?' he called.

At last, his vision cleared. And as the indistinct shapes finally materialised enough through the light-haze, Scott Weston's jaw dropped. He could not believe what he was seeing.

CHAPTER 25

La Madeleine - full title, L'Église Sainte-Marie-Madeleine - is Paris's second best-known church after Notre Dame. Built by Napoleon I in the style of a neo-classical Greek temple and originally planned, not as a place of religious worship, but a tribute to his *Grande Armée,* it lies in the Plâce which bears its name. Today it is fringed by high-end grocers of the likes of Fauchon and Fortnum and Mason. Their tempting wares attract not just the gawping attention of the tourists, but also the hard-earned cash of Paris's great and good.

Carver had visited there once before, but as he stepped through the impressive portal into the back of the church, he realised he had forgotten the wonders within. The cavernous, single nave runs the length of the interior to the High Altar. Hanging above it, gloriously lit by a clever combination of concealed lighting and sunlight filtering through the half-dome above, a marble statue depicts Mary Magdalene's ascent to Heaven, accompanied by two angels. Flanking the nave on both sides, romanesque columns continue the temple theme. Equally spaced in the high ceiling are three domes, each lavishly gilded in Renaissance-inspired décor. All around the walls are frescoes and carefully-crafted depictions of key characters and events from Christianity.

Ingrid whispered, 'Impressive, yes?'

Carver nodded, still taking it all in. 'Very.' Like him, other than for weddings and funerals it was Ingrid's first visit to church in years. For that reason, they allowed themselves one complete circuit around the walls before turning to the business that had brought them.

Returning to the back of the church they looked round in vain for a priest, having seen none during their tour. Sitting at a plain wooden table over to their right was a late-middle-aged woman. In front of her on the desk, a folded card read, 'Pour Vos Questions.' They headed over. The woman had delicate, bird like features and was wearing what Carver imagined his late grandmother would have called, 'Sunday-best'. He immediately stereotyped her as either a retired librarian, or school teacher. As they reached her table she looked up, smiling sweetly. The smile stayed, even when Ingrid explained who they were and what they needed.

Fluent, according to her lapel badge, in French, Italian and English, the woman grasped what they needed quickly, but didn't pry for details. Crossing to a bookstall in the far corner, she spoke briefly with a younger man, indicating Carver and Ingrid when he peered round to see what sort of police they were. He picked up a telephone, spoke into it, then nodded to the woman. She was still smiling as she returned to them. 'Father Masson will be with you shortly.'

Some minutes later, Carver was studying the stuccoed ceiling when a voice behind said, 'Monsieur? Mademoiselle?' He turned.

Dressed in the traditional black cassock, Father

Masson looked to be in his late fifties. Grey-haired and wearing wire-framed spectacles with oblong lenses, he bore a studious look. Behind the glasses ice-blue eyes shone, bright and lively. Carver thought he had the sort of cheerful visage all priests should have, but not all do.

After first checking that the priest was comfortable with English - he was - Ingrid introduced them, saying only that they wished to speak with him regarding a 'delicate matter.'

Masson showed puzzlement, but said nothing and beckoned them to follow. He led them down the nave then right into a room which Carver snatched at a memory from his youth and recalled as probably being the Sacristy. Indicating a long table with ancient wooden chairs arranged round it, the priest bade them sit. He made sure the sturdy door was shut before joining them.

'How can I help?'

Ingrid told him of their involvement in the series of murders presently afflicting the city, of how their investigations showed the victims were all church-goers, and how it appeared that at least two of the victims had visited his church shortly before their deaths.

The priest's face registered shock, then concern. 'Are you saying there is some sort of connection with La Madeleine?'

'We do not know of one, but that is what we need to find out. The victims had to come to the killer's notice somewhere. If we can find out where and how, we may be a step closer to identifying him.'

'You say these poor souls were visitors to Paris? And that they were all of a Christian faith? Could there not be other places they visited? Notre-Dame, Saint Sulpice perhaps?'

'It's possible, but we know for certain only that they came here. We are interested in discovering if there is any particular reason why they did.'

The priest's gaze slipped down and to the right. Carver saw it. 'Something occurs to you, Father?'

At that moment the door behind them opened. Carver turned. In the doorway stood another black-robed priest. Considerably younger than Father Masson, he was also several inches taller and a good deal broader. Seeing them, he excused himself and made to retreat but Father Masson beckoned him in with a wave of his hand.

'Entrez Migue. S'il vous plaît.'

The newcomer did as asked. Closing the door behind him, he came forward.

Carver's first thought was that with his athletic build, the priest looked more like some sporting idol than a man of the cloth. Then he chided himself. *And why shouldn't he?* The tanned, mediterranean features positively glowed with health and vitality. A quick glance right told him that Ingrid was maybe thinking the same.

Indicating for the younger man to join them at the table, Father Masson introduced him as Father Alonso, the Church's curate. He went on to explain that as Alonso was responsible for much of the church's day-to-day running, he should be made aware of the matter they were discussing. But he asked their permission before doing so.

'No problem,' Carver said.

In his native language, Father Masson explained to his colleague the reason for the detectives' visit and where they had got to in their conversation. As Father

Masson spoke, the other priest's expression turned through interest, horror, surprise and, finally, puzzlement. When he was finished and Father Alonso turned to them, some of the colour had left his face. About to say something, Father Alonso stopped himself, made the sign of the cross and kissed the crucifix on the end of the Rosary at his waist before uttering a muted, 'Jesu Christi.'

Father Masson's pointed, 'Ahem,' drew their attention. He seemed embarrassed by the younger man's oath, understandable though Carver thought it was. 'Now, where were we?'

Carver picked up. 'My colleague had asked if there was any reason you could think of why the victims may have visited here. I believe you were about to say something?'

He remembered. 'Ah, yes,' but then stopped, as if wary about speaking. 'Tell me, is there anything that links the victims? Anything they had in common?'

Ingrid said, 'We know of no direct connection between them. However-' She glanced at Carver. He nodded. 'We believe it is possible that they all harboured some sort of secret. Something they had not shared with their family and friends.' She told of Marianne's affair. The possibility that she was not the only one.

'Ah.' Father Masson nodded, knowingly. But Father Alonso looked away, as if such things embarrassed him.

'What is it, Father?' Carver said.

The older priest regarded them both, then turned to his colleague. Something passed between them. The younger man still looked uncomfortable. Father Masson spoke.

'What do you know of Sainte-Marie-Madeleine?'

Carver and Ingrid swapped blank glances. 'We know that this is her church.'

'Of course. But I am referring to the saint herself?'

Carver drew on his early schooling. 'Didn't she wash Christ's feet, or something?'

The priest smiled, patiently, then nodded again. He seemed to come to a decision.

'Sainte Marie-Madeleine is one of the holiest of saints. An icon of the church. Many of the Christian faith, not just Catholics, pray to her.' Carver waited. 'Those who pray to her believe that here, in her own holy church, their prayers will have the best chance of being heard.' He paused, letting his words sink in. Carver began to feel like he was listening to a sermon. 'Do you know why people pray to Sainte Marie-Madeleine, Chief Inspector?'

Carver shrugged, shook his head. 'I assume they do it for all sorts of reasons.'

'And so most non-believers might think. And not unreasonably. But actually, the process is not as random as you may imagine. Like many saints, Sainte-Marie has come to be associated with many causes over the years. In fact she is claimed as a patron by all sorts of groups, apothecaries, glove makers, even hairdressers.'

Carver put off considering why hairdressers might need a patron saint for another time. 'Fair enough. So what-'

'She is also the patron saint of penitent sinners.'

Lapsing to silence, Carver tilted his head back, digesting the priest's words. He glanced again at Ingrid, also working on it. Eventually he said, 'Sssooo, some people might pray to her for...'

'Forgiveness,' Ingrid finished.

The priest nodded, gravely. 'You say that some of these unfortunate victims had secrets. And that this most recent woman was harbouring feelings of guilt for having broken her marital vows. It may be that she came here to pray for Sainte Marie's forgiveness.'

Carver sat back in his chair, thinking on it. 'That might fit. But it's a long way to come from Souterraine just to pray.' He turned to Ingrid. 'What do you think?'

She frowned. 'I am not sure. . . but then I am not... I don't-' She changed tack, addressed Father Masson directly. 'Would a woman these days feel such guilt over just having an affair that she will travel all the way to Paris to ask for forgiveness?'

Carver held his breath. Halfway through her question he'd seen the priest bristle. As she finished, his eyebrow arched upwards.

'*Just* an affair, Mademoiselle? Do you not consider an affair outside of marriage to be a mortal sin?'

Perhaps realising her mistake, Ingrid was about to say something when the priest continued.

'I am aware that, these days *some women* think nothing of entering into a relationship with a married man.' He paused, looking at Ingrid in a way that was almost accusatory. Carver sensed her discomfort, surprised by the sudden change in the priest's manner. 'But in fact, there are many, women *and* men, who *do* feel such guilt, and who *do* travel such distances to pray for forgiveness.'

Ingrid stood her ground. 'I am sorry, Father. I did not mean to offend your beliefs. I was just trying to put myself in their shoes.'

The priest smiled again, but this time Carver thought he saw something other than amusement in it. 'I suspect that for a modern young woman such as yourself, Mademoiselle, that may be difficult. You indicated earlier did you not, that you are not a believer?'

Seeing Ingrid beginning to colour, Carver sensed the need to move on. 'Are you saying, Father, that you know of people who have come here to pray for forgiveness after having had an affair?'

The priest hesitated a long time before answering. 'People come here to pray for many things.' Then he added, 'And do not forget, this is a working church. We also take confession.'

Carver nodded, long and slow. He glanced at Ingrid. She was just sitting there, tight-lipped. 'I'd forgotten about confession.'

'I take it then, that you are not of the faith either?'

Carver sensed more dangerous ground. The priest's words were clearly meant for him but he was staring at Ingrid again, who was staring back.

'If it's all the same with you Father, I prefer to keep my beliefs to myself.'

'Of course.'

Sensing they needed to get back to the reason for their visit, Carver reached inside his jacket for the photographs he had picked up from the Murder Control on their way out.

'These are the two women we believe came here. Could you say if you remember seeing them at all?' He laid them on the table for both priests to see.

Thus far, Father Alonso had remained silent. Now he leaned forward to get a better look. But as he did so he seemed to feel the older man's gaze on him, looked up, saw it, and shrank back again. Carver picked up on it. Father Masson seemed to be making a point of avoiding looking at the photographs.

'I'm sorry, is there a problem?'

Again, the older priest hesitated before making his reply. 'Please Chief Inspector, try to understand. It is not that we do not wish to help, but the Sanctity of the Church, especially the confessional, must be respected.' As the older priest spoke, Carver sensed a tussle within him. 'It is possible that one or both of these poor women may have come here, either to pray for forgiveness, or perhaps even make their confession directly to God through one of us. If that were the case, then they came here seeking absolution, which is always given subject to the rules of the confessional. I am sure you must be aware that, as with lawyers, such things are privileged. I could not possibly breach that privilege by identifying those who may have sought God's absolution.'

Carver bit his lip, counted to three. 'I understand, but I'm not asking about anything they may or may not have said either in, or outside of confession. All I am asking is that you look at the photographs and tell us if you can remember seeing them in church?'

Father Masson eased himself back in his chair, folded his hands on his stomach, and stared at Carver, smiling his benevolent smile.

As they came through into the sunlight, Ingrid was blazing.

'They say the church is responsible for many deaths. They are right. There was nearly one back there.'

Carver grimaced. He felt similarly, but was taking it better, though only marginally. Then again, he hadn't suffered the indignity of being labelled a sinner, even if it was by inference. After reaching the impasse, he had worked hard at trying to convince Father Masson that simply looking at the photographs and either shaking or nodding his head would not breach the sanctity of the confessional. He soon discovered that his first impression of Father Masson as an easy-going sort was misplaced. In fact it seemed that the good priest was the sort who, once decided on a course, would not bend for anyone. Carver noted that Ingrid stayed out of it, which was probably as well. He sensed that anything she may have said would not only fall on stony ground, it may render any later attempt to get the priest to change his position, redundant. Since leaving the sacristy with Father Masson's, 'Believe me, I have no wish to be obstructive,' ringing in their ears, Ingrid had made up for her silence. Between closing the door behind her and leaving through the portal they'd entered earlier, Carver had been glad he wasn't religious. Such language in a house of God, particularly directed at a priest, would have had him worrying about being an accomplice to blasphemy.

Halfway down the steps, he was still trying to get her to calm down when a cry, 'Monsieur! Mademoiselle!' made him turn. Father Alonso was scurrying down the steps after them, holding up his cassock so as not to trip. Stopping on the step above, he turned to glance over his shoulder, as if fearful he may be being observed.

'I am sorry about what just happened. Back there I mean. With Father Masson. Please do not judge him harshly. He has very strict views about the Sacraments.'

'As do we,' Carver said, 'About murderers.'

As if unsure whether Carver was attempting humour, the priest smiled, weakly. He turned to Ingrid. Her face was like stone, unlike when she first saw him.

'Mademoiselle. Please accept my sincere apologies for what my colleague said to you. I am sure he intended no slight.'

Her reply was stark. 'And I am sure he did.' Then she seemed to remember that the young priest was innocent of any crime. She gave, just a little. 'But thank you for the apology, even if it is not you who owes me one.'

Alonso's smile widened. She almost returned it. He made to say something, but stopped. Carver sensed confliction.

'What is it Father?' Carver checked the top of the steps. There was no sign of Father Masson.

'Not all of us see things as black or white as Father Masson does. Please, may I see the photographs again?'

Carver dug them out, passed them across. As the tall figure bent over them, Carver was conscious of Ingrid studying him.

After a few moments the priest said a hesitant, 'Yess.' Carver waited. 'Perhaps...' He hesitated again, turned to look back up the steps.

'We also respect confidences, Father,' Carver prompted.

The smile came again, directed squarely at Ingrid this time. Whatever she was thinking, she returned it.

'This one.' He pointed at the second victim. 'I think I do recall her visiting the church. It was over a weekend, I believe. I seem to remember seeing her more than once.'

'When was this?' Ingrid said.

'Let me think... It would have to be some months ago. In the early part of the year, perhaps.'

Ingrid and Carver exchanged glances. Theresa Plusset's body had been found on the twenty-first of

January, a Monday.

Carver tested. 'It was a long time ago. How certain can you be you that it was her, on a scale of ten'

The priest thought on it. 'Seven, maybe eight. I remember because she was very upset about something. She was crying. I asked her if she needed counselling.'

'You spoke with her?'

'Briefly. She refused any counsel, but she did ask me to pray for her. She wouldn't say why apart from saying she was a sinner.'

Carver turned to Ingrid, flashed her a look. *That's it*. 'Was she with anyone?'

Alonso shook his head. 'I cannot say. I recall seeing her talking to a man on one occasion, but I would not be able to say if they were together.'

'What did this man look like?'

He tried to remember. 'He was quite tall. I seem to recall him wearing some sort of long, dark coat. More than that I couldn't say. I'm afraid I didn't get to see his face at all. I'm afraid I didn't pay him much attention. I was more interested in seeing how she was.'

'Don't worry Father, it's something.' Carver waved the photograph of Marianne Desmarais. 'And this one?'

'I am not sure... There was a woman a few days ago... I saw her as she was leaving the church and I was coming in. But it was just a glimpse. I cannot say for certain it was her, though I do know the one I saw was on her own. When was she... When did she... die?'

'Three days ago. She is the latest victim.' The priest's mouth gaped. Carver continued. 'I take it from what Father Masson said, it is not unusual for people to come here seeking forgiveness?'

Father Alonso nodded. 'I would say every day.

Amongst the faithful, the church is famous as a place of pilgrimage and absolution.'

'You must hear of many sins,' Ingrid said.

The priest turned to her. 'We do. Many require a great deal of penance to receive absolution.'

'I take it you would not want to go on record about this?'

'I am sorry. I cannot. As Father Masson said-'

'Don't worry about it, Father. You've been very helpful. We appreciate it.'

As they made to leave, the priest said. 'If I can help again in any way, please don't hesitate to ask.' Carver sensed the words were more for Ingrid's benefit than his.

'What about Father Masson?' she said.

He gave a wan smile. 'Father Masson is what some would call a traditionalist. He means well, but these days, the church has to live in the real world.'

'Amen to that, Father.'

Throwing her a last smile, the priest turned and retraced his steps back up the steps. As he disappeared back through the portal, Carver turned to Ingrid.

'If we need anything more from him, I'll leave it with you.'

She tutted. 'He is a priest, Jamie,. You should not say such things.'

'Hmm. He's also a man, and I did not get any sense that he may be gay.'

She shot him a shocked look that turned to withering. 'Come, we must tell Remy of what we have heard.'

As they headed down Rue Royale, the detectives did not look back. Even if they had, they would not have picked out the searing gaze that followed them all the way to where they turned into the Place de la Concorde, and out of sight.

CHAPTER 26

The young man from Boston stared, open mouthed, at the fiancée he barely recognised. In Scott's eyes, Tory Martinez was naturally beautiful, a legacy borne of her Nordic-Latin genes and what he put down to a wholesome-American upbringing. But the figure now standing before him was a different Tory altogether. Caked in more make up than he'd ever seen her wearing before, blonde hair styled like a Hollywood starlet, her well-proportioned figure sheathed in a shimmering, off-the shoulder red dress with matching opera gloves, Tory tottered on heels that were even higher than those she'd bought for their graduation ball, and which nearly broke her ankles. A diamanté choker with matching bracelet and earrings completed the ensemble. Scott gasped at the transformation. It was the sort of look he sometimes saw on the covers of the Vogue magazines his mother took each month.

'Tory? What are you... what have you done?'

Beaming a smile as wide as the day he proposed, Tory made a mincing pirouette, stretching out her arms so as to maintain her balance on the heels that click-clacked on the stone patio. 'Like it? Michelle's given me a make-over.'

Lost for words, Scott could only mumble, 'You're not kidding.' As he turned to where Michelle stood off, he saw her regarding him closely.

'So,' Tory said. 'What do you think?'

'It's... it's....'

'Yes?'

'Amazing.'

Excited, Tory read his reaction as approval. She turned to Michelle. 'Thank you so much, Michelle. It's something I've dreamed of for years.'

Scott looked flummoxed. 'You have?'

As if amused by his hesitancy, Michelle approached and linked her arm through his, turning him so that together they could examine her creation. 'Scott, you should know that all pretty girls long to see how truly beautiful they can be. And do you not think that now, like this, your Tory looks really beautiful?

'I... uh, I guess so.'

Tory put her hands on her hips, making a show of looking offended. 'You *guess* so? Well thank *you* Mr Enthusiastic. I'll have you know Michelle went to a lot of trouble for your benefit. She even took in this dress so it fitted. The least you can do is show some appreciation.'

Sensing danger, Scott tried to recover himself.

'I *do* appreciate it. You look great. It's just.. uh...'

'Just what?'

He appealed to her. 'Hell Tory, you *are* beautiful. You don't need any of this... this....' He cast a hand in mute gesture.

'This... ? Go on. What were you going to say?'

'This... stuff. The make up. The dress. The shoes. You know I think you'd look beautiful in a sack. All this stuff does is make you look like a hooker'

Tory froze. All trace of excitement vanished from her face.

'Did you just call me a *hooker?*'

Scott realised his mistake at once, tried to recover it.

'No I didn't call you a hooker, What I said was-'

'You said, 'hooker'. She turned to Michelle. 'Am I mistaken Michelle? Did you hear him call me a hooker?'

'Well.. yes. I heard him use the word, but-'

Suddenly angry, Scott turned on her. 'No I didn't. I mean...' He turned back to Tory. 'I may have used the word. But I wasn't referring to you. What I said was-'

'I heard what you said. You said I looked like a hooker.'

'Aw c'mon Tory, you know I didn't mean-' He stopped, an alarm ringing. 'In any case, why is Michelle fitting you with a dress anyway? You've got lots of dresses at home.'

'But not with me. If we're staying for her party I'll need something to wear. Michelle said I could wear this.'

'But we won't be here for her party. We're moving on.'

'We haven't decided that yet.'

'Haven't we? I thought we had.'

'No, you said you were thinking about it and we would talk about it again.'

'That's not how I remember it.'

'Well just to be clear, I'd like to stay for it.'

About to come back at her, Scott was suddenly conscious of Michelle following the argument like a spectator at a tennis match. Turning to her, he thought he saw traces of a recently-vanished look of amusement.

'I think we should talk about this in private.'

'You do, do you? Well I'm not sure there's anything to talk about.' Stepping out of the heels, she pulled off her earrings and the rest of the jewellery. She handed them back to Michelle. 'Here Michelle. Thank you for all your efforts. I loved what you did and really appreciate it.' She turned to Scott. 'It's just a shame that some people obviously feel it just makes me look like a *hooker*.' She stomped off towards the house.

Scott made one last appeal, '*TORY,*' but knew it was useless. He watched as she disappeared back into the house.

He took a deep breath before turning back to Michelle. She was standing with her arms folded, regarding him with a neutral expression that gave nothing away. He wondered what she was thinking. A second later he knew as a smile he could only describe as snakelike spread across her lips and she shook her head, slowly, in mock rebuke.

'Hooker? Oh Scott. My dear, dear, Scott. I think you've really done it now.'

In that moment, Scott Weston knew with a certainty he had not felt before, that the situation he and Tory were in was more complicated than even he had imagined. More than that, as he met the older woman's gaze and recognised for the first time the murky depths that lay behind the beguiling features, he felt the first tingling awareness that not only was it complicated, it was also in some way, dangerous, though exactly how, he could not begin to imagine.

Lifting a finger, he pointed it at her. 'Whatever game you think you're playing Michelle, forget it. Tory's my girl, and always will be.'

The sly smile showed again. 'Is she now? Well perhaps that is something you need to ask her.'

For long seconds he stared at the older woman, as if seeing her for the first time. About to point the finger again, he couldn't find the words to go with what he was thinking. Turning on his heel, he headed after the girl he loved.

CHAPTER 27

When Carver reported back to Remy and his team on their visit to La Madeleine, he tried to play it down. A possible connection between two of the victims and the church was a line of enquiry that certainly needed chasing down. But as yet it was also inconclusive, its relevance uncertain.

That didn't stop Remy's detectives falling on it like hyenas on a discarded kill.

As soon as Ingrid finished translating Carver's report - just so there could be no mixed messages or misunderstandings - the conjecture began. Most of it focused on the religious connotations. La Madeleine. The church-going natures of the victims. The killing ritual itself. Theories ranged from the already postulated, 'religious-zealot' killer, to the possibility that he frequented the church and used the opportunity to identify 'penitent' victims. Another was that the victims had met the killer online, via some dating/sex web-site and arranged a 'safe' meet at the church before being lured to their deaths. Those like Carver who urged caution, or even went so far as to disparage the likelihood of a connection at all, were quickly overridden by the clamour for positive action.

There was no shortage of suggestions.

Remy should immediately authorise twenty-four seven CCTV coverage of the church's entrances and exits to monitor visitors' comings and goings. Visitors should be 'leafleted' in an appeal for information and prior sightings of the victims. Someone went so far as to suggest that round-the-clock surveillance should be put in place on anyone and everyone associated with the church. It led Remy to cast a pained glance in Carver's direction. Carver knew why. Murder Detectives tend to forget that while for them, catching a killer has to take precedence over all other policing operations, not all senior officers see things the same way. That said, Carver could hardly blame them.

By their nature, every long-running investigation generates lines of enquiry that appear promising but peter-out in a dead-end, or are left hanging because a vehicle cannot be traced, someone has moved with no forwarding address or a suspicious sighting cannot be verified. The longer the enquiry stays 'live,' the longer the list grows. Within police circles, tales abound of cases that are solved overnight when a piece of information that had been sought for months clicks into place, resulting in the sort of 'sudden breakthrough' that plays so well in the news bulletins. Not so with the, 'Pension-Boucher' investigation, as the Paris tabloids had dubbed it. When Carver first began the arduous task of familiarising himself with the then five murders and the many facets of the formidable investigation that had grown in their wake, he was surprised to find only one unresolved line of enquiry that appeared to hold any promise at all. And it required a stretch of the imagination. It concerned a teenage youth seen close to the scene of the third murder. He was riding a motor scooter while plugged into some device on ear-phones. Variously described by witnesses as 'black,' 'Asian,' or 'white but wearing dark clothing,' Carver had severe doubts he would prove to be involved. The killer they were stalking was apparently capable of talking his way into victims' hotel rooms, overpowering them in a way that didn't attract attention, butchering them in the bloodiest manner imaginable, then leaving the scene sufficiently bloodless as to not attract attention. It hardly fitted with the image of a Vespa-riding killer leaving the scene while listening to the latest download from his favourite indie-band.

But for all that, the Madeleine connection *was* progress, of sorts. Which was why, when he rang Jess with an update that evening and to find out how she was, he tried to sound matter-of-fact about it. She sussed the deceit at once.

'You think it means something?' she said when he finished describing his encounter with Father Alonso.

'There's no way to tell yet.'

'But you're hopeful?'

'Like I say, we have to wait and see. It could be something, it could be nothing.'

'It's the first firm connection anyone's found between the victims.'

'I know.'

'So what are you going to do?'

'Me? Nothing. It's up to Remy to decide. I'm not involved, remember?'

'Bullshit. What have you said to him?'

'I told him we should look for any signs of a Madeleine connection with the other victims and in the meantime plant a watcher in the church, just in case.'

'Undercover you mean?'

'No, they'll wear a placard saying, "Police. Please tell us if you are planning to murder someone".'

'Hmmphh.'

For several minutes they talked investigation matters, Jess's Analysis and what it was showing, or not. Familiar with her ways, he noticed at once when, having covered everything they needed to, her voice drifted like she was waiting on his permission to change the subject.

'What is it?'

'I had a call earlier from Dave Shaw.'

Carver sat up. 'Oh yes?' Shaw was the DI in charge of the Force Information Bureau. Astute, intelligent and with spies all over, he was usually amongst the first to pick up on anything newsworthy buzzing around Headquarters. Carver had known him for years.

'Someone's been asking questions about what you are doing in Paris, who authorised it, how long you are there for, that sort of thing.'

'Someone like who?'

'Dave's not sure. He heard it through Jenny, the ACC's secretary that he took a call yesterday. It supposedly came from someone at Interpol. Whoever it was, said they wanted to confirm that all the protocols governing cross-channel Police cooperation had been followed.'

'That's bollocks. I'm not here in any operational capacity and my coming over was agreed between the Chief and the Paris Prefect by way of informal arrangement. It's got bugger-all to do with Interpol.'

'Which is what the ACC said. According to Jenny,

whoever it was didn't query it but rang off when the ACC started asking questions about how Interpol had got hold of it in the first place. So what do you think it means?'

Carver thought on it. 'It could mean that someone over here is getting twitchy.'

'About...?'

'Dunno. Maybe we've struck a nerve somewhere.'

'Over you helping them out with their murders, or the other thing?'

'The other, most likely. We know Megan had friends in high places in the UK. I suspect it'll be the same here.'

'So you think someone is looking to put pressure on to get you pulled off?'

'It's always been a risk. I like to think she doesn't know I'm over here, but we can't be sure. It's why I've tried to keep what we're doing low profile. The fewer who know I'm here and what we're doing the better. Tell Dave I need to know if he hears any more about people asking questions.'

'Will do. Watch your back.'

She rang off before he could ask how she was. How her mother was doing. If she was sleeping better. He thought about ringing her back but decided against. She'd sounded not too bad and that she hadn't said anything was a good sign. Maybe.

He sat in his chair, pulling at his lip. He went to see Remy.

'What do you know about your examining magistrate, Monsieur Couthon?'

'In what way?'

'Can he be trusted?'

Remy thought about it. 'I've never had reason to think not. But, he is a member of the Judiciary. I suspect that he is as amenable to a bit of... persuasion, as most politicians. But his name has never come up in any enquiry I know of. What makes you ask?'

'Someone's rung my Headquarters asking questions about what I'm doing. I'm wondering who, and why.'

'You think it could be him?'

'Probably not him personally, but he would know who to contact to get the questions asked.'

Remy's gaze narrowed. 'Leave it with me. I will get someone to do some digging.'

'Thanks Remy.'

As he headed back to his lodgings, loaded with the papers he would read that evening, Carver's thoughts were on who else amongst those who knew of his mission to Paris would know who to contact to get questions asked. He could think of only two. Neither bore thinking about.

Back in his room, he checked his mobile. There was another message from Sue. It read, "How are you?" but then he remembered what day it was and recognised the subtext. The social services adoption team people had been due to make a home visit. At that moment, Carver's head was full of the events of the past few days. Hardly the best frame of mind to talk about Jason's future. But Sue deserved his time as much as anyone. And something told him that from here on in things weren't set to get any easier. He made the call.

As always, conversation was awkward to begin with. They were yet to find the pattern of greeting that allowed them to feel comfortable when answering the other's call. Carver wasn't sure there was one that fitted their unique circumstances. The one-time lover of a murdered daughter who was also the nominal father of her son. The mother and grandmother who still held the former lover responsible, at least partially, for her daughter's death. The fact that right now she was looking after said son/grandson on behalf of the 'guilty' father simply made it all the more complicated. Carver wasted no time asking after Jason.

'Is he in bed yet?'

Her hesitation was almost audible. *Deciding whether to lie.* 'I was just about to take him up.'

'A minute? Please Sue. Just one minute.'

Another hesitation, then, 'Jason, it's Jamie. He'd like to talk to you.'

Carver imagined him getting down off the sofa, coming to the phone.

'Hi Jamie. When're you coming home? Gramma got me a new Nintendo. I'll show you when you come. S'really cool.'

'What, better than the Xbox?'

'Way. I can use it in the car, in bed, everyfink.'

'Wow. Sounds excellent. I hope you're being good for Gramma?'

'I am.'

'Good boy.' He paused. 'Jason'

'Yeah?'

He fought for words.

'What?'

They wouldn't come.

'Nothing. Just you be good. I'll ask Gramma to read you a story in bed from me. How about the Gruffalo?'

He giggled. 'I'm seven, Jamie'

Carver's heart soared. He gave a sad smile. *So much missed.*

'Okay. Put Gramma back on.'

"Night Jamie.'

'Goodnight Jason.'

He heard her breathing. 'Thanks Sue.'

'What for?'

'The Nintendo. He obviously loves it.'

'He'd love a lot of things.'

Thanks.

But her next words took him by surprise. 'Perhaps you can buy him something next time?'

Was he mistaken or had some of the brittleness gone out of her voice?

'I'd love to.' Sensing an opportunity, he was about to go for it when she changed the subject.

'The adoption team came.'

Missed it. 'Okay. How did it go?'

'Good, I think. They had lots of questions but they seemed to go away happy.'

'Did they say how long they are happy for him to stay?'

'No, but there shouldn't be a problem. They said they have everything they need. Did you speak with your friend in Social Services?'

'Not recently but I'll give her another call. She said she'd let me know if there were any problems so I'm assuming no news is good news.'

'One thing did come up.'

'What was that?' As he heard her take a deep breath he winced, ready for it.

'They mentioned about paternity testing.'

Knew it. 'And what did you say?'

'That you think there is no need. That you have no doubts.'

'Good.'

Another silence.

'Can I say something, Jamie?'

'Go on.'

'Well, Paul and I have been talking. We know what you and Angie decided. But there is an argument.... As he grows up he may want to know for sure who his-'

'And if that's what he wants to do, I'll have no objection. It will be his decision.'

'But wouldn't it be better if he knew now? It would save all that wondering.'

'By who? Him, or you?'

'You know what I mean Jamie.'

He took a long breath. 'Yes, I do. But Angie was happy to accept things as they are. I'm sure she would want you to do the same.' As soon as he said it he regretted it. 'I'm sorry Sue. I didn't say that to blackmail you.' He waited. She didn't say anything. *You prick.* 'Sue?'

'I'm still here.'

'Listen, I know what you and Paul are thinking, and that you mean well. But have you...'

'Have we what?'

'Have you thought about what if... it goes the other way?'

'How do you mean?'

'A test.'

'The other way? But you've always said... That you are certain that-'

'I am.'

'So what do you mean, if it goes the other way.. I'm sorry Jamie. I'm not sure I understand what you are saying.'

Carver hesitated, searching for the right way to put it. Considering what they had been through and whatever their real thoughts were about him, Sue and Paul had been wonderful. He didn't want to hurt them. But there was a reality they had always avoided. Were still avoiding. Angie had known it. She had to have told them. Or had she? How does a daughter tell her mother that the child she is raising as her step-son may not be her boyfriend's, but that of a murderous rapist?

Too complicated.

'Don't worry. I'm not saying anything.'

'So why did you say-'

'Nothing. Leave it. We'll talk about it another time.'

'He's a lovely little boy, Jamie. He can't be-'

'He is a lovely little boy, Sue. He's our little boy.'

'I'm sorry Jamie. Sometimes, we find this is all so hard.'

'I know. And don't think I'm not grateful. Let me finish things here, then we'll get everything sorted out. I promise.'

It took a while but eventually, she spoke. 'Alright.'

'Give him my love.'

'I will. And Jamie?'

'Yes?'

'Will you promise me one thing?'

'What's that?'

'That you're going to get the bitch who took my daughter.'

'I promise.'

'Thank you.'

The line went dead.

He stared at the phone as it rested in his palm. He was still staring at it when his eyes flickered, then closed and darkness finally took him.

CHAPTER 28

The small town of Châtillon-sur-Seine lies some two hundred kilometres south and east of Paris. The train journey from the capital takes an hour and fifty minutes and passes through some of the most beautiful countryside in the region. As he rested his head against the carriage window, staring blankly through the glass, Scott Weston was oblivious to it. His mind was back in the Maison de Floret, as it had been since the minute the train pulled out of Gare Saint Lazare.

Thirty minutes into his journey he was already regretting the decision to go along with Tory's suggestion that he visit Jacques on his own, then return to pick her up. By that time Michelle's 'party' would have come and gone and they could then resume their travels.

With the benefit of distance, it was now obvious in a way it had not been at the house that the argument that began in the garden the morning before and continued, on and off, through the rest of the day, resulted from obstinacy on both their parts. Scott wanted to move on. Tory wanted to stay for Michelle's party. Simple as that.

What he should have done of course, was stay with her and see it through. That was his duty. To stay with her and keep her safe - not that Tory was the sort of girl who couldn't look after herself - not skulk off and abandon her in a hissy fit. It would after all only have amounted to another couple of days' delay in their plans. But she had seemed so bitter and so determined not to listen to his point of view that when she flung the suggestion at him – 'Why don't you just go and see Jacques on your own. He's your friend,' his reaction, fuelled by anger he now realised, was to show he would neither be manipulated, nor blackmailed into going along with her wishes.

'I might just do that,' he'd said, threateningly.

'Fine by me. Do it.'

'I will.'

Childish and foolish. Like all lovers' tiffs.

Afterwards, neither had been willing to back down with the result that after breakfast that morning he'd called for a taxi to take him to the station. As they parted, she'd proffered her cheek for him to kiss. Her response to his, 'I'll ring you when I get there,' was a curt, 'Okay.'

He knew now, with a certainty that made him squirm inside for not recognising it at the time, that what he should have done at that moment was sweep her into his arms and kiss her, long and hard, banishing the spat in a way that words alone could never have done. And he knew from the look in her eyes it was what she wanted as well. He had no idea what the outcome would have been, which one of them would have given way. It didn't matter. They would have worked it out somehow. Some other compromise maybe. One which didn't mean leaving her alone, in the clutches of a woman with motivations of which he was increasingly dubious.

But he hadn't taken her in his arms.

Stupidly, he'd quashed the instinct. To show how strong he was.

Another hard lesson learned.

Pride has a lot to answer for.

Taking out his cell he brought up her number, stared at it.

The train was due to arrive at its destination in forty minutes. Presumably it would be returning to Paris within the hour. If he waited at the station instead of carrying on to Jacques', he could be there by late afternoon. Back at the house by dinnertime. Plenty of time to repair the damage before bedtime, when they would seal their reunion - and how.

About to make the call, he wavered.

Whatever he did next, he would still need to call and see Jacques sometime. When he'd mentioned to Jacques the possibility they might visit, Jacques had been eager to welcome him to his home country. He remembered him mentioning something about arranging things so his parents would be there to meet him. Jacques' parents were great travellers, he recalled. They may have put themselves out to be there. He didn't want to let his friend down. He weighed the options.

He was halfway there now and Jacques was expecting him. If he stayed over the two nights they'd spoken of, he could return to Paris the morning after next. By then Michelle's party would be over. He could collect Tory and they could get straight off and be on their way to Milan some time that afternoon, free of other diversions. For all that he desperately wanted to repair things with Tory, he needed to get the visit to Jacques out of the way so that whatever time was left was theirs. Yes, he told himself. It was the best course.

The phone in his hand beckoned to him.

At the very least he should ring her and tell her what he was feeling, thinking. An apology – the one he should have made to begin with – would at least help them both sleep more easily, as well as set things up for when he did return so they could get right off and leave the conniving Madame Chartier and her strange ways for the next waifs and strays she may choose to entice into her home. He pressed the call button.

After a short delay, he got the caller unavailable message. He tried again. The same thing. He checked the signal. It appeared strong, and he knew reception at the Maison was fine. He'd rung Jacques no problem. Over the next few minutes he tried again, several times. All he got was the unavailable message. He wondered if she'd let the battery run down and forgotten to re-charge it. If so, it would be the first time, and she always set her phone to switch on if it was inadvertently left off. Then again, the past twenty four hours had been rather distracting.

Giving up, he resolved to try her again as soon as he reached Châtillon. And again at Jacques' if he didn't get her then. It didn't matter. He was bound to get her sometime before she went to bed. In fact thinking about it, a bedtime call may be even better. They'd done it before when they'd been temporarily parted. And while the telephone was not the same as actually lying next to her, a little imagination could go a long way. What better way of making up, long distance?

Feeling more relaxed than any time in the past forty eight hours, Scott Weston settled down to enjoy what was left of his journey. After less than a minute he roused himself again and reached into his rucksack. Taking out the Rough Guide to Milan he'd remembered to bring with him, he began flicking through it.

CHAPTER 29

Later that morning, Carver sat in while Remy and his team leaders decided what to do about the Madeleine connection. Most of the ideas put forward the previous day had been imaginative, but also impractical.

'Remember,' Remy began. 'This is one of the most important churches in all of France. We cannot treat it the way we would a sports stadium.'

He started by inviting Carver to remind them what they knew for certain. As Carver reeled off the several points, Remy translated, to make sure there were no misunderstandings.

He spoke about the victims, the secrets - possibly love affairs - that had brought them to Paris, the connection with La Madeleine, the possible sightings of at least two victims at the church, in one case talking to a man in a dark coat. Then Carver sat back and watched as the team debated what it all meant, what the right response should be. He was not surprised when, eventually, they came to the same working theory as himself. That the victims had come seeking Saint Mary's absolution for the sin of having entered into an affair, thereby betraying their families. But they were undecided about whether the killer was meeting his victims in the church, or just identifying, then following them. They asked Carver for his view.

'My guess would be that he identifies them when they turn up at the church. How he does that is unclear, but there are two possibilities. One is that when the victims visit the church for their absolution, he manages to engage them in conversation during which he picks them out as potential victims.'

'And the second?' someone said.

At this point Carver hesitated. It raised a host of practical problems. But he suspected at least some of the others were already thinking it. 'Confession.'

It led to a whole other debate.

The previous day Carver and Ingrid had established there were, in all, six priests who regularly practised the sacrament. No one had the faintest idea how to begin to investigate what went on in confession without approaching the priests themselves. In which case, if the killer was a priest – unlikely they agreed, but possible - he would be alerted to the fact the police were on his trail. The reluctance even extended to involving priests from other churches, or even far away from Paris. Whether their fears were justified or not, they were all wary of the famed closeness of the Catholic faith. Still, they had to do something.

As a first step, Remy ordered an undercover team be deployed into the church to see if they could spot anything that might fit with the little they knew. 'You never know, they may just see a distraught 'sinner' being comforted by a tall man in dark coat.'

'But what about the priests and confession?' someone asked. 'Is there anything we can do about that?'

Carver said, 'The only thing I can think of is to send

someone in to confess to some infidelity, then wait to see what happens. The trouble is there are six priests. If by some chance the killer is one of them, they would have to confess to each one to see which one acts on it.'

Remy shook his head. 'Too complicated.'

But with no other suggestions forthcoming, the meeting broke up, the detectives returning to managing the different strands of the investigation while they waited to see what the observations in the church produced.

The answer came within twenty four hours, when the first pair of undercover observers reported back to Remy. Identifying 'penitent sinners' was not particularly difficult, it seemed. What was harder, was trying to work out which, if any, could be a potential murder victim. 'They all look the same,' one of the officers said. 'Carrying their guilt like a badge, head down, praying, beating their chest, crossing themselves and kissing rosaries, crying. From what we saw, there are a great many ordinary people out there committing a lot of sin.'

The next day, frustrated and with nothing better to do, Carver decided to pay the church a visit himself, to try and get a feel for what might be possible. Having swapped his work suit for chinos and a blouson, he took a seat in the middle of the nave and settled down to carry out his own surveillance. When he spotted the pair of coverts, a man and a woman, posing as tourists wandering the church's interior, he pointedly ignored them. He soon saw for himself the difficulty they had reported. Even he had no problem telling the genuine worshippers from the tourists. Nor was it hard to spot the 'penitents' amongst the worshippers. The 'beating heart' descriptions from the undercover officers were spot on. In the course of an hour he counted more than twenty. Many prayed to the statue of Mary Magdalene herself.

Checking out the information desk, he saw that the lady they'd spoken to during his previous visit was not, there, another woman in her place. She was younger but, as he found out when he spoke to her, she bore the same sweet smile. In response to his query, she pointed out to him the 'confessional,' a small, freestanding glass box situated towards the rear of the church. Carver was surprised. He'd expected the traditional sort of wooden booths found in most old churches.

'We used to have them, but they were removed many years ago,' the guide explained. 'Confessors these days prefer something more modern, it seems.' Returning to his seat he considered whether, if they wished to monitor the confessional in some way, its open nature worked to their advantage or not.

He was still thinking about it when a voice from behind, said, 'Have you found what you are looking for, Monsieur Carver?'

He turned to find Father Masson sitting in the pew behind him. He wondered how long he'd been there, watching in silence. He appeared more jolly than when they'd last parted.

'I'm not looking for anything in particular,' Carver lied. 'I'm simply trying to work out what part, if any, the church may be playing in all of this.'

Smiling, Masson made a knowing face. 'Ah, yes. Trying to get inside the murderer's mind, like they do in the films, n'est ce pas?'

Given the circumstances, Carver didn't appreciate the priest's attempt at levity, particularly in view of his less than helpful stance. He made sure the priest could read it in his face when he made his point. 'This isn't some film, Father. This is real. People are dying. And not in a nice way. We have to explore every possible angle.'

Masson's face changed to how it was previously. 'Of course. Let me leave you in peace to finish your work.' He rose to leave but then stopped. 'One thing I must mention.'

Carver looked round. 'Yes?'

'Could I ask you to please inform whoever is in charge that the church would rather that you confine your policing activities to *outside*.' He nodded to where the undercover officers were trying to look interested in one of the artistically-rendered Stations Of The Cross encircling the nave. 'I know you have your job to do, but this is a House Of God. I must insist that those who come here to pray are allowed to do so safe in the knowledge that their communications with their creator are not being observed and recorded for later consideration.' He held Carver's gaze long enough to be sure his point had struck home. Carver didn't turn away from it.

'I'll pass on your message.'

'Thank you my son. God be with you.'

Leaving his pew, the priest crossed himself and bowed to the altar, before turning and heading for the sacristy.

Carver watched him go. *And with you, you wily old bastard.*

Outside the church, he tried Remy but got the engaged signal. He tried Ingrid instead. She answered at once.

'We have to pull the surveillance off,' he told her. 'It's

blown, and in any case, our friend Father Masson doesn't like it.'

'I'm not far away. Wait there.'

A few minutes later, Ingrid's battered Peugeot swung out of the passing traffic to pull up at the kerb. Carver got in.

'What happened?'

He recounted his and Father Masson's latest encounter.

'Is he being obstructive, or just following the rules of his church?'

'Difficult to say, but one thing's for sure.'

'What?'

'Preventing the next murder just got a whole lot harder.'

CHAPTER 30

Heading back to the Préfecture, Ingrid took them through Place de l'Opéra. As they rounded the baroque magnificence that is the Opéra Garnier, the inspiration and setting for Gaston's story of the famous Phantom, Carver experienced a sudden flash-back. Most times, thoughts of his now defunct marriage aroused feelings of bitterness. But for some reason, the week he and Gill spent in Paris remained untarnished. The last few days had been fraught. They weren't about to get any better.

'Pull in, Ingrid,' he said, sharply.

Ingrid didn't hesitate but swung the wheel right, at the same time hitting the brake. 'Is something wrong?'

'No, I er, just need to do something. I'll see you back at the Préfecture.'

"kay.'

Almost before he'd stepped out onto the pavement, she'd gunned the engine, then swung, seamlessly, out into the traffic heading down the avenue towards the Louvre. He watched her disappear.

Didn't even ask, he thought, before turning to look across to where the boulevard known as Les Cappuccines, joins with Avenue de l'Opéra.

On the corner opposite, the distinctive black and gold

frontage of the Café de la Paix, with its formally attired waiters carrying laden silver trays as they weaved between tables, was exactly as he remembered. Waiting for a gap in the streaming traffic, he crossed to it.

Ten minutes later, Carver was enjoying his café crème while engaging in Paris's second most popular pastime, people watching. The elderly gentleman whom he'd asked if he would mind sharing a table, had been gracious enough to pretend he didn't, before burying himself once more in his copy of Le Monde. What he really thought about some ignorant *Anglais* forcing himself onto his table, Carver could only imagine.

Remarkably, given the events of the past days, Carver was close to succeeding in the aim he'd set himself, on the spur of the moment when the Opera House first hove into view - pretending, just for a few short minutes, that his reasons for being in Paris were not what they were. And as his gaze swung, right and left, he felt himself being transported back to when he'd last sat there. Instinctively, he turned to check the chair to his right. Its emptiness shouted at him, to the point where he even let out a whimsical sigh. His table companion raised an eyebrow, but didn't shift from his paper. *Whatever*, Carver thought. *The coffee here's still the best.*

He turned his attention back to what many regard as the Opera Quarter's most distinguishing characteristic. Apart from the tourists, who dress as tourists do everywhere these days, with the emphasis on comfort and practicality, those who live and work there deport themselves, in the main, with a grace and style that the rest of the city struggles to match. For the next several minutes, Carver drank his coffee while letting his mind roam with the to-ing and fro-ing of the elegantly-attired passers-by. At first, he assumed it was random, but after several minutes he began to discern a pattern.

It was Saturday. Left out of the café, past the Opera House and across the Boulevard Haussmann was the venue that for thousands of Parisians is a weekly pilgrimage, the huge shopping emporium, Les Galeries Lafayette. It explained why the right-to-left flow past the café was predominantly female, predominantly well-heeled and well-dressed and, it seemed, also predominantly attractive. Carver checked out those at the tables closest. While the men seemed amiably relaxed, the ghosts of leery smiles etched in their admiring faces, the women were scrutinising, weighing those passing from the tops of their expensively-coiffured heads to the tips of their elegantly-attired toes. By the looks on the watchers' faces, they could have been attending some hot Paris Catwalk.

Something else Carver noted. While the ages of those passing varied, from teenagers to the indeterminately mature, it made little difference. There were few to whom most, men, or women, would not happily give a second, or even a third glance. The rule applied double to the mother-daughter combinations, of which there seemed many. Not a subject on which he'd ever much thought, Carver had no sense whether mothers and daughters shopping together while apparently trying to out-do each other in the style stakes was a peculiarly French, and/or Parisian, phenomenon. And as he mentally transposed his present situation to his home city, he couldn't decide whether it was his Manchester upbringing, or some latent prejudice that led him to imagine the Chanel and St Laurent giving way to bargain fashion store buy/wear/throw-away mix and match.

Lost in the moment, he shook his head and gave a wry smile as he imagined what Jess might say if she were there to read his thoughts. 'And what, pray tell, would *you* know?'

Eventually, conscious he was in danger of appearing leering, Carver sought a diversion, something on which he was more qualified to have an opinion. Turning his gaze, he re-focused across the road to where a smart black Mercedes had pulled up opposite the Opéra Garnier's side entrance. A moment later he shook his head again, this time in self-mockery as yet another, stunning mother-daughter combination got out and joined with those thronging towards *Les Galeries*. The mother, dark-haired and with a body many might kill for, was dressed classily; silky cream top, white skirt, tan jacket. Wrap-around sunglasses obscured her face, but he knew without having to look further she would be attractive, so too, her blond daughter. Not as curvy as her mother, her bright green leather jacket and fashionable yellow slacks fitted her youth. At that moment, the fact that she was very much fairer-skinned than her older companion, barely registered in Carvers' consciousness.

'Jesus,' Carver muttered as he turned away. 'They're everywhere.'

Later, Carver would recall that even on that first, brief sighting, and somewhere deep down within him, the mother's coal-black hair, model figure and haughty self-assurance stirred memories and associations that he wasn't, at that moment, inclined to acknowledge. It was a pleasantly-warm Saturday. He was sitting in the heart of the city's most elegant quarter. Here, now, the city was teeming with women who could match *Her* in everything but her taste for murder. If he wasn't careful, he could end up spending the rest of the day imagining seeing her on every corner, in every street café. Realising he was letting his imagination roam way too far, he shook his head again to rid himself of the distracting images. 'You bloody well *are* obsessed,' he admonished.

Sensing the spell of his brief sojourn breaking and having reached the coffee's dregs, Carver decided it was time to snap out of his reverie and get back to reality. But as he reached into his jacket for his wallet, something nagged.

He stopped, hand in pocket, looked round. *No sign*.

He stood up, glanced across the road again. *Not there*.

He looked to his left.

Fifty yards away, the mother and daughter from the black Mercedes were about to be swallowed up by the throng. As he caught the last glimpse of them before they became lost to sight and merged with the rest of the throng heading towards *Les Galeries*, Carver realised what had given him pause. Both women were tall in their heels, and full of the easy confidence beauty bestows. But that was where the similarity ended. While the daughter was fair, with blond locks that hung down her back, the mother's looks were much darker in tone all round, not just her hair. But it wasn't just their different colouring that was nagging at him. Carver was familiar with the emerging branch of Forensic Science known as, Forensic Gait Analysis, the identification of suspects through analysis of their body language, the way they walk. Research has shown that the way a person moves and carries themselves is as potentially distinctive as fingerprints, or DNA. During the time he 'worked' with Megan Crane, Carver had countless opportunities to observe, often from the rear, the way she walked and stalked. And as he caught his last glimpse of the mother and daughter before they were lost in the crowd, and cast his mind back to the moment they emerged from the black Merc and walked away, he realised, finally, what had lingered in his subconscious. The older woman's distinctive sashay.

He froze, staring towards where he had last seen them. 'Fucking hell,' he said.

Across the table, the elderly gentleman looked up from his paper to regard him with undisguised disdain.

CHAPTER 31

Most assume that the investigation of crime is all about the systemic application of science, logic and plodding, methodological enquiry. In most cases it is. But what they would be surprised to know is how often coincidence and luck plays its part. Rather, how they do for those prepared to do something other than sit around waiting for the telephone to ring. Carver had learned the lesson early, as a young DC at Salford.

At the time, the prevailing view amongst members of The Robbery Squad was that it would be a waste of time to take seriously the threat made by the brutal leader of the Chinese gang who smashed their way into Ling's Fish and Chip Shop on the Salford New Road late one night. As the robber dangled the owner's baby granddaughter over hot fat by her ankle, he'd promised to return unless Ling's youngest daughter – the baby's mother - brought the family gold they'd come for to a meet in the middle of the city's China Town, two days hence. Apparently acting on old information, the gang hadn't known that following an earlier break-in, old man Ling had decided a bank vault might be a safer option than the old floor safe with the wonky door. That the thug went so far as to specify a midday rendezvous made the supposed handover, in the detective's eyes, all the more unlikely. The squad's longest-serving DS, Terry Lunt, summed up most's thoughts on the subject. 'It was spur of the moment bullshit. They'll have sussed the police are involved by now. Come the day, you won't find a one of 'em within ten miles of the drop.'

DS Barry Cody, Carver's immediate supervisor at the time, thought otherwise. Quieter than Lunt and generally more thoughtful, the two DSs enjoyed an uneasy relationship, suspicious yet no less respectful of the other's methods. 'The way they terrorised the family, I wouldn't mind betting they'll assume they're too scared to involve the police,' was Cody's take. 'There's nothing to be lost running it, so why not?' But it took all of Cody's considerable powers of persuasion to muster enough cover for the stake-out.

But by half-past two on the day of the supposed meet, even Carver was beginning to think that on this occasion, Cody's known enthusiasm for following unlikely leads might be proving a stretch too far. Fifty yards away, on the street corner the thug had specified, now littered with the butts of the twenty or so cigarettes she'd smoked her way through the last three hours, sweet-looking Lai-Lai Ling looked bored to tears. By three o'clock, Cody was prepared to accept defeat.

'Wrap it,' his command came over the radio. 'Everyone stand down. See you back at base. We'll pick up the girl.'

As the others did as ordered and headed back to Salford, Carver and Cody pulled out of the abandoned garage they'd been using as an OP the past four hours and headed for the corner where Lai-Lai stood. As they pulled up beside her, she bent to check the car's occupants. Her face lit up as she recognised the two detectives and Carver barely had to indicate the backseat before the door was open and she was on it, sighing relieved sighs and muttering, darkly, in Mandarin. Through the rear view mirror, Carver smiled at her and said, 'Everything okay?' The muttering continued. Lai-Lai spoke not a word of English. Carver pulled a U-turn and headed for the road that would take them out of China Town.

They'd gone less than thirty yards when both detectives jumped as Lai-Lai started shouting and shrieking. As Cody spun round in his seat to see what was wrong, Carver checked his mirror. Lai-Lai was banging the flat of her hand against the right-hand window, turning in her seat and pointing at something, or someone, they had just passed. It took Carver only a second to realise that the subject of Lai-Lai's sudden excitement was a straggly-haired youth in a woollen bobble hat loping along, hands in pockets, in the opposite direction. Carver acted on instinct. Executing another U, he caught up with the youth and eased to a stop next to him. Cody leaped out and grabbed the youth, before the surprise in the young man's face could turn to something else. Holding onto his arm, Cody dipped his head to check out Lai-Lai. It was hard to distinguish any words at all now as she shouted and screamed and continued to point at the youth, at the same time twisting and turning in her seat as if maybe thinking it was time to find an alternative means of transport.

'Him?' Cody said, pointing at the young man he was holding onto. He admitted later it was probably the most stupid single word he'd ever uttered in his life. All that came from Lai-Lai were more shrieks and panicked nods. Cody asked the youth his name, but was not at all surprised when, through shrugs and shakes of the head he indicated that he spoke no English. With the youth standing there, looking dazed and doing his best to feign innocence, Cody had no choice but to do what he did next, which he also admitted later and with hindsight probably wasn't the brightest. Opening the rear passenger door, he pushed the youth into the back seat right next to Lai-Lai. Pausing only to make sure the child safety catch was on, he slammed the door shut.

Lai-Lai promptly fainted.

As Peter Goode, the barrister charged with prosecuting the case through the Crown Court would later comment, 'It was no more than one might expect from a young mother who suddenly finds herself rubbing shoulders with the man she last encountered threatening to kill her baby in the most horrific fashion.

For as Cody and Carver discovered when they eventually got Lai-Lai and their prisoner back to Salford and brought in an interpreter, that was who the youth was. It transpired that following the robbery he had never given a moment's thought to keeping his rendezvous with Lai-Lai and it was pure coincidence that he chose to pop out for cigarettes the same time that the officers were giving up on the stakeout.

'Sheer luck,' Lunt called it.

'In this job you make your own luck,' was Cody's take. Carver never forgot it.

Memory of the lesson was bubbling somewhere in the back of Carver's brain as he pulled a ten-euro note from his wallet and dropped it on the table next to the bill he hadn't even checked yet. Then he was moving, fast, round the tables, out onto the pavement and across the road towards where he'd last seen the two women.

'MONSIEUR.'

The shout came from behind. Carver turned.

One of the café's waiters was coming up on him, fast. Not the young one who had served Carver, but one of the older, more experienced ones. Carver stopped. As he approached, Carver saw the ten-note in one hand, the bill in the other. The waiter held them out for Carver's inspection. The look on his face said he was well used to dealing with bunkers. Any other time Carver would have argued. One coffee and a pain-au chocolate and ten euro wasn't enough? He didn't have time. It was Paris. As he dug in his wallet for another note, he checked over his shoulder. Not a sign of them. He thrust the first note that came to hand in the general direction of the waiter. He didn't look to see what it was or what happened to it as by then he was off and running, ignoring the shout of, 'Monsieur, votre change?'

CHAPTER 32

Carver stopped as he reached the crowd waiting at the lights to cross over Boulevard Haussmann to Les Galeries Lafayette's south east corner entrance. He checked the heads in front. No sign. He looked left and right. All he could see was a seething mass of shoppers.
Fuck.
The pedestrian signal turned green and the crowd surged forward. He went with them, head turning, eyes searching. Further down the Boulevard, fifty yards to his left, those waiting to cross to the store's main, middle entrance, also started to move. Chinks appeared in the solid wall of pedestrians, which was when he caught a glimpse of blond and black with an accompanying white/tan, yellow/green. His heart skipped. Was it them?
Too far away to be sure.
As the kerbside neared, Carver weighed options. As things stood, he would enter the store at the same time as the two women - if it was them - though via different entrances. On the other hand, he could break from his crowd, join theirs, and follow after them through the middle door. Either way, he would lose them for a period of time, and that was assuming he was able to

pick them up again once inside, which was by no means certain. He had visited the store just once before. The details were hazy but he remembered being blown away by its sheer scale. Picking them up again would depend on where they headed once inside, the location of stairs and escalators, how busy it was. The last he already knew - *very* busy. He made his decision.

Keep going.

Inside was like any big city department store on a Saturday, only ten times worse. 'Manic' hardly did justice to the heaving mass of pushing, jostling sea of browsing humanity on which Carver found himself tossed. Desperate for some sign, he strained to peer over heads, trying to gauge where they might be if they had kept going straight after entering. Nothing. Ahead of him, in the middle of the ground floor was the 'up' escalator, a continuous line of shoppers ascending. The tidal flow was pulling him towards it. He didn't resist. Right now, any direction was as good as any other. He tried to think if he'd ever heard of some set of rules that governed women's shopping behaviour, that determined where they went when they entered a department store. Up, down, straight in or round the margins? He had no idea. As the flow carried him round a jewellery display wagon he lost sight of the escalator. When it reappeared, he just caught a flash of green-yellow half way up before it rose above ceiling level and out of sight. Heart pounding, he pushed forward, earning black looks from those he elbowed aside. As he stepped onto the conveyor he looked up. Whoever he'd seen, they weren't there now. At the next floor, he scanned around quickly, before following the line heading up once more. Committed now, he just hoped he was following in their wake.

Next floor, same again, then up. He was aware that using the escalator was risky. Once on, there was no getting off, not in this crowd. But at least the first half of each ascent gave him a bird's-eye view of the floor he'd just left. As he rose and scanned, the germ of an idea came to him. He took out his phone, called Remy.

'Where are-'

'Don't talk, just listen.' It took two more ascents to explain what was happening, to find out what he needed to know, and then make his proposal, all the time scanning the floors.

After listening in silence, Remy's reaction was as Carver expected.

'Are you mad? This does not qualify as-'

'I know Remy, but what else is there?' He had one chance. At the end of the day he and Remy were friends. Conscious of where he was, he lowered his voice. 'Remember what she *did*, Remy. And not just to me.'

There was another silence, then, 'I'll call you back.' He rung off.

As he started towards six, Carver took stock. He had no way of knowing if his idea was viable. Even if it was, was there enough time? Whichever, it was out of his hands now. He needed to think on what he could do in the meantime. The store guide on each floor showed seven floors. One more flight and he would need another strategy anyway. Six was toys and hardware; Seven, restaurants, toilets and hair dressing. Male logic, probably not the most reliable under present circumstances but it was all he had, told him that for two women shopping together, Seven had to be a fair bet, but when? He tried to remember Gill's shopping habits. Would she ever have managed seven floors without succumbing to the temptations along the way, even if only for some advance browsing? No chance.

At six and still with no sign of his quarry, he stepped off-line. He turned left, intending to head round to the down escalator and retrace his route, scanning floors as he had on the way up. He stopped. Before him was the feature that makes *Les Galeries* one of the most unique buildings of its kind. The central atrium that runs from the roof-top glass dome to the ground floor was designed to 'improve the shopping experience' by letting natural light permeate into the very heart of the building. Around it on each floor, a circular balustrade gives shoppers a clear view of the floors below and, to a lesser extent, above. Too good an opportunity to miss, he approached the rail. For several minutes he stood there, peering down, up and around, scanning as much of the floor-space as he would see from anywhere apart from the store's CCTV Control Room, wherever that was. All the time he wondered how Remy was doing.

By now Carver's brain was racing, seeking options other than scouring the store, and waiting on Remy. One floor down, one of the grey-blazered security officers of whom he'd glimpsed several already was walking the floor. He would be in radio contact with his Control Room. Maybe it was time to-

Carver froze. On the floor directly below the security officer, two women were browsing amongst rails of garments.

It was them.

Carver focused straight in on the 'mother', age, height, figure, the way she carried herself. They all tallied with the memories now swooping in from whichever corner of his brain he'd mentally stored them the past couple of years. Yet as the seconds ticked, what he needed most eluded him. Perusing the displays, checking labels and prices, she either kept her head down, or turned away from him. And as he stared across the fifty-metre gulf between them, Carver suddenly found himself invoking two powers he'd stopped believing in long ago, telepathy, and prayer.

Look up. Just once. Dear God, that's all I ask.

As he waited for the glimpse that was all he needed, he barely dared to breath.

Then it happened.

In the act of flicking fingers along a row of hangers the way browsers do when looking for a particular size or style, she suddenly stopped, hand hovering over the items as if she might resume her search any second. Only she didn't. What she did sent Carver's pulse sky high. Angled slightly away from him, she began to turn slowly towards him, at the same time lifting her head, as if responding to some sensory alarm.

She was no longer wearing sunglasses.

CHAPTER 33

It was one of those occasions when, just for a few moments, the world stands still.

As Carver stared across the void, the woman he had last seen getting into a car in dead of night outside Kayleigh Lee's home appeared to be staring directly back at him.

Or was she?

In line between them, the blond girl was holding aloft two blouses, one red, one black, as if waiting for a steer on which to buy. For a moment, Carver wasn't sure whether the older woman's gaze was directed at the blouses, or him. Clarification came as the girl turned to look up and over her shoulder, searching for whatever it was had captured her companion's attention so fiercely she could not answer a simple question. In that moment, Carver experienced something he had not felt in a long time - the discomfort that comes when neck hairs rub against a shirt collar as they stand suddenly proud. A chill as marked as if he had just entered a walk-in-freezer rippled through him. For long seconds, the face of the woman staring back at him stayed blank. But then slowly, chillingly, a thin smile spread across the features he remembered so well.

Holy Mother of God.

For several seconds more the woman who had once sworn to kill him held his gaze. Like a rabbit caught in a car's headlamps he could only stare back.

Without warning, the spell shattered as the smile vanished, suddenly. At the same time, Megan Crane reached out and grabbed the girl's arm. The blouses she was holding aloft fluttered to the floor as she was jerked almost off her feet. Spinning on her heel, the woman he'd been searching for all this time headed away, no pausing for explanations. Within a split-second the pair had disappeared from Carver's view, heading deeper into the store. Finally free of her imprisoning gaze, he moved.

He raced for the down escalator. She would be heading for the quickest way out of the store. He had to either stop them, or regain line-of-sight before they did so. They had a two-floor start. His chances weren't good.

No time for politeness and consideration now, Carver pushed, shoved, jostled and elbowed his way around and in front of those before him, forcing his way down the conveyor as fast he could safely manage. Dark looks and curses he couldn't translate but could guess at followed his progress. As the floor below came into view he searched in vain for signs of the pair. There were none. He calculated time. They'd been on the fourth floor. From there it would only take them five minutes, six max, to exit the store.

Too much of a start.

Suddenly, the in-store public address system began to blare. A female voice, so calm and assured that it had to be taped, announced 'Mesdames et Messieurs, votre attention s'il vous plait...' Though the meaning of the words that followed was beyond him, Carver's heart leaped as those around stopped in their tracks to listen, heads cocked to hear better. Puzzlement, followed swiftly by hints of alarm crept into faces.

It had to be Operation Funnel. Remy had come through.

A British Police-devised anti-terrorist response tactic, Operation Funnel's primary purpose is to enable a surveillance team, or officers in 'hot pursuit' to re-establish contact with a suspected bomb-carrying terrorist. It is designed for use in circumstances where contact has been lost within enclosed public venues such as shopping centres, sports stadia, concert venues, hotels, etc. Such places invariably have a multiplicity of entrances and exits - hence the term, MEPP; Multi-Entrance/Exit Public Place. MEPPs are often deliberately used by target suspects to shake off any suspected surveillance by the simple means of leading the surveilling officers on a merry dance into, out of, and around the venue until such time as the surveillance is so dispersed or confused that it falls apart, allowing the suspect to resume their nefarious activities unobserved.

The need for some such counter-tactic grew in the wake of 9/11 and the ensuing rise in global terrorism. The tragic shooting to death of the innocent Brazilian student, Jeane Charles de Menezes by police in London in two-thousand-and-five focused minds on that need. In Britain, those in charge of MEPPs were tasked with drawing up contingency plans whereby all exits bar one could, on receipt of a coded signal from the police, be closed and an evacuation of the venue initiated with visitors being 'funnelled out' through a single, pre-designated exit. The idea is that pursuing officers station themselves at the exit where they can pick up their 'lost' suspect as they came out, thus regaining the capability to thwart any intended attack. For the plan to work of course, a credible justification for the evacuation is needed - a mains gas leak or similar, being the recommended option. The scheme is not foolproof. The uncertainties inherent in any such operation can never be entirely overcome. If a device-carrying terrorist comes to suspect what is happening, he or she may choose to press the button anyway. But at least Funnel provides an option that may not otherwise be available. To Carver's knowledge Funnel had only ever been used twice in the UK. Leicester's Highcross Shopping Centre, and London's Waterloo Station. In both cases it achieved the desired outcome.

Carver also knew that Funnel's principles had been shared with governments and police forces across Europe, having had a hand in doing so. His call to Remy was to find out if it had been adopted locally, and particularly by the owners of Les Galeries Lafayette. Remy's immediate concern was over the fact that the case did not involve terrorism, a universally agreed pre-requisite for authorising activation. But from what Carver was now seeing, and regardless of whatever concerns he may have had, Remy must have overcome them. God alone knew how, or what story he had concocted to get authorisation. But that was for later. Right now, hearing the announcement, Carver's excitement grew. There was still a chance he might catch her.

Even before the announcement ended, security staff

were visible on the various floors, making their way quickly to cover whatever exit points they'd been designated during training. And while Carver knew that whatever the outcome, he and Remy would soon have to answer some serious questions, there was only one that mattered right now. Would the response be fast enough to trap Megan Crane inside the building, and would he be able to pick her up at the designated exit provided he got there first?

His phone rang. It was Remy. Carver confirmed that Funnel had been activated.

'The designated exit is at the back of the store,' Remy said. 'Tell security to direct you to Exit Twelve.' Ingrid is on her way with other officers. They should be there in five minutes'

'Thanks Remy. I owe you.'

As he made his way down, Carver witnessed, for the first time, the impact of what he had only ever imagined on paper. The faces around reflected a mix of bewilderment, anxiety and annoyance. But there was no sign of the panic many said would inevitably transpire. Instead, everyone appeared to be making their way down through the store purposefully, but calmly. Until they reached the ground floor.

As it hove into view, Carver could hear raised voices and saw groups of people milling around. Before the escalator grounded, he used his last moments of elevation to look over heads and check out those exits he could see, the central main entrance and one over in the far corner. A crowd was gathered at each, harassed-looking security guards doing their best to direct them to the rear of the store. At the corner exit, Carver could see there was some sort of melee which the two guards present were struggling to contain. Carver saw at once what the problem was. They had not been quick enough to get the door shut. Shoppers were still forcing themselves through, ignoring the guards' demands that they should leave via the rear. Carver sensed a mini-panic in the making. And there, a split second before he lost his view amidst the pushing and jostling, he glimpsed the two women, pushing their way towards the still open doors.

Shit, no.

Without waiting for the escalator to level out, Carver vaulted over the moving handrail. He landed amongst a young Asian family, mother, father and a gaggle of children. Seeing the looks in their faces that his sudden appearance triggered, he realised they feared a general panic was about to break out. Throwing them a wholly inadequate, 'Pardon,' he sprinted for the exit, dodging customers and weaving around floor displays. As he neared, he could see the crowd thinning out. The guards must have finally got the door shut. Those who had not managed to force an escape had no choice now but to follow their directions, though some were still lingering to argue. As Carver arrived, one of the guards, a sturdily-built black man with short dreadlocks, put out an arm to block his way, directing him to the rear.

'Pardon monsieur. Allez à l'arrière du magasin, s'il vous plaît.' *Please go the rear of the store.*

Carver looked around. The crowd was dispersing quickly now. There was no sign of the two women.

'S'il vous plaît, monsieur,' the guard repeated, more assertively this time. Having had his fill of uncooperative customers and misinterpreting Carver's hesitation, he seemed set on reimposing his authority.

Carver made to comply. With luck he could still hope to catch them at the rear exit. But as he turned away, he glanced out through the now-locked glass doors. On the pavement outside, those who had made it through still lingered, peering back into the store, interested to discover the cause of the disruption. Amongst them, less than ten yards away, stood the unmistakable figure of Megan Crane, hand in hand with the blond girl. Like everyone else, they were watching what was happening inside. Only Megan Crane wasn't just looking back into the store, Carver realised. She was staring at *him*.

'FUCK.'

Instinctively, desperate to get as close to his quarry as he could, Carver, pressed forward, pushing passed the guard's outstretched arm. *If he could get them to open the door, he could still...*

'MONSIEUR,' the guard shouted. A heavy hand wrapped itself round Carver's bicep, hauling him back.

'POLICE,' Carver yelled to the guard's stony face. 'JE SUIS POLICE. POLICE ANGLAIS.'

He reached inside his jacket, pulled out his warrant card, waved it at the man. He didn't look at it. For all Carver knew, he might not even recognise written English. He tried again. Turning back to the doors he pointed to where the two women now stood out, the only stationary figures in a sea of dispersing passers-by. 'HER,' he shouted, pointing through the doors. 'This is all about HER.' Even as he said it, Megan Crane edged nearer, as if to better witness the collapse of his efforts. Turning to the guard, Carver saw him looking blankly outside, clearly struggling to make sense of what this mad Englishman claiming to be a policeman was saying. To his eyes, all he would see were curious shoppers, no one that looked *remotely* like a terrorist. Panic began to rise in him as Carver saw the end scenario looming. Sure enough, the guard babbled back at him in French, gesturing emphatically, insisting that Carver do as ordered.

He tried one last time. '*You don't understand.* It was me who ordered the shut down.' He banged his chest several times, desperate now to make the blank-faced guard understand. '*ME*. The POLICE. That woman, out there.' He pointed at Megan Crane, now drawing nearer to the glass. 'She is wanted for *murder*.' So great was his frustration at not being able to make himself understood, Carver almost spat the words out. Never before had he so regretted not sticking with French at school. In desperation he tried to convey, 'killer', miming the act of plunging a knife into himself. Firing a gun. It succeeded only in confirming to the guard that he was dealing with a madman.

'S'il vous plait,' Carver pleaded. 'Ouvrez la porte.' *Open the door*. One of the few phrases he knew.

But while the guard was beginning to look less certain, he didn't move to obey. Instead he lifted his radio, showing it to Carver. 'Un moment, monsieur.' He spoke into it. Calling his supervisor, no doubt, to come and assess the situation. More wasted time. More than ever, Carver sensed the opportunity draining away. As the guard spoke with his control, Carver took a step toward the door. This time the guard didn't try to stop him. The door was locked. Whoever he was, the madman wasn't going anywhere. Carver pressed against the glass, staring out at the woman who had haunted his dreams the past two years. To his horror, she approached to stand within inches of the glass. She stared through, as if to finally confirm, beyond doubt, that the man staring back at her was, indeed, the man she had once vowed to kill.

The beginning of a sly smile began to play about her lips. She mouthed words he could not hear, but he read them, hearing in his head the soft, seductive tones. *Jamie? Is it really you?*

His left hand was pressed flat against the window. He watched, fascinated, as she lifted hers to place it, oh so deliberately, over his. Her eyes bored into him. A memory stirred. Suddenly he couldn't breathe. He was suffocating. He whipped his hand away. The spell broke. Her smile widened. Still into her games. Behind him the guard was still jabbering into his radio.

The blond girl materialised at Megan's shoulder, a quizzical look on her face. Carver saw she was young, pretty. She said something. Carver tried to read her lips, was surprised to realise he could. 'What is it? Who is he?' *She was speaking English*. He took in her blonde tresses, the blue eyes, perfect white teeth. Something about her shouted, *American*.

Megan glanced at the girl, then back at Carver, seeing him weighing her, noting his interest. Her smile widened, a perfectly plucked eyebrow arched as if to say, *Let me show you*.

What happened next made the blood in his veins run cold.

Stepping away from the window, she took the girl's hand, then proceeded to parade her round in a circle before Carver's horrified gaze as if she were some fashion designer showing off the ingénue she intends will be the world's next super-model. As she passed Carver, the girl's eyes met with his and he realised. *She has no idea what is going on.* As the girl completed her circle, Megan let go her hand and returned her gaze to Carver. The girl was behind her now. She didn't see the way the older woman's gaze slid in her direction, momentarily, then snapped back to Carver. A sly, curious look came into her face. It took Carver a moment to read it.

As realisation hit, he froze. At the same time, all colour drained out of his face. *Oh my God.*

'NO.'

Megan Crane waited only as long as it took for her to be sure he had interpreted her message. Then she reached out and took her young companion by the hand. Lifting her other, she waggled fingers at him the way lovers exchange farewells after an intimate rendezvous. Then she turned and disappeared into the milling throng of shoppers.

Carver reacted as any man would in the circumstances, policeman or no. He banged both fists on the glass and shouted as loud as he could. 'MEGAN. COME BACK. YOU CAN'T. YOU MUSTN'T. MEGAN.'

Then the guards were on top of him, wrestling him to the ground, responding as per their training to deal with someone who was clearly disturbed and in need of being brought under control before he did something that might endanger members of the public, or themselves.

And as Carver struggled against the hands trying to restrain him, uttering cries that alternated between 'You don't understand. Call the police,' and 'Megan, come back. Don't do it,' in his mind's eye he saw only one thing. The horrifying sight of Megan Crane showing off, for his benefit, the beautiful young girl she had somehow managed to draw into her web and whom she had already marked for her deadly amusement.

CHAPTER 34

By the time Ingrid convinced the store's Security Team that the madman they were holding really was a policeman, albeit an English one, then got Carver back to the Préfecture, the inquisition was well underway.

They waited an hour for Remy to return from his grilling. He'd been called upstairs by his Directors, demanding to know how a 'manche' – French for 'sleeve', their equivalent of Operation Funnel - came to be activated without proper authority. As in the UK, the protocols governing such measures are stringent. The incident has to involve terrorism. There must be a potential threat to life. Authority must be sought from the most senior operational police commander available. As Remy later told Carver and Ingrid, when he admitted to his shocked chiefs that he'd ignored the rules and authorised it himself – he had no option but to tell the truth - he expected he would be immediately suspended from duty. A discipline enquiry would be called. The end result would, if he was lucky, see him put back into uniform, pounding the streets.

But while his Directors' response was the expected explosion of outrage coupled with demands to know, 'Who is this Englishman? Why is he here?' it lasted only as long as it took them to realise the precariousness of their position. Even as Remy was being interrogated, a call came from the Managing Director of Les Galeries Lafayette requesting a full briefing on the situation so he could explain away the loss of a day's trading to his board. A figure of several hundred-thousand Euros was mentioned. Suddenly the possibility of substantial compensation payouts loomed, which was when the Directors' collective outrage changed to something more like panic. The rest of Remy's interrogation consisted of them grilling him on what he knew, seeking an angle by which they might claim the police acted in good faith and, of course, to protect the public. Remy was impressed by the level of imagination on show as they sought to fit the activities of a murderous fugitive from British justice into some definition of urban terrorism. Eventually, perhaps realising that they were in danger of exposing too much of themselves to a junior officer, they dismissed Remy, informing him that they would consider his position at a later date. Their only demand was that he submit a full report on the incident before the end of the day. As he was about to leave, they summonsed him back to issue one further instruction. There was to be only one copy of the report and, after printing, it was to be erased from Remy's computer. He decided at once that he would comply with the instruction. But a copy would find its way onto a data stick first. Recognising a cover up in the making, he knew the time may come when he could be grateful for some leverage.

The day ended with the three detectives engaging in much soul-searching and what-if-ing in the darkest corner of Les Deux Chats Noirs they could find.

Afterwards, Carver slunk back to his lodgings where he spent a sleepless night, haunted by the image of Megan Crane leering at him through the glass, seconds before he was wrestled to the ground.

CHAPTER 35

As she drank her coffee, Jess did her best to hide the shock that had taken hold during the couple of minutes her host had spent making them drinks.

It actually started the moment Tracy Redmond opened the front door. If Jess had not known that as recently as two years before, Tracy was still practising, she would not have believed it. And though at that time she was a long way off from being at the top of her game, she was, nevertheless, still well regarded enough within the legal profession to be offered the occasional brief. And that was despite all the disclosures about her private life, the people she had come to be involved with.

Now, the shoulder-length blond hair Jess remembered as always being clean and well-coiffured, was limp, straggly, and in sore need of a treatment. The complexion that was once glowing, was now sallow. The flesh on her arms, pale, loose and blotchy. Jess read the signs. It was clearly either crack or heroin. All she had to do was ask Tracy to roll up the sleeves of her jumper and she would know. But there wasn't much point. Whatever she was on, the overall effect was the same. A pale shadow of the woman Jess first met in

Megan Crane's playroom that fateful night.
Another life ruined.
Jess had last seen Tracy less than four months before. Already then on the slide, she had slipped further since. A lot. Jess understood the reasons why. Following Megan Crane's trial, it had taken the Bar Council another twelve months to complete its investigation into the activities of the member who was revealed to have been the lover and, as the tabloids slavered over, 'sometime-sex- slave' to not one, but two serial killers. And with her not ever having been charged before the court with any criminal offence - the CPS dropped the charge of Aiding and Abetting in return for testimony - it was a further three months before the Reporting QC found the right form of phrasing and presentation of the 'known facts' to show that Tracy Redmond had breached enough of the rules laid down in the Bar Standards Board Handbook to be guilty of Professional Misconduct - at the very least.

At the time, Jess had expected that Tracy would put up a fight against her disbarment. She wasn't exactly the only member of her profession involved in the activities that so many of her erstwhile colleagues now seemed prepared to 'tut' over. Megan Crane's archive revealed that much at least. Sympathetic to Tracy's fall from grace from the start, Jess had even hinted she might be willing to supply her, in confidence of course, with insights she might find useful in constructing a defence. To her credit, Tracy would have none of it. She accepted her disbarring without objection, or criticism. Jess still wasn't certain as to why, but she suspected that someone, somewhere, knew enough that Tracy was still vulnerable. So far, the identity of whoever had driven

Megan Crane to and from the scenes of some of the Worshipper Murders remained to be proved.

Tracy's descent into darkness began the day she removed herself from her Manchester Chambers. And though Arthur Carrington tried, initially, to give her the support she so clearly needed at the time, there was only so much he could do. Apart from the fact that Tracy seemed determined to reject all offers of assistance, Arthur was left in no doubt that unless he disassociated himself, completely, from the now disgraced barrister he'd once loved, his own associations with Megan Crane's circle might come under greater scrutiny than they had heretofore. Jess never got as far as examining the reasons for the difference between the way the profession dealt with Tracy and Arthur. But she had her suspicions. At the end of the day, and for all its claims to have moved with the times, The Bar Council remains highly traditional, and still very much a patriarchy.

Now, as she watched Tracy chain smoking her way through another packet of B&H, all the time flicking non-existent ash into the crowded ashtray, Jess couldn't help but wonder what the future held for this woman who was once so widely admired. Hell, the night they first met, even she had been fascinated to realise that there really are women prepared to allow themselves to be used for another's sexual pleasure for days on end. She'd always thought they were only ever the product of a certain type of man's imaginings. It made her wonder if that woman might ever return, or was she gone forever?

For a quarter hour or so, Jess went with the small talk that was now the pattern of her occasional visits, catching up with each other's lives, though only as far as

Jess was prepared to reveal, before turning to the subject that had brought her. In that time, Tracy spoke of having finally taken a job, clerical work at a local high street insurance broker, and registering, just that week, for a detox programme run by the local Drugs Action Team. The way she seemed desperate that Jess should believe her, Jess wasn't at all sure she did. Tracy made no mention of Arthur Carrington, and nor did Jess.

Eventually, sensing Tracy about to launch into some new fantasy about what she intended to do with her life once she got things back on track - surely she could not seriously believe anyone would give her application to be readmitted to the profession serious consideration? - Jess broke in.

'I need you to tell me what else you can remember about this place outside Paris Megan took you to, Tracy. Were you able to recall any landmarks, like we spoke about last time?'

At their last meeting, Tracy had revealed how, before Megan embarked upon her killing spree, she had accompanied her to a large house outside Paris. Owned by an older, suave Frenchman she only ever met once and never heard Megan speak of again, she was kept there for several days. During the time she was there, Megan 'introduced' her to several men and women, some of whom Megan obviously knew, others she seemed to be meeting for the first time. Jess didn't enquire as to what took place while Tracy was there - she could imagine - but she was keen that Tracy tell her everything she could about the place itself, the people she met. It wasn't much.

Most of the time, when she wasn't taking part in

some 'scene', Megan kept her locked in an upstairs room. Bare apart from an iron-framed bed to which she was often chained, she got the impression it was used to house others such as her, from time to time. She ventured out only once, with Megan and a younger man, when they went into Paris and took dinner at a 'very nice' restaurant, 'somewhere overlooking the Eiffel Tower.' For once, Tracy said, they behaved, 'normally', enjoying the ambiance of Paris at night as friends do. Tracy described the man as best she could remember - Jamie had said it sounded like Henri Durcell - but she could give few details of others she met at the house. Much of the time she was hooded or blindfolded.

'All I can remember,' Tracy said in response to Jess's questions, 'Is that on the way back from Paris, we passed a big sport's stadium, a football ground I think, all lit up, just off the motorway. I would say the house was about twenty minutes drive from there.'

Jess noted it to pass on to Jamie. She knew the Stade de France stood to the north of Paris, and was just off the A1 Motorway. But she suspected there would be other stadiums that would also fit the description. For another ten minutes, she continued to pump Tracy for anything that might give Jamie a pointer to Megan's present whereabouts, but nothing more was forthcoming. As she began to wind the conversation up, Tracy seemed to sense it.

'Will you excuse me for a moment?' Tracy said. 'I'd like to show you something?' She left the room.

During the several minutes she was absent, Jess rinsed their coffee mugs under the kitchen tap and checked her mobile for messages. There was only one that mattered, a reply from her mother to one she had sent earlier that afternoon. 'Managing ok. But would be nice if you could call sometime.' It ended with a sad-face emoji. It had the desired effect. Jess felt the guilt pangs returning. *Ohhh.*

Behind her, the door opened. Tracy returned. Jess could tell at once that during her absence she had attended to her appearance. Her hair was brushed and neat, and she had applied fresh make up. She looked somewhat better than when she left the room, but still a long way from how she had once appeared. As she returned to her chair opposite, Jess sensed nervousness in her. Only when she sat down did Jess notice the small, black velvet sack, secured with a drawstring, that Tracy was carrying.. She held it out for Jess to take.

'What's this?' Jess said. But as she took it off her and heard the metallic 'clink' from inside and felt it's weight, she came on alert. *Uh-oh.*

Tracy looked at her, but her face gave nothing away. 'It's something I wonder if you may like to use sometime.'

Jess stared, first at the bag, then back at Tracy. Her instincts shouted at her. *Don't open it. Just leave. Now.* But she found herself saying, 'Use? When, how?'

Tracy gave a hint of a wan smile. 'Look inside. You will see.' Then she leaned forward and bowed her head, presenting Jess with her long, slender neck - and stayed that way.

Jess stared down at the pale, white flesh before her. And in that moment she knew, exactly, what she would find if she were to undo the bag's drawstring and peer inside. Her heart started thumping.

Oh, shit.

CHAPTER 36

As the lights of the taxi that had brought him from Gare Lazare disappeared back down the track towards the main road, Scott Weston stood rucksack in hand, and stared across at the Maison de Floret. The front of the house was lit up. So too, from what he could see, was the side overlooking the pool. The driveway leading up to the house was jammed with smart Mercedes and BMWs. The strains of music he thought he vaguely recognised but couldn't have named - some opera aria maybe? - reached his ears.

Michelle's party looked to be in full swing.

Taking out his mobile, he tried one last time to give Tory warning of his arrival. It was no good. As it had been doing since the first time he tried on the train the day before, the 'unavailable' message rang out. He put it away. Hefting his bag, he started towards the gates.

On waking that morning after a restless night's sleep, he'd tried Tory again. As soon as he heard the familiar message, he knew he could not go another day worrying why she wasn't answering. He gave it until lunch time. When there was still no response, he made his apologies to Jacques and his parents. By then they were aware of his concern. Gracious hosts, Jacques parents expressed their regret over his early departure but empathised with his dilemma. 'I am sure it is only a technical problem and she is fine, but we fully understand why you would want to get back.' Scott didn't mention he'd also tried both the house number and mobile numbers Michelle had given them the first day, 'In case of emergencies'. All his calls had gone unanswered.

Jacques ran him to the station to catch the evening train to Paris. An accident on the line somewhere outside the capital added an unscheduled hour and half to his journey. It was gone nine by the time he arrived at Gare St Lazare and grabbed a taxi. Traffic out of the city was the worst he'd seen yet. It was a further hour before the taxi dropped him off.

The high, iron gates were shut. Sensor-operated, he'd seen them open and close automatically during their comings and goings. An intercom and buzzer was built into one of the gateposts. About to use it, he hesitated.

Scott never knew what made him decide not to announce his arrival openly but seek an alternative method of entry. Something to do with wanting to keep the element of surprise as long as possible. One thing he'd gleaned about Michelle Chartier was, she liked to be in control of things. *Well not tonight, lady*. Besides, he preferred to have an idea of what to expect, rather than just walking in, blind.

Leaving the gates, he followed the high brick wall anticlockwise until he reached the woods overlooking the garden's east side. During their first garden tour, he'd noted how most of the trees were cut right back so they did not protrude over the wall. 'I like to protect my privacy,' Michelle had explained. But he remembered one stout beech that, devoid of overhanging branches nevertheless leaned at an angle that brought it pretty close.

In the dark, trudging through thick bracken, over and around fallen trunks it took him a while to find it. Luckily, there was enough light spilling from the upper parts of the house so he eventually got there without doing himself injury. Leaving his bag at the base of the tree to collect later, he shinned up the trunk until he was a foot or so higher than the wall. He judged the gap to be about a couple of metres. He was athletic, and strong.

'No problem.'

Gripping the trunk firmly in both hands, he bounced and swung back and forth, mentally rehearsing the spring that would take him over. Bracing his feet against the trunk, he launched himself into space.

Whether overconfident or deceived by the darkness, he misjudged it, totally. He landed clumsily, chest down, across the top of the wall and had to scrabble, feet and hands, to stop himself falling back the wrong side. But he overcompensated and before he could stop himself, toppled over into the vegetable patch the other side. He fell heavily, winding himself. At the same time he felt an ankle twist under. The pain was acute and he had to work at not crying out.

'Shit-shit-shit.' He hissed the words through gritted teeth.

He lay there for several minutes, recovering, before getting up and hobbling towards the house. The ankle wasn't broken, but he wouldn't be running any races for a while. As he reached the side of the house, Scott was conscious that, soiled and bedraggled, he was hardly looking his best to make any sort of entrance. He wondered whether he should have just pressed the buzzer.

The main lounge with the French windows was the other side of the house. Hugging the darkness close to the walls, he made his way round the back. Passing the kitchen, the lights were on and he saw the remains of what looked to have been a formidable buffet. Used plates and platters containing remnants of sliced meats and finger food and half-empty salad bowls were stacked on the table and work surfaces. Seeing them reminded him him he had not eaten since a grabbed baguette, earlier in the afternoon. There was no sign of anyone. He carried on towards the other side of the house but it wasn't until he neared the open lounge windows he heard the sound of clapping. The drapes were only partly drawn, and he retreated back onto the lawn to make sure he was out of the light before peering in. It wasn't what he expected.

When Michelle first mentioned her 'little soirée' she'd made it sound like an informal gathering. A handful of friends and acquaintances. Drinks and canapés, that sort of thing. But the event Scott witnessed taking place in Michelle Chartier's spacious lounge that evening was of a different order altogether. A dozen or so couples were formally attired, men in black tie, the ladies in sparkling evening wear. Most had champagne flutes in hand. But rather than the informal mingling and mixing Scott expected, they were all arranged on chairs around the edges of the room, but angled to face towards the doors leading into the room from the hallway. Before them, draped in a figure-hugging black velvet dress slit almost to the waist, Michelle appeared to be giving some sort of speech. He couldn't hear her words but whatever they were, her guests seemed appreciative. Every now and then they interrupted to give a short round of applause. As he tried to work out what it was all about, he looked for Tory. She wasn't amongst them.

So where is she?

The answer came a minute or so later when, ending her delivery, Michelle stepped to one side and made a presentational arm-sweep towards the doors, which opened on cue. Scott's blood froze as Tory entered. She was wearing the spectacular red outfit that had sparked the argument of two days earlier. With one exception. Attached to the diamante collar round her neck was a silver chain, the end of which was being held by a young black man who was leading her into the room as if she were some show-pony. He was accompanied by a girl with long dark hair and a coffee-coloured complexion. They were both wearing skimpy outfits that revealed lots of flesh.

Scott could barely believe what he was seeing. 'What the fuck?'

In other circumstances, with another woman playing Tory's part, Scott *might* have found something to appreciate in the tableau he was witnessing. But this was his Tory, and while there was no denying that right now, she looked like every man's fantasy, the sight of his fiancée being exhibited in such a way sent his head spinning and his gut into turmoil. His first thought was to burst right in and drag her away, but instinct restrained him. Instead he simply gawped as Tory was led into the centre of the room, to appreciative clapping.

'Tory?' he hissed to himself. 'What the hell are you doing?'

Letting go the chain, the man and girl retired to the back of the room, leaving Tory alone, in the middle. As the clapping continued, Tory stood there, half-smiling and looking round at the audience, as if acknowledging their appreciation.

Scott was transfixed. For all Tory was blessed with natural beauty, he'd never known her play on it. Nor had he ever seen her try to capitalise on what God had given her by preening herself or going out of her way to attract attention - of either sex. Yet right now that was exactly what she appeared to be doing.

Or was she?

As she continued, seemingly, to drink in the admiring glances and comments, Scott suddenly had the sense something wasn't right, apart from her uncharacteristic behaviour. Eventually he realised. *It's the smile.*

Tory's smile had always been bright, and lively. When she released it, her whole face lit up. But the smile now on show looked artificial, as if it had been painted on. And the more he looked, the more he saw that her expression had a dreamy quality about it. The eyes in particular, rather than shining and full of fun and laughter, were dull, lifeless.

She's been drugged.

The realisation hit him like a punch to the gut and gave rise to two conflicting thoughts. The first was relief that however it looked, Tory was not the willing participant she'd first appeared. The second, more worryingly, was fear.

What the fuck have we got ourselves involved in?

CHAPTER 37

Like most of his college's male fraternity, Scott's occasional late night channel-cruising included the sort of 'lifestyle' programmes that seem aimed at those for whom sex is a primary leisure activity. Now and again, they ran features on fringe-group activities that revolved around elaborate, role-play fantasies. They usually involved dressing up and acting out ritualised and, to the uninitiated, dramatic, even frightening scenarios. The young and inevitably attractive reporters who fronted the features always went out of their way to present such 'games' as harmless fun. The mantra trotted out at the end of each report was that however things might look, everyone featured in the programme was a willing participant. The intimation was that such activities – the ones featured at least – only took place by way of mutual consent.

But as Scott witnessed the scene developing in front of him - people were now leaving their chairs, approaching Tory to examine her as if she were some exhibit - he had the clear impression that for those present, 'consent' was not a matter about which they would worry unduly. And for all that the behaviour on show so far had been civilised and non-threatening - no-one had yet laid a finger on Tory - he had a growing suspicion that for all the cultured restraint on show, beneath the surface lurked something sinister. Above all, he sensed danger.

A change was taking place in the room. Michelle was ushering people back to their seats. They responded, but slowly in some cases and only after completing their appraisal of the beautiful young woman on show. At a sign from Michelle, the dark couple came forward again to take up Tory's chain and lead her to the back of the room. She followed them, meekly, as Michelle again took centre stage.

It took Scott a couple of minutes to figure out what was going on in what followed.

To begin with Michelle led some sort of discussion. When it was over, a strange thing started happening. Every now and again someone in the audience – usually a man – raised a hand. People would look round and, occasionally, respond with polite applause.

A minute later, he realised.

'It's a damn auction. She's auctioning Tory.'

Desperate and increasingly fearful, Scott knew he had to do something. But what? He thought again about bursting straight in, but decided against. Right now Tory was in no immediate danger. Such an interruption might trigger the sort of reaction he would rather avoid. If he bided his time the opportunity may still come to slip in and spirit Tory away. In the back of his mind the thought lingered that whatever happened, he would be referring the whole matter to the police the first chance he got. By now he was settled to the fact that regardless of how accepting Tory appeared, she was a kidnap victim. Someone – Michelle Chartier for one – needed to be held to account for it. But such thoughts were for later, when he'd got Tory safely away. Right now he needed to-

Within the room, another change was taking place. The 'auction,' if that was what it was, had ended. Guests were leaving their seats, mingling, smiling. Some were making their way over to congratulate a distinguished-looking late-middle-aged couple. The man was of average height but barrel-chested, sporting a thick mane of silver hair. His oriental-looking wife or girlfriend was full-figured, with dark hair piled on top of her head in an elaborate style. Well-preserved for their age, their tanned complexions hinted at healthy, sunny lifestyles. Scott switched his attention back to Tory, just in time to see her being led from the room by her escorts. He waited only a moment, checking to make sure everyone else was staying put, before making his way, swiftly, around to the back of the house. His ankle throbbed but desperation drove him to ignore it. He'd seen no open windows on his way round but he was betting the back door would be unlocked. He was right, and the kitchen was still unoccupied. Slipping inside, he closed the door quietly and made his way through to the hallway. He just caught a glimpse of the girl escorting Tory as they reached the top of the stairs and turned right towards the bedroom he and Tory had shared. Hesitating only to make sure the lounge door was staying closed, Scott limped across the hall, and up the stairs, taking them two at a time, despite the pain. He reached the landing and peered round the corner to the corridor where their bedroom was in time to see his fiancée being led inside. The door closed.

Breathing hard and heart pounding, Scott weighed

his options. From what he'd seen of them, he was confident he could handle the young couple if he needed to. They didn't look the sort who would resist if he walked in and took Tory from them. But they would certainly raise the alarm, in which case the chances of getting Tory out of the house undetected would be zero. There was still no sign of movement from downstairs. There could still be time.

He approached the bedroom door, grateful for the strip of carpet that ran the length of the wooden floor. Putting an ear to the door, he listened. Low, measured tones - not Tory's voice – and the sounds of drawers being opened and closed spoke of some activity within. Hearing metallic chinks and clicks, he remembered her collar-chain. But there was nothing to suggest any violence or aggression was being used against her. He remained there listening, his other ear cocked for signs of any approach from downstairs. After several minutes the murmurings within sounded closer. Someone was coming out.

Springing to the other end of the corridor, he secreted himself as best he could in the recessed doorway to one of the other bedrooms.

The door opened and the young couple came out. The man shut the door firmly behind him, but didn't appear to lock it. Together, they made their way back along the corridor the way they had come. As soon as they turned the corner out of sight, Scott ran back to the door. Trying the handle he found the door unlocked. *Thank God*. He went in.

The room was dimly lit. The only light was from a shaded lamp the far side of the bed. His gaze went straight to Tory. Lying under a silken coverlet, she looked to be asleep. He went to her side.

'Tory. It's Scott. Wake up.' Getting no response, he touched her shoulder, shook her, gently. 'Tory. Wake up.'

She turned her head on the pillow. 'S'awrigh...' she murmured. 'I'm just having... a...' She went under again.

He shook her again, harder. 'Come on baby, we've got to get out of here.'

This time she roused a little, but seemed to have difficulty moving. 'Scott? S'at you?' Something chinked beneath the covers.

Scott started. 'What the fuck-?' He stood up. Gripping the edge of the bed cover, he swept it back. 'Ahh, Christ.'

Clad only in her underwear, still wearing a garter belt, stockings and heels, Tory was secured to the bed's corners by slim chains attached to leather cuffs around her wrists and ankles. The thought of the black couple, preparing her, sent a chill through him. Any lingering doubt about the exact nature of the 'auction' he'd just witnessed disappeared completely. Panic gripped him. He needed to get her away from here, fast.

He bent to the nearest wrist cuff. 'Wake up Tory, we're going.' He stopped. The buckle was secured by a tiny padlock. The other was the same, so too the cuffs round her ankles. 'Shit.'

Tory stirred again, tried lifting her head. 'Scott? Wha- What's going on?'

He pulled hard at the chain. Thin but strong, it held fast. 'Don't worry Tory. I'm going to get you out of here.' He needed tools. Turning, he looked around to see what he might use. His eyes went to the dresser. What he saw there stopped him dead. Lined up on top and on a table next to it, was an array of sex toys and paraphernalia that would do justice to an adult store catalogue. Vibrators and dildos of all shapes, styles and sizes lay amongst a host of other equipment. Some of it he recognised or could guess at. Handcuffs, gags, straps, paddles, tawses. Other items – rubber tubes, metal clamps, devices of polished silver he'd never seen before, and didn't like to imagine their purpose.

'Oh my God.'

Averting his gaze and trying not to think of what would have happened had he not come back when he did, he began rifling through drawers, searching for something he might used to remove the cuffs or the tiny locks. There was only bed linen and items from Tory's travelling wardrobe.

He was still searching when the door opened.

Michelle Chartier stood there.

CHAPTER 38

It is late, yet still he waits, watching from his vantage point, conspicuous yet invisible, as always. He knows she will come soon. Several times during his vigil he has seen her pass across the tall windows, talking to her colleagues, on the telephone, perusing documents while drinking from a cardboard cup. During that time the building's lights have switched off, room by room, floor by floor. Now only one remains lit. Where she works.

Earlier, the English detective had left alone, disappearing into the evening gloom, head down, a look of concern in his strong features that was not there the day before. He wondered briefly, where he was staying, but didn't dwell on it. It is of no matter, not yet. Tonight his focus is her. And unlike the previous evening, there are no intruding commitments that will prevent him following where she may lead.

The air is chillier than of late. For the first time he can see his breath, a sign that autumn draws near and beyond that winter, with its dark nights, closed shutters and drawn curtains. It makes him wonder if, when it comes, he should step up his work rate. Perhaps, in light of recent events, he ought to take full advantage of the seasonal changes that add thickening layers to the cloak of anonymity his missions require.

His most recent completed mission was the first for some while, and he had almost forgotten its effect, its heady potency. Even now, days later, traces linger still of the buzz that comes with completing the act. A by-product of the work itself, he imagines it an example of his master's beneficence. A small reward for his willingness to undertake what most would consider hard and distasteful work. A lesser individual could find it reason enough to work harder. Not him. His reasons are pure, driven by higher needs than the mere physical. Nevertheless, and not for the first time he thinks of how the recent changes to his situation may work to his advantage. More opportunities to meet those in need of his particular services. Those such as the woman for whom he now waits.

He knew as soon he saw her she was one of, *them*. By now he can tell just by the way they look at him. The way they carry themselves. No longer does he have to wait for them to confirm it. It is already there, written in their faces. Corruption and Damnation. Which is why they must be stopped before they visit ruination on those who deserve it least. The innocent. Those such as him.

At that moment the lights across the square blink once then black out. She is coming. Thrusting his gloved hands deeper into the coat's pockets, he steps back into the dark beneath the archway. He must be careful in case she heads his way as she leaves, able to secrete himself elsewhere if the need arises. A few moments later, the door at the top of the steps opens, and she comes out.

She pauses to button up her coat before descending,

heels clicking on the stone, treading carefully in the dark lest she slips. There is, he thinks, a sensuousness in the way she moves. He has seen it before in such as her. A feline grace that goes with the composed elegance. But he also knows that, together, they are merely the lures she uses to attract those foolish enough to take the bait.

At the bottom of the steps she turns left, away from where he waits. It means that he can slip from his hiding place and follow without fear of discovery. It is unlikely that she will look back. There is no reason for her to think she is in any danger. After all, she is more used to hunting, than being hunted.

As he follows her across the sweep of square that lies at the foot of the great cathedral's two towers and towards the bridge that will take her south across the river, he smiles to himself. She will know soon enough how quickly the roles can be reversed.

CHAPTER 39

Michelle Chartier stared in mute shock at the young man who appeared about to ruin her plans. Beside her, the middle-aged couple looked simply bemused. When they first entered the room behind their host, they were all smiles, looking forward no doubt to their night of pleasure. When they saw Scott vault across the bed to place himself between Michelle and the young woman they'd paid for, the smiles vanished, replaced by bewildered concern. The man recovered first.

Throwing a question at Michelle that Scott could not understand, he gestured, animatedly, at the interloper who seemed out to spoil their night of fun.

For several moments, Michelle Chartier stood, mouth open and rooted to the spot, staring at the young couple she'd taken in. As the man continued to babble, her hand came up sharply, cutting him off. He stopped babbling. She took a deep breath then, as if someone had thrown a switch, recovered herself. A smile came into her face.

'Why, Scott,' she cooed. 'I didn't realise you were returning so soon. How nice to see you again.' She turned to the older couple, making ready to say something. Scott could almost hear the cogs whirring.

Amazing.

He got in first, squared himself. 'Whatever it is you were planning here tonight Michelle, it's over. So you better make sure they-' he jabbed a finger at the couple, 'understand.'

The man rocked back. 'Est-il l'Anglais?' He babbled at Michelle again.

She turned on him, red fury in her face. 'SILENCE!'

The man shrank back, so too his wife. The looks on their faces registered their realisation that whatever was happening, it was not something Michelle had anticipated. Nor did it look like it might be resolved easily. But when Michelle turned back to Scott her face was composed again.

'My dear Scott, I think you may be confused about what is happening. Come with me and I will explain.' She offered him her hand, as if she expected he would take it.

He was in no mood for explanations, true or otherwise.

'Fuck off, Michelle. I'm not playing your games. I want you to release Tory, right now. Then I'm taking her out of here. And you can tell all those people downstairs there'll be no more auctions tonight so they may as well fuck off as well. I'm telling you now, you haven't heard the last of this.'

His hope was that a display of anger, together with an intimation of possible consequences, would be enough to convince Michelle that her only hope lay in appeasement, starting with releasing Tory. The first sign the tactic may not have worked as intended came when, instead of rushing to comply, Michelle let a fleeting smile play around her lips. Calmly, she turned to the other couple and whispered something in the man's ear. Already eager to leave, the man nodded once, threw a wary glance at Scott, a last, lustful one at Tory, then left the room. His wife scuttled after.

Scott's sense of unease deepened as Michelle closed the door behind them and leaned back against it. The signal could not have been clearer. Scott felt the first flutter of panic in his stomach.

'Move away from the door, Michelle. You can't keep us here.' To his dismay, her response was a throaty chuckle.

In that moment the fear that had been growing finally rooted itself within Scott Weston. He had hoped that harsh words and the threat of retribution would be enough to convince her that her warped enterprise was over. That she had no choice but to let them go. But her cool manner and the way she seemed to be deriving amusement from a situation that only moments before had rendered her speechless, left Scott wondering what he was missing. He weighed his options.

On the bed Tory looked to have slipped back into whatever had her in its grip when he first came in. There was no way he was going to get her out if Michelle and her friends sought to stop him. He thought about the window, but he was on the first floor and he was already carrying one damaged ankle. His only way out was through the door that Michelle was now barring. He drew himself up to his full height.

'Get out of my way Michelle. I'm leaving.'

'Without your lovely, Tory? Oh Scott, you disappoint me. Surely you are not going to leave her here, alone, with all these... admirers.'

Scott forced himself to stay calm. 'Don't you worry.

I'll be back very soon. And I won't be alone.'

'Oh dear. In that case I suppose I have no option but to let you go.'

To Scott's surprise she stepped away from the door.

Unsure whether it was some trick, he hesitated only a second before deciding he had to take the chance while it was there. Taking a last glance at Tory he bent to her. 'Don't worry sweetheart, I'm coming right back for you.' Then he headed for the door.

As he passed Michelle, her hand shot out to grab his wrist. The strength in her grip surprised him. He spun round. Two dark pools bore into his.

'Are you sure you don't want to stay? You never know, you may find what happens during my little gatherings more to your taste than you imagine.' Her gaze slipped back to Tory before returning to him.

He screwed his face in distaste. 'You twisted, bitch. Touch her while I'm gone, and I swear, I'll-'

Her eyes flashed. 'Yes? You'll what?'

'I'll... I'll kill you. That's what.'

She made a mock-scared face. 'In that case I'd better do as you say.' She let go his wrist.

Opening the door Scott stepped out into the corridor and turned towards the stairs.

Something hard and heavy struck at the base of his skull. A sickening feeling rose in the pit of his stomach and his world began to spin. His knees buckled and as the floor runner rose to meet him he managed a single word, 'Tory...' before the blackness took him and he saw no more.

CHAPTER 40

Ingrid opened her eyes. The bright red figures on the clock read two-thirty-two. She remained still, listening for whatever had woken her to come again, but the only sounds were the ones drifting in through her window. Montparnasse at night.

A draught across her shoulder set her heart thumping. Her back was to the door. She always slept with it shut. She waited as long as it took to mentally rehearse what she was about to do. Then she moved, fast. In one fluid movement she slipped out from under the duvet, yanked open the bedside drawer, pulled the Glock 9 pistol from its holster and came up and around in a two-handed grip, facing the door.

There was no one there.

She scanned the rest of the room. Likewise.

On tiptoe she ran to the door, peered round into the hall. Empty. She went back to the window. Parting the curtains with the gun's barrel she looked right to where the balcony, crowded with her pot-plants, fronted the living room. The lace voiles were billowing out through the glass doors, caught on the night breeze. She clamped a hand over her mouth, stifling a gasp. She'd checked the doors were locked before retiring.

Her mobile lay next to the bed. Grabbing it, she dialled 112. In as low a voice as possible she said, 'Police.' When the operator answered she didn't wait to be asked but identified herself as an off-duty *policier*. 'There is an intruder in my apartment. I need backup, now.' She gave her address and telephone number and before ringing off told the operator to make sure whoever was coming knew she was armed. Dropping the phone on the bed she went back to the door.

Widening the gap a few inches, she slipped out and stood with her back to the wall, listening. Nothing. The door to the bathroom was almost opposite. She began there.

Pushing the door open, she hit the light switch, leaned in, swept the room and backed out again quickly, ready in case someone chose that moment to charge her. She did the same in the other bedroom, the kitchen, and the small utility area next to it before reaching the living room. She leaned against the wall and breathed deep, readying herself. By leaving it to last she'd given any intruder plenty of time to depart the way they'd come. Police or not, her first priority was self-preservation. She would worry about catching the bastard later.

'I have a gun. I'm coming in. If you are there and you move, I will shoot you. Speak now and I won't.'

She counted to five then threw herself forward, at the same time dropping and rolling before coming up on one knee, gun pointing and ready. Another sweep. Nothing. The only movement was from the voiles, still billowing. In the distance, the sound of sirens growing louder echoed through the open glass doors.

She let out a long, 'Phhhew.'

She went out onto the balcony. One of her pots was

on its side where the visitor had knocked it over on his, or her, way out - the noise that had woken her. She checked the doors. The metal frame was buckled where the lock had been forced. The first time she'd suffered a break–in, she made a mental note to find a better glazing company than the cowboys who'd installed it to carry out the repair. She checked the balcony each side, above and below. It was clear. The apartment was on the third floor. The balconies were in line above each other with ladder-fire escapes hanging off the ends. Scaling them wouldn't be a problem for any reasonably fit person. They'd complained to the landlord many times over the years about the risks. His response was always a shrug accompanied by, 'What can I do? Fire regulations.'

Returning inside, she checked around. As far as she could tell, nothing seemed disturbed. No. Something was registering in her subconscious. It took her a few moments to place it. On a table next to the sofa was the oriental table lamp she'd picked up for a song at Le Marché d'Aligré, the renowned bric-a-brac market near the Bastille. As she stared at the empty space beneath it, her skin crawled.

It wasn't a particularly precious photograph. Just her, her parents and her brother. Taken on holiday years before when she and Anton were teenagers. But it was one of their last 'happy family' pictures before Anton left for university and she and her parents fell out over her decision to drop her medical studies in favour of the police. She squirmed at the thought of the intruder choosing it as their one souvenir of their visit.

The sounds of cars screeching to a halt below jerked her back. She went back out onto the balcony. In the street below officers were running for the entrance, looking up. She waved to them. 'It's okay. He's gone.' They waved back, but kept running.

Taking one last look out over the sleeping city she muttered, 'Who are you? Where are you?' Then she went to let her colleagues in and brew the coffee they would expect her to provide before they left.

CHAPTER 41

Next day, the official line from the Director's office was that the matter that had given rise to the 'Sleeve' activation at Les Galeries was so sensitive that details could not yet be shared with the store's owners. Remy duly communicated this decision to them in a phone call. As he replaced the receiver he said to Carver. 'If they believe that, then I am the great-grandson of Napoleon.' They all knew that the Directors of the Paris Police Force were buying time while they consulted the lawyers to find out where they stood before saying more.

Concern over Ingrid's night visitor added to the tension. After going over it with her several times, the conclusion was they had no way of knowing whether it was some random but bold intruder, or if she'd been targeted because of who she was, or something she was involved in. Carver hoped it was the former, though his gut told him otherwise. Dark memories stirred. *God forbid, not again.*

Remy made phone calls to get her apartment more fully alarmed. Beyond that, they all accepted there was nothing else they could do. Even Ingrid agreed. Their attention returned to the investigation, all the time waiting to see what the day would bring.

As the morning passed, it became clear that the directors' apparently measured response to the incident of the day before masked feverish activity. It was all aimed at casting Carver, and his UK masters, as the villains of the piece. Carver had rung The Duke as soon as he could after returning to the préfecture the previous day.

'Just letting you know to be ready, John.' He began. 'There's a shit-storm brewing.'

It was not long before he received the first of what would become a stream of calls alerting him to what was happening at his Force Headquarters. Predictably, it was from the always-in-the-know, Dave Shaw.

'I hope your ears are burning because they damn well ought to be. What the fuck's happened? Did you shoot the French president or just shag his wife?'

'You need to speak to The Duke, Dave. He'll want to know because he's the one they'll call first.'

'They already have. He's on his way here now. And there's a reception committee gathering. My source in personnel tells me they've asked for your file.'

After that the calls came steadily. Jess was next.

'Word is the Chief's blazing. His secretary says that when she took in coffee, she heard Mick Cooper saying they needed to remember, "-what this Crane woman did to him." A former Detective Superintendent who had risen to Assistant Chief Constable, Cooper was a long-time friend to the CID. Most regarded him as the most even-minded of the force's Chief Officers. Carver was grateful for Jess's report. Never had he needed allies more.

Clive Moody, the public-school educated head of

Special Branch rang towards lunchtime. He was furtive as ever. 'I'm being asked to find something that might connect this Crane woman with Terrorism, and Paris. I assume it's something to do with you. Would you mind filling me in on what the hell's happening?' Carver did, as best as he could.

After lunch, Shaw rang again. 'The Chiefs' meeting's broken up. The Deputy's handling it. He's talking to someone in Paris as we speak.' Carver noted the Deputy Chief Constable's involvement. Next to the Chief, he was the force's highest disciplinary authority. Major cock-ups invariably landed on his desk.

'How's The Duke? Have you seen him?'

'I'm told he came out looking like he'd gone ten rounds. He's gone to ground and right now no one's sure where he is.'

Probably consulting with his good friend, Mr Macallan.

It was mid-afternoon when The Duke rang again.

'Give it me straight,' Carver told him, knowing he would anyway.

'Not good,' The Duke said, blunt as ever. 'Apparently the Foreign Office has got involved.'

Shit.

'I'm due back in with the ACC at four to brief some Secretary of State who wants the full story. Chapter and verse.'

'Where's it going?'

'Cooper's on our side but he's up against the Chief and the Dep. If it turns political, which is where it's heading, they'll be wanting their pound of flesh.'

'Thanks anyway John. Given the stroke I pulled I can't really blame them. I just hope they put it all on me and not Remy.'

'Bugger that. If you'd caught her, everyone would be congratulating you on a brilliant piece of initiative and counting the lives you'd saved. I'm not done yet, and neither is the ACC.' Before ringing off, Carver made out he shared his optimism and thanked him for his support. Inside, he felt hollow.

Further calls came from Shaw and Jess but they added little. By then the HQ shutters had come down and everyone was simply waiting for the final decision. It came late in the afternoon.

The Duke was the bearer of the news Carver expected. After briefly describing the shouting match he'd been part of before making the call, he gave his former deputy the bottom line. 'They want you back. As in yesterday.'

'Okay.' Having spent another sleepless night working it all out, Carver thought he could best protect The Duke from the next storm he would set off by sharing as few of his thoughts as possible.

'I told them that when you get here, they speak to you only in my presence. I've nominated myself as your friend.'

'So they're taking it to discipline?'

'No one's said as much yet, but I'm taking nothing for granted.'

'Thanks, John. I know you've backed me as best you can. I'm grateful.'

'When will you be back? There're daily flights to Manchester aren't there?'

'I'll let you know soon as I know.'

There was a pause. 'You're taking this too calmly. I hope you're not thinking what I think you're thinking.'

'I'll see you when I see you, John.'

'Jamie, you're in enough shit already. Don't be doing anything stupid.'

'I'll speak to you soon, John.'

'JAMIE-.'

Carver disconnected. Switching off his mobile he put it away inside his jacket before turning from the window he'd been facing as they'd talked.

Three pairs of eyes waited. Remy, Ingrid and Carissa had witnessed the call, his side of it at least. One way or another, they all stood to be affected by its outcome. *Some more than others.*

Remy broke the silence. 'What did he say?'

'I'm recalled on the next flight back. My best guess is my bosses have done a deal with yours and I'm the trade-off.'

Disappointment showed in their faces, especially Carissa. Her investment in what they'd worked on so long was as great as Carver's, more in some respects. *Depends how close she was to her sister.*

'I am sorry, Jamie,' Remy said. 'I know how much this all means to you. How hard you've worked at it.'

Carver nodded.

Only Ingrid stayed silent, staring at him, waiting. The night before they'd been the last to leave Les Deux Chats. As they finished their drinks, talk had turned to what Carver would do if the worst happened. Carver had given little away. But she was as good at reading people as she was crime scenes. So far, she had shown no surprise over anything that had happened.

'Is there anything we can do?' Remy continued. 'Any appeals we can make to anyone?'

'Thanks Remy, but no. No need for that.'

'But surely your Chief will listen if someone from here speaks on your behalf. They must know what you've been through? Why you did what you did?'

'Oh they know alright. And as for listening, well you've never met my Chief. He's got his eye on a HMI's job.' Seeing Remy's puzzled look he explained. 'A Home Office position. A bit like your Ministry of Justice. Where ambitious Chiefs like to end up.'

Carissa spoke up, her voice trembling with emotion. 'Do not worry, Jamie. One way or another, I plan to continue with what we started. I will not rest until this demon is either returned to prison or dead. I promise, I will keep you informed every step of the way.'

Carver shook his head. 'Like I said, no need for that, Carissa.'

'But I want to Jamie. I know how much this means to you.'

'No, I mean there is no need to keep me informed. I can see for myself.'

Her brow furrowed. 'What do you mean? How can you see if you are back in England?'

'I won't be back in England. I'll be right here. With you.'

'*What?*'

Finally, realisation dawned in Remy's face. During his conversation with The Duke, Carver's responses had been matter of fact, controlled. Like he'd already decided what would happen and was resigned to it. Ingrid's face was still blank.

'Jamie?' Remy said, disbelief in his voice. 'Surely you are not thinking-.'

'I'm not going anywhere, Remy. I've invested too much to give up now. If I hadn't seen her I may have thought otherwise. But the way she looked at me, the way she showed me the girl. There is too much riding on it. If I don't carry on and that girl, whoever she is, ends up dead, I won't be able to live with myself. Whatever they do when I return home is up to them. But I'm due some leave. I'm taking it. As of now.'

Carissa's face lit up. 'You mean-'

'I mean I'm carrying on as before, if you are still with me?' Carissa nodded, eagerly. 'But we need to be getting on with it. Start making things happen instead of waiting. I can't see them trying to send someone after me. Even if they do I haven't committed a crime, so there's nothing they can do.'

Remy's expression was grave. 'This could be dangerous, Jamie. People here will not like it. If I am seen to still be working with you, they will remove me as well.'

'I know that Remy, and I don't expect you, or Ingrid, to do anything that might expose yourselves. From now on I must have nothing further to do with your investigation. Carissa and I will carry on on our own. We've started a ball rolling. Let's see where it ends up.'

'No,' Remy said. 'You cannot.'

Carver made ready to dig his heels in. 'I'm sorry, Remy. You're a good friend, but what I choose to do in my own time is my affair. I promise I'll make clear you tried to talk me into going home.'

'You misunderstand. I am not arguing with you. What I mean is, you cannot do it on your own. When the time comes you will need help. Most of all, you still need Ingrid.' He turned to where she was following the conversation keenly, face as expressionless as it had been throughout. Something passed between her and

Remy that was invisible to Carver. She nodded.

'What are you saying, Remy?'

'I am saying that if you wish to continue, then I, we, will still help you. Officially you are no longer here. As far as we know, you went back home. But we will have to be careful. Very careful.'

'You don't need to do this, Remy. Or Ingrid. We can-' He stopped as Ingrid's hand came up.

'Enough. It is decided. Without you we would not have picked up on the victim's secrets, or Madeleine. This is more progress than in the past two years. For all our sakes, mine and Remy's, and yours and Carissa's, we must continue to work together. But as Remy says, from now on you must be like a ghost. Invisible.'

As Carver digested her words, he looked from one to the other. Resignation was there in each of the faces. In Carissa's case it was mixed with hope. His slow nod sealed their pact.

'In that case, let's get to it.' He turned to Remy. 'I've been thinking about how we get round the problem of monitoring Madeleine without permission from Father Masson.'

'And?'

Carver's expression had never been more serious. 'If we continue as we have been, then you and Ingrid will be breaking many rules, yes?'

'Oh, yes.'

'We have an expression in England. "In for a penny, in for a pound".'

'I have heard it. What, exactly, are you thinking?'

CHAPTER 42

Scott Weston tried to open his eyes, but couldn't. Groggy, head spinning and feeling horribly sick in his stomach, it took him a few moments to work out why. Something was tied, tightly, around his eyes. A knot pressed, painfully, against the back of his head. He tried to move, but could not. His wrists and ankles were tied to the arms and legs of the chair on which he was sitting. As he tested his bonds, he felt the burn of rough rope against his flesh. He tried to say, 'Where am I?' but it came out as, 'Waaahhgg?' Only then did he realise. A bitter tasting cloth of some kind was stuffed in his mouth, secured by whatever was wrapped around his head. Feeling a vomit coming, he fought to stop his gut spasming. He could choke to death.

Disoriented, confused, it took a minute before his head cleared enough for him to remember. When he did, an image of Tory came to him, chained to the bed. Anger gripped him, bringing him back to full consciousness. Straining against the ropes binding him to the chair, he screamed through the gag.

'Nnngghhh.'

The ropes held. He was going nowhere.

The effort brought on the nauseous feeling again. He

felt dizzy. He collapsed back in the chair, fighting against it. He concentrated on his breathing, keeping it slow and steady, as deep as the gag would allow.

When her voice sounded, it was accompanied by an echo of the sort a basement cellar might produce.

'Ahh, so you're awake at last. Thank goodness. I was beginning to worry that you weren't going to come round. That idiot, Franc, hit you harder than he was supposed to. How are you feeling?'

'Ungghh.'

'I take it that means not very well. Never mind. It won't be very long.'

The ambiguity in her words chilled him. *What won't be very long? What's going to happen*?

She said something he couldn't make out, but got the impression her words were directed at someone other than him. Footsteps sounded. Heavy. A man's tread. A door banged, the echo reverberating. Where *was* he? He waited. He could do nothing else.

Heels click-clacked on stone, authoritative, determined, growing louder. They stopped next to him. A familiar, musky-sweet smell was in the air. The perfume she'd worn that day outside the Café Rive Gauche. He felt warm breath on his right cheek. *What was she doing?* A drawn-out sigh sounded in his ear. It seemed tinged with regret. Like her words, it chilled him, hinting at something ominous. And as he sat there, waiting for her to do something, wondering what it all meant, worrying about Tory, Scott Weston felt something creep into his bones he had never experienced in all his twenty-five years. Stark terror. He began to shiver, but not from the cold. Time hung motionless.

Eventually there was a loud click and the squeak of hinges. The door opening. Muted voices began to echo. People entering. The sounds of chairs scraping against the hard floor. An audience gathering. *For what?* He heard her intake of breath as she rose from his side. She had been there all this time, watching him.

More heel clicks, then, 'Hello everyone. Make yourselves comfortable. As you can see, he's back with us again.'

Click-clack, click-clack. Coming back again.

'The light please, Franc. Thank you.'

Fingers pulled at the knot behind his head. Suddenly the tightness around his eyes was gone. He opened them. A spotlight stabbed like knives into his face, blinding him, forcing them shut again. He waited for the pain to ease. He tried again, more slowly his time, blinking into the light, once, twice, three times.

A movement in front of him, then she was there, silhouetted against the spotlight. The way she kept shifting her position, moving in and out of the light, it was as if she was weighing him, from different angles. *What for?* He feared finding out.

'Now then,' she said, as if talking to herself. 'Let me see... Franc, help me.'

A man came from behind her. They both approached. Following her instructions, he helped her man-handle the chair, moving it a few feet to the right. She stood back again. 'That's better.'

Why is it better? What difference does it make?

Eyes finally adjusting to the light, Scott saw that she seemed to be gauging something. Her gaze kept flicking to something above him. He looked up. A rope noose dangled above him, its anchor point cloaked in darkness. His eyes widened in terror. He looked from it to her then back again. She was looking right at him, smiling. He felt a looseness in his bowel.

Off to her left, just beyond the light's reach, dark shapes shifted, coming forward, watching, waiting... *for what*? He prayed his suspicions were wrong. They had to be wrong. This could not be happening. Not to him, Scott Weston, the all-American boy from Boston whose college tutors all agreed that he had a bright, no, a *very* bright, future at the Bar. He thought of Tory. His bladder failed.

'Oh Scott.'

His eyes snapped to her. She was shaking her head, regretfully. 'Tch. Look what you've done. Now do not spoil things. You look so nice sat there like that. And some of my friends have come quite some way to be here. Please do not let me down.'

He stared at her, eyes wider then ever. His heart was beating so fast he couldn't even try to say anything.

What's happening? Tory, where are you? What has she done to you?

She came forward, stopped in front of him. Reaching out she tucked him under the chin, forcing his head back. He stared into the face that, only days before, he had found so seductive. In keeping with whatever role she was now playing, her expression was one of regret.

'Such a lovely boy,' she said. 'So bee-ootiful.'

Turning, she addressed the audience, softly, in their native language. 'Trés, trés beau, n'est-ce pas?' There were murmurings of agreement. Someone even clapped. She turned back to him, still tipping his head back. 'Such a shame.' Bending to him, she brought her face close to his. She waited, staring deep into his eyes, as if looking for something. *What?* All she would see there was fear. Then he realised, that was what she was hoping to see. Without warning she leaned forward and kissed him, or at least she closed her mouth over the cloth covering his, cupping the back of his head and pulling him towards her. His eyes stayed wide as hers closed. She stayed like that for several seconds. Just as suddenly she let go. Giving him one last smile – no sign of regret now – she stood up. She reached up and his gaze followed as she took hold of the noose above him and pulled. There was enough slack that she could gather it in both hands. Bringing it level with his face, she showed it to him.

'Now then Scott. What do you imagine this is for?'

He stared back at her, shaking his head. He was having difficulty thinking straight.

'You don't know? Silly boy, of course you do.'

He shook his head again, groaned into the gag. His eyes pleaded with her. *No, Michelle. Don't. Please. You can't. You mustn't.*

'There, you see? You *do* know.'

She slipped the noose over his head. He felt its weight, loose, on his shoulders. His breath started to come in pants and grunts. He groaned, louder, into the gag. She nodded to someone behind. He felt the noose stir. As it drew tight, he felt its roughness against his neck. She nodded again and it stopped tightening. She looked down at him, her face suddenly serious.

'You spoilt my party last night, Scott. I suppose this will go some way to make up for it.'

He shook his head, gurgling like a baby. *No Michelle. Please God, no.*

Then, taking one last look at him, she spun on her

heel and turned away as if to join the rest of the audience. At the same time she lifted her arm and flicked her hand out to the man behind.

'ALLEZ.'

With a jerk, he felt the rope tighten around his neck, pulling him up, cutting off his air, the chair to which he was attached rising with him. As his feet lost contact with the floor, Scott Weston screamed into his gag as loud and as long as he could.

CHAPTER 43

From his seat in front of the Café Madeleine, Carver stared across the road at the stocky figure in the crumpled brown suit scurrying, head down, along the pavement. The man's haste and apparent preoccupation caused Carver to wonder if Marcel Brossard even remembered which cafe they had agreed for their rendezvous. Carver put down his coffee and was about to call out when Brossard suddenly stopped. Looking up, he turned his gaze to where Carver was holding up a hand. Finally recognising the man he had met for the first time only the day before, he returned Carver's wave - and stepped right off the pavement.

Carver leaped out of his seat to yell a warning when Brossard saw the approaching city-bus just in time and hopped back onto the kerb. Carver heaved a sigh of relief. *Jesus.* If their new recruit got himself run over now, the trouble they had already stored up for themselves would be as nothing to what would follow.

Seconds later, having managed to survive the traffic rolling east along Boulevard Haussmann, Brossard plopped himself down in the chair opposite. Breathing heavily, he dug out his tobacco tin and proceeded to roll himself a cigarette. As Carver listened to the wheezes and grunts emanating from the bedraggled figure, he wondered again about the nature of the medical condition he was suffering. Their meeting of the day before had been Remy's first contact with him for over a year, he later admitted.

After a couple of deep, restorative drags, as if embarrassed by his display of ineptitude, Brossard ran a hand through the thinning grey hair. 'This is why I hate Paris. Too much traffic.'

'Remy told me you've lived here all your life.'

He nodded. 'Born here.'

'If you hate it so much why don't you move? There's a lot less traffic in the country.'

The man looked at Carver as if he were a moron, before giving a gallic shrug. 'You think there is demand in the country for my sort of work, heh? Perhaps the farmers will pay me to listen to their animals, shagging each other through the night, n'est-ce-pas?'

Carver gave a wan smile. *Point taken.* Nevertheless, he added the man's lack of affection for the city of his birth to the list of contradictions he'd begun compiling almost from the moment they first met. Remy had described Brossard as the finest, *'oreille électronique'* - electronic ear – in all of Paris. Whether true or not, Carver's impression so far was of someone barely able to look after himself, never mind be relied on to set up a listening operation so sensitive it could, if discovered, see them all in prison.

When Carver first suggested bugging the confessional, the morning his 'recall' was confirmed. Remy's conspiratorial smile vanished. His immediate response was to dismiss the idea as being, 'Out of the question.' Not only would a Magistrate never contemplate authorising such a step, no one in the church would either. As in the UK, the consent of the 'property owner' in such a case is essential. But when Carver went on to make clear that he was not talking about an official operation, subject to all the necessary prerequisites and permissions, but something unofficial, 'below the radar' and using whatever 'private resources' Remy could muster, the French detective's face took on a grave expression. When Carver pointed out that it was the only practical way by which they might hope to identify any potential victim, Remy signalled him to silence. After making a couple of calls to put other things on hold, they retired to Les Deux Chats. There, over cognac and whiskey, they resumed their conversation.

'This is a dangerous step you suggest, Jamie. Apart from losing our jobs we could both end up in prison.'

'If you have a better suggestion, I'd be glad to hear it.'

Remy stared at him, slung back his drink, ordered another. Carver had never seen him so hesitant.

'I... know a man. He sometimes takes... private commissions.'

'You've used him before?'

Remy gave a measured nod. 'He used to do occasional work for the DGSI, our Security Service. Unofficially, of course.'

'Of course.' Carver waited. He knew someone in Manchester with similar skills who had done work for the British Security Services in the past. 'Would money be a problem?'

Remy gave a dismissive wave. 'He owes me a favour. And he likes Cognac.'

Carver looked wary. A liking for Cognac was not the sort of qualification he would look for in the sort of technician they would need.

The silence stretched. Carver said nothing, letting Remy get used to the idea. They were moving into uncharted territory. Not long after they first met, he and Remy had discovered they had several things in common. One was a belief that when it came to catching killers, rules should be followed as far as practicable. And where it wasn't practicable, they both agreed. The police's most basic function is to protect life.

After a minute's contemplation Remy straightened in his chair. 'I will make some calls. See if he's around.' He lifted his glass. Carver did the same.

'Salut,' they said together.

Now, sensing Marcel Brossard's nervousness, Carver thought a coffee might help calm him down. He was about to hail a waiter when Brossard leaned forward and clamped a hand on his arm. His mood was suddenly serious.

'What game are you and Remy playing? Do you take me for an idiot?'

Carver sat back, blinking. 'What are you talking about? What makes you think we take you for an idiot?' He didn't mention that in other circumstances and without Remy's reassurances, the accusation may have held up.

Instead of answering, Brossard dug in his pocket and placed a device resembling a mobile phone on the table. Carver leaned forward. Above a row of buttons was a screen display. It showed some sort of recurring wave-type signal.

'What is it?'

'A sweeper.'

'Right. What does it do?'

'I use it whenever I place a new installation. It detects anything that may interfere with the signal.'

'So what's the problem?'

'The problem, Monsieur, is that Remy did not tell me everything he should have told me when he asked me to do this thing.'

Carver glanced at the device, then back at Brossard, none the wiser.

'I'm sorry Marcel, I'm not with you. What do you think we haven't told you?'

'Neither of you mentioned having already tried this with someone else.'

'What do you mean, 'already tried'? Already tried what?'

'To place a listening device in the confessional. As I have just done.'

Thinking either he had misheard, or Brossard was mixing his English, Carver dug deeper. 'Let me get this straight. You are saying someone else has tried to place a device before today?'

'Not just tried. Succeeded'

'What the hell gives you that idea?'

'This.' He poked a stubby finger at the device.

Carver eyed it, warily. 'What is it saying?'

'It is saying that there is already a bug transmitting a signal from within the confessional.'

'WHAT?'

Brossard eyed him suspiciously.

'You know nothing about another transmitter?'

'Absolutely not. Where is it? Have you got it?'

He shook his head. 'I was only able to place my device under and behind the table ledge. I had no opportunity to look for another as I had to think about confessing my sins. But I activated the sweeper in my pocket while I was in there and checked the reading when I came out. It shows another signal, operating on a different wave-length.' Carver stared at him. After a few moments, Brossard said. 'If it is not yours, then whose is it? What does it mean?'

It was some seconds before Carver responded. As he took out his phone and brought up Remy's number he turned to the man who looked nothing like any surveillance expert Carver had ever met.

'It means we know how the killer is identifying his victims'

Carver and Brossard waited as Remy listened, cupping a hand round his ear to shield it from passing traffic. Every now and then he glanced at them, then went back to listening. Eventually he removed the earpiece and passed it back to Brossard, shaking his head.

'What can you hear?' Carver said.

'A son confessing that he lied to his mother. He told her he could not visit last month because he was ill.' He threw Carver a wry smile before explaining. 'France were playing Australia at Stade De France.' Carver nodded. Rugby was another of Remy's passions.

Remy turned to Brossard. 'You are sure this is not coming from your device?' Brossard said nothing but returned him a pointed stare. Remy shrugged. 'I am sorry, my friend. It is just, so unlikely.'

'Unlikely or not,' Carver said. 'It's there, and it's working.'

Remy nodded, 'But to who and where is it transmitting?'

They turned to Brossard. He showed his palms. 'It is impossible to say where the signal is being picked up. But it is not very strong, so it would have to be within a radius of no more than five hundred metres.'

Carver looked around. In the centre of Paris, five hundred metres covered more ground than they could ever hope to check in the time available, even if they were acting officially. The three exchanged glances. Eventually Carver said. 'It shouldn't matter. So long as we pay close attention and be ready to move the moment we identify a likely target, we can still catch him.'

Remy let out a sigh.

'What's up?' Carver said.

'I am just thinking, I will need to come up with some good reasons why a couple of my team will be missing each day.'

Carver gave a pointed stare. 'You are sure you can trust them not to tell anyone what we are doing?'

'Do not worry about that, Jamie. They are very discreet.'

Carver gave him a hard stare. 'Let us hope so.'

CHAPTER 44

A short walk from the Place de Bastille, the Marché D'Aligré is renowned throughout Paris for the quality of its fruit and vegetables, as well as its colourful street market. The opposite side of the city to Montparnasse, where her apartment was, Ingrid nevertheless tried to get there at least once a week, if only for the kiwis and mangoes she needed for her morning juice. That morning, she had taken advantage of a rare, free Saturday to visit and was delighted to find the Beauchamp family stall carrying stocks of her favourite Rainier cherries. Encouraged by Phillipe, the eldest and most dashing of the family's three sons, she was in the act of tasting, when a tap on her shoulder made her turn. For no reason she could think of other than her mouth was stuffed full of cherry, she blushed when she saw Father Alonso standing there, smiling.

'Farrer,' she tried, struggling to get her words out. 'Whar a surpri-'

'Please' he said, realising her predicament. 'Do not choke. I only wanted to say, "Hello".'

After several swallows, she managed to recover herself.

'I am sorry, Father. I was just-'

'Sampling. Yes, so I can see. I hope you are known to this young man. It could be embarrassing if he had to report you to the police for eating his stock without payment.'

'No more embarrassing, I assure you, than being caught in the act by a priest.'

Seeing Phillipe enjoying her discomfort, she thrust a bag of the fruit at him together with a note. 'I'll take these. And wipe that smile off your face.'

'Of course Mademoiselle. And will you be taking your usual box of complimentary produce as well?'

She glared at him. 'Don't be clever, Phillipe. The day may come when I have to ask to see your trader's licence.'

'And nothing would give me greater pleasure than to produce it to you.'

With one last shake of her head, she exchanged the bag for a handful of change and turned away. 'Come Father, let me lead you out of this den of thieves. This is no place for a man of the cloth.'

As they strode away, Phillipe called after. 'Look after your cherry, Ingrid.' It drew raucous laughter from some of the other stall holders. Trailing a hand so the priest would not see, she gave them the finger. Whistles and cat-calls followed their retreat.

When they were out of range she turned to him. 'How are things at the church, Father? How is Father Masson?'

His face seemed to grow darker. 'The church is fine, Mademoiselle-'

'Please, call me Ingrid.'

It brought on the schoolboy smile. 'Ingrid.' He continued. 'It is the matter you are pursuing that continues to be troubling. I take it there are no further developments?' She shook her head, but kept it non-committal. 'As for Father Masson, well Father Masson is...' to her surprise he changed tack. 'I take it you heard he stopped your officers watching inside the church?'

'I did.'

'I imagine that causes you great difficulty.'

Recognising the danger, she skirted the subject. 'Murder enquiries are full of difficulties. There is always another way.'

'Even so, I can imagine the pressures you must face. It cannot be easy, especially for a young woman like you.'

Ignoring the implied sexism in his words - *he probably knows no better* - and unsure as to whether his empathy was genuine or simply his default, 'Priest Mode', she looked deep into his face. The clear, blue eyes stared back at her. No trace of the embarrassment she imagined some priests might feel being scrutinised by a woman. They were outside Bridgette's Coffee Bar. Right now Ingrid was between partners. She missed confiding.

'Do the church's coffers stretch to coffee?'

Later, Ingrid put it down to a combination of being caught off-duty and off-guard, and the priest's practised abilities as a listener and giver of succour. Certainly, until she began talking she had never fully recognised the tensions and conflicts so deep within her.

To begin with she spoke only in general terms. Of the pressures of the investigation. The long hours. The stresses of dealing with the victim's families. The awfulness of the crimes themselves. As in all such cases, the politicking carried on by Mayors, Magistrates and others, was not helping.

Alonso's response surprised her. 'I understand. I have had similar experience.'

'In what way?'

'I once had to deal with something... It was very disturbing.' It was his turn to be discreet. 'It involved children. You understand?'

She nodded. In her experience, child abuse was the only thing that came close to murder or rape in terms of its long-term effects. She wondered what he meant by, 'deal with', but felt it inappropriate to ask. The priest spoke of how he'd often wondered how detectives and other emergency service workers cope with the horrors they sometimes have to deal with. For once with time to spare and goaded by his apparent interest, Ingrid began to talk about other aspects of her work, her own experiences. At one point Alonso mused on how difficult it must be for detectives to stop their work intruding into their private lives.

'You are right,' she said. 'Though I never realised just how difficult until recently.'

Soon after, his observation that evil often lurks among normal society unrecognised drew a wry smile. 'Very true. It is even harder to spot when it disguises itself as something beautiful.' It drew a puzzled look from the priest.

After discussing how they both in their different ways had to avoid letting their work affect them, she became reflective, staring into her coffee cup. Eventually she said, 'That is when it is useful to have someone you can talk to who can help put things in perspective.'

'You are missing that, I see.'

'Why do you say that?'

Reaching across, he placed a hand, lightly, on hers. 'I meet many who are troubled by matters they cannot discuss openly. I sense such things in you now. Something other than these horrible murders perhaps?'

She stared at him, bit her lip.

'If it helps, I am good at keeping confidences.' His manner reflected something more than just offering reassurance.

Withdrawing her hand, she sat back. A sigh escaped her. 'I am involved in something... It involves someone... horrible. Evil. What we are doing requires that I do things which I find... disturbing. And yet-'

'Yes?'

'And yet, there is an aspect to it that is strangely fascinating. Am I wrong to feel that way, Father?'

His expression was grave. 'Everyone slows down to look at the accident on the other carriageway, Ingrid. It is human nature.'

'I know that, but...' He waited, neither inviting, nor encouraging. She made a decision. 'You say I can talk to you in confidence?'

'Of course. But let me warn you, when you have finished there is something I must also discuss with you.'

'Fair enough, I have time. There is a woman. Her name is Megan Crane.'

CHAPTER 45

Jess was viewing the video of Marianne Desmarais' murder scene when the notification popped up in the top right corner of her laptop screen. The logo and subject heading, "Re Your Post", told immediately where it had come from, though the sender's handle - "AntonyWithoutCleopatra" meant nothing. And while her first instinct was to dismiss it - she really needed to finish going through the new material Jamie had sent over before the evening was out - the few seconds she hesitated while she debated was long enough to make her realise, she wasn't going to.

Jess had always been curious. Even when very young, her mother had used to berate her for going through her drawers and cupboards. 'You're a real little Pandora, you are,' she would say. This, before she even knew Pandora's story. As she matured, that curiosity had, in many ways, come to define her. Growing up, she always wanted to know what she would find if she opened the door, what the next day would bring, what lay just around the bend. During the years she read books - she rarely had time now - once started on a novel, she could never put it down until she'd finished. The desire to know what happened next was always too strong. It was that curiosity, largely, that had drawn her to CID work. As Jamie had said on more than one occasion, 'It's what makes you the detective you are.' But it had also on occasion got her in trouble, both at work, and in her private life.

Like now.

Some while ago, Jess knew, she had started out on a journey, one unlike any she had embarked on before. Still continuing, it had taken her thus far to places that, in her younger days she would never have believed existed, brought her into contact with people whose lifestyles were strange to the point of being almost beyond understanding. Not without its risks, even now she remained uncertain as to where the journey might take her, who else she was still to meet along the road. Given her job, a more prudent person might have chosen to step off that road some time ago. Indeed, there had been times the past couple of years when she considered doing exactly that, only her curiosity would not let her. Despite the risks, she needed to discover how long the journey would continue, where its end point was, and what she may find when she got there - if she ever did. Until then she was happy enough to continue, though carefully, taking one step at a time. The notification that had just popped up represented, maybe, one such step.

Knowing that until she had at least investigated the source of the interruption she would not be able to return, fully, to the work she was doing, she clicked on the notice box. At the same time she gave a terse, 'Tch,' acknowledging her own weakness.

A message box opened up. In the top right corner was the sender's avatar, a photograph of a face, focused in tight. Probably a selfie, she thought. Jess scanned it enough to satisfy herself that there was nothing about it that shouted any immediate warning as regards proceeding further, and read through the message. It took her less than thirty seconds.

To her surprise - she hadn't really had any idea what on earth to expect - she discovered that it appeared to have been written by someone who seemed reasonably educated, appropriately courteous, and sufficiently self-effacing as to suggest that the writer might possess a sense of humour not unlike her own. The message itself was interesting, containing just enough information about the sender to allow her to judge whether it warranted a reply. She decided it did.

Closing the message - she would be able to retrieve it through the website when she was ready - she returned to what she had been doing. And while she was able to focus enough on the material she was reviewing so as to not miss anything, somewhere within her subconscious, a part of her brain was already beginning to play around with the 'what-ifs' and 'maybes' enough to bring on the merest hint of an anticipatory tingle.

CHAPTER 46

Taking care not to mark the bright lemon duvet cover, Simone Bessette placed her case on the folded coverlet at the end of the bed, then paused to inspect the room. As usual with budget hotels in central Paris, there was barely space to walk around the bed. But everything looked and smelled clean. More importantly, the charges were such Oliver would not notice anything unusual when he came to check their account balances at the end of the month.

Satisfied the room suited her purpose, she turned to the windows, already partly open. Opening them further, she stepped out onto the narrow balcony. Four storeys below, the noise from the shops lining the busy thoroughfare of Rue Malisherbes drifted up to meet her. But she could only see a couple of bar-restaurants, which meant she should at least get a good night's sleep.

Leaning out over the handrail, she looked to the south. Sure enough, there, in a direct line from the end of the street, between two blocks of buildings, she could just make out a section of the church's famous, classical portico. The hotel's web page had said 'Within three hundred metres.' She judged it a little more than that, but was not concerned. It was within walking distance.

She hated the metro. Too smelly and cramped.

But seeing the church so close, thoughts of what had brought her to Paris in the first place bubbled to the surface. Her stomach tightened and a shiver rippled through her. Courage, Simone, she told herself. You have planned this many weeks. Let us not now take fright. Three days from now we will be on our way home, free of the shadow that has hung over us so long.

To her surprise, the thought lifted her mood and she found herself humming a tune from Les Misérables, her favourite musical. It made her smile to realise it was The Song Of Angry Men with its oft-repeated refrain... *will not be slaves again...* How appropriate.

Feeling a good deal better than when she'd left home that morning, Simone turned to see to her unpacking.

CHAPTER 47

He stands, naked, in front of the mirror, surveying the scars that define him, counting them in the order they were inflicted. His fingertips trace their length, feeling the hardness of those he has borne longer, the softer tissue of those still healing, the painful sharpness of the most recent. It is a ritual he performs daily, so that none passes without he reflects on the burden he carries, the guilt he yearns to shed but knows he never will.

As he counts, images form in his head. Imprinted memories of the precise moment of each mark's birth. Where he was, the time, even the weather. Together, they form a historical record which testifies to the ongoing process of atonement that is as important to his well-being, as sustenance and sleep are to the body he inhabits.

Yet the images he associates with the marks are not all he sees. As they form then recede to make way for the next, they do so against a backdrop of a series of interlinked episodes. A repeating storyline that haunts not just his sleeping hours. A reminder of the sin that can never be forgiven.

It starts, as always, with an innocent accident. A young boy returns home after a playground fall in search of his mother's succour. Mounting the stairs, he hears strange noises from her bedroom. Rounding the door, he is confronted by something that is alien to his childhood experience. His mother sits astride his uncle. At first he imagines they are playing 'horsey' like he does with his father. Only the strange noises coming from her are not those he associates with playtime. Frightened for her, he begins to cry. They hear him. Their hysterical reactions only make it worse.

Cut to the next scene.

His mother and father are in the kitchen, arguing, again. He has no sense of the matter they are discussing, he wishes only they would stop. Each time seems worse than the one previous. Suddenly his father's angry face appears before his. He asks a question, about his uncle. Behind him his frightened mother shakes her head. '*No*'. But he has been taught that a good boy never lies, certainly not to his father. He gives his answer. 'Yes.' His father looks at his mother, strangely, then back to him. She begins to cry, terrified now. His father asks another question. He cannot lie, but he fears what the answer will bring. So rather than say the words, he raises his gaze to the ceiling, indicating the room above.

Cut to the next scene.

It is his birthday. It should be a happy day. Instead, he is standing in the doorway to his mother's bedroom. Her naked body lies strewn across the bed, her dead eyes staring up at the flaking ceiling, lips apart, as they were when she drew her last breath. Her porcelain skin, once so soft, so pure, is riven by the multitude of cuts to her arms, legs, torso and, worst of all, the once beautiful face. Blood, so dark it is almost black, still oozes, wet and shiny, testimony to the fact she has not long departed this Earth. On the floor, next to the bed his father crouches, knife in hand, crying. Cut to the final scene.

It is his birthday again. The uncle with whom he now lives but wishes he didn't, stands in the doorway to his bedroom. He has been drinking. In his hand is the knife the boy has seen him playing with several times of late when, in unguarded moments he has turned to find him watching him, a strange look in his face. He shuts the door, comes forward. The look in his uncle's face terrifies him.. He stands over the bed, looking down on the cowering figure, who starts to cry. Two words pass the man's lips. 'Your fault.' Then he reaches out, takes the boy's arm, and pulls back his sleeve. He wields the knife the way the boy's father used to do when gutting the fish they caught together in the stream.

And so it begins.

The image is such as would stay sleep in most for days, if not weeks. Not for him. Instead of revulsion, fear, panic, it generates pity, shame and, most of all of course, guilt. Overriding everything is the yearning that comes with each moment of reflection. The never-voiced but no-less heart-felt pain of regret. *If only I hadn't told.* But it is too late. The damage wrought can never be undone. Hence his guilt. The penance he must make to atone.

His counting finished for another day, he picks up his shirt from the bed and pulls it over his head, wincing as the fabric's fibres catch on the raw edges of his most recent wound. No longer bleeding, it nevertheless still gapes. Without the benefit of sutures it will be days before it stops seeping. The only treatment he allows himself is the iodine he applies to ward off infection. He accepts the pain without complaint. It is all part of the atonement process.

As he turns away from the bed, he glimpses the photograph he has only recently acquired. It had lain under the shirt. Reaching for it, he peruses the four smiling faces. Previously, he had thought to separate her from the others, discarding them in a way he had thought would be symbolic, given his intentions. But he is having second thoughts. Since he visited her, together with all he has learned since, he is beginning to wonder if his early assessment may have been too hasty. True, she has the same look and bearing as the others. And her values, he senses, do not accord, fully, with those his master has laid down. Nevertheless, having taken the time to explore her nest, to observe her as she slept, he knows now she is not as he first thought.

To start with, the apartment was surprisingly homely, not at all the gaudy boudoir he expected. And instead of flimsy items designed to display her wantonness, her wardrobe was stocked, in the main, with garments that were surprisingly conservative. The contents of her drawers and cupboards also indicated a mundaneness that was at odds with the amorality he associates with his victims. But more than anything else, it was her sleeping face that struck him. Lying there, she looked sweetly innocent. There were even traces of the same qualities he used to see in one who was once close to him, one he thinks of often. It has left him... confused.

Not enough to raise doubts about his work of course. Nothing could do that. Having experienced the lifelong pain that his victims cause, he does not doubt that the punishment he metes is apt.

But having identified her as one needing God's

punishment for the evil she generates, he now realises that perhaps she herself needs protection. If someone, one such as him perhaps, can watch over her, steer her away from the paths of evil, then perhaps she may yet be saved. He has no idea yet how he may accomplish such a task, he will need to think on it. But having had the thought, he wonders if it may not be a pointer to another route to the atonement he seeks. Perhaps he should offer them all the same sort of guidance? It would not hurt to try. And if they refuse, then no matter. He can always revert to the punishment that is always there. The confusion gives him pause. He ought not decide such things too quickly. His mission has been defined over many years. Any deviation from the established pattern will require proper and careful consideration.

Meanwhile there is work to be done. If she is not to be his next recipient of salvation then he must find another. Doubts and confusions over how best to carry out his mission in the future have not dampened the urges that drive him. If anything, the opposite.

Though he cannot fully explain why, recent events seem to be pushing him to step up his work rate. Perhaps it is the result of having been given the opportunity to see his work as others see it. Or the insights he has gained of late that make him realise that while God is clearly on his side, others are not. There are those – she is one – misguided enough to believe that it is *his* work that must be stopped. And while he would relish the opportunity to convert them to the path of wisdom, he is not so blind as to think such a thing is possible. The indoctrination they have suffered means it is they who are blinkered. Would that he had time to change that, but he does not. He realises now that the day could come when he is forced to halt his mission. What will happen if and when that day comes he has no idea. But until then, his duty is clear.

Finishing dressing, he takes one last look at the picture. Somewhere deep down within him a feeling he has not felt for a long time stirs. Recognising it as another potential distraction, he drops it on the bed, and goes to work.

CHAPTER 48

Staring out through the car's passenger window, Carver was oblivious to the way the terrain had changed since they'd left the A6 at Nitry to follow the signs for "Parc Naturel Régional du Morvan." The route south from Paris may be known as the, "Autoroute Du Soleil" - *The Motorway of the Sun* - but for the first couple of hundred kilometres the title reflects more the hopes and aspirations of the holidaymakers who flock to the Riviera each summer, than the mostly featureless landscape they pass through in the early stages. Now, as they neared the Parc, the farmland and rural industry that had dominated had finally given way to the rolling hills and forest Carver first imagined when Carissa floated their destination as the ideal venue for their purpose. Only two hours from Paris, private but not so isolated as to make it impractical, it would she suggested, fit nicely with the story they had been peddling the past weeks. But for all that Carver hoped she was right, right now his focus was not on the appropriateness of the venue, nor the changing scenery. Rather, he was still pulling apart Ingrid's account of her chance meeting with Father Alonso. Carver's initial interrogation, the one that began right after her first casual mention of her 'interesting encounter ' of the previous day and continued all the way down the last section of motorway before they turned off, had ended ten minutes before. Since then silence had reigned. In back, Carissa was maintaining a tactful silence.

Eventually, Carver realised that his search for significance in what he had heard - *there may not be any* - was threatening to confuse his recall of her account. Turning to Ingrid, he just caught the upward glance that pointed to her regretting having ever mentioned it. He ignored it.

'Run the bit about what Alonso said about Masson past me again.'

Shaking her head, Ingrid muttered French. Throwing him a wary glance, she took a deep breath.

'As I have already told you, twice, he spoke of having learned of something that was causing him concern. He *thinks* it may involve Father Masson, but cannot be sure. It *may* be something that will assist our investigation, but he wants to make sure of his facts first, and will tell us as soon as he has done so.'

'And he would not say what this "something" is?'

'NO. By the time I finished interrogating him the way you are doing me, I think he was sorry he even mentioned it. I know now how he felt.'

Carver gave a long sigh. 'I'm sorry, Ingrid. I'm losing patience with these bloody priests. They seem to think the Church is exempt from any police enquiry and that they can pick and choose what information to give us and when, and that we've no choice but to accept it.'

'I feel the same, but what could I do? I could not arrest him for withholding information when I have no idea what that information is, nor even if it is relevant to the investigation.' As the road began to snake, Ingrid's grip on the steering wheel turned her knuckles red.

After a short interval Carver said, 'Could it be something he heard in confession?'

'I DO NOT KNOW.' Rounding a bend, Ingrid swung the wheel, fiercely, before easing off as the road straightened. She took a long breath. 'I have told you everything he told me. There is no more. We cannot do anything else until we get back to Paris. Then we can go and see him again and you can ask him the same questions I did and see if you can do any better, okay?'

He caught her sideways look. It was withering. 'Alright, calm down. I'm not doubting you did everything you could and I'm sure I wouldn't have done any better.'

'Thank you.'

'It's just so bloody annoying.'

Behind, Carissa said nothing. The Paris murders were not her concern. Her turn was coming.

Carver gave it one last try. 'Let me just check I've got it right. You bump into Father Alonso at the market. You start talking. He buys you coffee. Right?'

'Right.'

He tells you he has been meaning to call you as something is worrying him, yes?'

'Yes.'

He definitely said, worrying, not interesting, or suspicious?'

The look again, then, 'Worrying.'

'Okay. So. Worrying suggests he is facing some sort of dilemma, doesn't it? Like he has to make a decision whether he can tell us?'

Another shrug. 'Possibly. We don't know.'

'But if it was something he'd heard in passing, or even if he'd seen something suspicious himself, he could just tell us, right? He wouldn't have to worry about it.'

'I am not..'

'But if he had heard something in confession, or if it concerned another member of the clergy, that would certainly put him in a dilemma, wouldn't it? He would have to think long and hard on what to tell us, yes?'

'I think so.' She looked uncertain. 'I'm not sure we can read too much into what he said. He was very anxious when talking to me, not always clear.'

'Like he was conflicted?'

'Yes,'

'Well there you are. If someone had confessed something to him, he would certainly be conflicted. The sanctity of the confessional, and all that.'

'Umm... maybe.'

'The thing is. How likely is it that someone is going to confess to a priest that he is responsible for a series of ongoing murders?'

'I do not know. Not very likely?'

'Agreed. An old crime, committed twenty years ago and which has been playing on someone's conscience ever since, yes. But an ongoing series of murders? I doubt it. Don't you?'

'Yes. I mean, no. I mean-'

'And he definitely said it concerns Father Masson?'

'THINKS, it MAY, concern Father Masson.'

'Which means he must have heard it from someone else, or learned it from a source that is not Father Masson. If he had heard it directly from Father Masson he would know, wouldn't he? He would be sure.'

'Er....'

'So that suggests that he suspects Father Masson of doing something but doesn't want to tell us until he does know for sure.'

'That is one possible interpretation.'

'What others could there be?'

'Perhaps he thinks Father Masson himself may have information, and he is trying to get him to share it with us.'

'Hmm, maybe but-'

'Jamie, until we know more, *anything* is possible.'

The silence returned. Eventually Carver said, 'When we get back, I'm going to sort these bloody priests out, once and for all.'

Ingrid caught Carissa's eye in the mirror. Neither said anything.

For several minutes there was silence in the car. Eventually, a body of water appeared on their left.

'This is the lake,' Carissa said.

Carver sat up. He had been thinking of throwing another question Ingrid's way. He shelved it. A minute later, as they crested a hill, Carver saw the aptly-named, Lac Du Crescent, meandering it's way south through the Parc's forest. Halfway down the lake's western shore, a rocky promontory jutted out into the water. Perched on the end, silhouetted against the sun's reflections on the water, was a Château. Even from here, it looked impressive.

Carissa pointed over Carver's left shoulder. 'There it is,' she said.

As Jamie Carver got his first view of the location he hoped would finally see an end to the darkness that had blighted his life these past three years, a feeling of foreboding, deeper than any he had experienced before, came over him. And as he felt it taking root, he hoped to God it was merely his overactive imagination stirring things up again.

CHAPTER 49

The road dropped to follow the lake's contours on its western side. As they meandered their way around the shoreline, Carver kept getting glimpses of the château, coming ever closer. As the setting and the building itself became clearer he realised, Château de la Roque was even grander than he had imagined.

Comprising several storeys - he could make out at least five though there could be more - its limestone walls supported a steeply-pitched roof of dark grey slate. At the promontory's furthest point, the wall on the side of the chateau overlooking the lake rose sheer in line with the cliff. From the topmost floor, a rounded turret protruded out over the water.

'Hell, Carissa,' Carver said. 'You said this guy was a friend. You didn't say anything about him being royalty.'

'Do not be over-impressed, Jamie. The Gavroche family are not what they were. Nowadays Giscard has to work for a living.'

'Shame.'

As he gazed on the property, Carver didn't dwell on what lay between the château's owner and Carissa. Whoever Gavroche was, whatever his involvement, he must have once been rich enough to indulge his fantasies. What they were was no business of Carver's. To her credit, Carissa had said as much when she first spoke about a property that may suit their purposes. 'The owner owes me,' she said, but little else. At first, Carver had tried to wheedle the story out of her. But when it became clear he was wasting his time he gave up. Even so, he'd concluded it must involve something fairly significant if Gavroche was willing to turn his house over to them for several days while he, his family and staff took an impromptu holiday.

One thing Carissa had shared. Giscard Gavroche had once moved in Megan Crane's circle. Carissa wasn't certain, but suspected Megan may even have once visited the château herself. The news alarmed Carver, until Carissa pointed out that it would actually lend credibility to their enterprise. It may even entice her to attend. And whatever the cause of Gavroche's turn around - it seemed he now hated her with a passion - he had assured Carissa that Megan would have no reason to suspect he may conspire against her. Carver didn't ask further, but was reassured to know that Megan Crane had enemies apart from himself. It sometimes seemed as if everyone she met fell, eventually, into her thrall.

As they hugged the shoreline, Carver's gaze stayed on the château. All he knew of its history was that it had been occupied, briefly, by the Nazis during the second world-war. It lent the place a sinister air and made him wonder what secrets might lie hidden within its thick walls. He still had no way of knowing if the bait they'd been dangling had come to Megan's attention. But if it had, and she'd taken it, he couldn't imagine a more suitable venue at which to see an end to their interminable game of cat and mouse.

A few minutes later, at the point where the promontory grew from the shoreline, Ingrid swung left between stone gateposts adorned with shiny brass plates proclaiming, "Château de La Roque" The gravel driveway ran some two hundred metres along the promontory before ending at a turning circle in front of wide steps leading up to the front doors. At the foot of the steps, a silver Daimler waited, facing back down the drive. Across the other side of the circle, a builder's van stood with its rear doors open, tools and building materials unloaded and awaiting collection. Next to the Daimler, a black-suited driver observed their arrival with casual interest. Ingrid parked behind the van.

As they got out, the front door opened and a tall man, impeccably dressed in Scottish tweed, stepped out. Seeing Carissa, he descended the steps to greet her warmly with an exchange of kisses. Carissa introduced him first to Ingrid, with whom he shook hands, then Carver. Carver noted the firm, dry grip, as well as the way Gavroche subjected him to searching scrutiny. After some seconds, the Frenchman seemed satisfied and relaxed into a more welcoming smile.

'I have heard much about you, Monsieur Carver.' His English was almost perfect. 'There are few who can claim to have bettered The Devil Woman. A shame it was not more permanent.'

'Don't worry Monsieur Gavroche. Next time, it will be.'

'In which case I wish you every success.' He turned back to Carissa. 'I am just leaving for Rennes. Claude is inside. He is at your disposal.' With a final nod to Carver and a rakish smile to Ingrid, he got into the Daimler. They watched it disappear down the driveway.

'Is he always so talkative?' Carver said to Carissa.

'You and he have more in common than you might imagine.'

But Carver could imagine. She had to be thinking of a certain female psychopath.

Carissa started up the steps. 'Let us see how the work is progressing.'

In the wood-panelled hallway, the sounds of electric tools and hammering echoed from one of the reception rooms off. A butler, formally-dressed in waistcoat and tails appeared to greet them. He made a little bow to Carissa. 'Welcome back, Madame. A pleasure to see you again.' Carver was surprised to realise he was English.

'Thank you Claude. You look well.'

'All the better for seeing you, Madame.'

Carver had no idea whether the studied politeness was genuine or being played for his benefit, but he waited while Carissa made the introductions. He responded to Claude's courteous nod with one of his own. As the butler went off to organise refreshments, Carissa led them through to where all the noise was coming from.

It was a spacious reception room. Light flooded in through two large bay windows which looked out over a well-tended garden. Most of the room's furniture and fittings were covered by white dust sheets. Nevertheless, the decorative ceiling and ornate wall carvings Carver could see peeping out from under some of the sheets, hinted at the Château's history.

But it was the construction work they had come to inspect, not the house. In the middle of the parquet floor in front of the windows, a metre high modular stage, was being set and clamped together by two men wearing traditional, French 'workmen dungarees'. Fronting the stage was a steel frame, split into vertical sections. A large glass panel, was already fitted into the section on the extreme left. Over by the window, a glaziers rack contained several more.

Recognising Carissa, the elder of the two left off levering a section of stage into place to approach, wiping his hands on a rag. Carissa greeted him with a smile.

'Bonjour Eric, ça va?'

'Bonjour Madame.' He made a polite bow of his head, but not so much that Carver read anything into it. After a brief conversation, Carissa turned to him and Ingrid. 'This is Eric. He is providing all the equipment.' They nodded and shook hands, but it became quickly apparent that Eric spoke almost no English. As he and Carissa conversed, Carver wandered over to inspect the work in more detail.

Standing in front of the 'stage', Carver was conscious of a weird feeling inside and tried not to think too hard on its purpose. When completed, he judged it would measure some three metres deep by five in width. The right hand edge butted up against a door to the adjoining room - the one through which it was intended Inger would enter. Once all the glass panels were fitted into the frame, the stage would be fully enclosed in glass, effectively turning it into a glass cage. Carver's intention was that things would never progress to the point that it would come into play. But if by some chance they did, he wanted the security of knowing that no member of the audience could reach Ingrid, or seek to involve themselves in the events on stage. The stage itself had but one notable feature. An upright frame comprised a stout wooden beam, three metres long, the ends of which were housed in brackets attached to the top of steel posts at either end. The beam hung a good two metres or more above the stage. Towards the back of the stage, two sets of wooden steps, the wood matching the cross beam, looked like they were meant to be placed beneath it. Seeing them, Carver turned to look for Ingrid. She was stood off to one side, staring at the structure as if realising, for the first time, it's purpose. She looked paler than normal. He went to her.

'Remember it only has to look the part. We don't intend that it will ever be used.'

She continued to stare, her gaze slipping from the beam to the steps. 'I hope to God not.'

At that moment, another man entered the room and joined Carissa and Eric. Younger and more casually dressed than the carpenters he was carrying coils of electrical cable.

'Jamie,' Carissa called. 'This is Anton, the camera engineer.'

'Ah. Just the guy I want to speak to.'

Unlike Eric, Anton spoke enough English that Carver could make his requirements understood. For the next several minutes they talked camera angles, monitoring positions and other technical requirements. Carissa joined them as they were finishing. 'Come,' she said. 'I will show you round.' Dragging Ingrid away from her morbid musing, she led them round the house. As she went she filled them in on what she knew of the château's history. Gifted to General George Gavroche by Napoleon during the Spanish campaign - when the Emperor still imagined his European ambitions would bear fruit, the house had been the Gavroche family home ever since. As they made their way, up floor by floor, Carissa seemed to delight in revealing the locations of the several priest holes, 'secret' passages and otherwise-invisible doors between some of the rooms and inter-connecting corridors. Carver listened, interested, as she described how the château's relative closeness to Paris meant that over the centuries it had provided refuge to both royalists and republicans, depending on where the incumbent Gavroche generation's sympathies lay. But while he was impressed by the house's architecture and history, he wasn't certain when Carissa showed him the unused first floor bedroom Anton had already earmarked as the most appropriate location to set up his monitoring equipment.

'I'm going to be a long way away from the action.'

'Only while everyone is arriving. Any nearer and we run the risk someone may take a wrong turn and discover you. Here you will be safe unless someone deliberately goes looking. And if they are that wary they probably won't come in the first place.' Carver nodded at her logic, but he couldn't help recalling two previous occasions when circumstances had forced him to monitor events from somewhere his instincts told him was too far away. On both occasions he had been proved right, but right now he couldn't see any viable alternative.

After wending their way up more flights of stairs and along corridors, they found themselves on the top-most attic floor, the fifth, Carver worked out. Claude was already there, preparing the guest rooms his employer had instructed be made available for their use. He showed them which was whose.

Carver's room was plain but comfortably furnished,

and criss-crossed with low wooden beams. In the centre was a huge bed, so high a wooden step was placed next to it. Off to the right, an en-suite shower was the room's only nod to modernity. He couldn't help thinking that, were it a hotel, a few days in such surroundings would do him the world of good. The sound of laughter from along the corridor drew him out and he wandered down to the room at the end. Inside he found Carissa watching Ingrid as she tested the springs of her four-poster bed. The room was similarly appointed as his, but was three times as big. Vast areas of floor lay between the bathroom on the right, the bed in the middle, and a floor-length window set in a rounded recess in the far wall to the left.

'This is the turret we saw overhanging the lake,' Carissa said, walking to the window and flinging it open. 'Take a look.'

Joining her, Carver and Ingrid leant out. A long way below, the lake's waters lapped against the cliff base. 'Whoa,' Carver said, stepping swiftly back. He was never comfortable with unguarded heights. 'Shouldn't there be a rail or something?'

Carissa chuckled at his nervousness. 'This used to be the house's main store room. Before there was a decent lake road, boats would moor below and supplies would be winched up.' She pointed out through the window and upwards. 'See?'

Following her indication, he saw that the end of one of the thick ceiling beams extended out through the wall above the window. Attached to the end, directly over the lake, was a pulley mechanism. A coiled length of thick rope hung from a hook outside the window, one end threaded through the pulley to an anchor point somewhere. By now Carver was conscious of the depression that seemed to have settled on Ingrid as something that had thus far lived only in their imaginations began to harden into some form of reality. He tried lightening the mood. He nudged her elbow and nodded at the rope and pulley.

'Fire escape,' he said. It drew but a wan smile.

Returning downstairs, they found Eric and his team of workers tucking into platters of sandwiches and a carafe of red wine. They declined Eric's offer that they should help themselves. As they made ready to leave, Carver passed by Eric's young apprentice, sitting on the edge of the stage. He was holding up a newspaper, skimming through the pages. The front page was facing and as Carver passed he glanced at it, did a double take, then froze, continuing to stare at it.

'What the-?'

'What is it?' Ingrid said.

Stepping forward, Carver snatched the paper from the youth.

'Monsieur?' the startled lad cried.

Ignoring him, Carver poured over the page. Ingrid joined him, alarmed by his sudden anxiety. She leaned across.

'What are you looking at?'

Folding the paper over, he showed her the article and photograph that had caught his eye. It was of an attractive young couple, blonde haired and with wide smiles that spoke of young love.

'What does it say? Tell me, quickly.'

As puzzled as she was alarmed, Ingrid scanned the article. Carissa joined them, intrigued to find out what was going on.

Carver was impatient. 'What's it about?'

'MOMENT,' Ingrid barked, trying to digest it in the face of his badgering. Finally she turned to him.

'It concerns two American law graduates who are supposed to be travelling through Europe.'

'What about them?'

She checked the article again.

'The young man's body was fished out of a quarry-lake outside Paris two days ago. Members of a scuba diving club found it during a training exercise. The police think it had been there less than twenty four hours. The girl is still missing.'

As she concluded her summary, she lowered the paper to look up at Carver.

He was as white as the sheets covering the rooms furnishings.

CHAPTER 50

The plan had been that they would meet with Remy after visiting the château, to work on the details of the event that was now only days away. Instead, the afternoon and evening disappeared in a blitz of phone calls and hastily-arranged meetings. Remy knew the detective in charge of the investigation into the American boy's murder. His name was Bernard Dupois and he was working out of the police station in the town of Beauvais, close to where the body had been found. When Remy contacted him to tell of Carver's sighting of the boy's missing fiancée at the Galeries, he was ready to drop everything and come straight to the Préfecture. But as it was now out-of-bounds to Carver, Remy said they would come to him. They arrived just after six and met with Dupois and his deputy in the cramped office they had commandeered off the local Police Inspector. When Dupois started by confirming they were talking, 'off the record', Carver guessed that Remy must have made him aware of the difficulties surrounding his involvement.

Dupois was some years older than Remy. They knew each other as colleagues rather than close friends. Carver thought he had something of the drained look some detectives acquire as they approach retirement age. His English was sketchy at best, which made the meeting difficult. Remy and Ingrid interpreted as necessary as first Dupois, then Carver, shared their stories.

Scott Weston's body had been found less than seventy-two hours before. Carver was interested in how he had been identified so quickly, given he was found naked. The answer was a tattoo. To begin with, the police had assumed that the Greek letters, kappa, lambda, delta, tattooed on the underside of the deceased's right bicep pointed to him being Greek. But a young police graduate entrant who'd studied in the US remembered how American University Fraternity Houses often use letters of the Greek alphabet as a Frat House identifier. She was right. After a day and half of making phone calls and being passed from Frat House to Frat House, she eventually spoke with the President of one in New York. He knew of a recent Yale graduate, Scott Weston, who was travelling through Europe with his fiancée and whose description fitted with the body now lying in the police morgue. Local police were sent to Scott's family home in Boston, as well as that of his fiancée, a Tory Martinez.

Confirmation followed quickly. Understandably, the families were distraught. Tory's parents were almost hysterical for news of their daughter. The families themselves had little first-hand information about Scott and Tory's movements the past week, other than that they had decided to linger a few days in Paris. However social media posts to their closest friends had mentioned how, through a stroke of luck they had met and were staying with 'a sophisticated Frenchwoman' in a 'nice house just outside Paris.' They did not specify where, and while Scott had mentioned posting photographs later, he had not got round to it. An IT team had already been put to work analysing the missing pair's digital data trails. However, as of that afternoon, Dupois' team had no information as to the circumstances under which Scott Weston had met his death, other than that the postmortem showed he had died from being either violently garroted, or hung by the neck.

That sealed it for Carver.

For the next hour, aided by Ingrid and Remy, Carver briefed Dupois on Megan Crane, her case history and his mission to Paris. Dupois barely interrupted as he listened with growing horror to Carver's story. The only thing Carver held back on was the finer detail of the plan by which they were hoping to lure Megan Crane into the open, though he did refer, obliquely, to 'steps we are taking.' When Dupois heard about The Woman's predilection for asphyxiating her victims he needed no more convincing as to who he and his team were looking for. He asked Carver for photographs and full details so they could go to an examining magistrate and obtain a warrant for her arrest. Carver had them with him and handed them over, but not before checking with Remy that the examining magistrate in question would be someone other than Marc Couthon, the man overseeing the Paris investigation. Remy confirmed that as the body was found beyond the city boundaries, a different magistrate would preside. He asked Carver about his concern.

'There was something about Couthon's interest in her made me uneasy,' Carver said.

Remy nodded, but said nothing.

Eventually, Remy pulled the strands of what they knew together. They were all agreed that Megan Crane was, almost certainly, involved in Scott Weston's murder. She was clearly living somewhere close to Paris, as Carver had suspected all along, though presumably under an assumed name. Most likely she was being harboured or enjoying the protection of people with money and influence. Whoever her protector was, he or she had to know she was a killer on the run. Which made it unlikely that any fresh appeal would lead to her unmasking. There was a strong likelihood that the missing girl would soon end up dead as well, if she wasn't already. As Carver pointed out however, there was reason to hope there may still be time to find and save her. One thing they knew about Megan Crane was, she enjoyed drawing things out. Their chance meeting at Les Galeries was four days ago. She'd kept poor Tracy Redmond chained up in her cellar far longer than that many times.

By now, Dupois had heard enough to surmise that the 'steps' Carver had mentioned they were taking to find Megan Crane were not altogether official.

'Correct,' Carver said.

Dupois didn't hesitate. 'In that case, if there is anything I can do to help, let me know.'

That evening, as the three detectives travelled the Autoroute back into Paris, they all thought the same. The plan by which they hoped to lure Megan Crane into the open could wait no longer. Tory Martinez's life depended on it.

CHAPTER 51

After successive nights of into-the-early-hours phone calls, Carver was relieved to hear that Jess seemed to have finally accepted that nothing she could say would move him to change his course, though she remained anxious.

'I can't help worrying, Jamie. Eventually you'll be back here, facing the music. And remember, it'll be me helping you pick up the pieces.'

The strain in her voice added to his guilt. 'I know that, Jess. And believe me, when that time comes I'll be grateful. But I've no choice but to see this through. It's the best chance we're ever likely to get. And now that there's the girl to think of, I couldn't walk away, even if I wanted to. The sigh that greeted his words confirmed her capitulation. Two nights ago she'd have launched into another argument.

'Is there anything I can be doing at this end?'

'Just keep watching my back, like you are.'

Earlier, she had described the latest conversations she'd had with Dave Shaw and her various other contacts. The way it sounded, there was only one topic of conversation around Headquarters. *Jamie Carver's gone rogue.* He was just glad when she didn't make any reference to, '*again.*' She had heard a rumour that The Duke himself might be sent over to 'persuade' him to come back. But so far, nothing had come of it. Carver wasn't too concerned. He was sure Jess would hear from The Duke direct if that were to happen. Since their last conversation, Carver had kept his UK mobile switched off, and with the sim removed, and had bought a 'burner' to keep in contact with Jess, Ingrid, and the others. He had not shared the number with The Duke. He hoped he would understand.

Carver remembered something. 'Have you heard anything about anyone having contact with someone over here? Anyone asking questions?'

'Not according to Dave Shaw. He thinks the Deputy is keen that the Paris authorities don't know you've not arrived back yet. Too embarrassing. But the longer you stay away the bigger the bang will be when you get back.'

'So long as I know I've given what's happening here my best shot, I'll live with it.'

'Fair enough.'

As the silence stretched, Carver realised that for the first time he could remember, they'd run out of things to say. 'Look after yourself, Jess.'

'You too.'

He hung up.

CHAPTER 52

The cane-weave chairs were never built for comfort. Simone Bessette was glad she didn't have to sit through a whole mass. Just waiting her turn was bad enough. Conscious of the fluttering feeling that had been growing in her stomach all morning, she closed her eyes and concentrated on trying to stay calm.

The night before she had slept fitfully. Wanting to be fresh and at her best the next morning she had retired early. It was a bad decision. She'd have been better staying up late. Maybe even polishing off the rest of the wine she had chosen to go with her dinner, instead of restricting herself to the single glass she thought sensible. In the pitch dark she had tried to force sleep. But each time she emptied her mind to welcome it, thoughts kept coming of what the next day would bring. She lost count of the times she found herself mentally rehearsing the words she would use, the process that would follow. Having imagined it so many times the past weeks, it needed no conscious effort on her part for the sequence to play over, like a vinyl record stuck in the groove. Even when she tried to focus on happier thoughts – her renewed devotion to her husband, the girls, how they would have spent their evening - the moment she relaxed, her mind drifted back to what the morning would bring. And so she had tossed and turned through most of the night, tracking the bedside digital clock's progress. 23:32, 00:45, 01:58, 03:10. Eventually, she must have managed to drop off.

Yet despite it all, she did not feel tired. If anything, she was more awake than she'd been in a long time. As if she'd spent the past few weeks in a semi-trance and was finally coming out of it. She even felt - and this really surprised her - a little excited. But it wasn't the thought of what she was about to do that was making her heart beat faster. It was the anticipation of what would come after. Less than an hour from now, God willing, the burden she had been carrying so long would be gone. No longer would she be living each day under the cloud that had grown so heavy, that just smiling needed a conscious effort. Simone had always been known for her joyfulness. The girls in particular loved the way their mother always made sure that at least part of each day was set aside for 'fun-time'. The last few days maintaining the pretence had been almost unbearably hard. Now, the thought that the next time they were together her smile would be as natural as it ever was before the foolishness took her, made her heart soar. A sudden, mischievous thought struck her. Before returning home that evening, she may even find time for-

'Madame?'

She opened her eyes. A late-middle-aged woman with a wrinkled but kindly face stared down at her. Simone recognised her as one of the guides she had seen earlier. Their job was to note the order of people's arrival. To usher them forward when their time came.

'S'il vous plait?' She gestured towards the confessional.

Taking a deep breath, Simone Bessette crossed herself and rose from the chair. Crossing the aisle she paused outside the glass door, then rapped a knuckle, lightly, against it. A voice said, 'Enter.' She opened the door and stepped inside.

'Come in Madame. Please, sit.'

The voice was kindly, forgiving. In front of the table was a chair, identical to the one she had just vacated. She went to it. As she sat, she realised her nervousness had vanished. Even so, she did not yet dare show her face to the man opposite and kept her head down. She went straight into the familiar recital.

'Pray, Father, give me your blessing, for I have sinned. It is three weeks since my last confession....'

And as she spoke the words she knew so well, Simone Bessette felt the burden that had lain around her shoulders these past months start to lift.

CHAPTER 53

Carver noted their grim expressions as Remy and Ingrid approached the small café on the Bastille end of Rue de Rivoli. He said nothing but waited while they took seats and ordered coffees. During breakfast, Remy had rung to say that he and Ingrid had been called in to see their Director before starting work. After they'd settled he said, 'Tell me the worst.'

The pair exchanged troubled glances. Remy spoke first. 'Someone suspects you are still here, Jamie. That we are still in touch.'

'Over the murders or the other thing?'

'Our Chief did not say. He spoke only of you, and us. He asked if we knew where you are, what you are doing.' Carver waited. He had no intention of asking. 'I told them that as far as I know, you have returned to England.'

Ingrid leaned forward. 'As did I.'

Remy looked embarrassed. 'Of course. We *both* said-'

Carver waived it away. 'I understand. Did he say why someone thinks I am still here?'

They shook their heads, faces blank. 'No. But he suspects we are keeping things from him. Things were said between us that should not have been said.'

'Threats?'

'Not direct, of course. But he made clear that if we are proved to have lied to him, our careers will be over.'

Carver grimaced, remembering a similar conversation he'd once had with an Assistant Chief Constable. He survived only because of what he knew about an episode early in the man's career. Remy and Ingrid would be feeling the pressure. He was particularly concerned that someone suspected he was still around. According to Jess, no one back home was letting on he had not returned. Could the leak be at this end? By now he regarded Ingrid as close a friend as Remy. They could do no more. The time had come.

'You must pull out. Things are getting too hot. If you two end up in the shit because of me-' He shook his head. 'I wouldn't want that. Besides, things are all set for tomorrow night. Carissa and I can handle it.' He turned to Ingrid. 'It won't matter if you're not there. She'll either turn up or she won't. Your presence won't be crucial.'

Ingrid shook her head. 'You don't know that, Jamie. People will be expecting to see me. If I am not there they will ask questions. If *she* gets to hear of it before she arrives, it may alert her enough to put her off. All our efforts will have been wasted.'

Carver looked for the counter-argument. He couldn't see one. They had spoken many times about how important it was that everything should look as genuine as possible for as long as possible, even to the end point if necessary, though he still hoped they would never get that far.

'Anyway,' Remy said, continuing from where Ingrid

left off. 'What's done is done. Even if we did pull out now, we have done enough that they can destroy us if they wish to. Another couple of days will make no difference.' He even managed a chuckle. 'My God, what we have done in the Church alone is enough to see us in prison. What can they do that is any worse?'

To his surprise, Carver found himself moved by their show of loyalty, and was embarrassed when he realised it must have showed as Ingrid placed a hand on the back of his, saying, 'We both know how much this means to you, Jamie. We are not going to leave you now.' Remy settled for an affirming nod. Carver gave it a final check.

'You are both sure about this?'

Remy waived the question aside. The decision was made. 'Get out your papers. Let us go over tomorrow night one more time. We still have a murder investigation to get back to.' He held up a finger. 'Which reminds me. Martin and Brigitte have confirmed that Madame Furay had also recently ended an affair. Her sister told them she had spoken about feelings of guilt and shame in the weeks before she died. She even spoke about seeking God's forgiveness, but gave no details. The sister didn't mention it as she thought it was not relevant.'

Carver nodded. Janinne Furay was the killer's second victim, but the last to be confirmed as having had an affair. That made all of them. And they were all now known to have been strongly Catholic. The theory was holding up. He would be interested to hear fuller details. But it could wait.

Reaching into the knapsack that was with him constantly now, Carver took out the papers for the following night's operation. They were becoming increasingly dog-eared. Little wonder. The last few days they'd rarely been out of his hands. He got as far as spreading them out on the table when Remy's phone rang.

'It is Marcel.'

Carver came alert. Marcel was the trusted detective Remy had put in charge of the confessional listening team. He usually reported in the early evening, after confessional activity had ended. Something must have happened. Remy's face confirmed it. As he rose from his seat, Carver and Ingrid rose with him.

'Quand?' Remy said. *When.* He began to gesture at them. *We must go.*

Carver grabbed up his papers. They would go over it another time. If there was to be another time.

'Vous êtes certain?' Some basic phrases Carver had no trouble translating. Remy's car was parked across the street. They started towards it. 'Trés bien, Marcel. We are five minutes away. Talk with Ingrid.' He passed Ingrid his phone, instructed her to keep talking. He turned to Carver. 'A woman has just made her confession. She was seeking forgiveness for an affair she had with her husband's best friend.'

As they piled into the car, Carver asked the key question. 'Who did she confess to?'

'Father Masson.'

Remy started the engine, waited for the first sign of a gap in the traffic streaming down Rue de Rivoli and took it.

As they shot forward, Carver thought, *Here we go.*

CHAPTER 54

As Remy dodged traffic, Ingrid relayed Marcel's commentary from the back seat.

'They have her in sight. She is leaving the church. They are following. Wait. . .' As she listened, excitement grew in her face. 'A priest has come out of the church. He seems to be looking for someone. He is-'

'What?' Remy said. 'He is what?'

'Un moment. He is. . . Oui, Marcel. They think he is going after the woman... He is following her. Marcel is telling his team to hang back so they can follow him. They are-'

'What?'

'Something else is happening. Marcel is talking to... Oui Marcel. Qu'est ce que c'est?' Confusion spread over her face.' Un autre?' A pause. She turned to Carver, all the time listening to Marcel. 'Another priest? After the first?'

Carver couldn't wait. 'What is he saying? What about another priest?'

She took the phone from her ear. 'Marcel says there is another priest. It looks like he is following the first one.'

'WHAT? What the hell's going on? Who are they? Is

one of them Masson?'

Before she could comply, her own mobile rang. Digging it from her bag, she checked the screen. 'It's Father Alonso.'

She has him in her contacts?

She listened, intently, a phone to each ear. 'Oui, Miguel. Oui.' Carver noted the first name terms. 'Oui...' There followed a blast of French that to Carver seemed to go on forever. At one point she interrupted to shout down the other phone at Marcel. Carver guessed she was telling him she was talking to one of the priests. He could imagine their confusion. Remy said nothing but drove in furious silence, weaving in and out of traffic. Eventually, Ingrid lowered her own phone but kept Remy's to her ear. She shook her head as if having trouble digesting what she was hearing. Putting her mobile in 'secrecy' mode, she filled them in.

'Father Alonso is following Father Masson. He is concerned about what he may be up to. Masson came to him after taking the woman's confession. He was babbling about her being one of those women the police were looking for. He kept calling her a sinner and saying something about having to make sure she did her penance. When Masson went to the chapel, Alonso followed. He saw him watching the woman as she said her prayers. When she left, Masson grabbed his coat then followed her out of the church. Alonso thought he should follow. He didn't know what to do so he phoned me. What do I tell him?'

'Tell him we are on our way.' Carver said. 'Where are they?'

She jabbered into the phones. Marcel first, then Alonso.

'Along Rue Tronchet towards Boulevard Haussmann.' She listened again. 'Marcel and his team are still hanging back. Alonso does not know they are there. Shall I tell him-'

'Say nothing,' Remy said. 'Let us see what happens.'

For the next couple of minutes Ingrid juggled conversations, updating Remy with the route so he could home in on the chase. Between talking to Marcel, she kept imploring Alonso to be careful.

'They are turning into...' She pointed. 'A gauche. On the left. Ici.' As they turned the corner, Carver saw the street sign. Rue de Provence.

Ingrid had Alonso to her ear. 'She is going into a Hotel. Hotel Burghoff on-'

'I know it,' Remy said.

Ingrid's tone became suddenly urgent. 'NON, Miguel. Nous sommes-' A pause then, 'Miguel? MIGUEL?' She looked up. From the look on her face Carver guessed she had lost contact.

'What happened?'

'Masson has followed the woman into the hotel. Alonso was going to follow them inside. I was telling him not to, but he's hung up.'

'Where's the hotel?'

'Two minutes,' Remy said. He floored the accelerator.

CHAPTER 55

As she started repacking her suitcase, Simone Bessette felt even better than she had imagined she would. To find all her anxieties, all the guilt, so completely gone and so quickly, all for the sake of an hour in church, was immensely liberating. She'd heard people speak of being, 're-born.' Usually after overcoming serious illness, or following divorce. But she'd never really understood what they meant, until now. It really did feel as if her life was about to start over, with all the opportunities that presented. She was not yet forty. Not even middle-aged by today's standards. Another lifetime lay before her. This time she would not make the same mistake.

Thank you, Sainte Marie.

Booked on an evening train home, Simone's plan was to spend a leisurely afternoon browsing the shops, enjoying the odd glass of wine, before making her way to Chez Muraq for a late lunch of one of their cheese platters. But now she felt like she could not wait to return to her children and husband, to begin the new life that was hers. She imagined them at home, waiting for her when she walked in. Oliver in his favourite chair, the girls curled up in his lap. Just picturing it made her want to laugh out loud.

One thing. When she did get home she would have to be careful about letting her new-found euphoria show. If she appeared too happy, Oliver might wonder what had happened during her three-day visit to see old school friends to bring about such a change. Hard though it would be, she would have to remember to keep her feelings in check. At least for a little while.

A knock came at the door.

In the act of folding her nightdress Simone straightened. She turned to the door as if she might see through it. Who could that be? She was not expecting anyone. Nor had she called the desk for help with her bags. She took a step towards the door.

A shout from somewhere down the corridor stopped her mid-stride. A single word, but full of alarm. As she hesitated, there came a second cry, followed by a roar like a wild animal, right outside the door. Starting to feel frightened, she took a hesitant step back, which was when all hell broke loose. Shouts, screams, bangs and thumps, then a crash, told of a fierce struggle taking place. Someone cried out. *Was it pain, or despair?* Either way, Simone did not wait to find out. With nowhere else to go, she dived into the bathroom and slammed the door, setting the lock that she realised was ridiculously inadequate. As the rumpus continued, she shrank back against the sink.

My God. What is happening?

As suddenly as it began, the commotion stopped. At least it died down to the point where she could no longer hear it. Quelling the panic that was threatening to well up inside her, she tried to think rationally. Across the corridor from her room she remembered was an

Emergency Exit. Presumably stairs would lead down to outside. She had no idea what the commotion was, but she was already recalling some of the terrorist atrocities of recent years. Either that or some maniac was loose in the hotel. Either way, she did not want to end up trapped in her room, or alone on the floor at someone's mercy.

As the silence stretched she slipped the bolt back and ventured out. It was still quiet. She moved to the bedroom door, put her ear to it. All she could hear was a strange, wheezing noise – a bit like the noise a party balloon makes when it springs a leak and begins to deflate. In the middle of the door was a spy-glass. Having checked when she took the room she knew it gave a view along the corridor in both directions. She looked through, but could see no one. Perhaps now was her chance. Slowly, she opened the door.

The sight that greeted her was one she would remember the rest of her life.

Seeing Marcel waving, Remy slammed on the brakes. The car screeched to a halt outside the Hotel Burghoff. Even before it had come to a stop, Carver was out and heading for the steps, Ingrid following.

Carver saw the confusion in Marcel's face as he reported to Remy. Carver had no idea what he was saying, but the way he was pointing into the hotel needed no translation. Bounding up the steps with Ingrid on his heels he burst into the lobby. Remy followed them in. The reception desk was to his right. Behind it, an Asian girl with long black hair and wearing a grey uniform was speaking frantically into a telephone. She dropped it as they charged in. The look on her face told Carver she was probably speaking to the 112 operator.

'POLICE. Where?'

She lifted a quivering finger in the direction of the stairs across the lobby. 'Le premier étage.' *First floor.*

Remy was nearest the stairs. He bounded up them. Ingrid was about to follow when Carver grabbed her arm and dragged her back, behind him. Even as he did it, he knew there would be hell to pay later. But the memory of an occasion when he should have jettisoned chivalry sooner had never left him. He would apologise later. Three-in-line, they raced up.

As they reached the first turning on the stairs, a woman's scream, shrill and piercing, sounded above. A chill ripped through Carver's bones. Adrenalin flowed, lending impetus to his charge.

Simone Bessett could barely make sense of what she was seeing. Two men were slumped on the floor. To the left of the door, they were below the range of the spy-hole, which is why she hadn't seen them. The older of the pair was wearing a grey raincoat. He was flat on his back, the black handle of a knife sticking out of his chest. The wheezing sound she'd heard was coming from him. As she gazed on him, she realised his breathing was growing fainter. The other man was slumped over the first, an arm outstretched against the wall, supporting himself. Blood was dripping from somewhere up near his neck. As Simone appeared, he lifted his head. Tears tracked his cheeks and she realised that the other sounds she'd heard were his anguished sobs.

Simone let out a scream that bounced off the walls and reverberated along the narrow corridor. She clamped a hand to her mouth, shutting off the wail. She stared down at the man with the knife in his chest, then realised. His face was familiar. Surely it could not be... The black robes and white collar peeping out from under the raincoat confirmed it. Less than an hour before she had been confessing to him. Shock hit her. Her head spun and a shaking started in her legs. She staggered and fell back against the wall. As she fought against the oncoming faint, the second man stretched out a blood-stained hand. Still sobbing he implored her. 'Ambulance, Madame. Vite.' Even as he spoke, blood dripped from under his chin, like paint dripping from a brush. She saw that he too was wearing a collar. It was too much. As she slid down the wall, her last impression before the darkness claimed her was of blurred figures, rushing headlong towards her. The one in front shouted something. By then she was too far gone to assign any real meaning to his words. But as she hit the floor, she wondered how it was that she had suddenly been transported to England?

CHAPTER 56

Carver was on his mobile to Remy when Ingrid returned to the hospital waiting room.

'She's just come back. Hang on.' He threw her a questioning look.

As she flopped down into one of the vinyl easy chairs she shook her head, still trying to make sense of it all.

'*Merde*. What a mess.' She looked up. 'Tell him you'll ring him back. We have to talk.'

'I'll call you back Remy.' Carver put his phone away.

Before he could say anything further she rose from the chair again. He could see she was agitated. 'I need water.'

'I'll get it,' he said. 'You look like you need a moment.'

When he returned she was calmer, sitting staring out of the window that gave a view across the river.

He had a list of questions. But first things first. 'How is he?'

She shook her head. 'Not good, and in shock, I would say. He cannot come to terms with having killed his own Monsigneur.'

'And his injuries?'

'Not as bad as they looked. The cut to his neck bled a lot, but it wasn't too deep. It just needed a few stitches. There are cuts to his hands where he tried to take the knife off Father Masson, but that is all.' Something in her head drew a smile. 'Typical priest. Apparently he wouldn't let them take his collar off. Physically he is fine. Mentally, I fear it will be some time before he recovers.'

'He's a lucky man. It could have been a lot worse.'

'That's what I told him. He was stupid to try to tackle Masson on his own.'

'On the other hand, if he hadn't, the woman might now be dead. Did he say how long he has suspected Father Masson might be the killer?'

'Since Masson began obstructing our efforts at surveillance. He thought it strange, seeing as it was his congregation who were at risk.'

'What else did you get out of him?'

'Only bare details. The doctor kicked me out while he does a full evaluation. I will speak with him again when he is finished and get the full story. But from what he told me so far, it seems that when he saw Masson follow the woman out of the church he was worried what he might be up to so decided to follow them. When he saw Masson follow her into the hotel he feared the worst, rightly it turns out. He did not know he was being followed and thought that if he waited for us, it might be too late, so he went in after him. He saw Masson outside the woman's door with the knife in his hand and realised what he was about to do. He called to him to stop and tried to pull him away but Masson turned on him and they fought. He believes now that Masson would have killed him if he got the chance. As it happens, during the struggle, Alonso managed to turn the knife, which is how it ended up in Masson's chest.' Ending her account, she caught Carver's eye. 'I am afraid for what will happen to him, Jamie.'

Carver rubbed her arm, reassuringly. 'Don't worry. From what you say it is a straightforward matter of self-defence. I cannot think any prosecutor will-'

'Not the legal side. I am sure you are right about that. But I worry what it will do to him as a man, especially as a priest. Can you imagine what must be in his head right now? He has killed another person. Worse, he has killed another priest.'

'But a priest who was himself a murderer,' Carver said.

She shook her head. 'I doubt that will matter to Miguel. It would not surprise me if he cannot carry on his vocation.' She looked about her, as if deciding what to do next. 'What was Remy saying? Where is he?'

'He's at Masson's apartment. They have found a box under the floorboards. It contains some trinkets, jewellery, handkerchiefs, that sort of thing. Remy thinks we will find they belonged to some of the victims.'

'Trophies?'

'Looks like it.' He hesitated to tell her. 'Your missing photograph is among them.'

She turned ashen. 'My God. So it was *him* in my apartment.'

Carver said nothing. A shudder rippled through her. She buried her face in her hands. He imagined what she was thinking. *I could have been next.* She fell silent. He gave her time.

Eventually she said, 'So, why did he do it? Why kill all those women?'

'Right now, it's looking as we were thinking. Remy has spoken with Madame Bessett. She admits that she came to Paris to seek absolution from Sainte Marie for an affair she ended some weeks ago, and that is what she confessed to Father Masson. My guess is, he has been targeting women with children who have had affairs and, by doing so, put their marriages, and children's happiness at risk. That would fit with his, 'Pray For The Children' message. You will need to do some digging, but I think you'll find the answer there somewhere. Maybe his parents split up after an affair and he never got over it. Something like that.'

For a while longer, they ran hypotheses. They came up with several. Eventually they fell silent. They all needed time to digest what had happened.

Eventually, Ingrid said, 'What now? What about tomorrow night?'

Roused from his musings, Carver turned to her. 'I need to speak to Remy about it. There's obviously a lot you've all got to do to link Masson to the other killings, but as he's dead and you won't need to worry about court appearances, I'm hoping we will still be okay to go ahead.' He checked his watch. It was nearing seven o clock. It wasn't the sort of conversation to have over the phone. 'What are you doing, coming or staying?'

'Staying. As soon as the doctors have finished with Miguel, I need to take his statement. It will be a long one, I think.'

As Carver left her, he could see she was still coming to terms with the day's events and, probably, the fact of her own narrow escape. He shut the door quietly.

Ingrid had to wait longer than she expected to speak

again with Father Alonso, nearly two hours. Eventually the Indian doctor showed up to tell her they were finished and she was free to see him.

'Is everything alright?' she asked the doctor. 'What took you so long?'

His response was a simple. 'He is fine, now. You can see him.' About to press further, Ingrid decided there was little point. She'd had to accept long ago that the police are no longer exempt when it comes to patient confidentiality.

Alonso was sitting up in bed, wearing pyjamas. Tubes were attached to the back of one hand, as if they were responsible for his drained look. As she entered he was looking out of the window but turned towards her. She threw him a weak smile. 'How are you feeling?'

He shook his head, slowly. Tears welled. She took his hand. He grabbed at it, squeezed.

'You did what you had to do, Miguel. God knows that.'

He nodded. Swallowed, hard. 'I hope so.' He paused before turning a sad face on her. 'But I killed a man, Ingrid. Me. A priest. How can I live with that?'

'Live with the fact that by killing him, you saved others. And they were innocent. He was not.'

He almost laughed. 'Innocent? Are any of us innocent, Ingrid? Is there such a thing? I am beginning to wonder.' There was another long pause during which he held her hand, tightly. Eventually he said. 'Do you know why?'

'We have some theories. Something in his past, we believe. But we will find out. We will be making many enquiries over the coming days.' She waited in case he had other questions, but all he did was stare at her. The life seemed to have gone out of his eyes. 'Do you feel up to talking about it, Miguel? I need to take your statement, but I could leave it until the morning.'

He shook his head. 'No. Let us do it now.'

She took out her papers and pen.

It was after nine o'clock when she finished writing and took him through signing the several sheets of paper. She felt as exhausted as he looked.

As she made ready to leave he said, 'What will happen tomorrow?'

She blew out her cheeks. Where to begin? 'Like I said, there are many enquiries to be made. Masson's background. His past history. Other matters as well. We have to start making our report to the Magistrate. There is much to do.'

'Will I see you?'

She looked into the handsome face, saw the anxiety there. Something else as well, she thought. 'I will call in. But it will have to be in the morning.'

'Why? What is happening?' When she hesitated to answer and he saw the look in her face, he sat up. 'Is it to do with the matter you spoke of when we met in the market?'

She nodded, reluctant to acknowledge it.

'It is tomorrow?'

She nodded again. 'Yes,' she whispered.

Concern showed in his face. 'Can you not postpone it?'

'It has to be tomorrow. Everything is set.'

He stared into her eyes. 'You are scared.' A statement, not a question.

She took a deep breath. 'Yes. I am scared.'

He stretched out his free hand. She hesitated, then took it. He drew her towards him. 'Would you allow me to say a prayer for you?'

She hesitated. It was years since she had prayed. 'You know, Father, I think I would.'

He bade her sit on the bed. 'Give me your other hand.' She did. He clasped them together in his. 'Now close your eyes and tell me about it, so I shall know what to pray for.' She did his bidding.

She was there for another half-hour. At one point her phone pinged to say there was a message. She ignored it.

CHAPTER 57

Carver lay on the bed to make his calls. Sleep would be a long time coming anyway.

The first was to Jess, his second call to her that day. Leaving the hospital, he'd rung to update her on the afternoon's events.

'We're still on.'

'Thank God.' Then she realised what she'd said. 'I don't mean... I mean it would be a shame to waste so much-'

'I know what you mean. And you are right. It would.'

'How is Ingrid?'

'I'm not sure, but I think she's okay.'

'And Remy?'

'He's good. There's not many could keep as many balls in the air as he is right now.'

Her short silence heralded the obvious question. 'Do you think she'll show?'

'Honestly?'

'Honestly.'

'I've no idea.'

'I hope she does, Jamie. For your sake.'

'I hope she does, for *all* our sakes.'

It raised a chuckle. Against the backdrop of the day's

events it was a warm sound, and mightily comforting. 'I guess you're right.' There was another pause before she added, 'Ring me before it begins?'

'I will.'

'And say 'hello' to Inger for me.'

'Ingrid.'

'Yeah, her. And Carissa. I'll have to meet her sometime.'

He smiled. 'One day. Goodnight Jess.'

'G'night Jamie.'

Next was Ingrid. She sounded sleepy.

'Are you in bed yet?'

'Not yet. I've just got back from the hospital.'

'This late? Was there a problem?'

'No. It just took longer than I expected.'

'Everything okay?'

'Yes. I took his statement.'

'Anything new?'

'Nothing of any significance. It was all more or less as I told you before.'

'You got my message about us going ahead tomorrow?'

'Yes. But I knew we would be going ahead anyway. Remy would not want to cancel.'

'How are you feeling?'

'Do not worry about me Jamie. I am okay.'

'I know you are. But if you want to talk about it...'

'I have done that already.'

He hesitated. 'Right. I'll see you tomorrow then.'

'Yes. And Jamie?'

'Yes?'

'Thank you for all your help.'

'I've done nothing. It's me should be thanking you.'

After bidding her goodnight and hanging up, Carver mused on what she'd said about speaking to somebody. 'I've done that already....' *Now who would that be?*

He turned on the pillow.

Just for a second, the spill of auburn tresses on the pillow tricked him into thinking they were Rosanna's. But the eyes waiting for his were brown, not green. They stared at each other for long seconds.

'Jess says she would like to meet you sometime.'

'And I her.'

He waited. 'This time tomorrow it could all be over.'

'I hope so.'

'Me to. What were you thinking about?'

'When?'

'Then, while I was on the phone.'

'My sister. What were you thinking of when you turned to me?'

'Rosanna.'

'So neither of us will sleep tonight.'

'I guess not.'

A minute passed.

'Jamie?'

'What?'

'Would it be wrong if we stopped thinking about them, just for a little while?'

He considered it. 'I don't think so.'

Like magnets, they drew together. The last thing she said before they lost themselves was, 'Look after me Jamie.'

CHAPTER 58

There were three monitors in the room. The one on the left was set so that every five seconds the display rotated between the camera covering the main gate, and the one in the entrance hall. Right now, the only activity was at the gate. There, the two detectives playing, 'Event Security', were pacing to and fro, swinging their arms to ward off the chill. The middle screen showed the invited audience, beginning to settle into their seats. The third screen showed the stage within the glass chamber where all the action would be taking place - or rather not, Carver hoped, fervently. Empty apart from the wooden frame with the cross-beam and the sets of steps beneath, it set Carver's heart thumping every time he looked at it, especially the noose dangling from the beam. And despite knowing that the whole set-up was a sham, Carver could not escape the feeling of foreboding that had been with him since waking that morning.

The trouble was, for the plan to succeed, those attending needed to be convinced that the event they were all paying to see was going to take place. It was why so much effort had gone into making sure everything looked right, from the gate security team, to the glass chamber itself. And Carver knew that, depending on how things went, he may have to let things run right up to the point where Ingrid may have to be seen preparing herself for the final act itself.

But no further.

Definitely, no further.

Whatever transpired over the next hour, Carver had sworn to himself, long ago, that things would never move beyond allowing Ingrid to make her final walk into the chamber. If by then their quarry had not shown, he would call an abort. There was no question she would ever get as far as stepping up onto the step. Certainly, nowhere near a rope. He had been there once. He was not going to venture that way again.

Next to him, the radio blared. Ingrid's voice. 'What's the decision? What are we doing?'

Carver hesitated a few seconds longer, giving himself a last opportunity to consider. It was the scenario they had feared. They were already some twenty minutes behind schedule, but as yet there was no sign of Megan Crane. But two of the twelve-strong audience were still to arrive. Inevitably - how could it be otherwise? – they were Henri Durcell's guests.

Right from the beginning, Durcell's past connections with Megan Crane and his present ones with those who shared her interests, meant he was the operation's key target. To Carver's mind, there was still a good chance one of the latecomers could be Her. Durcell had given the names, Michelle Chartier and Elise Turec for his missing guests. The checks they had been able to make so far remained inconclusive. Carissa thought she could recall having once met a Michelle Chartier. If it was her, she was a former hostess who used to frequent the same sort of private clubs and house-parties as Carissa.

As far as Carissa could recall, she had caught herself an oil-rich Arab and departed, long ago, for a life of supposed luxury in one of the more obscure Gulf States. Of an Elise Turec, there was no trace whatsoever. Until the pair arrived, *if* they arrived, they had no way of knowing if they were genuine names, or aliases. Carver was doing his best to ignore the fact of the initials, M.C. It is a myth that criminals like to keep their initials when they adopt an alias. But occasionally, they do. If Carver allowed his gut to rule and was a betting man, he fancied the odds that Michelle Chartier, would, if she showed up, turn out to be Megan Crane. Too soon to assume their plan had failed, there was only one option.

'Let's go with it,' he said. 'But tell Carissa to be ready to start stalling once things get underway. We need to let things run as long as possible. They could arrive any moment.'

'Okay,' Ingrid said. 'Wish us luck.'

More than that, Carver thought.

As he stood back from the radio, Carver hoped his decision fitted with what the audience would expect. The last time they'd checked with Durcell, as the reception drinks were being served in the dining room, he'd insisted that his missing guests were 'on their way' citing heavy traffic leaving Paris as the probable cause of their lateness. It sounded likely enough to be genuine. The rest of the paying guests would accept a short delay in proceedings to accommodate latecomers. But if it went on too long, it could start to arouse suspicions.

A few minutes later, the lights in the room where the stage was dimmed as the connecting door leading into the glass chamber opened. Carissa came through first.

She was wearing a full-length, black gown with lace attachments that flowed and swirled as she moved. Her hair was a mass of cascading curls. With dangling hoop earrings, and bangles on her arms and wrists, Carver thought she looked like some exotic gypsy. Behind her came Ingrid, and there was a appreciative murmur from the audience as she came into view. Also in black, she was wearing a short, figure-hugging dress, black hose, and stilettos. Carissa had seen to her makeup, accentuating her dark eyes and high cheekbones, and styling her hair so that it was very different to her normal look. Carver had seen her transform herself for her role before. Over the course of their several 'pitches' and under Carissa's expert tutelage, Ingrid had become adept at changing herself from workday detective to an object of someone's fantasy. But he had not seen her like this before. In fact he was finding it hard to reconcile the Ingrid he had come to know, with the one now being gawped at by the audience. He had no way of knowing whether the murmur from the audience when she first appeared signalled appreciation, lust or something else, though he suspected the middle of the three. He turned his mind to other matters.

One of the glass panels surrounding the stage was actually a door, with an electronic lock. Carissa entered the code, before leading her charge out. Another buzz circulated amongst the audience as she stepped down from the stage. Two chairs were already arranged in front, video cameras mounted on tripods pointing at them. Ingrid took one, while Carissa settled herself in the other. As they looked up to face their audience, spotlights came up on them. An expectant hush settled.

'Good evening ladies and gentlemen,' Carissa said.

They had decided early on they would use English. The audience was of mixed nationality and besides, it suited Carver. The few responses that came were muted. 'Welcome to Chateau de la Roque, and thank you for honouring our agreement.'

'I would not have missed it,' a man with an Italian accent said. It drew nervous amusement, which dissipated quickly.

Carissa continued. 'We all know why we are here.' She gestured towards Ingrid and gave a respectful nod. 'Tonight you will witness something none of you are ever likely to see again. It is a unique event brought about by a combination of fortuitous and tragic circumstances. Most of you have already met Nicole,' - Ingrid's 'alias' - 'and are aware of the circumstances I refer to. You also already know what is to happen here tonight. But for the benefit of those we have not met before, and the video record, Nicole will now explain in her own words why she is here and why she is about to do what you are here to witness.' She paused before continuing. 'Before Nicole speaks however, I should inform you that, as you are probably aware, the legal status of an event such as this is uncertain. It is possible that at some time in the future, questions could arise as to whether any law has been broken and, if so, whether any person concerned with tonight's events should be held to account. While such questions will be of no concern to Nicole, they could be for the rest of us. For that reason I have taken legal advice and am taking certain precautions. These are aimed at ensuring, so far as may be possible, that in the event of any authority seeking to impose legal sanctions, civil or criminal, on any person here present, then we as individuals will be distanced from any such liability. For these reasons I am videoing this introduction and everything Nicole says and does from here will also be recorded. I will describe the other precautions as the evening proceeds. Nicole.'

Taking her cue, Ingrid sat up and turned to face the camera. She gave a smile, before becoming serious. 'My name is Nicole Canavalet. I am thirty-one years of age. I am here of my own free will and not acting under any form of duress. In the last twenty four hours I have consumed one medium-sized glass of wine which I took with a meal this afternoon. At six o'clock this evening I took two tablets of Diazepam, a form of Valium. These are the only substances present in my body at this time. Before coming here today I submitted myself to a psychological examination carried out by a qualified and competent clinical psychologist. The results of that examination are in this envelope.' She held aloft the buff envelope she'd taken from her chair. 'They show that I am of sound mind and not suffering from any condition affecting my ability to think and act freely.' She turned to Carissa.

'Thank you Nicole. Now, for the benefit of the recording, can you just confirm that you understand exactly what is going to happen to you tonight?'

'Of course. I am going to be hanged by the neck until I am dead.'

CHAPTER 59

As always, the words sent an icy chill through Carver's veins. Though he'd seen her rehearse them several times, he still found them deeply disturbing. An image, buried deep in his brain threatened to force its way to the surface. Recognising the need for a diversion, he turned to the monitor showing the audience and reached for the camera joystick.

Although he could not see them at that moment, Carver was aware that Remy and another officer were somewhere at the back of the room. Dressed smartly in dark suits, they were acting as part of the security team and event 'supervisors'. Those comprising the audience were dressed formally, black-tie for men, evening-dress for women. With their faces hidden behind masquerade-type masks, they could have been attending some celebration ball or up-market charity event. The men's masks were simple, covering only their eyes. But the women's were colourful, elaborately decorated with crystal and feathers. During the planning stages, the masks had been a point of discussion between Carver and Carissa. He was concerned that it would make it harder to spot Megan Crane if she showed up. She waved his argument away, pointing out that those attending would expect to be able to preserve their anonymity on camera, just in case. If their expectations were not fulfilled it might prompt questions. In any case, once assembled, the audience would be under the detectives' control. If needs be, all they had to do was tell them to take off their masks. 'And in any case,' as she finally put it, 'Do you really think you will have difficulty spotting her amongst a handful of other women?' He had to admit, he thought not. Nevertheless, right now it was frustrating that their responses to Ingrid/Nicole's statement were shielded.

The audience was arranged in two rows, eight at the back, six in front. At the end of the back row were the pair of German lesbians. Cinched into tight corset-dresses with lots of ties and stays, they could barely keep their hands off each other, with much stroking, caressing, and kissing on show. Then there were the two married couples. The middle-aged French pair were aloof and quiet. So far, they had kept themselves very much to themselves. The other couple were younger, in their thirties maybe. The husband was Italian, his wife, Finnish. Loud and given to making coarse remarks, they both came across as immature and over-sexed. Carissa knew him to be heir to a famously-rich motor manufacturing magnate. Carver suspected he'd never done a day's work in his life and wished there was some criminal offence they could arrest and charge him with just for being there. But then he realised, he could say the same about them all. Considering what they had come hoping to witness, both couples seemed remarkably at ease. It made Carver wonder what other 'special events' they might have attended in pursuit of their interests. At the other end of the row, was the older

Japanese man and his much younger, Thai 'girlfriend.' Carissa was still uncertain regarding her gender. 'I can't tell whether she's transsexual or a transvestite,' she'd said after meeting him/her. The front row was reserved for Durcell's party. Durcell himself was at one end, alongside the woman Carver had chased after at the hotel that day in the vain hope she might have been Megan Crane. Next to them was a younger, bearded Frenchman together with a dark-haired girl who Carissa was convinced was high on something. 'He's a real weirdo and she seems totally out of it,' she'd reported to Carver. 'I can hardly get a coherent response from her.' Apparently the Frenchman had managed to unnerve her – no mean feat - by leering at her, constantly, and responding to her questions with monosyllabic quips and sly smiles he seemed to imagine made him appear, 'cool'. 'There's something about him I don't like at all,' Carissa had said. 'Apart from the fact he's interested in events such as this, I mean.' At the end, two empty chairs awaited the late arrivals.

As Carver zoomed in on the audience, Carissa played for time by getting Ingrid to lay out her supposed back-story, 'for the record.'

Clearing her throat, Ingrid began. 'Twelve months ago I was diagnosed with a rare form of Huntingdon's disease, a hereditary and incurable degenerative brain condition. It is still in its dormant stage but once it takes hold, which doctors say will be within the next three to four months, my brain cells will start to die off at an increasingly rapid rate. Less than twelve months from now, I will be dead. As the disease progresses I will become increasingly dependent on others. Eventually I will need full- time care. My parents are not wealthy and my mother is ailing. I cannot bear the thought of them having to watch me die while spending what little savings they have in trying to keep me alive, as I know they will.

'Sexually, I have always been a natural submissive. I have been a 'breath play' fetishist for several years and have sometimes fantasised about being hung, in front of an audience. When I first learned about my condition, I considered suicide, simply to spare my family suffering. But after speaking with certain people, I realised that if others with similar leanings were willing to pay to watch me act out my fantasy for real, I may spare my parents a great deal of anguish and secure their financial future. I have known Carissa for many years and knew she would know how to contact people such as yourselves. To begin with she tried to talk me out of it.' At this point Ingrid reached out and took Carissa's hand. *Nice touch*, Carver thought. 'But when she realised I was serious, and that I was going to die anyway, and so horribly, she agreed to help me. Carissa, I will be forever grateful for what you have done for me, and for my family.'

There was a catch in Ingrid's throat as she said it. To his surprise, Carver found himself similarly affected. 'If that doesn't convince them, nothing will,' he muttered. Once again, he could only marvel at Ingrid's acting skills, especially considering how she hated the role she was playing. 'Distasteful and demeaning,' was how she'd described it. Carver knew Ingrid still had some difficulty with the whole premise of 'Nicole''s 'motivation.' To begin with, she was sceptical that people would actually pay large sums to witness her supposed death. But then Carver showed her some of the remaining material from Megan's archives and some he had gathered whilst researching her past activities. She was astounded and repulsed in equal measure. But while she remained troubled, she agreed to play the role.

With two guests still to show, Carver's hope was that someone – Durcell most likely - was waiting until he was sure everything was as it had been purported before sending some sort of 'all clear' message via mobile or some other means. Carver imagined Megan Crane waiting in a car, close enough so that she could arrive just in time to witness the finale. He didn't mind how 'last minute' her arrival was, so long as she showed. He checked the gate again. Still no activity.

In the room below, Carissa had moved on to explain to the audience how the event would be staged.

'As you can see, there are two entrances onto the stage, this glass door at the front, and the one at the side of the stage that connects to the library next door. The glass is shatter-proof and strengthened. The locks are electronic, operated by a digital code known only to myself and Nicole. Soon, Nicole will retire to the room next door so she can mentally prepare herself for what is about to happen. When she is ready, we will enter through the connecting door which will then be locked. I will help Nicole into position on the podium and place the noose around her neck. I will then strap this to the palm of her hand.' She held up a small oblong device with a red button in the centre. 'It is a remote control. It operates a trap door, like this.' She pointed it through the glass and pressed the button. A trap in the middle of the step fell open. 'I will secure her hands behind her back then leave the cage, lock the door and join you here. When Nicole is ready she will press the button.

The trap will open, and she will fall. You will play no part in her death, nor will you be able to do anything to prevent it. From a legal standpoint, you cannot be held liable. Does anyone have any questions?'

The Frenchman spoke up. 'What if she changes her mind at the last minute?'

'The apparatus is set up so that if Nicole presses the red button twice in succession, the noose will be released. I will then enter the chamber and release her. In the event of that happening, your payment will of course be refunded.'

'Do not worry, Monsieur,' Ingrid said. 'I have no intention of changing my mind.'

It drew a satisfied nod from the questioner.

'Any other questions?'

One of the lesbians raised a hand. 'How are you feeling, right now?'

'Nervous. Excited. Frightened. Sad. Happy. A rollercoaster of emotions. It is difficult to explain.'

'Are you aroused?'

Carver winced. It was a horrible question for Ingrid to have to deal with, but given the nature of the audience and their interests, one they'd anticipated. Again she handled it as she had rehearsed with Carissa.

'Earlier today I was not, but I have to admit that as the moment draws near, I am beginning to experience strong feelings of arousal, mixed with the others I describe.'

Which is what they'll want to hear.

With no other questions, Carissa rose. 'You now have the opportunity to meet with Nicole one last time before she retires. I will return in a few minutes.' She left the way she had entered, leaving Nicole alone with her adoring 'fans'. Seconds later, Carver's mobile rang.

'Any news Jamie? I cannot stall much longer.'

'Nothing. The only thing you can do is drag Ingrid's preparation time out as long a possible.'

'I will, but there is a limit. If it goes on too long, they will become impatient.'

'They can please themselves. If needs be Remy will stage the police raid and arrest them all. I suspect they will choose cooperation over facing a magistrate, even if they are confident they have not broken any law.'

They were still discussing options when Carissa interrupted to say, 'Ingrid needs to speak with me. I will ring you back.' Two minutes later she did. 'Something unexpected has come up. The Frenchman, the weird one with the beard, is asking if it would be possible for his girlfriend to meet Nicole privately. Apparently she would like to ask her some personal questions. He is prepared to pay an extra five thousand for the privilege. He says it is a birthday present for her, to make the whole occasion more memorable.'

'Jesus Christ,' Carver said. 'How much more memorable does it need to be?' He shook his head. 'These people. They're even more twisted than-' He pulled himself up. They weren't playing by normal rules. 'What does Ingrid think? How does she feel about it?'

'She says she can handle it. Besides, it will give us a little more time.'

Carver nodded. An extra few minutes could make all the difference. 'Then go for it. Every little helps.'

A few minutes later, Carver watched as 'Nicole' said her last goodbyes before following Carissa out through the glass chamber to the room next door. A minute later

Carissa returned alone and took the Frenchman and his girlfriend to one side. After a brief conversation she told everyone to help themselves to drinks and snacks laid out on a table at the rear of the room and returned next door. She rang Carver again.

'I've told them they can have ten minutes with 'Nicole.' I'm going to go over things with her one more time so we don't trip ourselves up, then bring them in.'

'Right. If anything happens while they're with you I'll call and let you know.'

Standing in front of the monitors, Carver wiped the sweat from his brow. He checked his watch. Now some forty minutes behind schedule, he was doing his best not to let the sinking feeling take hold in his stomach. They had worked so hard, risked so much.

On screen, the connecting door to the stage opened. Carissa came through, beckoned to the Frenchman and his girlfriend and held the chamber door open as they stepped up onto the stage, then followed her through to next door.

'That's it,' Carver said. 'Ten minutes, then its all over.'

He turned to check the monitor covering the gate one last time. As he did so, a car drew up and stopped.

Carver froze.

CHAPTER 60

As the Frenchman helped his girlfriend stumble into the chair, Ingrid regarded her with alarm.

'Is she alright? She looks like she is about to pass out.'

The man turned to his companion as if only just realising her condition. Her head kept dropping forward. Ingrid wondered how much she had drunk during the delay when drinks were served. For the first time, the Frenchman showed concern. 'I am afraid the excitement is getting to her. Perhaps this is not such a good idea after all.' He turned to Carissa. 'I am sorry Madame. A little *restoratif* perhaps? Do you have any cognac?'

'Not here, but I can get some.' She checked with Ingrid, who nodded. 'I will be back in a moment.' She left the room.

As the door closed, the Frenchman put his arm round his girlfriend's shoulders. 'I am sorry about this Mademoiselle. I think maybe I should not have brought her here.'

Ingrid was in full agreement. She wondered what sort of man would bring a girl in such a state to something like this. But she needed to stay in role. 'Do not worry Monsieur. I am sure- Oh my God.'

Seeing the girl starting to pitch forward, Ingrid lent forward to catch her. As she struggled to hold onto her, the Frenchman rose, coming round to Ingrid's side. In front of the curtained window was a sofa. 'There,' Ingrid said, nodding towards it. 'Help me get her on the-'

The words cut off as the Frenchman's arm suddenly wrapped itself around her throat, pulling her back and off balance. At the same time, something soft and sickly-sweet smelling pressed over the lower part of her face. Had she reacted instantly, Ingrid may have used her training to escape the attack. But burdened by the girl, and disoriented by the suddenness of the attack, she hesitated to let the girl fall. And though that hesitation lasted only seconds, it proved decisive.

Carver stared at the screen showing the main gate. 'Please God, let it be.'

The radio crackled. One of the gate officers said, 'We have two women at the gate. A Michelle Chartier and an Elise Turec. What are your instructions?'

Yes. Carver grabbed the radio. The officers were using earpieces. No danger of him being overheard. 'Direct them to the front door. I will meet them there.' As an afterthought he added, 'In fact you two follow them. We may need you here.' No point taking chances.

Carver clenched a fist. About to radio through to Carissa, he remembered that she and Ingrid had company. He rang her mobile. No reply. He called Remy on the radio.

'Michelle Chartier and the other woman are here. She'll be at the front door in two minutes.'

'Do you need me to come out?'

'No. Your men are bringing her. I'll let you know

soon as we've got her.'

Leaving the room, he made his way to the stairs. He was halfway down when he saw Carissa crossing the hall carrying a glass. He was about to call to her when the sound of crunching gravel sounded from outside. He reached the bottom of the stairs just as Carissa disappeared into the library. The door closed behind her. Crossing to the front door he stopped and took a deep breath before flinging the door open.

Two women were making their way up the steps. Their heads were down and they were picking their way carefully so as not to trip in their dresses. The one in front was tall, with shoulder-length hair, as black as coal. They were flanked by the officers from the gates. This time there could be no escape. Startled by the door's sudden opening, the woman in front stopped to look up. For the first time, she saw Carver, waiting. They stared at each other.

Carissa closed the library door then turned toward the chairs where she had last seen Ingrid and the girl. They were empty. Looking around, she saw the girl over on the sofa. She looked either half-asleep or semi-conscious. Alarmed, Carissa started towards her but stopped as she saw the figure lying on the floor across the other side of the room, not moving. Her eyes widened as she realised it was Ingrid. About to rush to her, a voice came from her right.

'Good evening, Carissa.'

She turned. A shock-wave hit her.

'*You.*'

Before she could react, there was a blur of movement and something thin and dark looped over her head and pulled tight round her throat, cutting off a scream. The glass fell from her hand. She scrabbled, desperately at whatever was round her throat, her nails drawing blood. Realising she could not get a purchase on it and panicking, she grappled, desperately, for a grip on her attacker's wrists to try to relieve the pressure. But her attacker was strong and shrugged away her already weakening efforts. And as her strength began to ebb, her vision to blur, a voice, calm but unmistakably malevolent said, 'Say hello to your sister, bitch.'

And as the chill words that spelt out her attacker's intentions rang in her ears, Carissa Lavergne finally realised. For all their planning and preparation, she and Carver had still made the fatal mistake of underestimating her sister's killer's ingenuity.

CHAPTER 61

The words of greeting Carver had ready died in his throat as he stared at the woman he had never seen before. Confusion must have shown in his face as she returned him a similarly puzzled look.

'Monsieur Carver?' the woman said. She said something in French he could not understand. He turned a vacant face to the accompanying officers.

'She is asking if you are the man they are supposed to meet,' one said.

'What man? How did she know my name?' He turned back to her. 'Who are you? Why are you here? Who gave you my name?'

All he got was more French.

'English,' he said to both women, louder than he needed to. 'Parlez-vous anglais?'

Alarmed, they shook their heads. Michelle Chartier said, 'Non. Pas d'anglais.' She turned to the two officers, started talking to them. Carver broke in.

'Tell them we are Police. Ask them what they are doing here. How have they got my name?'

At mention of the Police, the women became guarded. But as the officers fired questions at them, they fired others back. Hands waved. Voices rose. Carver sensed things falling apart. He heard his name mentioned, several times. Finally one of the officers turned to him.

'They are escorts. From Paris. They say they were paid to turn up at a party here tonight. They were told it was a joke someone was playing on an old friend and that when they got here they were to ask for you and you would explain.'

Carver rocked back on his heels. How could someone...?

'Who?' he said. 'Who paid them to come here?'

The policeman put the question to her, then turned back to Carver.

'An English woman. She said her name was Anna Davis.'

Carver froze. Anna Davis was the name of Megan's - the Worshipper Killer's - third victim. And Carissa's step-sister.

Carver stood motionless, staring out into the night as he struggled to grasp the meaning that lay behind the two women being sent here. *And being told to ask for him.* It had to be Megan of course. It could be no other. She would know that only he would recognise the name Anna Davis. A thought began to form. He turned to look back into the house, where everyone was still awaiting the latecomers' arrival. Megan would know that once the two women arrived and told their story, he would know she was onto him and was not going to risk showing herself. So why go to all the bother? Why let them carry on as if the event was going to take place? And why would Durcell show up if he knew the falsity of it all? He thought about Carissa. Could there be another significance in her using Anna Davis's name for this particular deception? He thought about the audience, inside, waiting. He remembered the weird Frenchman with the strange girlfriend who wanted to meet Ingrid. And as he did so, an icy fear gripped him. The girl was too young to be Megan Crane. But nevertheless, had there been something familiar about her? He thought back to his encounter at Les Galleries. And as he pictured Megan parading the young American, Tory Martinez, in front of him, he focused on the girl's face, and his heart skipped several beats.

'OH GOD. NO.'

He sprinted up the steps and back into the house. As he went, he called back over his shoulder. 'Keep them here. Don't let them go anywhere. I'll need to speak to them.'

He stopped at the library door, tried it. It was locked. He knocked once, then again, louder. 'Carissa?' He waited only seconds. 'Carissa?'

No response came.

Inside the room, the buzz among the audience fell away as the connecting door opened, and stayed open. On the front row, Henri Durcell slipped out of his seat and made his way quietly, to the back of the room. From his position in front of the double doors leading to the hall, Remy saw him coming and stepped forward to meet him. 'I am sorry, Monsieur. No one is allowed to leave.'

Durcell nodded and smiled in a way Remy thought strange. At that moment, he heard banging from somewhere outside, what he thought was a shout. It sounded like Carver. About to go and investigate, he paused as he followed the Frenchman's gaze as it returned to the stage. The connecting door was opening further.

Two seconds later a gasp of astonishment passed Remy's lips, and he instantly forgot all about Henri Durcell.

Carver dug in his pocket for the key Carissa had given him. She had the only other. Finding it, he unlocked the door and went in. His first thought was the room was empty. The connecting door through to the stage was shut. But a groan from his right drew his eye to the other side of the room. Ingrid lay on the floor, beginning to stir. He ran to her.

'What's happened, Ingrid? Where is-?'

He never finished the question.

Heavy drapes covered the bay windows that looked out over the garden behind the sofa. They were bunched at the bottom, as if concealing something. A woman's ankle with a black shoe peeped out. A sick feeling came to Carver's stomach. Bounding over, he wrenched the curtains aside. Carissa lay on her back. Her eyes were open, staring up at the ceiling. A black cord was knotted tightly, round her throat.

Carver felt his head about to explode. 'No, NO.'

He pressed his fingers to her carotid. But he'd seen enough bodies to know he would not find what he was looking for.

In his hand the radio blared, making him jump.

'JAMIE, WHERE ARE YOU?' It was Remy. Carver could hear panic in his friend's voice as he continued. 'SHE IS HERE. IN THE CHAMBER. SHE HAS THE GIRL.'

For the first time, Carver become aware of the sounds of some commotion emanating from the room next door. Leaping to his feet, he raced across to the connecting door. As he did so something caught his eye. Strewn across a chair, as if discarded in haste, was a man's black-tie suit and shirt. On top of it, a sandy-coloured wig and beard. Pieces clicked into place.

His fingers were shaking as he wrenched the door open and burst into the chamber. He managed two paces then stopped dead as his worst nightmare materialised before his eyes.

Teetering, shakily, on the podium, hands cuffed behind her and with a noose round her neck, was the, 'weird Frenchman''s girlfriend. Only now, close up and without the mask, and though her hair was cut shorter and dyed a different colour, he recognised the girl he had last seen arm in arm with Megan Crane as they slipped quietly away into the crowd outside Galeries Lafayette, the missing American, Tory Martinez. To his left, the other side of the glass, Remy was tugging, uselessly, at the door. Never expecting that he would need it, Carissa had not shared the combination. In the dark behind, shadows moved, the audience realising that their programme of entertainment was being hijacked, and that maybe an early exit was called for. But it was the black-clad figure hovering behind Tory Martinez that grabbed Carver's full attention.

Megan Crane was smiling in a way he had seen before, and made his skin crawl. Dressed now in the black body-stocking she had worn beneath her disguise, she showed no signs of either surprise or being put off her stride by Carver's sudden appearance. And when she spoke, it was like a dove, cooing to its mate.

'Hello Jamie. Welcome to the party.'

Carver ignored it. Less than ten yards separated

them. It was time to end it. He was about to leap forward when she lifted a hand, showing him the remote control with the red button in its centre. He froze again. Tory was standing over the trap.

'Don't, Megan,' he said. 'It's over. You can't get away.'

Her response was to arch an immaculately pencilled eyebrow, and smile even more widely. He had seen her do so once before. He knew what it meant.

To his left he was dimly aware of Remy stepping back from the glass, reaching behind and under his jacket.

'NO, MEGAN. PLEASE.'

Remy lifted his arms out in front, pistol in hand, pointing at the glass.

Carver opened his mouth to try again.

'As always, Jamie, you're too late.' She pressed the red button.

Everything happened at once.

The trap fell away and Tory Martinez dropped.

Remy pulled the trigger and the glass exploded.

The lights went out, plunging the room into darkness.

CHAPTER 62

Amidst the shouting and screaming, Carver's only thought was for the girl, though images of Angie as he had last seen her and now Carissa lying in the adjoining room, threatened to impose. *No more. Please, God, no more.*

Shattered glass crunched underfoot as he groped his way across the stage towards the podium, hands outstretched, listening for some sign of her. Something brushed passed him in the dark, making him jump. A fragrance trailed in its path, one he recognised. He heard Remy call, 'WHERE ARE YOU JAMIE? HAVE YOU GOT HER?' Which 'her' he meant, he could not tell. He didn't waste time replying. Right now he was Tory Martinez's only hope. If he gave his position away, she may yet try to stop him. They say cats can see in the dark. It wouldn't surprise him...

His shin banged, painfully, against something hard. The lip of the step. He waved his arms in front. She should be there, dangling. She wasn't. He moved forward. His foot caught on something and he stumbled. He landed on what he immediately realised was Tory, lying half in and half out of the trap. As he grabbed at her, pulling her up, searching for the knot at her neck he felt her move, trying to twist round. *Thank God. If her neck had broken...* He found the knot. Mercifully, it hadn't tightened as much as he'd feared. He pulled at it and it loosened. She must have been almost out of air as she gave a loud gasp, followed by a long 'whooping noise' as she sought to fill her depleted lungs.

The lights came on again.

Tory was across Carver's lap, gasping for breath. A few feet away, Remy stood in the middle of the stage, holding his pistol in both hands, twisting and turning as he searched for a target. Out in front, members of the audience were in various states of panic and disarray. As the room lit up, everyone rushed for the door. The connecting door to the chamber was wide open. Megan Crane was nowhere to be seen.

Remy didn't hesitate but started barking orders into his radio. Carver guessed he was ordering the lock down they'd planned to only ever use if things went badly wrong. As the responses started to come back, Remy turned to Carver. His face was full of questions.

Carver nodded towards the door. 'Call an ambulance. Ingrid-' His voice dropped as he added, 'And Carissa...' He shook his head. Remy turned white, and charged out through the door. Somewhere, a car's engine roared. Not willing to leave Tory, Carver shouted through the door. 'REMY. OUTSIDE. THE CARS.' An answering shout came from within. Carver left it with him. Right now his priority was the girl. He turned his attention back to her.

Half out of it even before it happened, she was still only semiconscious. As she coughed and gasped, still trying to catch her breath, she turned to look up at Carver. Terror showed in the clear blue eyes. She tried to say something, but either her voice-box was damaged or she was still too shaken. Pity welled in him.

'Don't try to talk. I'm a police officer. Everything's going to be alright.'

Whether she heard or understood he couldn't tell. As he looked down at her he remembered the happy smiling face in the photograph. Then he remembered her dead fiancée. She probably wouldn't even know. *Dear God...* He wondered what she'd been through the last couple of weeks, what she had seen, what she had suffered. He shuddered as the memory of a cellar, dank, dark and well-equipped came to him.

He stroked her cheek. 'You're okay, Tory. Don't worry. You're safe now.' A tear tracked her cheek.

Carver blinked, looked away. Movement from the room next door caught his eye. Remy's men were scurrying to and fro. He heard urgent shouts, followed by cries of dismay. He thought of Carissa, lying beneath the curtains. He closed his eyes, tight, and rocked back and to, clasping Tory to him.

CHAPTER 63

Carver waited while the ambulance made use of the turning circle in front of the house. As it pulled away, he raised a hand in a gesture of thanks to the driver. She waved back before putting her foot down. Her partner paramedic was out of sight in the back, seeing to Tory. A minute or so before, as Carver stepped down from the vehicle, he'd implored him to, 'Look after her.' The look on the man's face told Carver it was a redundant request, but he felt better for making it. By then the sedative was beginning to kick in and Tory was breathing easier. The plastic neck-brace made her look like a crash victim, nevertheless she was conscious enough to squeeze Carver's hand as he left her. She'd even managed a hoarse, 'Thank you.'

But for her Carver knew, the worst was yet to come. As the effects of whatever Megan had been plying her with began to wear off, she'd called out a couple of times for her fiancé, Scott. 'Just relax,' Carver had urged her, conscious how inadequate it was. She was easier now, but in the morning, by the time she'd slept and her head was clearer, she'd want to know why he wasn't there. Carver had already resolved to be there when she woke up, whatever the rest of the night brought.

The ambulance was halfway down the drive when the lights and wailers came on, warning someone coming up the drive to get out of the way. The house was now a murder scene. Car by car, the circus was arriving in response to Remy's calls. The police doctor and some of the forensics were already there. Soon, the long driveway would be choked. Remarkably, there were no press yet, though Carver knew it wouldn't be long. They would have a field day. He was still watching the ambulance when he felt Remy's hand on his shoulder. He turned to face him.

'Any news on the car?'

'Not yet.'

'Damn'

Only one car had made it away. The one that had bought the masquerading prostitutes, who were now missing. The officer who saw it take off, 'Soon after the shot was fired,' described seeing a 'bunch of women' run from the house and dive into it before it flashed past him and disappeared off down the drive. 'No I didn't see any faces, but the tall one in the front seat next to the driver had black hair.' The only other person unaccounted for was Megan Crane.

Carver shook his head, raised his eyes to the stars. 'Why the fuck did I take the men off the gate? It was stupid, stupid, stupid.'

'You thought you had her. I would have done the same. Do not blame yourself.'

Carver looked his friend full in the face. 'I DO blame myself, Remy. For everything.' He cast a despairing arm about. 'This whole debacle. The American girl. Ingrid.' A longer pause. 'Carissa.'

But by now in full SIO mode, Remy had no time for

recriminations.

'Enough, Jamie. That is for later. Right now there is work to do. Now she is wanted for murder in my country. We can still catch her.' He turned back to the house. Carver delayed only seconds before turning to follow. He caught up with him at the bottom of the steps.

'How is Ingrid?'

'Sore. Feeling sick. She would not go in the ambulance so I sent her to lie down. There will be much to do in the morning and I will need someone who is at least half-fresh.' He glanced at Carver. 'Why don't you go and-'

'I'm going nowhere until we hear word of her.'

Remy nodded. 'At least Ingrid was lucky. She could easily have ended up-'

'No,' Carver cut in. 'She wasn't lucky. That lunatic bitch doesn't leave things to chance. She plans her targets. She knew Carissa was helping us because of what she did to her sister, so she got her first. They were her targets tonight. Carissa, and the American girl.' He thought a moment. 'If anyone's lucky it's the girl.'

'Did you know that Carissa had cut halfway through the rope?'

Carver shook his head. 'We never got that far. The rope was never supposed to come into play so we didn't talk about it.'

'So why bother taking such a precaution?'

Carver shrugged. 'Carissa knew what Megan Crane is like. Maybe she knew there was always a chance she might get the better of us, no matter how well prepared we thought we were.'

'In which case, she saved the girl's life.'

'Yes...'

Inside, Remy went off to see how the team he'd assigned to the 'audience' was getting on. In the aftermath, they'd all been herded to the kitchen area at the back of the house where they were being detained. Earlier, Carver had seen Remy take no little pleasure in making clear that no one would be leaving until their stories had been thoroughly checked, and they had all made full statements. The protests were loud and long. Remy ignored them. Clearly, Megan Crane had known it was all a set up. Which meant that somewhere, there was a leak. Remy was determined to find it. They'd already started with Durcell, but the only thing out of him so far, apart from insisting he did not know anyone called Megan Crane, were demands to be allowed to call his solicitor. They were yet to be granted.

As he watched Remy's team pulling the early strands of what would soon be a full-blown murder investigation together, Carver ached to be involved. But he knew he could not. One of the first calls Remy had had to make was to Marc Couthon, the Magistrate Carver had met at the Palais De Justice, ages ago it now seemed. He was on his way, and was expected within the hour. Remy already had much explaining to do. Carver was not even supposed to be in the country. He did not want to make things any harder by flaunting himself in Couthon's face. Besides, he'd done nothing to be proud of. The opposite in fact.

Recognising that if he didn't find himself something - anything - to do that was productive, he would spend the rest of the night lost in recrimination, Carver remembered the cameras. They had been rolling all evening. Maybe they could tell him something useful.

He headed for the stairs and the first-floor bedroom-control room. As he passed the library, the door was open. White-suited figures milled about. A flash of light followed immediately by the whine of a recharging battery told of a scene photographer going about their business. A knot tightened in his stomach as he looked away. He mounted the stairs.

It took him a while to get his head around how to retrieve and view the recordings. He was not a natural when it came to computers and CCTV systems, but eventually, he got there. Keeping an ear out for any signs from downstairs that could indicate that the missing women had been located, he began with the video showing the audience in their seats.

The 'weird Frenchman' – *you were so close Carissa* – and his girlfriend were clearly visible on the front row. Carver paused the image and zoomed in. Not as detailed as it would have been in full light, it was just about good enough. Peering close, he thought he could just make out Megan Crane under the disguise. But he knew he was working with twenty-twenty hindsight. Would he have recognised her had they come face-to-face? He liked to think he would. But then, Carissa had spoken with her and she didn't spot that it was a woman in disguise. *Oh that she had.*

He moved on. It was the same with Tory. He zoomed in on an image that caught her full face, looking towards the camera. Behind the mask and beneath the make up he could just make out her clean-cut features. Or so he told himself. In truth he doubted he would have made either. He was familiar with the way the brain often doesn't recognise patterns, in this case faces, when they are out of context.

At one point the Frenchman/Megan Crane turned to speak to Durcell. It prompted Carver to realise he was looking at good evidence that Durcell was integral to Megan's plan. Someone had to have switched the lights off. Downstairs, he was still denying he even knew her. 'Explain this then,' Carver murmured as he noted the recording's time stamp on a slip of paper. He'd just finished when he heard voices, approaching. The door opened. Remy and one of his detectives entered.

'They've stopped the car, just outside Paris.' Carver's heart leapt but it lasted only as long as it took to register Remy's flat expression. 'It contained only the driver and the two prostitutes. They say there was no one else in the car when they left here.'

'They would.'

'They've been taken in for questioning. Do not worry Jamie, we will find her. Someone is going to have to talk.'

'Yes, but the problem is, when?' The information contained within the metal filing cabinet he'd recovered from Megan Crane's basement years before, showed she had friends all over. She had managed to live here, undetected, for close to two years. Where next?

Remy gave an acknowledging nod, then said, 'Also, Magistrate Couthon is here. It may be as well if you stay up here for a while.'

Carver nodded. 'I intend to.'

As Remy left, Carver returned to the CCTV.

Looking at the screens showing his nemesis but in another form, Carver set to reflecting on what he had tried and failed to do. Was it all a doomed enterprise from the start? Right now, it looked that way.

It was clear now that Megan Crane had known early

on that the whole thing was a set up. The charade with the two escorts, even going so far as instructing them to ask for him by name, proved it. He shook his head. He'd always known she had gall by the bucketful, but this... But then, why come at all? One thing he did know. Megan Crane likes to take revenge against her enemies. It was why she targeted him and Angie in the first place, luring him into the original Worshipper enquiry before. . . . Carissa working with him these past weeks meant that she too had now become Megan's enemy. Was that it? Was it all about targeting Carissa because she had dared to conspire against her, then using the set up they'd conveniently provided to see Tory hanged in place of Ingrid? Or was it something else, either instead of, or as well as? He remembered the look on her face when he first burst into the chamber. Her sly smile. As if genuinely pleased to see him. At the time, he'd put it down to her devious, calculating ways. Trying to unnerve him in a time of crisis, as she'd done before. She was effectively trapped, yet she was so cool, as if it was all part of some plan. But what sort of plan? And what stage was it at now, beginning, middle, or end? He rubbed fingers into his temples, where a dull ache was beginning.

She'd have known full well she was walking into a trap, yet still she came. And they so nearly had her. Had it not been for the confusion, and the dark, she may not have managed to slip away. It was lucky for her there were no officers on the gate or they'd have been there to shut them. She would have been... trapped.

He stopped.

No officers on the gate.

How could she have known there would be no one

on the gate? That was his decision. Made on the spur of the moment. The timing of her revealing herself, her attempt to substitute Tory for Ingrid, her subsequent getaway, they all appeared to have been planned to coincide with the two women's arrival. Not only did it provide a useful diversion – it certainly diverted Carver's attention – it also ensured there would be a car waiting when she came out, ready to whisk her away. Yet the plan could so easily have failed. Had the officers been at the gate to respond to Remy's lock down, she would have been trapped. Even if she had evaded those at the gate, a dog, or a helicopter with a dragon-lamp would quickly have tracked her down. Her coming here was a risk. In fact, the more he thought about it the more he realised. It was one *hell* of a risk.

So why do it?

She had to have known that any escape would depend on her being able to get as far away from the house as quickly as possible. But she could not have guaranteed that would happen. Carver's brain whirred. Megan Crane was no fool. And he'd never known her do anything that left much to chance. He'd said as much to Remy, not long ago. Yet a getaway by car left a lot to chance. He glanced at the screens in front of him, and smacked himself on the forehead.

'You bloody idiot.'

The answer, to one question at least, was right in front of him. Why hadn't they thought of it before? Because they'd all *assumed* they knew what had happened, that's why. The words he remembered hearing, so many times through his early training, came to him. 'If you *assume,* you make an *ass* out of *u* and *me.*'

He bent to the keyboard, programmed the search. Two minutes later he had it up on the screen. The view from the hallway camera, just before everything kicked off. He waited. Nothing happened. Too early. He fast-forwarded a few minutes. People were running around. Too far. He backed up. This time.

It started at the point where he came running back in after speaking with the two women outside on the steps. He disappeared out of shot as he ran across to the library door. Seconds later the two women appeared in the doorway. They came through into the hallway where they lingered, waiting for... what? As the video ran on, he mentally replayed what was happening out of shot.

Now, I'm unlocking the library door. Going in. Finding Ingrid. Then Carissa. *Oh God.* Remy's call on the radio. Opening the connecting door. Entering the glass chamber. Seeing first Tory, then Megan. Remy points his gun. He fires. On screen, the gate officers dashed across the hallway, towards where the shot came from. At the same time, the two escorts reacted with alarm, hands to their mouths. People began running back and forth. Carver started counting. 'One, two, three..' At the time, his groping in the dark seemed to last ages. In reality, it can only have been seconds. Ten. Twenty. Thirty. Another guard comes running in. Suddenly the escorts turn and run out through the front door. 'There.' He froze the frame, hit the rewind icon, played the sequence again. The shot. The guards running. Now the other guard running in from outside. The women fleeing... *On their own.* He let it run. The next person to appear was... Remy. Going out to check the front of the house. The car's gone, so he comes back into the hallway. He speaks into his radio. One of the gate officers appears. He gives him instructions. The officer runs outside. Remy disappears back towards the library. No one else appears.

Carver stopped the recording, leaned back in the chair. There had been no sign of Megan Crane. Certainly she did not leave the house through the hallway with the escorts as they'd thought. Yet the officer who saw them spoke only of seeing women leaving the house. When they'd asked him how many, his response had been, 'Two, possibly three.' Three matched their expectations. They'd gone with it. What if his first estimate - two - was correct?

Carver remembered his first visit to the house when Carissa showed them round. She had pointed out to them the several priest holes and hidden passages. 'There are others,' she'd said.

Jesus Christ.

Pausing only to grab his radio, he ran from the room.

CHAPTER 64

As Carver reached the top of the stairs and looked down, he saw Remy, talking to Magistrate Couthon in the hallway. He hesitated, then shook his head. 'Fuck it.' Skulking was never his thing.

He got as far as the top stair when a blur of movement somewhere along the corridor to his left caught his eye. He stopped. Turning back, he was just in time to glimpse a shadow disappear round the corner at the far end, beyond the room he had just left. Someone must have been lurking there as he'd come out. But he'd seen and heard no one. He could think of no reason why anyone should be moving about on the upper floors apart from him. The only possibility was if Ingrid had come looking for him but, seeing him in a hurry, had changed her mind.

He looked down at Remy and Couthon, still talking. He opened his mouth to call, then shut it again. It may have been nothing, in which case he could soon find out. No sense getting everyone wound up before he needed to. Couthon probably wouldn't hang around too long. If he could find out who it was without causing Remy any more trouble... He turned back and headed down the corridor, making as little noise as he could.

He peered left round the corner where he had seen the shadow disappear. It was another corridor with several rooms off. At the far end were more stairs and he just caught a flash of movement, heading up. He ran to the bottom of the flight. Of bare wood and with no carpeting, they were not as wide or grand as the main staircase leading up from the hallway. At the top, he could see part of the second floor corridor. No one was in sight. He mounted the stairs quickly, but quietly. Seeing no one on the second floor he carried on to the third, then the fourth, still without seeing anyone. As he neared the top of the stairs leading to the fifth floor, the last apart from the attics where they were billeted, he stopped to look through the railings before showing himself. Still no one. There were several doors, all closed. At the end were the stairs to the attics. He waited, listening. Above him, he caught the sound of soft footfalls, but they stopped almost as soon as he tried to home-in on them. He jogged down to the bottom of the stairs. Again, there was no sign of anyone. He ascended more slowly this time, conscious of how quiet it was in this remote part of the house. He peered down the corridor. The rooms they had been allocated were on the right, the doors evenly spaced, first Remy's, then Carissa's, his own, and at the end, Ingrid's. He moved down the corridor, stopping to press his ear to each door he passed. He heard nothing until he reached Ingrid's room, where he thought he could just make out the noises of movement within. Like the walls, the doors were thick. He worried about disturbing her if he was mistaken and she was sleeping. He rapped a knuckle, lightly, on the door.

'Ingrid? Are you awake?'

After a few seconds a voice said, 'Qui est-ce?' *Who is it?*

'It's Jamie'

There was a pause, then, 'Moment.'

He waited several seconds, imagining her putting on her robe. Then the voice said, 'Come in.'

Turning the handle, he entered the room - and stopped dead. His mouth gaped and his head span. For the second time that night he had walked into a nightmare.

Only this was worse than the first.

Far worse.

CHAPTER 65

Time didn't just stand still. The clock turned back three years, five months and twenty-two days. Back to the kitchen of the cottage he and Rosanna had shared out at Pickmere. In the middle of the floor, Rosanna was bound to a chair by ropes wound, tightly, round her body and arms. A cloth gag cleaved her mouth. At her shoulder, stood Megan Crane. Her fist was balled in Rosanna's hair and she was holding a broad-bladed knife to her throat. The shock was such that Carver had to put out an arm to the wall to steady himself. For several seconds he was so disoriented he did not know if he was awake, or asleep and reliving the nightmare that came so often.

'We'll have to stop meeting like this,' Megan Crane said.

The familiar voice triggered something. There was a 'whooshing' in his ears and he had to gasp as he finally remembered to breathe. Air rushed back into his lungs, the injection of oxygen reviving him enough that he managed to straighten, levering himself away from the wall. But as he gazed on the sight that still haunted his waking as well as sleeping hours, he realised. This was no dream, and they were not in his kitchen. This was real, and the woman tied to the chair was not Rosanna, but Ingrid. Barely able to comprehend how it could be happening all over again, he fought to suppress the wave of panic threatening to engulf him.

'You don't look well Jamie. Perhaps you would like to take a seat?'

As she spoke, she made a sweeping gesture. Following it, he saw the plain, wooden chair on its own in the middle of the floor, Looking up he saw it was positioned beneath one of the sturdy beams, a noose hanging from it. On the seat was a set of handcuffs. But though the sight filled him with the same, dank dread it had last time, for some reason he could not explain, he was not surprised to see it there.

As he took it all in, a strange, fuzzy feeling started to grow in the front of his head. He had already lost Carissa that night. Before her, he had lost Angie and, almost, Rosanna. Was it now to be Ingrid's turn? And following her, himself? If so it would be no more than he deserved. Penance for his failure to protect them all. The fuzziness grew in intensity. It was not an altogether unpleasant feeling. Somehow it made him feel warm inside, as if it held out the promise of relief from all that had haunted him these past years. Was the end, finally, in sight? Welcoming the promise, he closed his eyes, and went with it.

Terrified, sick to the stomach and aching where the ropes and gag were digging in, Ingrid was still able to recognise that something had happened to him. Seconds before, the way he suddenly straightened, she had thought he was about to launch himself across the room and tackle The Woman directly. What the consequences would have been, she had no idea. But now he looked like he had fallen into some sort of trance. It was as if someone had thrown a switch. One second he was there, breathing deep and steady, weighing options. The next he wasn't. She actually saw the moment when the lights went out in his eyes and his face took on the defeated look of someone who finally decides they can fight no longer. She remembered the few times she had tried to get him to talk about the events surrounding the death of the woman, what was her name, Angie? Whenever it looked like he might be about to talk of it, his face took on an expression similar to the one he was wearing now. At that point he always found some excuse to change the subject. The third time it happened, it was clear to her that he was avoiding. A couple of times since she had come close to mentioning counselling, but the time was never right. Looking at him now, she had no idea what was going on in his head but suspected it was something similar. And while she thought she understood, she wished she had pushed him further on those occasions. It might have stopped him switching off when the moment came, as he now seemed to have done. Ingrid was already scared half to death. But the sight of the only man who could save her apparently giving up, *really* terrified her.

She screamed into the gag. 'JAMIE.' It came out nothing like.

'QUIET,' Megan Crane yelled and yanked her head back. Pain exploded in Ingrid's scalp. It felt like her hair was being pulled out by its roots. Tears welled up. Not ready to risk a further dose of such punishment straight away, she tried to plead with him with her eyes.

Not like this Jamie. Please not like this. Then, to her

surprise, she felt anger flooding into her and she followed it up with a different exhortation. *Fight her, damn you, FIGHT HER.*

The Woman spoke up again.

'Now we've been through this before, Jamie, so let's not waste time like we did on the last occasion. You know what to do. Up on the chair.' She said it the way someone coaxes their dog to do tricks.

To Ingrid's horror, Carver turned to look at the chair, as if he was actually thinking about doing it.

She screamed again. 'DON'T JAMIE'. There was another yank, even more painful than the first.

'I told YOU to be QUIET.'

Ingrid felt the knife press harder against her throat and she caught her breath, expecting to feel its bite. It didn't come. Clearly, she wasn't ready yet.

'Come on, Jamie.' This time there was an edge to the voice. 'Do as you're told. Up on the chair.'

As Carver stepped towards it, Ingrid broke a sob.

'That's a good boy.'

Searing pain tore through Ingrid's head and scalp as her head was forced round and she was made to stare up into a face that seemed devoid of sanity. The eyes flashed and the demented grin that more rightly belonged in an asylum grew wider. 'You see? The Woman sneered. 'He does just what I tell him to do.'

Right then, Ingrid understood what Carver had meant when he once told her, 'You've never seen a crazy person until you've stared into Megan Crane's eyes.'

As Carver stepped closer to the chair, a low chuckle escaped the woman's throat.

A shudder of revulsion passed through Ingrid and she groaned into her gag.

Deep down, Carver knew what he was doing wrong. He should be resisting. But right now, doing as he was told seemed so much... *easier*. Besides, he wasn't sure he had any choice in the matter. It felt like he was no longer in control of his body, like he was watching himself doing her bidding from some vantage point, knowing it was wrong, but waiting to see what would happen. But then, he knew what would happen. He would get on the chair, put the noose round his neck and wait for Kayleigh to arrive. Only, he wasn't sure where Kayleigh was right now.

Carver had relived that night, many times over the past three years, mostly in his nightmares. And every time he did so, it triggered the same, horrible thought. What would have happened had Kayleigh Lee not shown up when she did? Sometimes the sequence ended with him watching Rosanna's life drain away as Megan Crane pulled harder and harder on the length of black ribbon around her throat while he dangled, helpless to stop her. Sometimes the events played out in his mind differently, with him not stepping up onto the chair, but choosing instead to charge across the room and overpower her, before she could draw the knife across Rosanna's throat. He never succeeded. Every time, the knife would draw and Rosanna's blood would spurt, arcing in the air to splash against the wall, before he completed even half the journey. He never got to see what happened after, to Megan or himself, because that was when he woke up. And in the instant he awoke, all he knew was that Rosanna had died because he had been too slow. But at least after, as he came round, he had the comfort of knowing it was just a dream. In real life he never made that mistake. In real life, right or wrong, he had stepped up onto the chair, and Rosanna had lived. It didn't matter how she came to live. All that mattered was, she didn't die because of his mistake.

Which was why, when Megan Crane ordered him, 'Do as you're told. Up on the chair,' it seemed entirely natural that he should obey. He didn't think about what would happen next. The important thing was to not put Rosanna's - no, Ingrid's - life at risk. Reaching out, he took hold of the back of the chair to steady it, lifted a foot, and put it on the seat.

Seeing what was about to happen, Ingrid knew she had no choice. It was now or never. If it meant feeling the knife's edge then so be it. It was going to happen anyway. Thrusting her jaw out as much as she could, she strained to loosen the gag. It gave enough so she could give a passable shout.

'SNAP OUT OF IT JAMIE.'

Something hard – the base of the knife handle – slammed into her temple with enough force to topple her sideways and send her crashing to the floor. As she landed, she let out a cry that was equal parts pain and anguish.

Hearing his name called, Carver stopped and looked round, just in time to see Megan Crane lash out, viciously, with her knife hand at her prisoner's head. For a split-second Carver expected to see blood spurt and he was about to cry out in protest, *'I'M DOING IT.'* But then he found himself watching as the chair toppled sideways and Rosanna/Ingrid hit the floor with a bone-jarring thump. Her cry of pain reverberated around the room. Carver winced in surrogate agony as Megan Crane reached down, took a firm grip on Ingrid's hair and, by no other means, pulled her back up to a sitting position. Ingrid let out another agonised scream. Even in his entranced state, it was more than Carver could stand and he cried out.

'STOP. Don't hurt her.'

Megan Crane rounded on him in a fury, like an angry parent yelling at a small child. 'BE QUIET. You just do as you're told.'

Carver hesitated, torn in several directions. He wanted to obey. That way he could avoid incurring her wrath. She held Ingrid's life in her hands. He didn't want to jeopardise it by attempting something he knew was impossible. She was too far away. He wasn't fast enough. But he also recognised another voice, growing louder, telling him he ought to be doing something to protect the colleague he had grown close to over the past weeks. An image came to him. They were in Les Deux Chats. She was there, smiling at him over her cointreau. A sly, teasing smile. Not unlike Rosanna's, in fact.

Suddenly, the 'whooshing' he had experienced came again. Only this time its effect was to flush away the fuzzy feeling that had seemed so comforting. He blinked, blinked again. Suddenly he was back. In the present. Facing the same dilemma he had faced once before. Only this time, for some reason everything seemed clearer. If he stepped on the chair and noosed and cuffed himself, he would be at her mercy. And this time there was no Kayleigh Lee around to come crashing through the window and save them. Not in France. And certainly not a hundred feet off the ground.

One thing Carver knew for certain about the woman he had been pursuing the best part of two years. *She doesn't do mercy.* At the same time, he had never forgotten what started it all. Edmund Hart's suicide. She had always blamed him for her lover's death. It was why she came looking for him in the first place. To avenge Hart's prison suicide. And though she had tried once and failed, and though he had since saved her life, he knew deep down that in reality, nothing had changed. Hart had hung himself. She had planned the same for him. And while the plan went on hold for a while - gratitude for him saving her from a similar fate - it would still be there. Leopards don't change their spots.

He looked across at Ingrid, helpless, terrified. By the look of her she was already resigned to dying. She'd given up on him. In that moment, he was flooded by a deep sense of shame. He had to do something, now.

The distance was about the same as last time. There was no prospect of the cavalry arriving. Remy and his team were busy downstairs, pulling out all the stops trying to work out where Megan Crane had gone to ground. There was nothing to make them think she was right here. On top of that, there was a murder scene to run. It could be hours yet before Remy thought to check on Ingrid to see how she was. By then it would all be over. He had two options. Easy really.

He made his decision.

Carver braced himself, took a deep breath, and-

A knock came on the door.

He stopped. Three pairs of eyes swung round. The door opened.

It was Father Alonso.

CHAPTER 66

It was one of those moments when something happens that is so out-of-place, so unexpected, no one knows what to do.

Ingrid's astonished stare betrayed the fact she simply could not believe he was there. Why would he be? How could he be?

Megan Crane's face betrayed a combination of surprise, puzzlement and annoyance that her carefully-staged finale had been interrupted, and at such a crucial stage. The hand holding the knife fell away from Ingrid's throat.

Like Ingrid, Carver had no idea how or why the priest was there. But he wasn't going to waste time trying to work it out. He saw the knife drop. Only a few inches, but it signalled where Megan Crane's mind was right then. Not on Ingrid, or him. He moved.

Flinging himself forward he'd covered a third of the distance before she even reacted. Her head came up and around to see him closing on her. Turning to look down at Ingrid, there was a moment's hesitation as she sought to realign the knife with Ingrid's throat. It was enough.

Even as the blade touched flesh enough to draw blood, Carver crashed into her, carrying her away from

Ingrid and bundling her to the floor. As they rolled round, banging into the bed, the furniture, he tried to lock his arms round her. But she was like a wild cat, arms flailing, trying to scratch, push or pummel him off. He couldn't get a firm grip. As their heads came together she saw her chance and sank her teeth into his shoulder. He roared with pain and writhed to free himself. But the act put distance between them. She was crouching above him, the knife still in her hand. He could only watch as it flashed down.

An arm shot out and a hand wrapped round her wrist stopping the blow in mid air. The point of the knife, hung, three inches above his chest.

Carver spun round and looked up. Father Alonso was standing over them. Seemingly without effort he lifted Megan Crane by the wrist, and held her in front of him, like a child examining a toy. Carver gasped. The priest was clearly a lot stronger than he looked. Writhing like a serpent in the vice-like grip, Megan Crane screamed the sort of bile a priest may not be used to hearing. At the same time flecks of spittle flew from her mouth. Some landed on Carver's cheek. What happened next caught Carver totally by surprise. As he looked at her, quite calmly, Alonso's other arm swung round and a fist the size of a ham smashed full into her face. She went immediately limp, hanging in his grip, feet off the ground. Then he tossed her onto the bed like a rag doll, where she lay still.

Carver shook his head, drew a deep breath and started to rise.

'Bloody hell, Father. That was-'

The huge fist crashed down again, catching Carver somewhere around the side of the temple and sending him crashing back to the floor, where he also lay still.

CHAPTER 67

Carver opened his eyes, but had to close them almost immediately as pin-pricks of light exploded in his head. He felt sick and dizzy. He tried to move, couldn't. He waited a few seconds before trying again, more slowly this time. Everything was blurred. The first thing he realised was that he was on the floor, tied in a sitting position with his back against something hard, arms behind him. Something - tape - was stuck across his mouth. A nauseous feeling swept over him and he shut his eyes again while he tried to work out where the hell he was, what had happened. Bit by bit, he remembered. Walking into the room. Megan Crane threatening Ingrid. They had fought. Someone had intervened to save them.

Father Alonso.

In a panic, scared of what he might find, he lifted his head and looked round. Ingrid was next to him, alive and tied as he was. The cloth gag had been replaced by a strip of black tape. She was looking at him, as if she had been waiting for him to wake up. She still looked terrified but as he came round enough to recognise her, relief showed in her face. She nodded at him. *Are you with me?* He hesitated, took as deep a breath as he could manage, nodded back.

She flicked her head, as if to indicate something in front of them. He turned his head, slowly, so as not to make the dizziness worse. In front of them was the end of the huge bed he remembered Ingrid bouncing on like a little girl when she first saw it. From their low position, the mattress was above their line of sight. Still dazed, it was a moment before his vision cleared enough for him to see something moving. A tall figure, hunched over, it's back to them. Every now and then the shoulders moved. Each time it happened a squeal, like an animal in pain, echoed in the room. As a thought came to him he closed his eyes and shook his head again, to make sure he wasn't dreaming. He wasn't. The figure he could see moving was Father Alonso. His bare back was scarred and red with cuts and wheals. Carver checked the rest of the room as best he could. There was no sign of Megan Crane.

In that second, Carver knew. He didn't try to work out how, he just knew. It happens like that sometimes. You think you understand a situation and know all you need to know about it. Then something new occurs, or you come across a new piece of information. Suddenly you realise that everything you thought you knew and understood was wrong and that the actual situation is the complete reverse. It was like that now. Between seeing Alonso at the door, witnessing what he did to Megan Crane, then waking up and remembering the crushing blow to the skull that laid him out, Carver realigned his understanding. And it told him that the man responsible for killing and butchering several women in and around Paris was not poor Father Masson, but Alonso.

As if to confirm it, the figure on the bed rose and swung itself, slowly to the floor. About to stand straight, he paused, looking back at something on the coverlet, then he turned and came towards them.

Father Alonso was naked and streaked all over with blood. The knife Megan Crane had been using to threaten Ingrid hung, limply, in his right hand. Seeing Carver awake, he approached to squat in front of them.

'So, Monsieur Detective Carver. You are awake again.'

Carver could only stare up at the figure that looked like it had walked in off the set of some Texas-Chain-Saw horror movie. Apart from the blood smeared all over, Carver saw something else. Beneath the smears, Alonso's torso, arms and legs were criss-crossed with scars, some old, others more recent. They varied in length and depth. Some were only a couple of inches, others extended across his chest, or the full length of his thighs or arms. Carver could tell that while some, the older ones, were fairly superficial, the more recent wounds appeared much deeper. As if the person responsible for inflicting them had experimented, over many years, to see how far he could go. A wound to his right side appeared recent, still seeping puss. Carver was amazed. The man had to be in great pain, yet he showed no sign of it.

As he squatted before them, Alonso stared first into Carver's face, then Ingrid's. Carver noted they way his features softened when he switched his gaze to her.

'I apologise that I did not intervene sooner. I would not have wished you to go through what you did, Ingrid.' He waited until Ingrid nodded to show she was hearing his words before continuing. 'Still, we must give thanks that I have been able to rid this world of one who was perhaps even worse than all the others together.' He half-turned to look back at the bed. They followed his gaze but from their position could only tell that whatever was on the bed, there was no movement, nor sound.

Alonso smiled at them. Another that chilled. 'You now realise of course the truth of it. Yes?' He waited for their nods. They gave them. He continued. 'Father Masson was never as clever as he thought he was. But he was beginning, I think, to work it all out. After you first came to the church with your story, he grew increasingly suspicious. It was only a matter of time before he stumbled upon the truth. Even for someone as dedicated to protecting the name of the church as he was, I do not think he could have stayed silent. Even had I explained to him the nature of the mission God has given me, to punish those women who risk more pain and suffering to their children than they can ever imagine by giving in to their carnal desires, he would have felt obliged to come to you, eventually.' He paused again. Letting it all sink in. Carver and Ingrid stared, transfixed.

'Yesterday I thought that perhaps I had done enough to make you think that Masson was the one you were looking for. That eventually you would move on and that after a suitable period of rest, I would be able to resume my work.' At this point he stared hard at Ingrid. 'But our last conversation, Ingrid, when you told me about the checks you would make into Masson's background? I knew you would not find what you were looking for. His childhood was, as far as I know, a happy one. Unlike myself he came from a family that cared. I realised it would not be long before that would put doubt in your mind. You would be forced to widen your enquiries. At some point you would learn of my childhood. The church records are very detailed. They show what happened to my mother and, later, to me. The suffering I went through. The guilt I carry round with me.' He heaved a heavy sigh. 'I knew then that if I was to continue God's work, I must kill you both. You were good enough to share with me what was to happen here tonight. We even prayed together, remember? That was when I decided to follow you here. Luckily, you were all so busy I managed to slip inside and hide myself away in one of the bedrooms until the performance you spoke of began. I had thought I may be able to make it look like something had gone wrong with your plan. That this woman was responsible for your deaths.' He gave a sad smile. 'It turns out I was right, only not in the way I had imagined. I certainly did not expect that I would be able to continue my own work at the same time.' He turned to look back at the bed. 'She was an unexpected bonus. Our Lord will be pleased.' He rose. 'Now forgive me but there is one more thing I must attend to before we can finish.' He bent down and cradled Ingrid's face in a huge paw. Her breathing intensified. 'Do not worry, my child. I have no intention of making you suffer in the way of these others. My first impressions of you were wrong. I know now you are not like them. I promise it will be as swift and painless as I can make it.' Ignoring Carver completely, he turned away and moved to a dresser set against the wall to their left. On it was a statue of Christ and a bible. Stopping only to buckle some sort of belt round his waist and pull on a cotton smock that was stained with dried blood, he knelt down, stretched out his arms in supplication, bowed his head, and started praying.

'Holy Father, hear my prayer. I send to you for your forgiveness another who has sinned. Not like the others, but in ways much, much worse. *Pray for the children*. I believe she is responsible for the deaths of many. That she has caused much suffering to those left behind. *Pray for the children*. Whether you find a place for her in your Heavenly Kingdom or feel she must be banished to Hell for her sins I know not. I know only that, like the others, she was brought to me for punishment, and punishment I have inflicted. *Pray For The Children*. Our Father who art in heaven. . .'

As the priest launched into his Lord's prayer, Carver strained at the bonds round his wrists. Ingrid did likewise. He had no idea how much time they had. Nor did he know how long he had remained unconscious while the priest sat astride Megan Crane, butchering her. He only knew that whatever time they had, they better make best use of it. Alonso was clearly every bit as mad as Megan Crane. But that didn't help to know how long he would pray. It could be two minutes it could be an hour. As he strained and pulled – the chords seemed expertly applied - every now and then he heard the blessing that was clearly a key part of the priest's offering ritual. '*Pray For The Children.*'

He was still working on his bonds, trying to picture the way the ropes were lying across his wrists so as to gauge where best to apply pressure, when he felt Ingrid's frantic nudging. He glanced round to see her nodding, urgently, towards the bed. He turned his head just in time.

Like a bloody corpse rising slowly from the grave, Megan Crane sat bolt upright.

CHAPTER 68

Of all that Carver had witnessed this night, nothing was as blood-curdlingly horrific as the moment he cast eyes on Megan Crane's once beautiful features. Her face, and what he could see of her upper body, bore the familiar pattern of cuts, gouges and lacerations he had witnessed on the other victims. Blood still dripped from them. As she sat there, she lowered her eyes and ran her gaze down her body, as if taking in the full horror of what had been done to her. Stretching out her arms in front, she turned them, slowly, examining the cuts to her flesh, before transferring her attention to her legs, abdomen, and breasts. Finally, hands shaking, she lifted them to her face, assessing the damage through trembling fingers.

Carver's first thought was, *How is she still alive?* The blood loss had to be enormous. He remembered the room in which Marianne Desmarais was found, the photographs of the other scenes. The way Father Alonso had spoken of her in the past tense, he had to be thinking she was dead, hence his 'offering' ritual. Then Carver remembered. During the run-up to her trial, he had discovered she was adept at a form of meditation. First learned when travelling in India, she was able to slow her heart rate, the way animals do when they hibernate. They suspected it was the trick she used to lure her victims into thinking she had lost consciousness during some BDSM game. After untying her, often in a blind panic, they would drop their guard enough so she could turn the tables on them, restrain them, then prepare them for the grisly killing ritual that back then attracted both the media's and Carver's interest, as was her plan. That has to be it, Carver thought. She must have practised it again right here, enough to convince Alonso she was dead at any rate. In the background, the priest's muttered prayers continued.

'...Amen. *Pray for The Children*. Also dear Lord can I ask that...'

Carver turned to Ingrid. She was staring at Megan Crane as if she could not believe what she was seeing. Sensing his gaze, she turned to him. She shook her head as if to say, '*What now?*' Carver had no idea. He returned his gaze to the bed.

Megan was staring back at them as if she had only just become aware of their presence. She looked across to where the priest was still praying, his back to the bed. As she turned back to Carver, she spotted the noose, still hanging from its rafter, unused.

Carver and Ingrid could only watch as Megan Crane swung herself, silently, off the side of the bed furthest from the praying priest. She stood up straight, but slowly, as if every movement was painful to her which, cut like that, it had to be. She took a step forward but stopped. Next to the bed was a full length dressing mirror. Carver watched as she stared at her reflection, seeing for the first time the full extent of the damage inflicted on her. He couldn't begin to imagine what was going through her mind. There are plenty of excellent plastic surgeons in the world, but are any that good? Turning away from the mirror, she took two steps forward, and reached up for the noose.

Carver wondered if she had lost her mind. If her hope was to sneak up on the priest and try and strangle him with it as he prayed, she didn't have a cat-in-Hell's chance. They had already witnessed Alonso's strength. She may succeed in getting the noose over his head and round his neck but as soon as he realised he would resist. In a battle of strength he would overcome her every time, then probably use the noose to finish the job he'd started. As Carver continued to watch, wondering about her intentions, he worked at the ropes round his wrists, pulling them first this way, then that. He wasn't sure, but they felt like they might be loosening.

But rather than take down the noose, Megan did something unexpected.

Until that moment, Carver had paid little attention to the means by which she had intended to hang him. He had assumed the rope was tied to the beam from which it hung, ready to bear his weight. But now he realised that in fact the rope was merely draped over the beam having been threaded through the several rafters that were spaced, at regular intervals, along the length of the room. The rope trailed all the way back to the full-length window through which its other end disappeared. He remembered the coil of rope he'd seen hanging outside the window during their initial tour. It was attached to a hoist fixed to the beam sticking out over the lake below. As he watched her work, an image of what she might be planning began to form in Carver's mind.

She'll never do it.

As Megan worked at the noose, the priest continued to chant. Lost in his offering and prayers for, 'those soon to come to you', by which he presumably meant Ingrid and himself, the priest still seemed oblivious to everything around him. And why not? As far as he was concerned, Megan was dead, and securely tied as they were, he and Ingrid were going nowhere. Nonetheless, Carver had the sense that the offering ritual might be nearing its end. He was hearing 'Amen' more frequently and the blessing, 'Pray For The Children', less than before. Also, instead of his arms staying outstretched, the priest was now bringing his hands together with each Amen, like he was closing down a series of linked prayers.

As he watched, Megan began to unthread the rope from the rafters, moving from one to the other, working her way back, swiftly but silently, towards the window. Her bare feet made no noise on the wooden floor, though a trail of bloody footprints marked her progress. As she came level with the priest's back Carver held his breath, but Megan didn't pause. Calmly, she unthreaded the rope from the last two rafters. Seconds later she was at the window, noose in hand, spare lengths of rope at her feet. The priest was nodding and bringing his hands together more than ever now. 'Thanks be to the Lord...' Carver pulled at the ropes. His wrists chaffed and burned like Hell, but he felt more movement. He said his own prayer. *Just keep praying another minute.*

Reaching out through the window, Megan gathered in the other end of the rope and pulled it back through. Now she had an end of the rope in either hand, one being the noose. Finally, Carver saw her plan. The rope was still threaded through the hoist attached to the beam. She was going to try and-

'Amen.' Alonso clapped his hands in a way that signalled his prayers had come to an end. Lifting his head, slowly, he turned his gaze on his prisoners. Behind him, Megan froze. Whether it told in their faces or he sensed it through some other means, his gaze flitted to the now empty bed. Alarm showed in his face. He began to rise. At the same time, Megan sprang forward, like a she-lion after prey. Passing from behind his right shoulder, she slipped the noose over the still-rising priest's head, at the same time giving a sharp yank on the rope so it tightened round his neck. Taken by surprise, the priest spun round, arms flailing, hoping to catch her. Skipping out of his reach, she ran down the room, taking the rope with her. His hands went to the noose but at that moment Megan reached the end of the rope's 'play'. As it tightened on the hoist and she continued to press forward, Alonso was hauled backwards, like a fish being reeled in on a line. Had he been ready, there was no way it would have worked. But caught off-guard and with nothing to grab at for purchase, the priest was pulled, staggering, back towards the window. As she reached the far wall, Megan turned and pulled in the rope's remaining play, at the same time maintaining the tension on the hoist. Unable to stop himself, the priest crashed into the windows, which burst open. Realising what was about to happen, he flung his arms out to the sides, searching for something, anything that might stop him being dragged out.

The walls around the window were made of sandstone blocks. Rather than square, the lip of the

stone around the frame was angled, so as to maximise the opening into the room – useful in the days when stores where hoisted up from the boats below. As he hit the windows, Alonso's scrabbling fingers grabbed at the stonework's edge, and held just enough to halt his progress. But the angle meant he could not get enough purchase to pull himself back in and upright. As Megan continued to pull as hard as she could on the hoist rope, Alonso hung on, balancing, precariously, half-in and half-out of the window, his fingers waging battle with the angle of the stonework around the frame. As he fought to maintain the grip he could lose any moment, Megan saw what he was trying to do. With a final yank she increased the pressure on the rope then raced forward to wrap her end round one of the bed posts. She did it several times then secured it with what Carver recognised as several expertly-executed half-hitches. Knots always were her thing.

Now Alonso was secured, still balanced over the window sill. With the rope tied-off to the bed-post there was no play he could use to relieve the pressure threatening to drag him out. All he could do was hang on, while his fingers scrabbled, desperately, for some relieving purchase he might use to try and free himself.

Wrists still working behind him, Carver had had no choice but to watch the struggle now poised so delicately with something close to fascination. But he knew that something had to happen to end it - and soon. If Alonso managed to free himself from his balancing act before Carver did his wrists, they were all dead. On the other hand, if Megan managed to pull Alonso out through the window he would hang, leaving her free once more to turn her murderous attentions on them. He pulled at his wrists with all his might. They felt on fire. Something gave. A shadow fell over him. He looked up.

Megan Crane stood over him, blood dripping from her several wounds. Seeing the blood pooling at her feet he realised that her exertions would have caused her heart to pump faster. Holding her arms out from her sides, she showed herself to him.

'Look at me Jamie. See what he has done to me?'

He tried to say something, couldn't. Reaching down, she ripped the tape off his mouth.

'Untie us, Megan. We can get an ambulance. A doctor. You'll be okay. We can fix it.'

She bowed her head, examining the lacerated mess that had once reduced rooms to silence when she entered. When she looked up, Carver saw something he never thought he would see in her eyes. Real tears.

'He's ruined me Jamie.' She appealed to him. 'Who will want me now?'

Carver was aghast. He had never seen her like this. He pulled at his wrists. There was more movement. 'Believe me, Megan' he said. 'However bad it looks, they can fix it. Just untie me.'

She gave him a long, scrutinising look. 'Would you still desire me like this, Jamie?'

It was a question Carver knew he could not answer, for all sorts of reasons. Next to him, Ingrid was following every word. He groped for some sort of response. 'Megan, we- We were never-'

What happened next took him completely by surprise. Squatting to his level, she took his face between her bloody hands. Like once before, a long time ago, Carver found himself staring into eyes that few were capable of resisting. His heart pounded. He opened his mouth to say something but before he could get the words out she pulled him towards her, at the same time she clamped her lips to his. Her tongue invaded his mouth, encircling his. Unable to resist, Carver could only hold his breath and stare, wide-eyed, as the woman who had vowed to kill him maintained the kiss for what seemed an age. Then, as quickly as it came, it ended.

Letting go, she stood up again. Somewhere beneath the bloody mask, a remnant of the sly smile he remembered so well lingered. 'Not quite as good as last time. But under the circumstances, it'll do.'

Stunned to silence, Carver could only stare up at her.

An urgent growling and nudging from Ingrid drew him back to the present. Turning, he saw at once the reason for her agitation.

Alonso had managed to get a firmer grip on the stonework with one hand. In the other was a knife. He must have had it in the belt under the smock and somehow managed to reach it. He was using it to saw through the rope above him. Already Carver could see one strand hanging loose where he had cut through. A few more seconds and he would be free.

Megan Crane reacted at once. A banshee scream like nothing Carver had ever heard in his life erupted from her. Her face transformed into a snarling mask of fury and she charged at the priest, arms flailing like a mad woman. As she ran, her screams bounced and echoed off the walls.

Carver put everything he had into a final tug at his bindings. They parted.

She was still some yards away when she launched herself at Alonso. Carver just caught the astonished look on the killer's face before she crashed into him, her momentum carrying them both out through the window and into the night.

Free at last, Carver tore at the rope round his ankles. Not as tight as that round his wrists, it came away. Leaping to his feet, he ignored the cramps and ran to the window. The montage that awaited him would stay with him the rest of his life.

The two killers were still there, dangling from the hoist, spinning round and round as they swung back and to against the backdrop of a nearly-full moon. Carver could tell from the angle of Alonso's neck that he was dead. Megan Crane was clinging to him like some demented harpy, legs wrapped round his middle, one arm cradling his neck. From her mouth she was emitting not so much a scream, as what Carver would later recall as more akin to a wolf-like howl as she swung, back and forth. Seeing him at the window she stopped howling and did her best to keep him in sight as she spun in circles.

'You see Jamie?' She called out. 'I saved you.' Then she looked down to her stomach where the hilt of the knife protruded, its metal boss glinting in the moonlight. 'But the bastard's killed me.'

Horrified, Carver watched as she reached down with her free hand, took a firm grip on the handle and pulled it, slowly, from her stomach. Dark liquid spurted as she withdrew it. Then she held it aloft against the night sky, like some sort of trophy as her blood dripped from the blade.

Above her something pinged. They both looked up at the rope. The strand Alonso had cut part-way through had parted. Another was unravelling, fast.

Carver and Megan Crane turned their faces to each other. For the last time, their eyes met.

'Love me forever, Jamie,' she said.

He stared back at her. There was a final ping. The rope parted and she fell, still clinging to the dead priest.

Leaning out as far as he dared, Carver watched as they plunged the seventy-plus feet to the lake below. There was a splash. Waves washed over, and they were gone.

CHAPTER 69

Carver was finding he was okay provided he had something to focus on. It was when he didn't he hit problems. Last night, at Les Deux Chats, he had focused on the second leg of the Champions League Quarter Final. Liverpool had played Real Madrid. For two hours he managed to lose himself. A bottle of Macallan helped. Liverpool had won, though the outcome did nothing to lift his spirits. Now he was focusing on other things. Apart from the meeting that would take place as soon as Examining Magistrate Marc Couthon got back from his early morning meeting with a High Court Judge, he was taking in the sight across the square from Couthon's office. Notre Dame looked magnificent in the early sun. It was only a few minutes after nine, but the tourists were already out in numbers, as were the beggars, practising the pathetic looks that would see them through another day. Behind him, Ingrid was checking out the paintings and shelves of ancient texts. Remy was on the Chesterfield, head down, playing with his mobile.

Carver had spent a good part of the past two days with Tory Martinez. That had given him plenty to focus on. Forty-eight hours before, he had kept his promise to be there when she woke up. He arrived at the hospital to discover her parents already there. They had flown from Boston the moment they heard she was missing. They already knew about Scott. Tory's father was a no-nonsense lawyer. He insisted that he and his wife should break the news. Carver waited outside.

After, following the first wave of grief, the Martinez family had questions. Lots of questions. Carver did his best to answer them all. Considering everything she had been through, Tory was remarkably in control. Overnight, the doctors had managed to flush from her system most of the cocktail of suppressants she had been fed the past few days, and through her tears she was demanding. She wanted to know all about the woman who had taken her fiancé from her. Carver thought he knew why. While she was as grief-stricken, angry and bitter as he would expect, her overriding need was for understanding. To know not just what had happened, but why. As they spoke, Carver caught glimpses of the steely young woman who would one day follow in her father's footsteps, once she got over the horror that Paris had become. That she would get over it, in some form at least, Carver was in no doubt. She just needed time. Her parents would see she got it. During the morning and into the afternoon he shared with them as much as he thought he could, and should, about Megan Crane. Her character. Her traits. Her history. Right back to Edmund Hart. Some things they did not need to know. He kept those to himself.

Then it was his turn. He wasn't sure she would be up to it. She was. Over the next day and a half she told him what they needed to know. Which was why they were waiting for Couthon to arrive back from his early morning meeting.

Ten minutes later, the door opened and 'L'Aigle' entered. Seeing them, he was all smiles. Or rather, his mouth was. His eyes said otherwise. He greeted them, individually, with a hand shake. And though he met their gazes, Carver sensed the difference from the last time. Couthon had met Ingrid once before. She had described how, on that occasion he had held onto her hand and made a show of trying to charm her. She described him as being, on that occasion, 'overly-tactile and creepy.' Not this time.

When he began to address Remy in French, Remy stopped him. He nodded towards Carver. 'Anglais, s'il vous plait.' Couthon showed some surprise, but did not argue. He rounded his desk and sat in his big leather chair. Safe refuge, Carver thought. Pulling up chairs, they arranged themselves before him. Couthon started again.

'I have read your interim report on the outcome of your investigations, Remy. It makes fascinating reading. And I congratulate you on your success.' They waited, saying nothing. Couthon continued. 'That the killer should turn out to be a priest is shocking, truly shocking. Believe me, it is shaking the city to its foundations.' Remy nodded. He and Carver exchanged glances. Couthon continued. 'But I have to say there appear to be some gaps in the report.' He hesitated, looked once at Carver then back at Remy. 'I think it may be best if we discuss these points in private?'

Looks passed between the three detectives. Remy smiled, weakly. Couthon read what was happening. 'Am I missing something here? Have I said something amusing?'

'No, Magistrate,' Remy answered. 'Nothing amusing at all.'

'Well then, what-'

'Only, we are not here to discuss my report.'

Couthon looked puzzled. 'No? What then?'

'Detective Carver will explain,' Remy said, passing the baton.

Carver waited until the eagle eyes met his. If Couthon had any issue with Carver's involvement, this time he chose not to raise it.

'As Remy's report makes clear, Father Alonso's unmasking is bound up, closely, with the outcome of the matter that brought me to Paris.'

'So it seems. Which is why-'

'It is that matter we are here to talk about.'

The tip of Couthon's tongue showed, briefly. 'But I have no involvement in that matter. Surely you must know that it is the Magistrate for the area where the young American was killed with whom you must speak?'

Carver almost smiled. For someone who professed not to speak good English, he could not fault his grammar. 'We already have.'

'You have? Well then, why are you here?'

'To execute this Warrant of Arrest.' He produced the paper from his inside jacket pocket.

Couthon pressed himself back in his seat. 'Warrant of arrest?' He swallowed. 'Whose arrest?'

'Yours.'

Another swallow, more pronounced than the first. He feigned a chuckle. 'Ridiculous. For what crime?'

'Right now it is for obstructing a police investigation. I am sure that other, more serious charges will follow in due course.'

'You are all mad. I have done nothing-' Carver's hand stopped him.

'The American girl has an excellent memory. She will be a good lawyer some day. It took us a day or so of wrong turnings and backtracking, but eventually she led us to the Maison de Floret.'

Couthon's face was blank. 'And what has this to do with me?'

'The people at the land registry have been most helpful. The house is owned by a gentleman by the name of Guillaume Rochelle.' Carver waited. The continuing silence told him all he needed to know. 'As you know, Monsieur Rochelle is a retired Judge. You and he used to work together, in Rennes I think?' Still no response. 'The one thing we could not work out is how Megan Crane knew of our plans. Not just enough to evade our trap, but to dare to use them for her own ends, which were to kill Carissa Lavergne, the American girl, and, if needs be, myself.' He paused again. Couthon's gaze was locked on him. 'Yesterday we traced Monsieur Rochelle to one of his other homes, outside Nice. You have visited there I believe? I have to say he was most cooperative, once we pointed out the possible implications of him providing refuge for an escaped killer. He was eager to demonstrate that he knew nothing of Megan Crane's crimes and thought he was merely providing temporary accommodation for an old lady friend of yours who had fallen on hard times. He did so by making available to us, his telephone records, amongst other things.'

At this point Carver stopped. Remy took out his phone and dialled a number. A mobile on Couthon's desk rang. About to reach for it, Remy got there first. Picking it up, he checked the number showing, and slipped it into his pocket. 'Evidence,' he smiled. Carver continued.

'The records show that over recent weeks, Rochelle has received several telephone calls made from your mobile. All the calls were made shortly after you met with Remy and received an update as to the progress of our investigations. Remy remembers that during each meeting you were as interested in how my search for Megan Crane was progressing, as you were the investigation into the murders themselves. Is that not right Remy?'

'It is, Jamie.'

Carver leaned forward, fixed Couthon with the gaze he had been waiting for. 'You passed that information to your friend, Rochelle. He in turn passed it on to Megan Crane.' Couthon said nothing, but the way his eyes were rattling in their sockets said much for the activity going on behind them. Right now his legal brain would be working, hard. 'She used that information to formulate her plan. In that sense it led, directly, to Carissa Lavergne's murder.' Carver rose from his seat. 'Remy?' Remy stood up, as did Ingrid. Carver passed him the warrant.

Remy read from it. He spoke in French. They needed to make sure there could be no procedural misunderstandings. Carver understood few of the actual words but knew, exactly, how it they would translate.

'I am arresting you for the offences of obstructing an official investigation into the whereabouts of a convicted felon, namely Megan Crane, as provided for under European Directive 117/94 on Inter-Community

Cooperation on Criminal Investigation. Also for failing to share relevant information with Investigating Officers in the case involving the kidnap and murder of Scott Weston and the kidnap and attempted murder of Tory Martinez....'

And as Remy continued to remind Couthon of his procedural and legal rights, Carver focused on witnessing Couthon's transformation from 'eagle' to 'sparrow.'

Epilogue

By their nature, cities are places of extremes. Within their physical, social and cultural landscapes, indulgent wealth lives alongside abject poverty. Stunning beauty contrasts with harsh ugliness. Acts of stirring human achievement bely pockets of utmost degeneracy. In some areas, chaos and darkness reign. Others are havens of tranquillity and innocence. City dwellers learn to avoid these extremes, or seek them out, according to their preferences.

To the south of the River Seine, in the quarter from which it takes its name, Le Jardin du Luxembourg caters for those who prefer the sunnier aspects of city living. Formerly the grounds of the Palais Du Luxembourg, which was once a prison but is now the home of the French Senate, *Le Jardin* is Paris's most popular public park. A place of refuge from the noise and bustle of the city, the garden is famed for its colourful flower borders as well as its shaded, wooded groves. Of a morning, the quarter's residents practise their preferred martial art amidst the trees. Tai-Chi is particularly popular. For the more active there is tennis, for the less so, boules. Coffee, croissants and light meals can be had in the garden restaurant and café next to the band stand.

For young families, the park's main attraction is its octagonal toy boating lake and surrounding terraces. At weekends, children learn how the trim of a boat's sail determines whether it will travel, serenely, across the lake, or sit on the water, sail flapping uselessly in the breeze. As the children play, parents and grandparents watch over them from the comfort of the green metal and wood deck chairs which the park authority thoughtfully provide, free of charge. Those who are free from such responsibilities simply relax or doze, seduced by the tranquillity of the surroundings.

On this particular Sunday morning there was a crisis. A boat's sail had come adrift from its boom and was sitting in the middle of the lake, going nowhere. It had been going nowhere for several minutes. During that time its young owner's voice had risen to shrill as he voiced his frustration. His implorings to his dozing father, lying semi-comatose in one of the chairs to, 'do something', were either going unheard, or being pointedly ignored. People were opening their eyes, looking round to see what the commotion was. The disturbance was threatening to disrupt their concentration on doing nothing. There were tuttings and murmurings. *Why does the father not do something? Can someone not take off their shoes and wade in to retrieve the stricken vessel? If he will not do it, then who?* Other fathers were coming under pressure.

From his chair on the stretch of gravel terrace furthest from the lake – too close and you can't take it all in – Carver watched, waiting to see what would happen. Facing south and east, the sun was directly in his face, though the sunglasses meant he could just about follow what was going on. He had witnessed similar incidents before. The usual outcome was that the father would rise to the occasion and step up to meet his responsibilities. But on this particular morning there was little sign of him doing so. The boy's voice continued to rise above those of the other children. At the edge of the lake, another father was instructing his own children, a boy and a girl. Distracted by the emergency, they weren't paying attention. Instead they were looking at the boat in the middle of the lake, then turning worried faces to him. He in turn was weighing the situation. Boat. Wailing boy. Sleeping father. Boat...

Carver judged it would not be long.

A figure stepped in front of him, blocking his view. The sun was behind her so she was little more than a silhouette. He leaned to the side to look round. She moved with him.

'You do know that if you keep on sitting here all day watching kids, someone's going to report you?'

He lifted his gaze, taking in the slim outline. Her pose was challenging, arms folded, leg braced in front. She was wearing a flowery summer frock and white cardigan. A tan leather bag hung from her shoulder.

'I've got away with it so far,' Carver said. 'Besides, the French are more relaxed about these things. Like love affairs.'

It drew a pointed, 'Hmmph.' She pushed the sunglasses up so they rested on top of her head, looked down at him. 'You look like shit.'

He shifted in his seat. Goaded to at least make an effort, he sat up straighter. Behind her, the father of the two boys was taking off his trainers. He was wearing cut-offs. No problem.

'Nice to see you too, Jess.' She was still shading him from the sun's glare. He took off his glasses so he could see her better. What he saw surprised him. Apart from the pointed look he was used to, she looked alert and healthy. Her ash-blond hair was longer, nearly on her shoulders now. Elegant. Classy. *In control.*

'You look good. What have you been taking?'

'Care of myself. Which is more than can be said for you.'

He looked down. Resigned himself to what was coming. 'Are you going to steal my sun all day?'

Looking around, she saw an empty chair, dragged it over, plonked herself down in front of him.

His view restored, Carver saw that Father number two was already in the water, heading for the boat. His excited sons were cheering him on to complete his mission. They had been joined by the boat's young owner. Soon they would all be friends. Retrieving the stricken vessel, he waded back to the wall surrounding the lake. Crisis averted.

'How did you find me?' Carver said.

'Ingrid.'

He showed surprise. She'd got her name right. 'How is she?'

'Good. She sends her regards. She said something about seeing you at. . . the two cats?'

He nodded, slowly. It had been three weeks now. 'What did you think of her?'

She thought on it. 'Nicer than I expected.'

'I told you she was nice.'

'I mean nice, nice. Not "wow" nice.'

'I never said she was, "wow" nice.'

'Yeah, right.' When he didn't come back at her, she continued. 'She must be made of tough stuff. She seems to have coped with it all better than some would.'

He glanced at her before returning to the lake. The

boat owner was running over to tell his father about the dramatic rescue. The way the man sat up and looked around, it was clear he'd been oblivious to the whole event.

'Ingrid was never a target the way I was. She just happened to be there. If she had been, a target I mean, she'd be dead by now.'

'She didn't target me either.'

'No. She had other plans for you.'

They let the conversation drift away on the breeze. Neither the time nor the place. Besides, they'd had it before, many times.

Carver heaved a sigh. 'I wondered when they'd send someone.'

'No one *sent me*. I'm on leave, due back next week.'

He turned to her. 'So why are you here?'

She sat back, gave him a look. 'Why the fuck do you think I'm here? I'm here to bring you home.'

'And what if I'm not ready to come home?'

'Tough. You're coming.'

He sighed. 'Jess, I know you mean well. And I appreciate it. But after what happened, I'm not sure-'

'I know you're not sure. That's why I'm here. To help make you sure.'

He took his time. 'What are they saying? Is there any...?'

'They've stopped talking about discipline if that's what you're asking. Looks like the ACC's done some sort a deal. We won't kick up stink about their bent magistrate helping to harbour an escaped con, if they forget about what happened at that Galeries place.'

'Doesn't matter. I'm still AWOL.'

'No you're not. You're on compassionate leave.'

'Am I? Who arranged that?'

'The Duke. At my suggestion. People were starting to ask where you were.'

He looked at her. She held his gaze, not a trace of doubt.

'Thanks.'

'Don't mention it.'

Strange, Carver thought. Twelve months on, and their roles had completely reversed. He thought on what to say, missed his slot.

'Listen.' He gave her his attention. 'You don't need to tell me what you've been through. I've been there as well, remember?' He looked away. 'And you've been here before and got through it.'

He squirmed. Thoughts of Angie, what happened after, always made him uncomfortable.

'It's not just that....' He searched for the right words. 'Christ Almighty, Jess. It's... God knows how many. Not just Angie, and then nearly Rosanna, but Gary Shepherd, the Hawthorns, and now Carissa. And it would have been Ingrid as well, if-' He let it ride. 'And that's not to mention all the Worshipper Killer victims. All these people, dead. Or could have been. All because of me. How do you think that makes me feel?'

'However you *think* it makes you feel, it's bullshit. They're not dead because of you. They're dead because of her. She was a killer. That's what killers do. They kill people.'

'But my job was to stop her killing people, and I didn't.'

'That's bullshit as well. Who do you think you are for God's sake? Some White Knight? The Lone-Fucking Ranger? Angie, Carissa, the Hawthorns, they were involved in all this long before you ever knew them. They all knew the risks, which is more than we did starting out. We had to go in blind. No one held our hand. In the end, we *all* underestimated her, Jamie. Not just you. What is it you tell people? That she was unique? Isn't that what you say?'

'Yes, but-'

'Well you were right. She *was* unique. More unique than any of us could ever imagine. That's the nature of evil. It disguises itself so we don't recognise it for what it is until it's too late.'

He remained to be convinced. 'Rosanna wasn't involved in it. Nor was Kayleigh Lee. I couldn't even stop her getting to them, and they were part of *my* life, not hers.'

'We didn't even know back then what she was. What could you have done differently? When the time came, you did as much as anyone could have done. It. Wasn't. Your. Fault. How many times do you have to hear it?'

He ran his hands through his hair, clasped them behind his head, tried to get his elbows to touch in front, dropped them again. He shook his head. 'It's hard Jess.'

'I know it's hard. We all know. The Duke as well.'

Mention of his old boss prompted him. 'Does he know you're here?'

She shook her head. 'I was going to tell him, but thought better. He'd have wanted to come.'

He nodded. 'Probably.'

'Definitely.'

He leaned back in the chair. Looked up at the cobalt blue sky. High up, a tiny white dot trailed a jet stream. Eventually he said, 'I just don't know whether I can anymore.'

'You can. Take it from me.'

'How do you know?'

'Because you're Jamie Carver, that's why. You were a good detective long before all this started. Before Edmund Hart even. You're still a good detective.'

'Says who?'

'Says me.'

'And what do you know?'

'I know who it was made me choose a career in CID.'

'Yeah? Well I'm sorry about that.'

'I've no regrets.'

'No? I have.'

She ignored the clumsy inference. She knew what he meant. 'There's nothing wrong in having regrets. But regret isn't the same as blame. Blaming yourself is wrong. Throwing away a gift is wrong. There's lots of bad people out there, Jamie. They all need catching. There aren't that many who are up to it.'

He was silent a long time. Eventually he sat forward again. He rubbed his hands together, slowly. 'They didn't find it, Jess. Her body I mean.'

'I know what you mean.'

'They found Father Alonso. Not her.'

'They also said the lake is deep. Lots of streams and rivers feed into it. They create down-currents, pot-holes. Ingrid showed me the Lake Superintendent's report. According to him a body is as likely to sink as get washed up. And they didn't find those two divers last year either.'

'They were wearing weights.'

She nodded, waited a while. 'So that's what this is all about. You're worried she's still out there.'

He shrugged. 'If Alonso got washed up, then why

didn't-'

'She's dead Jamie. Hellfire, cut up like that, the amount of blood she'd lost? There's no way she could survive a fall like that.'

'But if she was alive when she hit the water-'

'She'd have been concussed, and she would have drowned. Whatever she was, Jamie, she wasn't Wonder Woman.'

'But-'

'She's dead. Believe me.'

Another long silence. 'I'd like to.'

'Then do it.'

He didn't answer.

They sat a while. Eventually she looked to her right. She could wait no longer. 'The Duke didn't come with me. But someone else did.'

'Who?' He looked round, followed her gaze.

Over by the lake, two women, one older, auburn haired, beautiful, the other younger, wiry, still maturing, appeared to be doing their inadequate best to instruct the young boy between them how to set the sails on his hired boat. He sat up. 'Rosanna? Jason? And Kayleigh?' He turned to Jess, glared at her. '*WHAT* the fu-'

Her hand came up. 'Before you start don't blame me. It wasn't my idea. I was just i/c logistics.'

'Logistics? What logistics?'

'Finding you. Breaking you in.'

He shook his head. 'So whose idea was it then, if not yours?'

She cocked her head, gave him one of her, *are you stupid,* looks. 'Well, who do you think you prat?' She swung her gaze towards the three by the lake.

As he turned to look, he just caught the end of

Rosanna's backwards glance as she turned her attention back to Jason. *Giving me time. Letting it happen naturally.* The moment Jason saw him, that would be it.

'It's time to come home, Jamie. They want you back. They *need* you back. We *all* need you back.'

Sitting back in his chair, Carver looked up at the sky, feeling the warmth of the sun on his face. He closed his eyes. Took a deep, cleansing breath. The past three weeks he had thought about going home several times. Each time he'd convinced himself he wasn't ready, Hell, sometimes he thought he would *never* be ready. So much had happened. So many lives ruined. So many lives ended. The weight of the dead lay on him, like a shroud. He chanced another glance towards the lake. *They want you back*, Jess had said. *They need you.* Was it true? Did they want him, need him? He focused on Jason. Now seven, one thing was certain. He needed a father. End of. He thought about the fact that they had come all this way. He thought about what that meant. Finally, it dawned on him.

Christ Carver. What a wanker.

He stared at them some more, shook his head. Time to let go. Even as the thought formed, he felt the weight easing off him. Not all of it. Too soon for that. But some of it. A start at least.

He turned to look up at Jess. She was watching him, reading him. She was good at that. Better than Ingrid even. He imagined them getting on if they ever had the time. Heaving one last, long sigh, he raised himself up and out of the chair. He moved slowly, stiffly. *God you're a mess.*

For long seconds he stood there, staring at the young woman whose life, like his, had been changed by the events of the past three years. She stared back at him, saying nothing. Eventually, he lifted a hand and stroked the back of it, lightly, down her cheek. He broke a half smile. She returned it, nodded. Then he turned away and shuffled towards those who had come for him.

As he neared, Rosanna saw him coming, tapped Jason on the shoulder, pointed. He turned.

'JAMIE.'

Boat in hand, the boy ran to him. Carver squatted, let him run into him. They hugged. Carver lifted him up.

'They said you might be here, Jamie. Look at this. It's a real sailboat.'

'I can see that.' He looked at Rosanna, waiting. He felt awkward. 'Hi.'

'Hi,' she said back.

'Thanks for coming.'

She smiled. 'Why wouldn't I?' She looked him up and down. He waited for a comment. It didn't come. She came forward, wrapped him in her arms, held him, tight. Breaking the hug, she looked up into his face. There was a moment's hesitation, then they kissed, not too much - he still had Jason in his arms -but enough.

He looked across at Kayleigh, hanging back. 'Hi to you as well.' She pulled a smirk, moved in, and put her arms round his waist, squeezing. 'Hi.'

Jason pulled at his stubbly beard. 'You need a shave Jamie.'

'I know. Later.'

He squirmed in Carver's arms, impatient to get on with business. Carver put him down.

'I'm not sure if the sail's working. Do you know anything about boats, Jamie?'

Carver looked around. Jess was watching, smiling.

He turned back to the innocent young face.

'Do I know anything about boats? I'm from Liverpool.'

'Yeah, but do they have boats there?'

He chuckled. 'Yes they have boats.' He took the lad's hand, let him lead him over to the low balustrade surrounding the water. Kayleigh went with them, but Rosanna hung back, watching. Carver squatted. 'Let's have a look. If we don't do this right it might get stuck in the middle. Then someone will have to go in and get it.'

'Don't be scared, Jamie. It's not deep. You won't drown.'

Carver looked down at his son. The boy's face was full of expectation. He ruffled his hair, smiled at him. 'I'm not scared Jason. Not now that you're here.'

Jess watched her former boss playing with his son. It was only the second time she'd seen them together. For the first time in weeks she felt some of the tension that had taken up residence in her gut beginning to ease.

But not all of it.

She shifted her gaze to the far side of the lake. The woman was still there.

She'd first spotted her as she was making her way over to Carver, following Ingrid's directions and after leaving Ros and Kayleigh with Jason. She was sitting on one of the benches up on the grassy bank that overlooks the lake and surrounding terrace. It wasn't so much the woman herself, as the coal black hair that had caught Jess's eye. By now Jess was used to the involuntary double-take that came whenever she chanced upon women with similar colouring. She was trying to train herself to ignore it, especially now that she was gone. But she wasn't there yet. The thing Jess noted about this one was that though it was a warm, sunny day, she was wrapped up in a long skirt, jumper, boots and shawl drawn up over the lower part of her face. The wrap-around sunglasses meant that the only parts of her exposed to the sun were the hands she was using to hold the shawl about her, and the prominent cheekbones and high forehead, though given the way she was dressed, Jess imagined them caked in protecting makeup. Next to her, a distinguished looking man, bearded and slim in a way that suggested he was also tall, was dressed in brown tweed. Given the surroundings and the relaxed informality of those around, they made an incongruous pair. *Parisians,* Jess thought. *Even here, on a day like this, they have to dress to impress.* Sitting behind Carver and off to his right, they had remained in Jess's line of sight during the time she and Carver conversed. The way the woman sat, with her head angled towards them, she could almost have been watching them. Now, thinking on it again, she remembered that when she first saw her, her head was already turned in this direction.

But right now it wasn't. Right now she seemed to be looking towards the lake. Towards where Carver was kneeling next to Jason, instructing him on sailboat techniques. As the first hint of a thought came to her, Jess sat up. She looked over at Carver, then back at the woman on the bench. The sunglasses meant she could not be sure where she was looking exactly. She might simply be observing the boating activity going on around them. Only, she didn't look the sort who would be much interested in toy boats and kids.

But even as Jess began to wonder if she ought to do something to forestall any later musings of the, '*just suppose-*' variety, the woman stirred, interrupting the train before it could fully form.

As she rose from her seat, slowly and somewhat stiffly it seemed, her companion turned to lend her his assistance. It was then that Jess noticed the stick she was using for support. The woman cast one last look back at the lake, in Carver's general direction, before shuffling around the back of the bench, taking her companion's arm, and heading off along the bordered path that would take them back to the park's main entrance.

Jess watched her go. She walked with a pronounced limp. At this distance, and wrapped up the way she was, it was impossible to gauge her age. Still, Jess thought, she didn't look old. Yet she moved the way some do who suffer with bad backs, arthritis, or similarly debilitating conditions. Or like someone recovering from a serious accident. Jess bit her lip. As the woman passed out of sight behind a line of rhododendron bushes, Jess let go the breath she had been holding. Then she realised, and shook her head.

'You're getting as bad as him,' she admonished herself.

About to rise, a ping sounded from her bag. Taking out her mobile, she checked the screen.

The message read, *Thank you Madam. I agree, and await your instructions.* It was a reply to one she had sent earlier, the latest in a conversation that had begun several days before. She stared at it, considering. Looking up, she saw Carver and the others, all together now.

Jess Greylake turned on the spot, letting her gaze roam the terrace, the lake, the park and gardens. The woman with the stick was gone. Soon she would be but a memory. Her apart, Jess was struck by the sheer normality of what was going on around her. Children playing. Families enjoying time together. Lovers strolling arm in arm. Even Carver, playing with Jason, looked about as normal as she had ever seen him. She remembered something he had once said to her. *Everyone has secrets.* It drew a smile.

Lifting her phone, she typed her reply - *8.00pm. Chez Jules, Marais District. Do not be late* - and pressed 'Send'. As she put her phone away, she let one final, self-satisfied smile cross her face. Then she wiped it and went to join the others.

The end

Enjoyed reading? Please consider posting a review. Reviews are the lifeblood of authors as they help us stay visible to readers, and give us a better feel for what you like in a story. You can post a review by visiting the Amazon book page and clicking on, "xxx customer reviews"

Coming Next:- Finally, Jamie Carver is out from under Megan Crane's pernicious shadow. Or is he? Find out what fate next has in store for the detective who struggles to keep his private and professional lives separate in, *Family Reunion*.

How do you save a family from slaughter, when you don't know who or where they are - and your aren't allowed to find out?

Read on for a preview, or click on the button below to get it right now.

Enjoyed this book? Please consider posting a review. Reviews are the lifeblood of authors as they help us stay visible to readers, and give us a better understanding of what you like in a story. You can post a review by visiting the Amazon book page and clicking on, ["xxx customer reviews"](.)

Read on to learn what is coming next in the DCI Jamie Carver series...

Coming next in the DCI Jamie Carver Series

FAMILY REUNION

How do you save a family from slaughter when you don't know who they are, and you aren't allowed to find out?

A monstrous killer, newly escaped from a far-off asylum heads to the UK. His mission? To avenge himself on the family that betrayed him to the authorities. Alerted to the danger, but chained to a desk and still recovering from all that happened before, DCI Jamie Carver faces an impossible situation. Given a free hand, he knows how he could find the family in time to save them, but those charged with doing so won't listen, and his bosses won't let him get involved. When an innocent family are found slaughtered and Carver recognises it as merely the prelude to what is coming, he knows he cannot sit idly by and wait for others to die - even if it means risking his career, and breaking all his promises to the woman he loves.

The fourth in the DCI Jamie Carver Series, Family Reunion sees DCI Jamie Carver having to call upon all his skills and experience as he delves into the shadowy and dangerous world of illegal immigrants, foreign agents and victims who dare not show themselves in order to solve one set of horrific murders, prevent another, and catch a monster.

Read a sample, next.

Family Reunion

Chapter 1

Armenia, close to the border with Azerbaijan

A second after the high-pitched whistling stopped, the shell hit with a heavy, double 'WHUU-UMP."

The other side of the field, beyond the Institute's perimeter wall, a clump of olive trees rose into the air, seeming to hang there a split-second before exploding into a maelstrom of soil, rock and splinters. As the thunderous boom reverberated, the deadly cloud rushed towards the concrete building that now stood alone in the middle of the bleak landscape. But even as it spilled over the wall, through the pitted railings topping the brickwork, its momentum slowed, sharply, its lethal cargo discharging back to earth in a clattering hail of debris and charred timber.

Even before the dust settled, manic whoops of fear-tinged glee erupted from the building's third-floor windows. Covered only by chicken-wire - the glass had gone long ago - the yells and cat-calls echoed over the once fertile river valley that day by day was turning into a war-zone.

'Fuck ME, Melkon, did you see that?' Antranig Koloyan's cry mingled with the others as he turned to address his friend. But Melkon was down on his haunches, cowering against the wall, hands pressed to his ears.

Apart from The Monster himself, young Melkon was the only other inmate Antranig ever bothered with. Though his behaviour could be erratic, sometimes even as disturbed as the other shaven-headed residents of Ward G19 - particularly when he started with the howling - there were periods when he could pass for being as sane as Antranig himself, almost.

'Now THAT was CLOSE. Come see, Melkon.'

But rather than accept the wild-eyed Armenian's invitation, Melkon simply wrapped his arms even more tightly about his body and rocked back and forth on his heels. At the same time, a half-strangled wail – not quite the wolf thing - escaped him. When he looked up, his young face was full of fear.

'Come away from the window, Antranig,' he croaked, barely able to make himself heard over the clamour that had reigned since the shelling started up again. 'You'll get yourself killed.'

Intent on proclaiming his defiance, Antranig turned back to what was happening beyond the boundaries of what was the nearest thing to home most of them had ever known.

'I don't CARE. Come ON you bastards. I'm WAITING. Blow me up, you *FUCKERS*.' As if in answer to his prayer, another blast, closer this time, rocked the building.

Antranig threw himself to the side as a hail of dirt and debris hurtled through the windows, bouncing off the ceiling and walls to shower down over beds already covered in dust and ceiling plaster.

Not quite as ready to welcome death as he was making out, Antranig decided a few moments respite were called for. He back-slid down the wall to squat next to his friend.

'What do you think Melkon? Is this what we've been waiting for? The divine retribution that will cleanse us of our sins?' His eyes rolled as he laughed and he threw his head back to reveal a mouthful of stained ivory.

'Don't say that,' Melkon lamented. 'Someone will come. They wouldn't just leave us.'

The older man gave Melkon a pitying look. 'Of course they would you crazy bastard. Where do you think the orderlies are? Do you see them?'

Melkon turned to look towards the barred gate that separated the ward from the corridor leading to the stark offices and barely-equipped treatment rooms. There was no one in sight.

'I tell you,' Antranig continued. 'The cowardly bastards have legged it. That's fucking Kurds for you.'

'But what if we escaped?' Melkon grasped at another straw. 'What if, *He* escaped?'

As if reminded to check there was no immediate prospect of such an unthinkable event happening, they both turned to look down the other end of the ward. The gate to the purpose-built cell in the far corner was still locked, its single inmate clearly visible through the bars.

Vahrig Danelian, known to them all as simply, 'The Monster', was sitting on the floor, his back against the wall, head down, sunken eyes closed. His grey-flannel covered legs were stretched out in front, arms loose at his sides. To all intents and purposes he was sleeping. But even from here, Antranig could see the thin smile he recognised as marking the man's 'meditations'.

For a couple of seconds, the smile Antranig had stitched to his own face when the explosions resumed, flickered and almost died. But he forced himself not to dwell on the potential dilemma Melkon's question had raised. What did it matter? Even if *He,* or even any of them, did manage to get out, chances were they wouldn't last five minutes. The Azerbaijanis roaming the countryside didn't care who they killed. And a mad Armenian was still an Armenian.

So much for promises, Antranig thought.

'What do *they* care?' he said, dismissing his friend's hope. 'The only thing on their mind is staying alive. They don't give a shit what happens to the likes of us, certainly not Him.'

'But I don't want to escape,' Melkon pleaded. 'I just want the noise to stop. Make it stop Antranig, please make it stop.' With that he curled himself into a ball and started to let out a long wail that Antranig knew heralded the wolf-howls that always reminded him of the mountain forests outside Odzun where he had grown up.

For a moment, the haunting sound rose above the cacophony of yelling and yowling and everyone stopped. But when they realised it was only young Melkon, they all returned to what they had been doing, responding to the situation in their different ways, praying, crying or simply shouting obscene defiance at the yet-to-be-seen Azerbaijanis. Some had already retreated into themselves in the way they did when the world around became too much to bear, crawling back into their cots and wrapping themselves in the thin, grey blankets that years of washing had made transparent.

'That's it, Melkon,' Antranig said, grinning down at his friend. 'Howl like the devil. That will stop them.' But as he looked up, his gaze fell again on the cell at the far end of the room. A chill ran through him and his mood changed.

Though The Monster's head was still bowed, the black eyes Antranig was sure were the devil's own were staring right at him in a way he had seen only twice before.

The first was just before that time he went for the new orderly. It was the young man's first day on the ward and no one had taken the trouble to warn him properly. Or so they all thought at the time. It was only later that someone said that the man's mother was half-Azerbaijani. They never saw him again. Word was, he never recovered. The second time was the day they were visited by some Government Inspectors. Unusually, one was a woman. She looked good for her age and smelled nice in her neat grey suit and black shoes. As she stood outside the Monster's cell with the other inspectors, the man they had made an excuse to come and gawp at, came up to the bars, pressed his face between them and stared at her, fixedly, as he was now doing to Antranig. Without him even saying anything, the woman fainted away and had to be carried out. She didn't return either.

Over recent weeks, as rumours of trouble outside had grown, Antranig had finally succeeded, much to his surprise, in engaging The Monster in what could almost have passed for conversation. As far as he knew he was the only person in the place to have done so, save perhaps for Doctor Kahramanyan. But despite the dark matters they discussed, the gravity of undertakings given, Antranig now found the Monster's gaze as unsettling, terrifying even, as anything he had ever seen. He was sure it contained a message, one that right now, he didn't care to think about. It stirred him to action.

Jumping to his feet, he left Melkon to his howling and ran across to the entrance gate, remembering to keep his head low as he passed the windows. Grasping the cold iron in both hands he shook it as hard as he could so that it rattled, loudly, on its frame. At the same time he yelled down the corridor.

'SOMEONE GET US THE FUCK OUT OF HERE.'

Chapter 2

The hills of North Wales, above Colwyn Bay

The metallic clunk brought Carver awake with a start. For a split second, he wondered what in God's name was happening. But as the familiar low rumble kicked in and he recognised the sound he had already come to hate with a vengeance, he let out a long, low groan. Within seconds the noise changed, settling into a sequence of harsh growls interspersed with nerve-cringing grating noises. A dark-haired forearm stretched out from under the duvet to grab at the alarm, turning it towards the bed.

'Six-a-bloody-clock? I don't believe this.'

Driven by the annoyance surging through him, he swung his legs out of bed, got up and padded over to the window. As he went he trod carefully to avoid splinters, which was another thing. How long does it take to decide on flooring for Christ's sake?

The last few nights had been unusually warm for spring and he had discarded his usual cotton shorts after noticing they seemed more snug round his waist than previously. It had made him think again about getting back to the weekly badminton sessions that used to help counter Rosanna's cooking – as well as being a diversion from other things. Much as he enjoyed the succulent meat dishes and hearty soups that are the mainstays of Portuguese cuisine, he had long ago learned the truth of the phrase, 'too much of a good thing.'

Not bothering to cover himself, he pulled back the curtains. Dawn's early light flooded the room.

As he gazed down on the building site they hoped may one day be a garden, Alun Cetwin-Owen, Master Builder - or Odd Job Man, depending on who you spoke to - lobbed another spadeful of gravel into the mixer. About to stoop for another, the Welshman stopped and looked up, as if some Celtic sixth sense had alerted him to the fact he was being watched. Seeing the naked man at the window, he lifted an arm and mouthed what Carver knew would be, had be been able to hear it over the machine's incessant gloppetter-gloppetter - an excruciatingly cheery, 'Morning Mr Carver.'

'YOU WELSH BASTARD,' Carver mouthed back through the glass. The older man smiled and waved.

Carver was certain now that Alun's 'other project', the one he'd hinted about working on during the afternoon - hence the early starts - was a fiction. A few days before, he had mentioned it to Gwynn Williams at the farm where they got their eggs. Carver had gone to ask if Gwynn was interested in the hay-making opportunity the overgrown field at the back of the house presented. Carver had never suffered with hay-fever in his life but the past few weeks his sinuses had become increasingly irritated. During his last weekend off, his eyes had turned painfully red. When Gwynn asked how the building work was going, Carver had lamented over how Alun's other commitments were hampering progress.

'Work?' Gwynn had said. 'In the afternoon? Alun? Noohhhh. It's just he doesn't sleep, see? And if he's not in The Three Dragons by two o'clock, then something's wrong isn't it?'

At first Carver had wondered how it was that his supposed 'Wizarding Abilities' hadn't caused him to spot the lie. Then he realised. When Alun spoke of having, 'other things to do in the afternoons,' he hadn't actually mentioned building work. And whilst it would have been obvious to Alun that Carver assumed he was talking about another project, maintaining the illusion required nothing more of him than he keep his mouth shut.

Shaking his head, Carver thought on his options. If it wasn't for the fact that builders in that part of Wales were scarcer than the country's legendary gold mines, he'd have sent Alun packing long ago. They were already three weeks behind the 'rough schedule' he had let the man talk him into when they discussed the job. And just that weekend he had spoken of having to, 'Revise the original estimates.'

Then there were the rest breaks.

To begin with, Carver thought Rosanna was joking when she told him the boxes of tea bags he came across whilst rooting for his coffee one morning were just one week's supply.

'I didn' realise these *Wales-,'* – she still had difficulty with 'Welsh,' - 'These Wales drin' more tea than you Engleesh,' she had said, shaking her head.

That said, Alun's brickying was as good as any Carver had ever seen, and he was regular as clockwork.

A bit too regular, he thought.

But even as the thought came that it may be time for

him and Alun to sit down and thrash some things out, maybe over a pint in The Three Dragons, he felt the urge arriving that standing at the chill window had brought on. But as he turned from the window, the duvet over the still-occupied half of the bed stirred and he stopped. A face, bleary-eyed but beautiful enough under the gauze of flame-red hair stuck to it to remind him of what he stood to lose, poked itself out.

'No' again,' she said. It was followed by the string of expletives Carver had heard many times but was yet to discover their true meaning.

In that moment, the incongruity of her tirade, her natural beauty, their still-new environment and the awareness of what he, they, had been through the past couple of years, conspired to bring on a rush of emotion that stopped him in his tracks. Caught out, he gulped air to get over the catch that was suddenly in his throat. Still not strong enough to throw off the clawing memories, he looked back over his shoulder.

Away across the valley, through the morning mist and filling the gap between two mountains, he could just make out the stretch of the lake - Llyn Geirionydd, according to the map - that every now and then pulled his thoughts in the direction of another body of water. This one, also inland, was many miles away, mainland Europe, in fact. And as always happened when his thoughts turned in that direction, the image of a woman's body, hanging in the dark depths came to him. But even as his pulse started to quicken, Rosanna's tirade continued. For once, he was grateful.

'You mus' tell heem, Jamie. This is getting ridiculous.' As always first thing in the morning, her accent was thicker than it would be later.

'You wanted it finished,' he said, as he crossed to the still doorless en-suite.

Having come round a little, he was beginning to feel more forgiving about their early wake-up call. Besides, he'd set the alarm for six-twenty anyway, to give him time for one last run through the paper he would be putting before the Crime Committee later that morning. *Times past it would have been an Operational Briefing.* *And* he'd decided to call at Sarah's on his way in. His elder sister hadn't sounded good the previous evening. Despite her insistence that she was, 'alright,' he wanted to see for himself. But, turning the cold tap off, he forgot to do it slowly. As water-hammer triggered the juddering that echoed around the bare pipework and unfinished walls, his lighter mood evaporated.

'Shit,' he said, turning the tap back on. He waited for the jarring noises to stop before turning it off again, more slowly this time. Not for the first time, he wondered if maybe they hadn't bitten off more than they could chew.

At the time of course it had made good sense. At least it did to him. Given the associations parts of the North West still had with events he hoped to one day forget but suspected he never would, an abandoned barn conversion in the North Wales hills above Colwyn Bay seemed ideal. It was close enough for work – barring accidents the A55 and M56 were good roads and most mornings he made Salford well before half-seven. But, crucially, it was far enough away so he didn't have to live surrounded by reminders of what lay beneath the surface of a city that liked to talk up its cultural and 'cosmopolitan' aspects, and a county - Cheshire - that revelled in its reputation for 'poshness'. Given the problems they'd been having around that time, he also thought it would be good to have something they could pour their energies into as a couple. Something that might finally expunge both the memories *and* Rosanna's doubts about moving away from the cottage they'd both once loved, but was now contaminated by nightmarish memories neither would ever forget.

As he often did when he thought about such things, he recognised the never far away knot of regret that he'd had to abandon the places where he'd grown up; the areas where he'd honed his skills. Not for the first time, he wondered where else might end up so blighted before his career ended.

Of course the novelty of living in someone else's half-completed project had worn off long ago. Well-dodgy plumbing – the cash-strapped previous owner had done it himself – and an intermittent power supply soon saw to that. And while he wasn't entirely sure about Rosanna – she never talked about it – he knew that somewhere in his mind's deepest recesses, the doubts and fears still lingered.

'Besides,' he said, returning to the bedroom and picking up on the subject of Alun's early starts. 'You know the only person he ever listens to is you. Now why is that I wonder?'

A pillow hit him in the face.

'Policemen. You are useless at everything apart from catching the criminals who are so stupid they leave their DNA everywhere.' Then she remembered. 'And hounding-dog *motoristas*.'

Two weeks before, she had picked up her second three points on one of the coast road's many cameras, adding fuel to what he feared was a growing disillusionment with *his* - not *their* he always noted - choice of home. Knowing better than to rise to the bait, he sought a diversion.

'What time is this thing tonight?' Looking round for his shorts, he spotted them at the side of the bed. As he bent to step into them, her silence signalled a warning and he turned. She was propped on an elbow, glaring at him. Chiding himself, he made a mental note to not refer again to the Royal Northern College of Music's Mediterranean Folk Festival as 'thing'.

'Half-pas' seven,' she said, pointedly. 'I tol' you las' night.'

'Just checking.'

'*Please* don' be late.' The eyes became those of a little girl, a technique she could deploy to devastating effect. 'I am second on the programme. If you are late, you will miss me.'

He threw himself down beside her so that she bounced and her luscious tresses flew around her head before settling back about her shoulders.

'Would I miss you?' He reached for her, but she slapped his hand away, not willing to play until she had the commitment she was looking for.

'You missed me at Liverpool.'

He waved it away. 'That was a simple mistake. The doorman said. People always confuse the Empire with the Philharmonic.'

'If you had listened, instead of thinking always of your work you would have known.'

Recognising a loser when he saw one, he decided another change of subject was called for. 'How's the throat?'

She sniffed, gave a little cough, then reached for the

water bottle beside the bed. After a couple of sips, she hit and held a long, soft, 'Aaaaaaahhhhhhh.' She drank some more, then tried a couple of scales. 'Ah-ah-ah-ah-ah-ah-aaahh.'

'Sounds good,' he said, hoping to be sufficiently encouraging.

The ploy worked. Forgetting the cajoling, she got out of bed. Unwinding her sinuous body she stood straight, taking a long, deep breath. Her arms lifted into the pose she usually adopted at the start of a performance, and she sang.

Way too small, enclosed and echoey, the bedroom was hardly the best place to appreciate the seductive rhythms and subtle cadences of Fado, the mountain folk-music that is to the Portuguese what the Tango is to Argentina. Nonetheless, as Carver listened, relieved to hear the cold had cleared, the hairs on the back of his neck stood up, as they always did whenever he witnessed her transform from mere beauty, to angel.

But as he stood there, entranced, the words that still invaded his dreams from time to time returned. '..*and that other bitch. You're both dead...*'A shudder ran through him. With an effort, he willed the memory away. Pray God they would always remain just that. Words.

The singing stopped and she rounded on him - 'How was that?' - jolting him out of the morbid reverie threatening to take him.

'Wonderful.'

In that moment Carver decided. He didn't want to lose her, and would do whatever it took to make sure he never did, even if that meant staying away from the sort of cases that had ensnared him in the past. Which, unfortunately, would also mean delaying his return to CID beyond the eighteen months he had originally planned.

'An' you promise you won' be late?'

He crossed to her, took her face in his hands and placed his lips on those his father had once likened to the old Italian actress, Gina Lollobrigida. 'I promise.' But as they parted, he saw the green eyes narrow, the disbelief within them. Before she could say anything, he placed a finger to her lips, sealing them shut. 'I'll be there.'

Then, not wanting to risk going over the issues that seemed to raise themselves more often these days and knowing what she could be like in the morning, he decided it was time to answer the craving for caffeine that always grew rapidly once he was awake.

As he made his way down the stairs he remembered not to reach for the non-existent banister rail. He'd made that potentially debilitating - and painful - mistake once already, and didn't intend to repeat it.

Chapter 3

One floor below Antranig Koloyan's vain attempts to attract attention, Doctor Mikayel Kahramanyan was doing his best to stay calm as he spoke into the telephone. He was also trying to ignore the pain from his upper-left pre-molar. Two weeks before it had shed a filling, but there had been no time to seek out a dentist, even if there was one within twenty miles of the Institute, which he doubted.

'I understand that Colonel. But I still have over forty patients here. You promised me the rest of the trucks would be here the day before yesterday.'

'But that was before the rebels crossed the border at Damnah.' The voice was that of someone resigned to the inevitable. 'You must understand Doctor, I am fighting on three fronts and right now I need every transport available. Our Gorshki Division is on its way from Aliverdi and should be here tomorrow. You will get your trucks then.'

'TOMORROW WILL BE TOO LATE,' Kahramanyan yelled, frustration finally spilling over. *Did the man not realise what was happening? Did he not care?*

Across the room, the nurse with soft brown hair that seemed to be turning greyer each day carried on pretending not to listen. She did not want to further burden the man for whom she worked by letting him see how alarmed she was, especially when his, to her. transparent anxiety signalled well enough the seriousness of their situation.

Gadara Nalbantian had worked with Mikayel now for five years, ever since she accepted the post no one else wanted so she could be close to her ailing mother in nearby Martuni. And though her mother had died within the year, Gadara never thought to seek another position. By then she was happy working for a man who, unlike many of his peers, abhorred the ignorance through which their charges were classified as either 'demented' or 'evil'- save perhaps in one exceptional case.

During those five years, Gadara had never seen Mikayel lose his temper, not even during the laborious negotiations he had to suffer each month with the Health Ministry just to secure enough supplies to cover their basic requirements. But over the past few days, a change had come over the man she admired above all others. Gone was the caring clinician who had worked long enough within the country's rudimentary Health Service to both understand its limitations, *and* remain philosophical about what he could ever achieve as Head of Psychiatry and Assessment for the institution housing the country's *Forgotten*. In his place was a man increasingly desperate, worn down by The Ministry's prevarications over moving them somewhere safe. She knew, without having to ask, he hadn't slept well in weeks.

Of course, neither she nor Mikayel ever referred aloud to the desperate souls in their charge by the term in common use throughout the Ministry, *The Forgotten*. Whenever they heard it, they were quick to denounce the inference. To emphasise that the care given out to the one hundred and twelve inmates – the maximum number of cots available – was the best they could manage under their impoverished circumstances. In reality they both knew the truth. That as far as the Ministry was concerned, the rudimentary fragments of humanity housed within the Armenian State Psychiatric Institute and Correction Facility could disappear off the face of the earth tomorrow, and no-one would give a damn. Why else locate an asylum for the criminally insane so close to a disputed border which, even before the place was built, was prone to Azerbaijani incursions into the lands they still regard as their own?

As Gadara listened to Mikayel's tortured pleadings, at the same time continuing to pack the medicines and supplies they would need if the trucks ever came, her conviction that her efforts would prove wasted grew stronger.

'So, what do you suggest, Colonel?' Mikayel said. 'You are the sole authority in the region now. You tell me what to do with forty-odd men the authorities think are too disturbed for prison, but not enough, apparently, to merit proper psychiatric care.'

A weary sigh preceded the military man's answer. 'Leave them.'

A crackle on the line gave Mikayel hope he had misheard. 'I am sorry, Colonel, I didn't catch that. For a moment it sounded like you said, 'leave them'.'

Another sigh. 'I did.'

For long seconds, Mikayel stared at Gadara's back as she rooted over her boxes. But the sudden silence made her turn and as he saw the alarm flood into her face, he knew she had been listening.

'Y- You cannot mean that, Colonel,' Mikayel said, knowing in his heart he did.

'You have no choice Doctor. Even if I wanted to, and believe me I do, there is nothing I can do for you from here. According to intelligence the rebels will overrun that area within the next few hours. You know what will happen if you are still there when they arrive.'

Conscious of a growing feeling of dread, Mikayel persevered. 'But I can't just leave them for the Azerbaijanis. It would be as good as sentencing them to death.'

The casual tone in the Colonel's reply made clear that at that moment, the psychiatrist's problems were well down his order of priorities. 'Then set them free.'

'WHAT?'

'Either that, or leave them for the rebels. It is your decision.'

Mikayel's drawn face grew red and his voice rose. 'What you are suggesting, Colonel, is outrageous, and not worthy of your profession. It would be tantamount to a war crime.'

The Colonel's voice rose to match his. 'Face reality Doctor. This *is* a war. Or the nearest thing to it. In such circumstances we all have to take difficult decisions. I am sorry I cannot help you further.'

'But what about... Him?' the psychiatrist said, referring back to the problem they had considered when they first discussed the so-called evacuation plan. 'How can I set Him free? If by some miracle he avoided the rebels....'

The Colonel became abrupt. 'Then deal with him yourself.' He had more pressing problems to attend to.

'Wh- what do you mean... *deal* with him?'

'The box on your wall, doctor. We spoke about it during my assessment visit.'

As he pondered the little good that had come of it, Mikayel turned to the red wall-cabinet behind the door. He remembered now the interest the military man had shown in it. *Had he known all along it would come to this?* The psychiatrist's blood turned cold and his stomach lurched at the thought of what the Colonel was suggesting.

'But I- I am a doctor.' His breath started to come in gasps. 'I could not contemplate....' As he sucked air, pain erupted again in his broken tooth and he winced.

'In that case you must live with the consequences. I am sorry doctor. I cannot waste any more time on-.'

His words were lost as a thunderclap rent the air and the building rocked with the shock-wave of another explosion. But this time the noise was so loud, the shaking so violent, Mikayel's first thought was they had suffered a direct hit. He held onto the desk to stay on his feet while across the room Gadara pressed herself between two metal cabinets. Chunks of plaster rained down from a rent that suddenly appeared in the ceiling. After several seconds, as the shaking subsided and the leakage from above trickled to dust, an eerie silence descended. Mikayel waited long enough to be satisfied that the ceiling wasn't about to cave in, then returned to his conversation.

'Did you hear that Colonel? That was-. Colonel? COLONEL?' But the line was dead, and as he saw the blanked-out computer screen on Gadara's desk – it was usually connected to the creaking Health Service Network – he knew that their communications were gone. He imagined a large crater in the ground at the side of the building, where the service ducts were buried.

For long seconds he stared at the phone, stupidly, before placing it back on its cradle. He looked across at Gadara. Her face was a picture of fear.

'Wh-What did he say?' she said. As she spoke he saw her eyes slide in the direction of the cabinet. She had seen him look at it, probably guessed what was being suggested.

Mikayel swallowed. 'He said they are not coming. And that I must... deal with him.'

For long seconds neither spoke as the desperateness of their plight finally struck home.

Then Mikayel moved, quickly, like he had made a decision and needed to act on it before he changed his mind. He started opening desk drawers, rummaging through them, urgently.

'Where is it, Gadara? I remember I had it once.'

'What Mikayel? What are you looking for?'

'The key. It must be here somewhere.'

She joined him to help look. Eventually she found it, in the match box Mikayel had stuffed at the back of one of the drawers, certain he would never need it but keeping it safe in case some paper-wielding Government Inspector demanded he produce it. Taking it out, he crossed to the cabinet, unlocked it. As he pulled the doors open, he thought again how ridiculously large it was for its meagre contents.

A cardboard box, about three inches deep, rested on the upper shelf; another, smaller but more squarely proportioned, on the one below. Taking one in each hand – they were both heavier than they looked - he carried them back to his desk. Gadara appeared at his side.

The larger box was emblazoned with the logo of the American gun manufacturers, Smith and Wesson, a faded pen picture of a revolver, just like ones he'd seen in western films, beneath it. Mikayel lifted the lid. The gun was folded in stained oil-paper. As he took it from its nest and unwrapped it, a bitter, metallic smell caught the back of his throat. Though it must have been thirty years old or more, it seemed as new. Unused by the look of it. Its black metal was covered in a thin film of oil. As he weighed it, he noted at once how strange it felt. He was used to wielding instruments that in their various ways were designed for use on the human body, but not in the way this was intended. Another shudder ran through him. He turned the weapon in his hand, peering into the chambers. They appeared empty. He lifted the lid off the other box. Neatly arranged rows of bullets stared up at him, the rounded lead tips in their brass casings pointing up, six to a row. He took one out, but as he raised it to the gun he suddenly realised. Never having handled such a weapon in his life, he hadn't the faintest idea how to load it. He was wondering how the bullet fitted into the chamber when Gadara's hands appeared.

'Let me,' she said, taking the weapon from him.

He looked at her in surprise.

'My father was militia during the soviet. He used to let us shoot mouflon on the slopes behind our farm.'

As he watched her confident handling of the instrument, Mikayel suddenly realised, with regret, he knew almost nothing about her life before the Institute.

'Like this.' She pushed a catch and the revolver's cylinder flipped out to the side. She took a round and pushed it into one of the empty chambers.

'Okay,' he said, taking it back from her as she was about to reach for more bullets. 'It is my responsibility. I will do it.'

She stepped aside as one by one, his shaking fingers loaded five more rounds. When he was finished he pushed the barrel back into its housing. It locked in place with a loud, 'click'. Then he stood there, looking at her, the gun dangling at his side. In the distance, more explosions went off.

'You must go, Gadara. Catch up with David.' An hour earlier Mikayel had ordered the young American-Armenian who had recently come to work with them to leave.

But she shook her head and, to his surprise, smiled. At first he thought she was simply trying to convey her understanding of what he had to do. But then he thought he saw something more than just sympathy in her eyes.

'When we leave, we will leave together, Mikayel Kahramanyan.'

'But this is.... I would rather you-.'

'Hush.' She pressed a finger to his lips. 'I will go when you go.'

He looked down at her. There was a moment's awkward hesitation, then he put his arms round her and drew her to him.

'Pray God will forgive me,' he whispered in her ear.

In that moment, Gadara Nalbantian was almost tempted to surrender to the feelings she had held in check for so long. But then she remembered the gun in his untrained hand, and twisted in his arms so she could keep her eye on it.

Want to keep reading?

GET IT HERE

FREE DOWNLOAD

Get the inside story on what started it all...

Get a free copy of, *THE CARVER PAPERS,* - The inside story of the hunt for a Serial Killer, - as they feature in LAST GASP, Book #1 of The Worshipper Trilogy. Visit www.robertfbarker.co.uk/ to find out more and get started.

Robert F Barker was born in Liverpool, England. During a thirty-year police career, he worked in and around some of the North West UK's grittiest towns and cities. As a senior detective, he led investigations into all kinds of major crime including, murder, armed robbery, serious sex crime and people/drug trafficking. Whilst commanding firearms and major disorder incidents, he learned what it means to have to make life-and-death decisions in the heat of live operations. His stories are grounded in the reality of police work, but remain exciting, suspenseful, and with the sort of twists and turns crime-fiction readers love.

For updates about new releases, as well as information about promotions and special offers, visit the author's website and sign up for the VIP Mailing List at:-

http://robertfbarker.co.uk/

Printed in Great Britain
by Amazon